the image or images on the cover of this book depict
ns, such person or persons are merely models, and are
ortray any character or characters featured in the book.

BOOKS are published by

shing Corp.
reet
0018

Shelly Laurenston

d. No part of this book may be reproduced in any form
without the prior written consent of the Publisher, ex-
es used in reviews.

this book without a cover, you should be aware that
property. It was reported as "unsold and destroyed" to
neither the Author nor the Publisher has received any
stripped book."

tles, Imprints, and Distributed Lines are available at
scounts for bulk purchases for sales promotions, pre-
ng, and educational or institutional use. Special book
ized printings can also be created to fit specific needs.
or phone the office of the Kensington special sales
on Publishing Corp., 119 West 40th Street, New York,
ecial Sales Department, Phone 1-800-221-2647.

d the K logo are Reg. U.S. Pat. & TM Off.

57-1435-0
435-0
ack Printing: April 2018
Printing: September 2019

57-1436-7 (ebook)
36-9 (ebook)

2 1

d States of America

"Shelly Laurenston's
characters, strong fem
that can have you laughing out loud."
—*The Philadelphia Inquirer*

"Witty dialogue."—*FIRST for Women*

"Laurenston is the queen of paranormal romances
that mix over-the-top humor, eccentric characters and
sexy, crazy plots to produce addictive stories you won't
want to put down"—*RT Book Reviews,* **4.5 stars,
TOP PICK!**

"Quirky characters, madcap antics, snappy dialogue,
charged love scenes and sitcomesque humor keep
things move at a breakneck pace."—*Publishers Weekly*

"Hot and humorous."—*USAToday.com*

"Hilarious, sexy fun. The dialogue is smart and
funny, and at times outrageously shocking."
—**Heroes & Heartbreakers**

"A little bit of everything . . . humor, passion, and
suspense with a touch of paranormal."—**FreshFiction**

"Laurenston really scored with great humor,
conversations, and memorable moments galore in
this book."—**SmexyBooks**

"A wacky, crazy fun time that is sometimes crude and
outlandish, the dialogue is ridiculously hilarious and
the sexy scenes are smoking hot."—**FictionVixen**

"Clever, fun, and a really enjoyable read, with some
great characters and laugh out loud moments."
—**All Things Urban Fantasy**

W9-CKR-133
3 3288 10036742 6   AUG 2019
WITHDRAWN

shifter books are full of oddball
males with attitude and dialogue

Also by Shelly Laurenston

The Pride Series

The Mane Event

The Beast in Him

The Mane Attraction

The Mane Squeeze

Beast Behaving Badly

Big Bad Beast

Bear Meets Girl

Howl For It

Wolf with Benefits

Bite Me

The Call of Crows Series

The Unleashing

The Undoing

The Unyielding

The Honey Badger Chronicles

Hot and Badgered

In a Badger Way

HO
BADG
The Honey Ba

Sh
Laur

To the extent
a person or pe
not intended

KENSINGTO

Kensington P
119 West 40th
New York, NY

Copyright © 2

All rights rese
or by any mea
cepting brief q

If you purchas
this book is sto
the publisher, a
payment for th

All Kensington
special quantity
miums, fund-ra
excerpts or cust
For details, wri
manager: Kensi
NY 10018, attn:

KENSINGTON

ISBN-13: 978-1-
ISBN-10: 1-4967
First Trade Pape
First Mass Mark

ISBN-13: 978-1-4
ISBN-10: 1-4967

10 9 8 7 6 5 4

Printed in the Un

KENSINGTON
www.ke

*To my California family who taught me
the true meaning of sisterhood.
I love you guys.*

Charles Taylor didn't realize until that moment how fast life could flip on a man.

One second he'd been listening to two crazy women he'd known for years try to talk him into taking over the Pack from the young, arrogant wolf they all hated. The next second the doorbell rang . . . and everything changed. Forever.

He'd opened the front door to the main Pack house and found his twelve-year-old granddaughter standing there with her two half-sisters.

The other two weren't his granddaughters. His daughter had taken in the offspring of her worthless ex-boyfriend because that's what she was like, his Carlie. She'd taken those girls in and raised them like her own. Without question. Without resentment. And because it was the right thing to do, as far as Carlie was concerned.

So when Charles opened the front door and saw those three girls standing there, dirty, bruised, with that wounded look in their eyes . . . he knew. He knew his baby girl was gone. He knew it and was devastated by it.

But what could he do? Do what his daughter would

want. Take the three girls in. Raise them, even the two who weren't only *not* his blood but weren't even a tiny bit wolf. The middle one was full honey badger, like her idiot father and her criminal mother, who was doing hard time in a Bulgarian prison after a jewelry heist went bad.

The second one was half honey badger and half tiger, and his Packmates were not fans of cats. Not even a little. They didn't tolerate the house cats that roamed around their Wisconsin neighborhood. So what would they do to this little one with the big eyes and the stink of cat coming off her?

The girls did have one thing in their favor, though . . . they were young. The oldest twelve, the middle eleven, and the baby not even eight yet.

When the two She-wolves saw the girls, they gasped and immediately ushered the children in, leading them to the living room he'd just escaped from.

"What happened?" Lotti asked his granddaughter. "Where's your mama?"

His granddaughter looked up at him and, again, he saw the answer in her eyes. Just as he'd seen the answer when he'd opened the front door.

"My daughter's dead," he said flatly, still trying to process exactly what that meant.

Lotti and Jane went silent, hands stopping on the light coats the girls had worn to trek from Connecticut to Wisconsin to get to their mother's Pack. In the middle of winter.

Aghast, the two She-wolves looked up at him, then at each other.

"Let's . . . let's get you girls something to eat," Jane stuttered. "You must be starving."

Lotti stood and softly said to Charles, "We may have a problem . . . with two of them."

"If I have to leave, I will." He thought of his daughter, of how she would have handled something like this. "I won't separate them."

Lotti pressed her hand against Charles's chest. "I'll go talk to him."

He nodded and crouched down in front of his granddaughter to help take off her coat, but before he had a chance, Lotti quickly returned. "He wants to talk to them. Alone."

Frowning, Charles looked at his old friend over his shoulder. "What?"

She shrugged.

"Forget it," he said. He wasn't putting his traumatized granddaughter and her sisters through that idiot's bullshit.

"We'll talk to him," his granddaughter suddenly announced, sounding . . . adult. She might look like a little girl, but she'd never actually been one. Carlie used to say "my girl was born forty." And seeing the determined look on the child's sweet face, Charles believed it.

She stood and motioned to her sisters. "Where is he?" she asked a stunned Lotti.

"In the back. The yard. I'll show—"

"We'll find him."

While the middle girl held the youngest's hand, his granddaughter gently pushed the pair forward, and the three of them walked through the house alone.

That's when Jane growled. "I don't like this."

Neither did Charles. He didn't like it at all.

Betsey sprawled on the high branches of the big tree in the Pack's backyard and did her best to stay quiet.

She came out here to be left alone. She was too old to hang around the other pups and too young to hang around the adults. And at sixteen, she was counting down the days until she would go off to college and get the fuck out of here.

She loved her mom. She'd done the best she could for her only child, but Betsey had never fit in with the Pack because she wasn't full wolf. She was half wolf, half black bear. Her father had been a one-night stand her mother had still not gotten over. But being a bear among wolves was . . . challenging.

While Betsey was growing up, things had at least been tolerable. Until Billy Lewis had taken over as Pack leader. Now Betsey was praying nothing came between her and the scholarships that would allow her to go to an out-of-state college and get into a new life.

Until then . . . she'd sit in trees when she wasn't in school and hope that no one noticed her.

Like Billy Lewis, sitting on one of the benches in the Pack's backyard, looking over his domain like Richard the Third. But such a weak wolf wouldn't notice that Betsey was sitting in a tree watching him unless the wind suddenly changed and he scented her.

She watched as the three little girls came into the backyard. According to what she'd heard when Lotti came to talk to Billy, their mother had been killed and somehow those little kids had made it halfway across the country to the Pack house. Remarkable, really. At that age, Betsey wouldn't have lasted five seconds without her mother. But these girls . . .

Billy had insisted on a "private chat" with the pups, and that did not bode well. Billy didn't like what he called "half-breeds." An insulting term from an insulting idiot.

Sadly, Betsey had been forced to endure a "private chat" with Billy herself. It wasn't nearly as creepy as it sounded, but it was definitely cruel. He'd told her that come her eighteenth birthday, she was out, no matter what was going on in her life or her mother's. If her mother wasn't happy about it, she could go with her kid, but that would be up to Betsey.

A horrifying thought since Betsey knew how much her mother loved her Pack. Leaving it, even for her only daughter, would be too harsh for her. Betsey would never ask that. So, after that "private chat" she'd doubled up on her school work, began taking AP courses, and planned on graduating when she was seventeen. Thankfully, she was smart enough to make that happen.

But she didn't know anything about the little girls walking into the backyard to be left alone with Billy. She just knew her heart broke for them. Because no matter what their circumstances—yes, even the death of their mother, who'd been a former Packmate and daughter of the pack's Beta—it would mean nothing to Billy Lewis. Besides, this might be the chance he'd been waiting for . . . to get rid of Charles Taylor. An old-school wolf that the adults in the Pack desperately wanted as Alpha leader, whether Charles would take the job or not.

Betsey knew, though, that Charles would never let his granddaughter go into the cruel system of foster homes and state-run lives. That was not the best world for any child, but definitely not for a shifter. And for a hybrid shifter . . . nightmares were made of how badly those situations could end.

Still, to send the other two girls away simply because they weren't blood related or wolves . . . could Billy really be that cruel?

Who was she kidding? *Of course*, he could be that cruel!

The three girls stood in front of Billy now and he smugly stared at them, the corners of his mouth slightly turned up, his eyes heartless.

If Betsey had thought she could sneak away without being seen, she would. She didn't want to watch this.

"I hear you girls have had a bad time of it lately, huh?"

The girls stared at him, but said nothing. But the middle one, she suddenly waved at him. As if in greeting. Surprisingly—and just downright annoying—Billy winked back and pointed his finger at the girl. A move he considered "sexy."

Yuck.

He went on. "Look, I'm sorry to hear about Carlie. I always liked her. A weird wolf but fun. Ya know?"

Of course they didn't know! They were kids! *Idiot!*

Billy leaned forward, resting his elbows on his knees and clasping his hands in front of him.

His "sincere" look.

"I know this will be hard for you guys to understand but . . . you can stay," he told the oldest, an adorable brown-skinned girl with lots of curly hair and a pretty face. "But you two can't. I know," he continued, "I know this is hard to hear. But you might as well learn now how the real world works."

Something told Betsey these girls already knew how the real world worked.

While Billy blathered on, the middle girl sat her younger half-sister down on the bench beside Billy and abruptly walked off.

She moved over to the bushes and flowers that had been planted around the yard wall, head down, like she was searching for something.

And while she looked, Billy talked to Charles's granddaughter. Just like her grandfather, her face revealed nothing. It was blank. Impassive.

The middle sister, a very tiny Asian girl with black hair that had a white streak through it, picked something up and returned to her sister's side. Together they gazed at Billy until he noticed that the middle girl was holding something in her hand.

His smirk turned into a full-blown smile. Betsey had never met someone who enjoyed bringing out the worst in everyone like Billy did. Even desperate children who'd just lost their mother! "Is that for me, sweetheart? You going to hit the big, bad wolf with that little rock?"

He leaned in and his voice became so hard. Harder than Betsey had ever heard it.

"You swing that thing at me, little girl, and you'll be on the first bus to the closest foster agency. Maybe, after a few years, you'll meet up with your loser mom in prison. You can have a mother-daughter reunion behind bars."

If Billy was hoping to make the little girl cry, he failed. She didn't cry. She just slowly blinked and kept staring at him.

Then, without a word between them, the two oldest girls faced each other.

Charles's granddaughter nodded once and the middle girl pulled her arm back and with some mighty force for a kid, she swung her fist with the rock in it.

Knuckles made contact and Betsey blinked in shock when she heard something break in the oldest girl's face just before she hit the ground.

The youngest glanced up at the sound, but her expression was passive as well. Billy, on the other hand, reared back in shock.

"What in holy—"

While he was busy trying to figure out what was going on, the middle girl grabbed his left hand—and now Betsey understood the weirdly timed wave earlier—and placed it on the bench. She raised the rock and brought it down hard—onto Billy's knuckles.

Billy howled in pain as the middle girl tossed the

rock across the yard. Then, as if some silent cue had been given, she and the youngest burst into copious, dramatic tears.

The kind of sobbing that would get the attention of any She-wolf in a twenty-mile radius.

All the adults at home appeared in the backyard. And what did they see?

Two little girls sobbing hysterically. Another little girl nursing her bleeding, broken cheek while bravely attempting to hold back tears, and Billy . . . with busted knuckles.

The middle girl's knuckles were also bruised and bloody, but she held her baby sister close and had her hand curled into a fist and pressed against the child's side, ensuring that none of the adults could see it.

Charles moved through the adults until he stood front and center. Betsey had never seen the older wolf like that. He'd always been the calm one. The rational one. He was the great peacemaker of the Pack, making sure the small group didn't get into any fights they couldn't possibly win against Packs bigger and meaner.

But now . . . Charles was beyond angry. His brown eyes narrow, his breathing heavy, his entire body stiff, a slight tremor running through him every few seconds. And all while he gazed down at Billy.

Searching the crowd and seeing no friends, Billy shook his head and raised his hands, palms out.

"Wait a second, I didn't . . . *it wasn't me!*"

But with his hands raised like that, all anyone could see was the blood dripping between his fingers and slowly pouring down his wrist.

Desperate, Billy pointed at the middle girl. "It was her!"

As one, the adults all looked at the little Asian girl holding onto her baby sister. And, for a split second, Betsey saw the middle girl's face harden in a way that was a little too adult for a kid so young. The adults never saw it, though, because the youngest girl placed her sobbing face right in front of her sister's. Done on purpose? Betsey wouldn't have thought so. She seemed too young, but after everything that had happened . . .

"It was!" Billy insisted. "It was her! I would never hit a kid! I wouldn't!"

With a nasty snarl from the back of his throat, Charles reached down, grabbed Billy by his leather jacket, and yanked him off the bench.

The adults dragged Billy out, leaving the girls alone.

The oldest pulled the youngest girl onto her lap, her arms loose around her waist. The middle girl moved closer, finally resting her head against her sister's arm. For a brief moment, the girls looked their age, but they also looked weathered. Life had been hard on them already and the oldest didn't even look thirteen yet.

Charles returned to the backyard. He was scowling and now there was blood on him. He walked up to the girls and glowered down at them as was his way. Betsey was sure he had no idea how he must look to people who didn't know what was going on in his head. But the three sisters gazed back at him without flinching.

Sighing, he started to turn away, and Betsey knew he was trying to figure out what to do next. What to do about the two girls who were *not* his blood. Not related to him in any way except that his daughter had made them her own. But before he could walk away, the youngest girl reached out and gripped his forefinger with her hand, small fingers squeezing tight.

And like that . . . Charles suddenly had three granddaughters instead of one.

He reached down and picked up the youngest in his arms.

"Let's get you a room and something to eat," he suggested, although it sounded like the orders from a drill sergeant.

The eldest grabbed her grandfather's forearm and the middle girl, not as tall as her elder sister yet, grabbed the chain that attached his wallet to his jeans.

Together, in silence, they headed back to the house.

Betsey waited a few minutes before she crept down the tree trunk and shifted back to human. She put on her clothes and went around the side of the house, so she could enter through the front door.

As she came around the garage, the middle girl was waiting for her. And Betsey *knew* she was waiting for her.

Betsey froze in mid-step, gazing down at the kid with her mouth slightly open.

The kid stared up at her for what felt like forever and then, with a little smile, she placed her forefinger against her lips and said, "Shhhhh."

Without another word, she turned and walked away . . . and Betsey wondered if it was possible for her to take some more AP classes so she could get into college even earlier than she'd planned. Like, maybe next week . . .

Chapter One

Sixteen years later . . .

What had she been thinking? Using the "Ride of the Valkyries" as a ringtone? Because that shit waking a person up at six in the morning was just cruel. Really cruel.

And, as always, she'd done it to herself. Forgoing her anxiety meds so she could get drunk with a couple of cute Italian guys that she dumped as soon as the first one's head hit the table.

Charlie Taylor-MacKilligan slapped her hand against the bedside table next to the bed, blindly searching for her damn phone. When she touched it, she was relieved. She had no plan to actually get out of bed anytime soon. Not as hungover as she currently was. But she really wanted that damn ringtone to stop.

Somehow, without even lifting her head from the pillow she had her face buried in, or opening her eyes, Charlie managed to touch the right thing on her phone screen so that she actually answered it.

"What?" she growled.

"Get out," was the reply. "Get out now."

Hangover forgotten, Charlie was halfway across the

room when they kicked the door open. She turned and ran toward the sliding glass doors she'd left open the night before. She'd just made it to the balcony outside when something hot rammed into her shoulder, tearing past flesh and muscle and burrowing into bone. The power of it sent her flipping headfirst over the railing.

"What do you think?" the jackal shifter asked.

Sitting in a club chair in his Milan, Italy, hotel suite, Berg Dunn gazed at the man holding up a black jacket.

"What do I think about what?" Berg asked.

"The jacket. For my show tonight."

Berg shrugged. "I don't know."

"You must have an opinion."

"I don't. I happily have no opinion on what a grown man who is not me should wear."

The jackal sighed. "You're useless."

"I have one job. Keeping your crazed fans from tracking you down and stripping the flesh from your bones. That's it. That's all I'm supposed to do. I, at no time, said that I would ever help you with your fashion sense."

Rolling his eyes, the jackal laid the jacket on the bed and then stared at it. Like he expected it to tell him something. To actually speak to him.

Berg wanted to complain about this ridiculous job, but how could he when it was the best one he'd had in years? Following a very rich, very polite jackal around so that he could play piano for screaming fans in foreign countries was the coolest gig ever.

First class everything. Jets. Food. Women. Not that Berg took advantage of the women thing too often. He knew most were just trying to use him to get to Cooper Jean-Louis Parker. Coop was the one out there every night, banging away at those Steinway pianos, doing things with his fingers that even Berg found fascinating, and wooing all those lovely females with his handsome jackal looks.

Berg was just the guy to get through so they could get to the musical genius. And, unlike some of his friends, being used by beautiful women wasn't one of his favorite things.

It was a tolerable thing, but not his favorite.

"I can't decide," the jackal finally admitted.

"I know how hard it is to pick between one black jacket and *another* black jacket. Which will your black turtleneck go with?"

"It's not just *another* black jacket, peasant. It's the difference between pure black and charcoal black."

"We have a train to catch," Berg reminded Coop. "So could you speed this—"

Both shifters jumped, their gazes locked on the balcony outside the room, visible through doors open to let the fresh morning air in.

Another crazed female fan trying to make her way into Coop's room? Some of these women, all of them full-humans, were willing to try any type of craziness for just a *chance* at ending up in the "maestro's" bed.

With a sigh, Berg pushed himself out of the chair and headed across the large room toward the sliding glass doors. It looked like he'd have to break another poor woman's heart.

But he stopped when he saw her. A brown-skinned woman, completely naked. Which, in and of itself, was not unusual. The women who tried to sneak into Coop's room—no matter the country they might be in—were often naked.

What stopped Berg in his tracks was that *this* woman had blood coming from her shoulder. The blood from a gun wound.

Berg motioned Coop back. "Get in the bathroom," he ordered.

"Oh, come on. I want to see what's—"

"I don't care what you want. Get in the—"

The men stopped arguing when they saw him. A man in black military tactical wear, armed with a rifle, handgun, and several blades. He zipped down a line and landed on the railing of their balcony.

Berg placed his hand on the gun holstered at his side and stepped in front of Coop.

"Get in the bathroom, Coop," he ordered, his voice low.

"We have to help her."

"Do what I tell you and I will."

The man in black dropped onto the balcony and grabbed the unconscious woman by her arm, rolling her limp body over.

"Now, Coop. Go."

Berg moved forward with his weapon drawn from its holster. The man pulled his sidearm and pressed the barrel against the woman's head.

Berg aimed his .45 and barked, "Hey!"

The man looked up, bringing his gun with him. Gazes locked, fingers resting on triggers. Each man sizing the other up. And that was when the woman moved. Fast. So fast, Berg knew she wasn't completely human, which immediately changed everything.

The woman grabbed her attacker's gun hand by the wrist and held it to the side so he couldn't finish the job on her. She used her free hand to pummel the man's face repeatedly.

Blood poured down his lips from his shattered nose; his eyes now dazed.

Still holding the man's wrist, she got to her feet.

She was tall. Maybe five-ten or five-eleven. With broad, powerful shoulders and arms and especially legs. Like a much-too-tall gymnast.

She gripped her attacker by the throat with one hand and, without much effort, lifted him up and over the balcony railing. She released him then and unleashed the biggest claws Berg had ever seen from her right hand.

Turning away from the attacker, she swiped at the zip line that held him aloft, and Berg cringed a little at the man's desperate screams as he fell to the ground below.

That's when she saw Berg. Her claws—coming from surprisingly small hands—were still unleashed. Her gaze narrowed on him and her shoulders hunched just a bit. She was readying herself for an attack. To kill the man who could out her as a shifter, he guessed. Not having had time to process that he was one, too. Plus, he had a gun, which wouldn't help his cause any.

"It's okay," Berg said quickly, re-holstering his weapon. "It's okay. I'm not going to hurt you."

"Yeah," Coop said from behind him. "We just want to help."

Berg let out a frustrated breath. "I thought I told you to get into the bathroom."

"I wanted to see what's going on."

Coop moved to Berg's side. "We're shifters, too," he said, using that goddamn charming smile. Like this was the time for any of that!

But this woman rolled her eyes in silent exasperation and came fully into the room. She walked right by Berg and Coop and to the bedroom door.

"Wait," Berg called out. When she turned to face him, one brow raised in question, he reminded her, "You're naked."

He went to his already packed travel bag and pulled out a black T-shirt.

"Here," he said, handing it to her.

She pulled the shirt on and he saw that he'd given her

one of his favorite band shirts from a Fishbone concert he'd seen years ago with his parents and siblings.

"Your shoulder," Berg prompted, deciding not to obsess over the shirt. Especially when she looked so cute in it.

She shook her head at his prompt and again started toward the door. But a crash from the suite living room had Berg grabbing the woman's arm with one hand and shoving Coop across the bedroom and into the bathroom with the other.

Berg faced the intruder, pulling the woman in behind his body.

Two gunshots hit Berg in the lower chest—the man had pulled the trigger without actually seeing all of Berg, but expecting a more normal-sized human.

Which meant a few things to Berg. That he was dealing with a full-human. An expertly trained full-human. An ex-soldier probably.

An ex-soldier with a kill order.

Because if he'd been trying to kidnap the woman, he would have made damn sure he knew who or what was on the other end before he pulled that trigger. But he didn't know. He didn't check because he didn't care. Everyone in the room had to die.

And knowing that—*understanding* that—did nothing but piss Berg off.

Who just ran around trying to kill a naked, unarmed woman? his analytical side wanted to know.

The grizzly part of him, though, didn't care about any of that. All it knew was that it had been shot. And shooting a grizzly but not killing it immediately . . . always an exceptionally bad move.

The snarl snaked out of Berg's throat and the muscles between his shoulders grew into a healthy grizzly hump. He barely managed to keep from shifting completely, but his grizzly bear rage exploded and his roar rattled the windows. The bathroom door behind him slammed shut, the jackal having the sense to *now* go into hiding.

The intruder quickly backed up, knowing something wasn't right, but not fully understanding, which was why he didn't run.

He should have run.

With a step, Berg was right in front of him, grabbing the gun from his hand and spinning the man around so that he had him by the throat. He did this because two more men in tactical gear were coming into the suite through the front door they'd taken down moments before.

Using the man's weapon, Berg shot each man twice in the chest. They both had on body armor so he wasn't worried he'd killed them.

With both attackers down, Berg refocused on the man he held captive. He spun him around, because he wanted to ask him a few questions about what the hell was going on. He was calmer now. He could be rational.

But when the man again faced him, Berg felt a little twinge in his side. He slowly looked down . . . and found a combat blade sticking out.

First he'd been shot. Now stabbed.

His grizzly rage soared once again and, as the intruder—quickly recognizing his error—attempted to fight his way out of Berg's grasp, desperately begging for his life, Berg grabbed each side of his attacker's face and squeezed with both hands . . . until the man's head popped like a zit.

It was the blood and bone hitting him in the face that snapped Berg back into the moment, and he gazed down at his brain-covered hands.

"Oh, shit," he muttered. "Shit, shit, shit."

The other intruders, ignoring the pain from the shots, scrambled up and out of the suite. As far away from Berg as they could get.

Someone touched his arm and he half-turned to see the woman. She raised her hands and rewarded him with a soft smile.

That's when he calmed down. "Shit," he said again, holding out his hands to her.

She stepped close, held his wrists, studied the blade still sticking out of his side. She then examined the wounds in his chest. Unlike the intruders, he hadn't been wearing body armor. The bullets had hit him, had entered his body, but he was grizzly. Even as a human, you had to bring bigger weapons if you wanted to take down one of his kind with one or two shots.

Berg knew, just watching her, that she was going to help him. She was going to try. But she was in more danger than he was, and she needed to get out of here.

"Go," he told her and she frowned. "Seriously. Go."

He pulled away from her, went to his travel bag, paused to wipe the blood off his hands on a nearby towel, and took out a .45 Ruger, handing it to her. "Take this."

Her eyes narrowed again as she stared up at him.

"I get the feeling you need it more than me," he pushed. "Just go."

She took the weapon, dropped the magazine, cleared the gun with one hand before shoving the loaded mag back in and putting a round in the chamber.

Yeah. The woman knew how to handle his .45. Maybe better than he did.

She pressed her free hand against his forearm and, with a nod, slipped out the door and out of the suite.

"Can I come out now?" Coop asked from the bathroom. But before Berg could tell him no the jackal was already standing behind him.

"Well . . ." Coop said, "that was interesting."

"You could say that."

"You're bleeding."

"Yes. And please stop playing with the knife."

Coop pulled his hand away from the blade handle and attempted to look contrite. "Sorry. Does it hurt?"

Berg frowned at him and Coop nodded. "I'll take that glare as a yes. Maybe I should call the front desk." He started toward the phone on the side table by the bed.

"Think we'll make our train?" the jackal asked.

Slowly, Berg faced Coop and noted, "You're not used to real life, are you?"

"Not really. Why?"

"This is going to be big." When Coop's head tipped to the side like a confused schnauzer, he added, "The hotel room of some big-time penis was just violently invaded."

"It's *pianist*."

"Yeah. I said that." No. He hadn't. "Anyway, we'll have to get our stories straight. And we should leave out the girl."

"Oh." Coop thought a moment, the receiver held loosely in his hand. Finally, he said, "I'll call my sister first."

"Why?"

"If anyone can manage this, it's Toni." Coop winced. "But she's going to be annoyed at you. For, you know, letting this happen."

"You're alive, aren't you?"

"Yes, and I'm quite grateful. And I don't hold you responsible for this at all. But my sister . . . she won't be as . . . open-minded. You should prepare for that."

"I'm sure I can handle a She-jackal."

Using his cell phone to call his sister, Coop chuckled, "Yeah. Sure you can."

Staring at the open bedroom door, Berg asked, "Think I'll ever see her again?"

"The girl that was never here?" Coop asked. He shrugged while waiting for someone to answer on the other end of the phone. "If you keep an eye on the FBI's 'Ten Most Wanted' list . . . sure! Because let's face it. That's a woman who seems to have trouble following her around like a needy puppy."

Charlie avoided the elevator and found the stairs. She ran down until she reached the parking lot. She eased the door open, keeping the friendly giant's gun in her hand. She peeked around the door, didn't see anyone, so she ran toward the exit.

She dodged around the expensive cars, staying low and moving fast. She dashed past a car valet, and out of the lot.

Charlie moved down the street, cutting around the surprising number of people who were up this early. She'd just reached the corner when a man in a black tactical outfit and body armor stepped in front of her. They both raised their weapons at the same time, Charlie already pulling the trigger when a Lamborghini jumped the curb and rammed into the man. Both weapons missed their marks but now her attacker was pinned to the ground, screaming in agony as the passenger window lowered and Charlie heard the familiar—and shockingly casual, considering the circumstances— "Hey, shithead."

The petite Asian woman with the short pixie haircut dyed blue grinned at her. They were sisters but one would never know it by looking at them.

Max MacKilligan asked, "Miss me?"

"Can you just drive?" Charlie got into the passenger seat. "But be careful. You still have *human* stuck to the grill."

"I should let him shoot you? What kind of sister would I be?"

"One I don't have to visit in an Italian prison."

Chuckling, Max put the car in reverse and Charlie worked hard to ignore the short-lived begging and too-long crunching sounds coming from under the car as she pulled out. Charlie knew her sister was taking her time driving back over the gunman.

Max "Kill It Again" MacKilligan was known for being vengeful.

Once they were on the road and cutting through early-morning Milan traffic, Max pointed down. "Check by your feet."

Charlie did and found a small case. She opened it and let out a relieved sigh.

"Thank you!" she said, putting the eyeglasses on. Suddenly she could see again! She hadn't had time to grab her regular pair off the bedside table before she had to make a run for it and she hadn't gotten her contact prescription refilled in a few months. She kept forgetting. So for the last fifteen minutes, everything had been one blurry mess. Even the helpful giant was just a big, blurry spot. She'd have had to get close to his face to identify him. But he had *sounded* cute. And so nice!

"Better?" Maxie asked.

"Much. I can now *see* who's trying to kill me." She looked at Max and immediately cringed at the sight. "Oh, wow. They really beat the shit out of you."

"Excuse me," Max replied, indignant. "These lacerations and bruises are *not* because of the men who came to kill me. With my usual aplomb, I have dealt with those scumbags."

"Uh-huh. Then what did happen?"

"Why do we have to discuss that? Our lives are in danger."

Charlie gazed at her sister for a few moments before guessing, "Squirrels again?"

"They started it!"

"It's nice to see that nothing has really changed since we last saw each other." Charlie glanced out the window, but she had to look away. Her sister was moving so fast that it was kind of making her nauseous. "What about Stevie?"

"I'm waiting to hear back from her boss."

"Her boss?"

"She's not answering her cell and her assistants have no idea where she is."

"Is she still in Switzerland?"

Max shrugged. "Maybe. And stop glaring at me."

"How hard is it to keep an eye on one woman? I take six months. And you take six months. That was our agreement."

"Why is she still *our* responsibility?"

"Because she's our sister and we love her and if we don't watch out for her, she will get involved with the wrong people, and *destroy the world*. Is that what you want?"

"You always ask me that question, and you're always disappointed with my answer."

Charlie sighed. "Well, we need to find her."

"I know."

"She's in as much danger as we are."

"I know."

"They sent trained military after us."

"I know."

"And I know this car is stolen."

"Of *course* it's stolen."

"Well, that seems like kind of a problem since we have cops behind us."

"Buckle up."

"Oh, God." Charlie put on the seat belt. "We're going to die before we even get to her."

"Stop whining. You know how hard we are to kill."

"Hard to kill doesn't mean we can't lose body parts in tragic car accidents. And we can't exactly save our little sister if we're both in prison . . . and legless."

"What is your obsession with losing your legs?"

"It could happen!"

Max downshifted and swerved around a truck making a turn, barely missing the front end.

"I don't understand why you insist on worrying about something that may or may not happen," Maxie noted casually as a group of nuns dove out of her way, their panicked screams horrifying Charlie. "If you lose your legs, I'll get you a wheelchair with a Ferrari motor that goes from zero to sixty in four seconds. Wouldn't that be great?"

Hands pressed against the dashboard, Charlie admitted, "I'd rather have my legs still attached to my body."

"That's such a narrow view. What about bionic legs?"

"Schoolchildren," Charlie warned.

"Bionic legs would be so cool."

"Schoolchildren!"

"I see them. Calm yourself."

The car stopped—somehow—and Max patiently waited for the children and their teachers to get across the street. Out of nowhere, she began to whistle "H.R. Pufnstuf." Charlie had no idea why, but she blamed her mother. She loved that crap and made them all watch it in re-runs when they were too young to put up a fight.

Once the children were safely out of the way, Maxie hit the gas and roared down the street. Still whistling.

"We need a new car," Charlie told her sister when the cops caught up with them again.

"What's wrong with this one?"

"A lot."

Maxie's phone rang and she insisted on taking one hand off the wheel to answer it.

"Uh-huh. Yeah. Okay. Thank you, sir."

She disconnected the call and glanced at Charlie.

"What?" Charlie pushed when her sister didn't say anything.

"She needed a break."

"A break? She needed a break? What does that mean?"

"You know what that means, Charlie."

"I do?" Charlie thought a moment, then rolled her eyes. "Oh, come on! Again?"

"You know how she is. But hey! At least she's still in Switzerland. We'll get there in no time."

"But it's a mental hospital! *Not* a resort!"

"To her, all mental hospitals *are* resorts. Besides, it could be worse," Max said happily. "This could all be so much worse!"

Charlie shook her head. "Dude, I seriously don't know how."

Chapter Two

The black Mercedes-Benz AMG G63 SUV stopped in front of the mental health and rehab clinic.

Usually, it was only the wealthiest of European royalty who came to this place. Most Americans didn't even know it existed, but Charlie's baby sister had a gift. She could track down high-end mental institutions anywhere in the world. They all seemed to have spa-like amenities, five-star chefs making the meals, and group therapy, something her sister truly seemed to enjoy.

The first one Stevie Stasiuk-MacKilligan had ever checked herself into was somewhere in Malibu and cost a thousand a day. She never paid a cent, though. The lab she "interned" for took care of that, which could explain why no one bothered to question why a fourteen-year-old girl—at the time—was checking herself into a Malibu mental health clinic without a parent or guardian in sight.

And what did these brilliant and pricey psychologists discover about Stevie over the years? Exactly what Charlie already knew: That her sister was a high-strung prodigy who suffered bouts of extreme panic like any abandoned child would.

Stevie's mother, a Siberian She-tiger from a very wealthy family, had shown up at Carlie Taylor's door one day, asking for Carlie to babysit five-year-old Stevie for "a few hours." Charlie's mom, a She-wolf who never really learned how to say no to anyone but Charlie's grandfather, agreed. After three days, she told Charlie and Max that "it looks like your little sister is staying. Isn't that great?"

At the time, Charlie didn't think so. It was bad enough they already had one of their father's castoffs to take care of in the first place; now they had two. But that first situation had made more sense because Max's mother was doing hard time in a Bulgarian prison for armed robbery. She *couldn't* take care of her kid. But the She-tiger . . . she'd just walked away. From her own daughter.

Of course, Stevie didn't let any of that bother her. In her mind, she had so many other things to worry about "in the universe" that her mother's desertion didn't rate as important enough for her to hold a grudge.

So Charlie did it for her. She was very good at grudge-holding. Just ask her idiot father.

Charlie met up with her sister at the front of the SUV.

"All right," Charlie began, "you know the drill."

Max nodded and flatly replied, "Go in. Kill everybody. Get Stevie out."

Charlie briefly closed her eyes, took a moment to breathe and try to relax her shoulders. When she felt she wouldn't yell, she said, "That is *not* the drill."

"It could be."

"Could be, but it isn't. The drill is we go in, I do all the talking, you don't pick on Stevie."

"She's too sensitive."

"But because you already know that, you're not going to pick on her."

Max smiled. "What if I really want to?"

"Then I'll let her take your eye out this time. And you'll wear an eyepatch . . . and we'll call you One-Eye McGee."

Laughing, Max headed toward the front doors, Charlie right behind her.

When they stepped inside, both of them glanced at each other. Their sister really did have a knack when it came to finding beautiful places for the mentally ill.

There was so much white marble and beautiful white furniture. Stunning and expensive oriental rugs were laid out in front of white couches. White marble coffee and end tables rested on top of them. Floor-to-ceiling windows displayed the remarkable beauty of the Swiss countryside that surrounded the entire building.

"You have got to be kidding," Max muttered, staring up at the cathedral-like ceilings. "I think *I'm* feeling mentally ill because I could really use some Valium and a massage."

"Stop it."

Charlie grabbed Max's arm and pulled her to the desk, which was not white but clear glass. And perfectly clean. The stunning woman sitting on the other side in a white button-down shirt and tight, white skirt smiled, revealing perfect white teeth.

"*Hallo. Sprechen sie Englisch*?" Charlie asked.

"Yes," she immediately replied. "May I help you?"

"I'd like to see my sister. Stevie MacKilligan."

"Please have a seat. I'll contact her doctor."

"Thank you."

Charlie walked over to the couch, but it was so white that she was worried about putting her less-than-clean body on it. Max had had an extra pair of jeans and bright red Keds in Charlie's size—they always had backup clothes for each other—so she wasn't walking around in only a T-shirt, but Charlie hadn't had time for a shower. Just a quick stop at a gas station to wash the blood off, and let Max bandage up her shoulder so the bullet wounds could heal without a mess.

And for Charlie, nothing would be more humiliating than getting up from that bright white couch and leaving an unfortunate stain behind.

But Max didn't seem to have those issues, turning and dropping on the couch like she owned it.

Of course, Max didn't worry about much, which worried Charlie. She knew her sister could be reckless when it wasn't necessary. Max did, however, always manage to find a way to wiggle out of whatever situation she'd gotten herself into. And if she couldn't wiggle free, she would attack head-on without stopping.

It was the honey badger way.

Max pulled a baggie of honey-covered peanuts from the back pocket of her jeans and began munching, wiping her hands on the white couch after each handful she put in her mouth.

"Dude."

Max looked up. "What?"

"You're being sloppy."

"So?" She gave that lovely but still off-putting smile. "We don't have to clean it up."

"*Dude*."

Rolling her eyes, Max pushed the nearly empty baggie back into her jeans and brushed both hands against each other. She motioned to a spot behind Charlie and Charlie turned to see a man walking toward them. He wore a white coat and held a clipboard. He also had on a gold Rolex and Gucci leather shoes.

The doctor had expensive taste.

Smiling, Charlie immediately put out her hand for a shake.

"Ladies," the doctor greeted, grasping Charlie's hand. He went for Max's but Max just stared until he pulled his hand back. She didn't even bother getting up from the couch.

"Do you speak English?" Charlie asked.

"Of course," the doctor replied. "I am Dr. Gaertner. I am the director here. Come. Let's talk in my office."

He led them down the wide hallway, which looked out over the front of the building through more of those big, grand windows.

"Your center is beautiful," Charlie noted as they walked.

"Ahhh. *Danke*. Thank you, I mean. We are very proud."

He ushered them into a big office with white leather chairs and couches and even more glass windows revealing more amazing views.

No wonder her sister had come here for a break. It was way better than any spa Charlie had ever been to before.

"Please. Sit," he offered with a smile. Charlie immediately noted that except for a lamp, blotter, and phone . . . the man had nothing else on his desk.

Maxie plopped into a chair, her legs swinging up, about to land on the man's glass desk before Charlie punched them back down. With a warning glare at her grinning sibling, she sat down on the very edge of her chair and realized she should have left Max out in the car.

"Now, how can I help you ladies?"

"We'd like to see our sister, please."

"Ahhh, our dear Fräulein MacKilligan."

"*Doctor* MacKilligan," Charlie corrected out of habit. And, when Max raised an eyebrow at her, she reminded her sister, "She worked hard for those PhDs."

"True, true," Gaertner said, still smiling. "She is one of our favorite patients here. She is so helpful during our group sessions."

Max snorted, but Charlie quickly leaned forward to keep the doctor's attention. "I'm so glad she's here and getting the help she needs, Dr. Gaertner. But we'd really love to see her for a few minutes."

"I'm sure we can arrange something . . . in a few weeks. Right now it is too . . . uh . . . early in the process for family meetings. You understand?"

Before Charlie could explain that "no! I do *not* understand!" in the politest way possible, Max slammed her fist on that expensive-looking glass desk and announced, "Motherfucker, we wanna see our sister now!"

"*Max!*" Charlie barked, locking gazes with her sibling. "Could you let me handle this, hon? Thanks." Charlie turned back to the doctor, gave a helpless shrug. "So sorry. We've been under a lot of stress and—"

"I'm sure. But you understand, that's part of the problem, is it not?"

Charlie shook her head. "What do you mean?"

"Fräulein MacKilligan—"

"Doctor."

"—can't afford this kind of outside stress you and your sister bring. We are leaning toward a breakthrough. But you two . . ."

Blinking, Charlie asked, "You're saying that *we*"— and she motioned between her and Max with her forefinger—"are the cause of Stevie's problems? Is that what you're telling us?"

"Your sister loves you," Dr. Gaertner insisted. "But you both are . . . and I'm sorry for being so blunt . . . *terrible* for her."

Max sucked her tongue against her teeth and looked at Charlie. "*Now* can I hit him?"

"No." Not that Charlie wasn't tempted to unleash

Max on the good doctor, but as much as this place might *look* like a spa, it wasn't. It was a mental hospital. With large orderlies.

Charlie tried again. "I understand your concerns, doctor. I really do. But if I could just get three minutes alone with my sister, I would absolutely—"

"*Nein,*" the doctor said flatly, although with a smug smile on his face that Charlie desperately wanted to slap off.

The doctor stood. "But I will tell her that you were here when I think the time is right, and we will plan on a controlled meeting between you three. Very soon."

Charlie started to go across the desk just so she could tear the good doctor's nose off, but she didn't have a chance. She was too busy grabbing hold of Max and yanking her back before the badger could clear the glass and wrap herself around Gaertner's body like a python.

Charlie stood, bringing Max along, her grip tight on the tough flesh of her sister's back.

"Well," Charlie said, dragging her snarling sister along, "we look forward to hearing from you, Doctor. I'm sure you have my number on file."

"Of course."

Charlie walked toward the glass door and opened it. She pushed her sister out and hissed in warning when Max turned to go back into the doctor's office.

As they headed toward the front of the building, Charlie glanced back and saw that several orderlies were following behind them. Making sure they left the building without a fuss.

Once outside—the orderlies stood in front of the doors, preventing the sisters from reentering—Charlie and Max stopped by the SUV's passenger side and faced each other.

"Now can I go in and kill everybody?" Max asked.

"*No.*"

"You and your half-canine morals. It does nothing but get in the way."

"I know you're working hard to be a sociopath, but stop it."

"Sociopath is in the eye of the—"

"—forensic psychologist working for the prosecution?"

Berg was eventually sent to the local hospital to get his wounds checked out, but the local cops made it clear that they didn't like what Berg and Coop were trying to sell. The investigators knew the pair were hiding something; they just weren't sure what exactly.

It helped, though, that Coop wasn't just Coop but Cooper Jean-Louis Parker, master musician and former child prodigy. The Italian authorities could only push so hard, especially since they were already dealing with the repercussions of being the city where Jean-Louis Parker had been attacked. Every news service—even in the United States!—was reporting on the attack and what had happened to the much-beloved American maestro.

The first doctor that came into the exam room had been full-human and, after looking over Berg's wounds, had abruptly left. A few minutes later, a female doctor came in. She was older, with unbelievably long legs and a strong, lean body. A cheetah. Her nose twitched once and she smirked at Berg.

"You worried my associate," she said in charmingly accented English. "He thought you must be on steroids to be so big. Then he saw that you were already healing . . ." She washed her hands, dried them, and put on gloves. "He wanted to run many tests, check you in for the night. I told him that would not be necessary." She grinned, fangs briefly extending. "I am his boss, so he has to listen to me. He hates that, but for some reason," she added with a shrug, "I seem to scare him."

She leaned over and examined the wound in his side, her fingers pushing against the flesh. It hurt like a bitch, but he wasn't about to admit that to a cat.

"This is already healing. No point in doing more." She straightened and looked closely at the gunshot wounds on his chest. "These are already healing, too, but I will need to open them up to get the bullets out. We don't want the skin healing over those. That could lead to infection and fever." She pressed her wrist against his forehead. "Good. You do not have fever so far. I will make this quick. You don't need to go under do you? Before I do this."

"A local would be—owwww!"

"Do not be big baby cub," she ordered while she began digging in his flesh with sterilized metal instruments.

Berg was gritting his teeth as she worked, waiting for this to be over, when the exam room door flew open.

"What are you doing to my brother?" a female version of himself demanded. "I could hear him whimpering outside!"

"Helping his big, dumb bear ass," the doctor replied before she glanced back . . . and up. Her hands froze, and a small growl came from the back of her throat.

"This is my sister. Britta." Berg explained, knowing his sister's size alone was making the cheetah nervous. Female grizzlies were the most feared among the shifters. Not only were they psychotically protective of those they considered family—blood or otherwise— they were, like the males, easily startled. One wrong move could lose a shifter an arm. Or a whole head. "And my sister is going to be calm now. Calm, because I'm fine."

The doctor seemed to accept that until a male mirror image of Berg also walked into the room and, after slamming the door, glared around without saying a word.

Berg sighed. "And that's my brother. Dag. We're triplets."

"Your poor mother." The doctor motioned to the far side of the room. "You two, over there."

Britta angrily snapped, "You don't order me aro—"

"Britta . . . please?" Berg nearly begged. "Instruments digging into my chest. Think about that a moment before you say anything else."

With a nod, Britta immediately moved to the corner of the room, but Dag—oblivious as always—leaned in and watched the doctor trying to dig out that bullet.

Berg knew his brother was just curious. He'd always been fascinated by medical procedures. But that didn't mean the cheetah would understand. In fact, she was starting to sweat a little. And the room was cool.

But before Berg could warn his brother off with a growl, Britta came back and grabbed Dag's arm, yanking him over to the corner.

Could a cheetah take out three bears? With thumbs, access to lethal surgical supplies, medical training, and blinding speed . . . there was a definite chance. And why risk it when she was, in her own catlike way, trying to help?

"You know what's happening right now, don't you?" Britta asked from the corner. "Coop's sister is getting a private jet to come over here."

"Coop said that might happen."

"Don't worry. I'll handle her," Britta promised. She suddenly pointed at Berg. "When the cat is done—"

"I have name, big-bottom bear."

"—you and Dag will need to get Coop to Rome, then back to the States."

"Coop's still doing that concert?"

"There are some people you don't cancel on. The *Pope* is definitely one of them. But the remainder of the shows are going to have to be canceled."

Berg cringed. And not just from pain. "That's not good."

"It's not that bad. There are only two more after Vatican City," Britta reminded him.

"Yeah," Berg sighed. "But those two shows are in Russia. Those Kamchatka bears are gonna bitch if we cancel. They do love their Jean-Louis Parker."

"Don't sweat it," Britta said, her head down as she was busy texting on her phone. "Coop says he'll add St. Petersburg and some city in Siberia and that should quiet the bears and the tigers and the Cossacks."

Berg blinked. "There are still Cossacks?"

"Of *course* there are still Cossacks," Britta snapped.

"How am I supposed to know? I'm not Russian."

"Are you almost done?" Britta asked the doctor, her tone typically commanding, despite her lack of power with an Italian medical doctor who was also a cat.

"I'm done when I am done, sow. Do not pressure me."

"So who was the girl?" Britta abruptly asked, attempting to throw her brother off.

"What girl?" Berg asked, working to keep his face blank. A skill he'd picked up from their father.

"*The* girl."

The doctor paused in the middle of her work. "You went tense, bear."

Ignoring the doctor, Berg told his sister, "There was no girl. Just me and Coop in the room."

"Uh-huh," his sister replied before refocusing on her phone.

"The sow knows you lie," the cheetah teased softly, but Berg already knew that.

*   *   *

Stevie MacKilligan leaned forward, her elbows on her knees, her chin resting on her raised, clasped hands.

"And how does that make you *feel*?" she asked the patient across from her. "That your mother treats you like that?"

"Awful. I deserve better!"

"You *do* deserve better," Stevie insisted. "Just because your mother is the dictator of a small country and kills those she considers enemies of the state, doesn't mean that your opinion doesn't matter."

"You're right, Stevie. You're so right!"

Stevie turned to the man next to her. "And what about you, Jacques? How are you feeling? Are you still upset about losing that yacht race?"

"It is all my brother's fault!"

A throat clearing had Stevie looking over her shoulder. Dr. Gaertner motioned to her with a wave of his hand and Stevie nodded and stood. She looked at the man sitting across from her. "Why don't you take over, Dr. Schmidt?"

"Since I am the actual *trained* psychiatrist here," he sort of snipped back.

Stevie smiled at him. "And you are doing a *great* job." She gave him a thumb's up before walking over to Gaertner and following him out of the group therapy room.

He led her down the long glass hallway toward the back exit. They often liked to talk while walking in the beautiful garden behind the clinic. One of Stevie's favorite places.

"So what's up?" she asked.

"I wanted to let you know before you heard from someone else . . . your sisters came by today to see you."

Stevie stopped before they reached the doors and faced Gaertner. "My sisters, they're . . . they're here?"

"They were. I asked them to leave. I think we both know you're not ready to see them right now. Not when you're doing so well."

Stevie blinked and took a step back. "But . . . they were *here*. Here at the clinic? Inside the clinic? Is that what you're telling me?"

"I told them when the time was right, we'd call them for a controlled meeting. With you and the team and your sisters."

"Okay," Stevie said to herself, not really listening to the doctor anymore. "My sisters were here. They were here." She clasped her hands together and began to pace. "And you told them to leave. And now I'm alone. But I'm inside. So I should be fine."

"Stevie, please," Gaertner coaxed. "You *are* fine. I simply was not going to allow your sisters to come here and interrupt the work we have been doing. It is much too important to your health."

"If my sisters came here, it's because something's wrong." She turned away from Gaertner to walk back to the patient rooms. "I need a phone. I need to call them."

"No, no, Stevie. That is not a good idea." He gently took her arm and tugged her back around. "You need time away from your family. Time away from the stress you experience."

Stevie gazed at the doctor but she didn't really see him because she could only think one thing . . .

What did our father do now?

That was the only reason her sisters would bother her while she was at a clinic. Because he'd done *something*. Sadly, he was always doing something, and it was always up to Stevie to stop her sisters from killing him. Especially Charlie. Charlie loathed their father. Not that Stevie really blamed her, but he was their father. That mattered. At least to her.

She was sure of it. Something was really wrong if her sisters had come here to get her. Because they'd come to protect her. And this idiot doctor had sent them away. Had they really left, though? Had they really gone away? Maybe they were still around. Maybe she had time to catch up to them.

Stevie turned to Dr. Gaertner and calmly explained how she needed to find her sisters before it was too late and that she would, unfortunately, be forced to leave the clinic much sooner than she'd originally planned . . .

Oh, wait. That's how Stevie had *planned* to handle it in her head. With logic and reason and a calm, rational demeanor.

But when she faced Gaertner, just seeing his face made her angry. Angry that she was now alone and frightened because—without speaking to her—he'd sent her sisters away. He should have spoken to her first. He should have said something!

And her fear led to panic, which led to her hissing and throwing herself at Gaertner, knocking him to the ground, and wrapping her hands around his throat.

Sitting on his chest, she hissed again, this time right into his face, and she had a feeling her eyes had shifted color because his own eyes widened and she suddenly smelled urine, meaning the man had pissed on himself.

Huh. Maybe not just her eyes. Maybe her fangs had made an appearance too. That happened when she lost control. That's why she went to places like this. To get control of her panic disorder with the help of talk therapy and medications. To learn how to manage it and to fully understand it so that she didn't have what her coworkers fondly called "a MacKilligan episode."

And Gaertner had been right. Stevie *had* been doing well! She had been feeling better. More in control without any additional meds. But her sisters had come here, and they didn't bother her lightly. Her sisters never got in the way of her work or her mental health. They worried about her, and they sometimes babied her, but they never would have just "dropped by" for a "how do ya do?" That was not her sisters' way.

Stevie knew they kept an eye on her. She knew that one of them was always close by. But, again, that was not because they were obsessive about her. They were obsessive about what their father had, to quote Charlie, "Fucked up now."

She would have made that clear to Gaertner if she'd thought about it, but it never occurred to her that he'd stop her sisters from visiting. That he thought they were somehow the reason behind her panic disorder. If anything, her sisters were the reason Stevie hadn't spent most of her life in a straitjacket at Bellevue. Their pesky ways and less-than-stellar educations allowed Stevie some much-needed distraction from the cacophony of sights, sounds, and information that packed her brain each and every day.

The truth was, her sisters kept her sane, which was more than this damn doctor was doing!

Big, strong hands gripped Stevie and yanked her off the doctor, and someone shoved a needle in her arm. A strong drug was injected into her veins and she felt a brief moment of euphoria. A moment that allowed those holding her to think she'd been controlled. But Stevie wasn't completely human and, even worse for the staff, she was half honey badger. And thanks to her father's confused genes, her body didn't process drugs and poison the way an ordinary full-human or shifter did. Even the medications she took to manage her panic disorder had to be tested and retested continuously for *years* by a shifter-run medical group in Germany to get the dosage exactly right for her biological makeup.

So if they thought filling her up with whatever calming drug they gave the regulars was going to really do anything . . .

The euphoria passed as quickly as it came and Stevie yanked her arm out of the grip of one orderly, pushed the other orderly off her, and without much thought to consequences, yanked the needle out of her arm and rammed it into the eye of the third orderly reaching out to grab her.

He went down screaming and, in full-blown panic now—other people's screaming always freaked her out—Stevie screamed along with him as she made a mad run for the exit.

Chapter Three

They hadn't left the Swiss center yet, and Charlie knew the longer they stayed, the more concerned those orderlies were going to become. Already there were five of them standing outside the front doors, waiting for the pair to leave.

Hoping to calm them down, Charlie found a map in the glove compartment and spread it out on the hood of the Mercedes.

Max watched her and finally asked, "What are you doing?"

"Trying to calm them down by looking like we're lost," she softly replied.

"Why?"

"Because we're making them nervous."

"We make everybody nervous. Who gives a fuck?"

Charlie placed her hands on the hood and asked, "What's it like to be you, Max? Not to care? Ever?"

Max shrugged. "It's *awesome*."

Charlie let out that sigh she was convinced she only used when it came to her middle sibling.

"I'm not going to argue with you today," Charlie announced. More for her own benefit than for Max's because Max didn't give a shit. "We have too much going on."

"So, do you want me to look intensely at the map like it's still 1982?" Max asked. "You know, rather than just using my fucking phone to take us anywhere we need to go in any part of the world?"

Charlie briefly wondered if slamming her sister's head against the SUV's hood would be considered "arguing" when the front doors of the clinic burst open and her baby sister came rushing through.

An orderly instinctively reached out and grabbed the hysterical Stevie, but that was *not* a good move. Not a good move at all.

Stevie spun and slammed the palm of her hand up, ramming the orderly's nose and crushing it. He released her and, even though the others hadn't moved, Stevie kicked one orderly in the groin, another in the leg, breaking the fibula with a cracking sound that echoed around the quiet area. Another got a punch to the face that seemed to break his jaw and cheekbone, and the last was punched in the throat.

The orderly that had followed her outside had spun back around and returned to the safety of the center in order to get reinforcements.

That's when, screaming like she was on fire, Stevie ran for her life, so oblivious to everything around her, she didn't even see Charlie and Max standing there, watching her. She just took off running. And, with the tiger blood flowing through her veins, she hit forty miles per hour pretty damn quickly.

Max watched their panic-riddled sister tear off across the front lawn and hit the road that would lead out to the main highway. "Guess the doc told her we'd been here." Then she laughed because, well . . . it was kind of funny. "Look at her go! I think sparks are coming off her feet."

"Come on," Charlie ordered Max, tossing the map off the SUV hood. "We have to catch her."

They scrambled into the SUV and sped after their sister, heading down the long road that led to and from the clinic. On both sides were thick forests.

"If she goes into the woods—"

"She's panicking," Charlie reminded Max. "She's just gonna run until she can't anymore."

"She's so fast."

"In short bursts. She has no stamina." Not an insult, just reality. Again, it was the tiger in her. The wolf and honey badger in Charlie meant she could trot for hours. Not that she ever did. Why bother when she could just as easily rent a car?

Max suddenly hit the brakes and Charlie let out a relieved breath when she saw her baby sister standing in the middle of the road, taking in deep gulps of air and sobbing.

"I'll get her." Charlie opened her door. "And when I bring her back, you be nice!" she warned.

"I'm always nice!" Max laughed.

"Shut up."

Charlie walked around the car and over to her baby sister's side, but she didn't touch Stevie. She didn't put her arms around her and hug her. That was just a quick way to get her face torn off.

"Stevie." She said her sister's name flatly, with authority; her voice low. "Stevie," she repeated.

Blinking away tears, Stevie straightened her back and focused on Charlie.

"Charlie?"

"Hey, bubs."

"Charlie!" Now Stevie was in her arms, hugging her tight, and Charlie hugged her back because she was no longer worried about getting her face ripped off.

"You didn't leave me. You didn't leave me," she chanted.

"Of course we didn't. We were just trying to find

a way to get to you without the staff knowing." She stroked Stevie's hair. She'd started dyeing it a nice, safe blond. Charlie kept hers brown, and Max dyed hers any color she was in the mood to see for a few weeks or months. They did this to avoid the questions. So many questions about their hair.

"How bad is it?" Charlie asked.

Swallowing, Stevie took a step back, her gaze focused on the trees behind Charlie's head.

Charlie knew that look.

"Is anyone dead?" Charlie now asked, worried about her sister's answer.

"No! No." Her voice lowered even more. "No." Stevie cleared her throat. "Someone may have lost an eye, though."

"Okay." Charlie grabbed her sister's arm and quickly led her to the SUV, pushing her into the backseat and getting in beside her.

"Go, Max."

The car took off and Charlie held her baby sister's hand and calmly spoke to her. "Deep breath in. Deep breath out. In. Out. Close your eyes and just focus on the engine sounds. The road beneath the wheels. The air against the car."

"Your whining against my nerves," Max joked from the front seat.

Stevie's gold eyes popped open and she rammed the flat of her hand against the back of Max's seat.

"Hey!" Max barked.

"Do you know what I've been through?" Stevie yelled. "Do you have any concept?"

"Keep yelling at me, and I'll give you something to really whine about."

Unable to stand another second, Charlie slapped her hands together several times and yelped, "That is enough! We don't have time for you two psychotic females to be bickering like we're still in grade school!"

"Wait," Stevie said, the anger in her voice gone, unfortunately replaced by hysteria. "Do you hear that?"

"Stevie, you need to—"

"No. Listen."

Charlie did . . . and she heard it too.

"Is that a chopper?"

As soon as Charlie asked the question, the military-type chopper charged past them, so close, Charlie was surprised it didn't hit the roof of the car.

Max slowed to a stop.

The chopper turned and came back, hovering about fifty feet away.

"Dude!" Max demanded, trying to look back at Stevie over her seat. "What kind of mental hospital did you go to?"

The target and her sisters waited in the SUV.

"Stay here," he ordered the pilot. "Give them a minute to figure out what's about to happen."

"Got it."

The original plan had been to take the target in the clinic, but he'd just been heading toward the building when she'd run out, hysterically screaming. He'd immediately gone back to the copter. Especially when he realized the two older sisters were still alive.

His orders had been painfully simple. Pick up the target and bring her to the safe house. Two other teams had been dispatched to take out the troublesome older sisters so they couldn't get in the way. Apparently they had a reputation that had his clients concerned. But somehow those two had gotten away from full tactical teams. He still wasn't sure how they'd managed that.

The sister on the driver's side eased out and headed toward the back of the SUV.

"Want me to take her out?"

"No," he replied immediately. "We keep them alive until we have the target. They'll keep her pliable."

"She's probably going for a weapon."

He wasn't worried. The copter could handle a few gunshots.

Tapping the mic, he began the negotiation process.

Still in the backseat with Stevie, Charlie focused on her baby sister and ignored whatever the man in the chopper was saying. Most would be concerned with the chopper guy, but he was the least of her problems. Already Charlie could see the panic welling up again in Stevie. And if Stevie snapped . . .

"What's going on? Who are these people? They're not from the center! What did Dad do now?" Stevie spit out in rapid succession. Then she asked, "Why are they doing this? *What are we going to do?*"

There it went. That high-pitched squeal that said Stevie was moments away from going into full panic mode.

"Don't worry about them," Charlie told her sister. "Let's focus on your breathing."

Stevie calmed down enough to glare at Charlie. "Seriously?"

"I'm trying to help."

"I'm not an infant."

"Fine. Then balls the fuck up!"

"Don't snarl at me!" Stevie shot back, her panic finally overridden by anger, which Charlie welcomed. "If you only would—"

Both sisters screamed and ducked down, hands over their heads; the entire SUV bucked from the explosion.

They waited a few seconds before sitting up and staring out the front window with their mouths open, as the remains of the chopper landed all around their vehicle.

And with the chopper were the remains of several men, their charred bodies—and pieces from those bodies—banging against the vehicle and ground with nauseating thuds.

Charlie heard Max humming and turned to see that she had the back door open and was returning the weapon she held to its case.

"*A rocket launcher?*" Charlie exploded.

"Oh, my God!" Stevie gasped.

"*Have you lost your mind?*"

Max shrugged. "What? I wasn't about to get into a shoot-out with them. That's a *military* chopper. Did you see the Gatling guns on the sides?"

"I don't care, you idiot! What are we supposed to tell the Swiss authorities?"

Frowning, Max asked, "Why would we talk to anybody about this?" She closed the back door, went around the SUV, and got into the driver's side. She stared out the front window for a moment, got back out of the SUV, and walked around the front, kicking bodies and big, burning chunks of the helicopter out of the way to make a path through the debris.

When Max returned to the vehicle, she buckled her seat belt and glanced back at Charlie and Stevie. "Ready to go?" she asked, smiling. Chipper even. In fact, *extremely* chipper. Like they were going to brunch.

How did she do that? Unlike her sisters, Max was all honey badger, and yet she had the most pleasant, happy, almost *sunny* disposition Charlie had ever known.

Charlie had never met another honey badger like her.

"Stop smiling," Charlie ordered her sister.

And, of course, Max's smile grew until it took up most of her face.

Charlie nearly had her hands around Max's throat but Stevie wrapped her arms around her and dragged her back against the seat.

"What are you mad at me for?" Max asked, oblivious as always.

"Just go," Stevie ordered. "And shut up."

"Both of you are so moody." Max took the car out of park and drove through the path she'd created until she was able to enter the woods. This got them off the road and, hopefully, away from any law enforcement who'd be heading this way.

So this was what it was like to be a true "maestro." Berg thought he'd "gotten it" before, but he hadn't. Not until men came from the Vatican, sent personally by His Holiness so that they could escort Coop to his next venue.

Even cooler? They were waiting to board a private jet that was only used for His Holiness. The Pope had sent it to transport Coop and his entire team, and apparently he wouldn't take no for an answer.

Coop had tried. Politely. Not wanting to put the Pope and his attendees out in any way. And Coop wasn't bullshitting. He really didn't like to put people out, but again . . . His Holiness wouldn't hear it.

Of course, Coop had not asked for any of this, but his sister . . . ?

Well, Toni Jean-Louis Parker Reed was a different matter. Plus, she was trapped in Siberia at the moment and couldn't make her way to Italy just now. At least not in time to help. So she'd called the Vatican herself—of course she did—and had them make all these arrangements. For her brother's safety, she'd said. A sentiment that Berg could only roll his eyes over.

"Hey, Berg," Coop said next to him.

"Huh?"

"My sister is sending even more backup, to get us home."

Berg rolled his eyes again. "Oy."

The jackal chuckled. "Don't take it personally. It's just my sister's way. She can be obsessive when it comes to her siblings. Among jackal families, she's considered the gold standard of proper older sibling behavior."

"Is she sending someone I'm going to hate?"

"I don't think so. But I can never tell with you and your brother, which people you guys hate. Unlike your sister, who is very direct about her hatred."

"You do always know where you stand with my sister."

"I heard she'll be the one 'handling'"—he made air quotes with his fingers—"Toni when she gets here."

"Well, Dag and I weren't going to do it."

"Nope," Dag muttered.

"I don't blame you. She wanted to fire you guys, by the way. But I said, 'Absolutely not. They're my friends. And so what if they put me in grave danger and put my life and, more importantly, my God-given gifts at risk? A loss that would deprive the entire world, maybe even the universe, of something truly amazing. They're still my friends.'"

Berg gazed down at Coop. "How big of you."

"I thought so."

"We're friends?" Dag asked.

"The jet is ready, Maestro," one of the Vatican's men announced.

With Dag on one side of Coop and Berg on the other, the trio began to walk toward the door that would lead them to the private airstrip. But as they passed the front desk, Berg caught sight of the TV behind the attendant.

Both he and Coop stopped walking and briefly watched the Italian-language news announcement about a helicopter in Switzerland that had been shot down on a private road.

Coop didn't understand Italian but he got the gist of the story from the visuals.

He looked at Coop and the jackal stared back, both of them silently asking the question.

Then, after several seconds, they both said together, *"Nahhh."* And continued on toward the awaiting jet.

"Get out. I have to set this thing on fire."

Charlie stared at her sister. "Are you just on a rampage? What are you doing?"

"Don't worry. We have another car waiting right there. We're totally covered."

With another pleasant smile, Max walked off.

"She's going to get us killed or put in prison for the rest of our lives," Stevie informed Charlie. "I just want you to know that."

"I wish I could argue with you," Charlie admitted. "But I can't."

They got out of the car, each grabbing a duffle bag from the back of the SUV, and headed in the direction Max pointed out to them.

As Charlie walked, she smelled smoke from behind her just before Max ran up to them. Another bag was hanging from her shoulder. And the . . .

Charlie stopped and her sisters stopped with her. "You brought the *rocket launcher*?"

"You expect me to leave it? Do you know how much these things cost? Especially these really compact ones? Are you nuts?" she scoffed before heading off again.

"You know," Stevie noted, "we could kill her here and bury her and no one would ever know." She frowned, shook her head. "I guess that was a horrible thing to say."

"No, sweetie. It was just a honey badger thing to say. Nothing to worry about. I say honey badger things all the time but *never* do them."

They followed Max, reaching a brand-new Range Rover painted a very bright red.

"Subtle," Charlie said to Max. Her sister grinned, oblivious, and quickly began packing the trunk, stopping to answer her vibrating phone.

"We're all going to jail, aren't we?" Stevie suddenly asked as she and Charlie finished up the trunk packing.

"Not if I can help it," Charlie promised. "I've worked too long and hard for any of us to go to prison now." She paused a moment, then added, "But if we have to sacrifice someone, it'll be Max. She could handle prison way better than either of us."

After a few minutes, Max returned to their side and Charlie knew, as soon as she saw her sister's face, that something had changed.

"What?" Charlie asked when Max didn't say anything.

Max glanced at Stevie, then back to Charlie. "I just got a call . . . from New York."

"Oh, God," Stevie began. "Oh, God, Oh, God, Oh, G—"

"Stevie," Charlie said, raising one finger. "*No.*"

She could see her sister was readying herself for another panic attack, and Charlie simply didn't have the patience for it right now. Especially when Stevie could go from zero to hysterical in six seconds.

She was the Ferrari of panic.

"Breathe," she ordered Stevie before facing Max. "Who do we know in New York?"

"Not a lot of people. But . . ." She cleared her throat, glanced at Stevie who was now doing her deep breathing exercises. "It's Dad . . ."

Charlie briefly closed her eyes. "Let me guess. He's

in jail. He wants bail. Well, fuck him! I'm a thousand percent positive that we're on the run because of him. So he can stay in jail until he rots."

"He's dead," Maxie abruptly announced. "They need someone to identify the body."

Stevie put her hand to her chest and turned away from them, her head bowed, shoulders beginning to shake, her pain and grief clear to anyone who might be near.

Charlie and Max, however, didn't hesitate to silently bop around each other, performing dance moves they really shouldn't because they just didn't have the talent for it. However, it wasn't a dance of skill, but of excitement. Of relief. Of downright giddiness.

Neither sister spoke as they boogied around each other because words weren't necessary. But despite their silence . . .

Stevie slapped her hand against the Range Rover and snarled, "I know what you two are doing back there and *stop it!* He's still our father!"

Chapter Four

It took a few days to make it into the States, and it hadn't been easy. But Max had a lot of connections, which always helped when they were in foreign countries. Thankfully they were back now and able to drop their bags in the middle of the safe house Max had found through her birth mother's family.

"Wow," Charlie said, looking around. "This place is awesome. Your aunt hooked us up."

Max nodded. "It's not bad."

Stevie sat in the farthest corner and deepest part of the couch, her knees up, arms around her calves. "I don't like it."

"Why not?" Charlie asked.

Her nose crinkled. "It smells funny."

"That's just badger." Max took another sniff. "And something bear-ish."

Stevie's eyes grew impossibly wide. "Bears eat people."

"I'm taking a shower," Charlie announced because she couldn't start down this road with her sisters. "Then we'll figure out next steps. Okay?" When she got nods from both, Charlie grabbed her duffle and headed deeper into the Manhattan apartment.

The place was beautiful. Big, comfortable furniture.

Lots of windows allowing for light. And tons of cabinet space for the honey badgers to sleep in.

Charlie was surprised the Yang family had helped Max get this place for them to stay in. Even temporarily. Maybe Max hadn't mentioned that her sisters would be with her, but she didn't usually hide that from anyone. The Yangs had made it clear long ago that they would be more likely to help Max when she needed it if her half-sisters weren't involved. They'd never quite forgiven Max's mother for hooking up with Fred MacKilligan. Among the honey badger population, the MacKilligans didn't have the best reputation. Especially when it came to good ol' Freddy. The most useless of beings as far as Charlie was concerned.

To this very day, she still didn't understand what her amazing, feminist mother—or any other woman for that matter—saw in her worthless excuse of a father. He was . . . worthless! She had no other word for it. Or maybe she had too many words for the man. Many ways to describe how worthless he truly was.

But that was over now. Her father—thankfully!—was rotting away in a New York City morgue. Just waiting for her and her sisters to identify and bury him.

Charlie couldn't wait.

She knew it sounded cruel to those who didn't know her father. Who didn't understand *why* she disliked the man so much. But she had her reasons and those reasons were all she needed.

If nothing else, she hoped his death would end the bad luck that seemed to follow the man around and, in turn, follow his daughters around as well.

Daughters who hadn't asked to be born. Definitely hadn't asked for him to be their father. Three girls who'd had no say in what they'd already been through.

Yes. She blamed her father for all of it, but she wasn't

about to let that get in her way. Because it was a new day! She just had to be cool about it.

Stevie didn't like their father any more than Charlie and Max did, but she took the fact that he was their sperm donor much more seriously. She would want to mourn his death, and they had to respect that.

Which reminded her . . .

Naked, Charlie walked out of the bathroom, where the shower was now running. She went into the living room and found that Max and Stevie already had each other in headlocks. Max grinning. Stevie cursing Max.

"The never-ending, battling sisters," was what the Pack had called Max and Stevie. And it was true. The pair of them could and would go at it until someone separated them or an ambulance had to be called. The thing was, an ambulance rarely had to be called for either Max or Stevie. If there was one thing that was true about all MacKilligan females . . . they could take a beating. But teachers, coaches, strangers on the street, *anyone* who thought it was a good idea to get between the sisters to stop them from fighting always found out the hard way that it was *not*.

But Charlie wasn't some stranger on the street. She knew how to handle her sisters. It was the first thing her mother had taught her when she realized how poorly the two got along.

Going behind both women, Charlie grabbed Max by the tough skin of her back and swung her one way, then the other. Poor Stevie forced to go with her.

And while Charlie swung, she kept chanting, "Let her go, let her go, let her go." Until Max did what she was told to do.

"On the couch," Charlie ordered, pointing at Stevie. "You, on the chair." She motioned to the leather armchair until Max sat down.

Once both her sisters were sitting away from each
other, she said, "Now listen up. I'm going into the
shower. It will be a long shower. A luxurious shower."

"Why not a bath?" Stevie asked.

"I don't like baths. I don't like soaking in my own
filth."

Max started laughing but stopped when Charlie
snapped, "Shut up. Now, while I'm in that shower, you
two will not argue. You will not fight." She pointed at
Max. "You will not startle." She pointed at Stevie. "You
will not throw things. No matter what she says to you,"
she added quickly before Stevie could argue. "Let's just
be glad that we made it back to the States without killing each other or getting arrested. Let's enjoy this moment for what it is."

"The death of our father?" Max asked.

Charlie glared at Max for a moment before they both
raised their arms in the air and cried out, "Hurray!"

"Ladies!" Stevie barked, disgusted.

"Sorry. Sorry." Charlie didn't want to upset her sister. She wanted a shower too badly. A nice, normal, *relaxing* shower. And she couldn't have that if she was
worried the two of them were attempting to kill each
other in the next room.

"We'll get through this, Stevie," she promised her
baby sister.

Stevie nodded and moved deeper into the couch
corner until she couldn't move any farther. She placed
her feet on the cushions, wrapped her arms around her
calves, and rested her chin on her raised knees. Charlie
pointed at Max one more time, letting her know in no
uncertain terms that if anything happened while she
was showering, Charlie *would* absolutely blame Max
for it. Because most likely it would be Max's fault.

Max reached for the remote and turned on the enormous, high-end TV in the middle of the room.

"Oh, look," Charlie pointed out. "*Law & Order.*"

"Thank God," Stevie muttered. Funny, since Stevie always went on and on about how she didn't watch TV.

"Excellent!" Max chimed in. "One of the early episodes. Before cell phones and social media!"

Knowing they'd be entertained for a few hours at least, Charlie headed off to her very hot and relaxing shower.

Max was so tempted to fuck with her sister, but Charlie's warning had been very clear. Charlie was all about being clear. She didn't like vague. She didn't like subtle. She didn't like when people weren't direct. Why? Because Charlie was always direct.

When Charlie had told her once, "If you bother Stevie while she's taking that test, I'm going to break your arm," she'd meant it. Max had been forced to wear that cast for, like, two days, the break was so bad. But she'd learned her lesson. A Charlie warning was serious stuff, and you ignored it at your own peril.

Deciding to help make this easier for everyone involved, Max got up and grabbed Stevie's backpack. They'd run by that CERN place and picked up a bunch of her stuff so that she'd have things with her to keep her calm, like all her notebooks. And, at this point, it was all about keeping Stevie calm. Not a small order either. "Calm" was as foreign to Stevie as "uptight" was to Max.

She placed the bag next to the couch Stevie was on and started back to her chair. She didn't look at Stevie or smile. Because Stevie would assume Max was mocking her—and let's be honest . . . she probably was—and react accordingly.

But just as Max was about to drop her ass in the big armchair, both sisters looked at each other and then at the front door a few feet away . . .

*   *   *

Vic Barinov stood by his mate and smiled. They were finally home, and he couldn't be happier. They'd had to run over to Italy in a private jet to retrieve just one jackal. But that jackal was like family to his mate and she'd insisted that Vic and his panda partner be the ones to go pick him up. Then she'd insisted on going with them. It seemed like a big deal for nothing until the news hit the states about the brutal "hotel invasion" in Milan, involving Maestro Cooper Jean-Louis Parker. Suddenly Vic understood why everyone was freaking out.

But for someone who'd been through a horrible attack—one so bad his bodyguard had been shot *and* stabbed—good ol' Coop had seemed fine. More than fine. He'd still got to perform at Vatican City for the Pope and he'd flatly refused to fire the three grizzlies who'd been the core of his protection. Despite his older sister's near-hysterical rantings about cutting them loose. But nope. Coop wouldn't hear of it, which basically told Vic all he'd needed to know.

That whatever was going on, Vic didn't *want* to know.

Instead, he'd let his mate and her best friend get crazed about protecting a jackal old enough to breed.

Vic glanced behind him and saw the elevator doors open again. Coop walked out with two of his grizzly protection and Vic's partner, Shen.

He didn't know why, now that they were back on Coop's home turf, he couldn't get rid of them, but Vic wasn't going to complain. Instead, he'd just get into his house, go to his bedroom, and close the door—*before* the grizzly side of him got cranky and bit someone's head off, or his tiger side started clawing on human flesh to make it quiet. As a hybrid, he had many ways to stop people from getting on his nerves. Not that those options were morally right, but . . . you know . . .

Looking down at his honey badger mate, Vic immediately noticed that Livy Kowalski had the key in the lock but she hadn't opened the door. Instead, she stood frozen to the spot, her ears twitching right along with her nose. Then her eyes narrowed.

"Livy?"

She yanked the keys out of the lock and her lips pulled back over her honey badger fangs. Then, her dark eyes growing even darker, Livy growled out, "Badger."

"Livy, wait—"

"Badger!" Livy stepped back and kicked the door open, even though she had the keys in her hand and it was a thousand-dollar lockset on the door.

Vic grabbed for her, but she jerked away and charged into their apartment, throwing her entire body at the female honey badger standing by Livy's much-beloved armchair. Her favorite chair in the whole apartment.

Nope. This would not end well.

In horror, Berg watched two tiny Asian women go at each other like the wild animals they partially were. Snarls and snaps, blood flying, as they rolled across the floor of Vic's beautiful apartment.

And yet . . . Vic just stood there. Doing nothing. While his mate was possibly getting her ass ripped apart. Things were moving so fast, Berg really couldn't tell who was doing what to whom, but he took all that blood as a bad sign.

Maybe Vic was in shock or something. True, he had military training but maybe this was causing some kind of flashback. Yeah. That was it. A flashback. Why else wouldn't he be helping the woman he loved?

"Dag!" Berg called out to his brother before pushing Vic aside and rushing into the apartment.

Berg grabbed the unknown female from behind and Dag took hold of Livy around the stomach, lifting the tiny She-badger off her feet.

And, as soon as they did that, Berg knew exactly how stupid a move it was. The kind of move his sister would never let them get away with if she were anywhere near this situation. Why? Because she knew better. Size didn't matter when it came to shifters. Rage did.

And these two women were all about the rage.

The woman he held managed to twist around and latch her teeth into his neck, biting at the flesh of his throat, fangs digging for a main artery.

"Get her off me!" Berg screamed, desperately trying to push her away. *"Get her off!"*

But Dag couldn't help. He had his own problems. Livy had reached back with one hand and gripped poor Dag by the balls . . . and twisted. Then she kept twisting!

Berg's brother dropped to his knees, his scream so high-pitched that Berg was sure dogs in Brooklyn could hear him.

Livy pulled away from Dag and charged the other female.

Unlatching from Berg's neck—*Thank you, God!*— the female dropped to the ground and backed up, hissing, then charged Livy. Livy backed up, then lunged forward. It was like a dance. A weird, horrifying dance of death.

Berg fell back against the floor, his hand over his bleeding neck. He wasn't sure, but the tip of that woman's fang might have nicked his artery.

And that's when he saw her. She'd been sitting silently on the couch, but when he locked eyes on her, she suddenly seemed to . . . panic.

Like a house cat. Yeah. That was it. She panicked like a house cat!

The woman scrambled onto all fours, her back arched. She bared her fangs, her hiss of warning skittering across the room violently. So violently that the sound alone made the furniture move. So much so that both the badgers were briefly distracted. Blinking at each other and turning toward the female on the couch.

And when they did . . . she *really* freaked out.

Jumping straight up, she flipped in midair until she hit the high ceiling, her claws digging into the drywall . . .

And that's where she stayed, hissing at them all with a rage that shook the windows. The shaking becoming worse when she suddenly roared.

"What the fuck is happening?" a voice bellowed from the hallway that led to the bedrooms.

Berg forced himself to look away from the panicked female and over to the hallway—and he saw her. A woman he had assumed he'd never see again. She had on nothing but a towel, her wet brown hair resting against her shoulders, the strands already beginning to curl. Her dark brown eyes glaring at each of them, a vein in her neck and the side of her head throbbing.

"Somebody answer me!"

The She-badger pointed at Livy. "It was her," she said, her voice flat. Not like she'd just been in a life-or-death fight. More like she'd been in a life-or-death nap.

"You're in my house," Livy barked back.

"It's a safe house," the badger snapped. "It's not your fucking house. You have to share."

"It is *not* a safe house, you worthless whore!"

The badger's eye twitched the smallest bit. It was barely perceptible. But then she was reaching for Livy again and Livy was ready for it.

But the woman—*the* woman—clapped her hands together several times and both badgers stopped. Which was weird. Hand claps never got Berg out of his grizzly rage.

"Stop it. Both of you. This is completely un . . . un . . ." Her voice trailed off and she leaned down, eyes narrowing on Vic's mate. "Oh. Hi, Livy."

Livy gave a half-assed wave. "Hi, Charlie."

Vic, finally, spoke, his forefinger jerking between Livy and the other badger. "You guys know each other?"

With a small shrug, Livy admitted, "We're cousins."

Shen laughed from the doorway.

"But even if we are family—" Livy began.

Berg's attacker raised a brow at Livy. *"If?"*

"This is still *my* house and you can't just come here and act like it's yours!"

"Max?" the woman prompted when the other badger didn't say anything.

"What are you looking at me for?" the badger demanded. "It was on the list."

Livy frowned, nostrils flaring. "What list?"

"The safe house list. Online."

Livy went tense, her entire body vibrating. "My house is on the safe house list?"

"What's the safe house list?" Vic asked.

"It's where Yangs can go online to find a house to stay in when they're on the run."

Livy closed her eyes. "And *my* house is on the list?"

Max the badger shrugged. "Yeah. That's why we're here. It's not like I *wanted* to see you."

"I'll kill her." Livy shook her head. "I'll kill her."

"Livy—" Vic began.

"I will kill her!" Livy jumped up and yanked a phone from her back pocket. She speed-dialed someone and stalked out of the room.

Max smirked. "Let me guess," she asked Vic. "Her mother put her on the list just to fuck with her?"

"Probably."

Still dripping from the interrupted shower, Charlie looked around the room, her eyes not even stopping on Berg before moving on to everyone else.

She didn't remember him. He helped save her life, gave her his gun, and she didn't even remember him. Seriously?

"Where's Stevie?" she asked.

Grinning, blood covering her teeth, Max pointed.

Charlie looked up and sighed. "Could you please come down from there? *Now?*"

"I'm quite comfortable right here, thanks."

"Stevie MacKilligan!"

Claws were retracted and Stevie landed back on the couch. "No need to yell," she mumbled.

"Wait," Coop said, suddenly stepping in from the doorway. "Stevie MacKilligan?" he smiled. "Is that you? It's me. Coop. Cooper Jean-Louis Parker," he clarified when she only stared. "Remember? We studied under Maestro Raimondi and performed together for Europe's royal families. Is this ringing any bells at all?"

"No," she replied. Then, before Coop could say any more, she raised her hand, palm out, and informed one of the greatest, most-loved musicians in the world, "And to be quite honest, I can't deal with some obsessive *fan* right now."

"Not a fan," Coop corrected. "We studied together. We were *both* prodigies."

"Whatever. I'll get you an autograph later."

"No, no. You don't under—"

"Sweetie," Charlie cut in. "I really don't have time for this right now. Somebody just tell me what's going on."

Livy's cousin shrugged. "Nothing. Why?"

"Max."

Max grinned. "Sorry, couldn't stop myself." She

laughed a little and pointed in her cousin's direction. "Based on the yelling in Cantonese from the other room—"

"It's Mandarin," Vic corrected.

"Oh, what?" Max suddenly barked at the startled bear hybrid. "You think because I'm half Asian I know Chinese? Because I don't know Chinese."

"Told ya," Shen chimed in before sliding into the armchair, although Berg had no idea what the giant panda was referring to.

"But you two are family," Vic insisted. "How do you not know what dialect your people speak?"

"Well—" Max began.

"We don't have time for that conversation," Charlie announced. She was still standing there, wet, in only a towel. And she didn't seem to care. "Max, ignore the bears and talk to me."

"They are all bears, aren't they?" Stevie suddenly looked at each and every male in the room, sizing them up. After she finished, she leaned toward her sister and loudly whispered, "We're all going to die!"

"I'm actually a jackal," Coop corrected.

"Do you think that matters?" Stevie bellowed hysterically.

Charlie placed her fingertips against her temples. "We're not going to die and stop yelling," she sighed out.

"They're all *giant* man-eating bears except for my stalker."

"I'm not a stalker," Coop argued.

"Don't you see, Charlie?" Stevie leaned in, the scent of panic beginning to come off her in big, booming waves. "Bears kill. *Bears kill, Charlie! And they're going to kill all of us!*"

Charlie quickly walked to the couch and grabbed a backpack from the floor. She pulled out a bottle of pre-

scription pills, glanced at the label, then held it out for
the other woman.

"Take this," she ordered Stevie before focusing on
Vic and demanding, "Glass of water." Vic moved.
Rushing out of the room and returning in seconds. He
handed the glass to Stevie, and Charlie placed several
tablets into the woman's hand. "Take them."

"But—" Stevie tried.

"*Take them.*"

Stevie did as ordered.

"Now," Charlie said, facing them all again. "Where
were we?"

"You were trying to justify breaking and entering,"
Berg announced, "and you have absolutely *no idea who
I am!*"

Charlie stared at him across the room and, after a
few seconds, said, "Of course I know you! How could
I forget . . . you?"

"Then what's my name?"

"Deuteronomy?" She shrugged. "Dude for short?"

Coop burst out laughing but all Berg could do was
shake his head. "Seriously?"

Max briefly closed her eyes. "She doesn't know you,
Deuteronomy, because she can't *see* you."

"My name is *not* Deuteronomy!"

"Wow," Shen marveled at Charlie. "You're really
mobile for a blind person."

"She's not blind," Max said, laughing. "She's just not
wearing her glasses or contacts."

"*What are you doing?*" Stevie screamed at Max.
"Why don't you just announce to the world that we're
defenseless women just waiting to be *murdered by
bears*?"

"Defenseless?" Berg barked. "I'm bleeding from an
artery here!"

"Don't be a baby," Max said, glancing back at him. "I barely grazed that artery."

"We're all going to die here," Stevie insisted, pointing at Max. "And it'll be all your—"

Stevie's rant abruptly stopped and her head dropped forward. After a few seconds, she began to drool.

Max looked at Charlie. "What the fuck did you give her?"

"Her Xanax. To deal with her panic."

"Are you *sure* that's what you gave her? Because you're not wearing your glasses and she seems to be having a very . . . intense reaction."

Charlie reached down and grabbed the bottle of pills out of her sister's bag again. She brought the bottle so close, her eyes narrowing into thin slits, that Berg knew Max hadn't been lying. This was a shifter, who was not ninety years old, yet actually needed glasses because she couldn't see. She was nearsighted. A shifter? Nearsighted? That was so . . . weird.

"Uh-oh," Charlie said, the pill bottle practically touching her nose.

Max stared at her sister. "What?"

She cringed and held the bottle up. "It's lithium."

"Dude!" Max burst out along with a loud laugh.

"I know! I know." She dropped the bottle and grabbed a seemingly unconscious Stevie. She shook her sister. Then she slapped her.

"Stevie! *Stevie!*" When her sister didn't respond, Charlie released her and threw up her hands. "I've killed her. Of course I've killed her. I knew one day I'd kill you all."

Max finally got to her feet. "Good Lord! Get off the cross, we need the wood."

"What does that mean?"

"She'll be fine. At any point now, she'll projectile vomit and then she'll be good as new."

Every bear close to Stevie silently moved back.

"Just go get dressed," Max pushed. "So we can get out of here."

"And go where?"

"I don't know. A hotel? Like normal people."

"Normal people aren't on the run for their lives."

"Oh." Max nodded. "I forgot about that."

Charlie flung her arms out from her sides before crossing them over her chest. "How does one forget that?"

Max mimicked her sister by crossing her arms over her chest, too. "I have a lot on my mind."

"Name one thing you have on your mind. At this very moment."

The badger glanced off, gaze focusing across the room. And no, she never did answer the question.

Stevie abruptly stood, arms spread wide, body crouched. "*Bears!*" she suddenly yelled.

"It's okay!" Charlie said, standing in front of her, ready to sacrifice her body if her sister tried to get past her. "Stevie, it's okay. Why don't you take a little nap?"

"Okay." Stevie dropped to the couch, turned over and started snoring.

Charlie blew out a breath and suddenly smiled in his direction, although Berg was sure she still couldn't see him.

Still yelling at her mother, Livy paced back into the living room from the hallway. Without making a sound, Max charged her cousin. Livy was so busy being angry, she didn't even see her. But taking a step out, Charlie swung her arm in front of Max.

Max's neck ran right into Charlie's forearm—and it was like she hit a stone wall. Legs coming up while her head didn't move. Then she was flung backward.

The badger hit the floor hard . . . laughing and coughing.

Livy missed all of it. Swinging around suddenly and pacing back the other way, still yelling at her mother.

Charlie stepped over to Max, placing her bare foot on her sister's chest.

"Who's going to behave in her cousin's house?" she asked.

"Oh, come on!" Max said, still laughing.

Charlie leaned down and clapped her hands three times. "*Maxie!*"

"I promise! I promise! I won't start anything!'

"Or finish." Charlie raised an eyebrow. "Arguments begun at family dinners when you're nine years old do not need to be avenged when you're twenty-seven. Do we understand each other?"

"I told her I'd kill her one day. And I meant it."

"You were nine."

"I still meant it."

Charlie rolled her eyes. "Do we let it go?" she asked. "Or do I start dismantling body parts?"

"Fine. I'll let it go. It will not be forgotten," she added. "But I will let it go."

"Excellent. I'm going to get dressed so we can get out of here. You'll keep an eye on Stevie, yes? Make sure she doesn't choke on her own vomit or swallow her tongue. And I need you to figure out where we're going next. But be nice . . . and respectful."

Max gave a thumb's up and her sister stepped off her chest and walked away.

Wincing, Max sat up. She looked back at Berg and brushed her fingers against her own throat. "You still have a little blood dripping *right* there."

Berg growled at her, but she just laughed.

Chapter Five

Berg helped his brother up off the floor.

"I'm so glad Britta wasn't here," Dag said, one arm around Berg's shoulders, his other hand cradling his balls through his jeans. "She'd have kicked our asses for getting in the middle of a honey badger fight."

"We weren't thinking, that's all. Next time we'll know better."

"Agreed."

Berg's phone sailed past Dag's head. As it hit the wall and broke into pieces, Livy stalked back into the living room.

"I hate everyone," she announced to . . . well . . . everyone.

"Went that well with your mother?" Vic asked.

So upset she couldn't even respond, Livy walked out of the room again. When she returned a minute later, she held a bandage. She tore off the backing and without any preamble, slapped it against the wound on Berg's neck.

"Ow!"

"Don't whine," she snarled.

Hands on her hips, Livy said to Max without even looking at her cousin, "Now I guess I'll go talk to Charlie since she's the only one among you three that has any sense."

"You should go talk to her," Max agreed with a smile. "And make sure you keep that *great* attitude when you do. She'll love it!"

"No," Berg said quickly, seeing exactly where Max was attempting to lead her cousin. "I'll talk to her."

"You?" Max asked. "She doesn't even remember you."

"That was hurtful." Berg pushed his brother toward Vic. "Could you help Dag for me? I think he needs some ice."

"Or a new penis."

They all turned to stare at the other honey badger and Livy shrugged those massive shoulders and admitted, "I know, I know. I should stop talking."

Berg headed deep into the apartment until he found the bathroom Charlie was in. She'd put on jeans and was bent over at the waist, finger-combing her wet hair. Not wanting to startle her, he quietly waited. But Berg was having a hard time not staring. She looked really good in those jeans.

Then Charlie abruptly stood and Berg realized she wasn't wearing a shirt. Just a sheer, lacy bra. He was so surprised, he tried to turn away but rammed into the doorway instead, nearly knocking himself out.

Charlie was reaching for a comb when she heard that thud, followed by a "Dammit!"

She looked toward the bathroom doorway, but all she saw was a blur.

"Sorry," a voice said. "Didn't mean to startle you."

"No problem." She combed her hair off her face.

"And I thought you were more . . . dressed."

Charlie squinted down at herself. "The nips are hidden."

"Pardon?"

"Nothing, nothing." She looked at herself in the mirror, trying to figure out what to do with her hair. "So what do you need?"

There was a pause, then . . . "Do you know who I am?"

There was a room full of big guys in Livy's apartment and she still wasn't wearing her glasses. She was lucky to recognize Livy. So she took a guess.

"Deuteronomy?"

"That is *not* my name."

She didn't have time to worry about some sensitive guy's issues. She had so much on her mind at the moment that she really couldn't be bothered. Still, she didn't want to be completely rude. "How about you give me a hint," she suggested.

"Okay, I gave you a very nice, very *expensive* Ruger."

Shocked by that response, Charlie turned from the mirror and really studied the blur standing in front of her.

"You gave me a Ruger?" she asked, "No one has ever given me a . . ." She took a small step back. "Oh, my God."

Charlie couldn't help but smile. "It's you," she cheered. "My giant, helpful blur!"

"The name is Berg. Berg Dunn."

"I can't believe it." She really couldn't. "What are you doing here?"

"I live here."

She frowned. "With Livy?"

"No." He suddenly chuckled, shook his head. "No. Not with Livy. I live here in New York. Queens."

Rubbing her hands on her jeans, Charlie moved closer to the blur. "I am so sorry I didn't know who you were earlier. No wonder you were hurt. But I am really glad to see you again because I didn't have a chance to thank you—"

"It's not necessary."

"It is. Other than my sisters, no one ever helps me. Especially not strangers. You could have easily locked you and that smaller, paler blur in the bathroom and let me fight my own battles. You didn't. So I owe you big. I just . . ." Charlie briefly closed her eyes. "Well, right now, I have some other . . . issues to deal with. And your Ruger was dismantled and dispersed across a large swath of Italy." Charlie stood straight, refusing to let the shame of her life bow her. "But I *promise*. I will pay you back."

The blur leaned against the doorway. "What are you talking about?"

"I'm talking about paying my debts."

"For what? You were being hunted. What was I supposed to do? Not help?"

"Most people wouldn't."

"We look out for each other. We're shifters."

"Oh. Okay. Sure."

"Wow," he suddenly said. "You really didn't recognize me until I mentioned the Ruger, did you?"

"Not really."

"How is that possible? You're definitely a shifter. I saw your claws. You should at least know my scent by now."

"Allergies," Charlie admitted, pointing at her nose. "Can't smell anything right now. From May until at least October—sometimes December—I am living on decongestants and Benadryl. And, after making that mad dash out of my room and falling into your life, I don't have prescription strength anything, including my nasal spray, which I can't tell you how much I miss." She rubbed her nose. "It's so *itchy* right now."

"So you can barely see and you can't smell anything . . . but you can clothesline your sister?"

"I've been clotheslining my sister for a very long time now. And trust me when I say she deserved it."

Charlie turned back to the mirror and decided to put her hair in a high ponytail since she didn't have access to a blow dryer with a diffuser.

"I've never met a shifter your age who has eye problems that weren't caused by some kind of strange work accident."

"I believe that." Charlie began pulling her hair into a ponytail. "But ya know . . . it's my father's fault."

"Your father's fault?"

"He has the most fucked-up genes . . . ever."

"What do you mean?"

"I mean that the majority of my flaws and my sisters' flaws are due to our sperm donor. He is absolutely and unequivocally the reason that we're all freaks."

"I wouldn't say you're freaks," the blur said on a chuckle, placing her hairband in her palm.

"Oh, trust me," Charlie admitted. "We are *such* freaks."

"They are *such* freaks," Livy explained, dumping a tray of ice cubes into a plastic bag. She moved across the kitchen and was about to give the bag to Dag when Vic wrestled it from her hands.

"I think you've touched his balls enough today, don't you?" Vic asked before handing the ice to Dag, who appeared extremely relieved. Livy just didn't know why.

"Don't blame me for that."

"Then who do I blame?"

"Who gets in the middle of a honey badger fight?"

"I thought I was helping," Dag muttered as he gingerly placed the ice over his groin.

"Badgers don't need your help."

"It's not that I'm surprised you were fighting your own cousin," Vic said, resting his ass against the kitchen counter. "Because that happens so often. But this one didn't actually do anything."

"We have a past."

"Shocking."

"Why do you call them freaks?" Dag asked.

"Because they are." She lowered her voice a bit. "Can't you see that?"

"They're hybrids," Shen replied. "All hybrids are a little freaky."

Livy shook her head. "For every other honey badger mix, from the beginning of time, it never mattered what else a honey badger was mixed with. Our vicious DNA has always destroyed everything else, leaving only the honey badger and some human." She lowered her voice again to a whisper. "Except for those two. Charlie and Stevie are the only honey badgers I know who are *not* all honey badger. But they're not the problem."

"They're not?"

"No. I actually like them. Well . . . I like Charlie. I don't know what the fuck to say about Stevie. But my cousin who is all honey badger . . . still a freak." She motioned the males over with a wave of her hand. Vic and Shen stood next to her by the doorway while Dag kept his place at the kitchen table, nursing his balls.

"Just look at her out there," Livy said, pointing at her cousin, who was standing in the living room by the younger sister. "What do you see?"

"A woman quietly standing by her still-unconscious sister?" Shen asked.

"Vic, do you see what's wrong with her?"

"Yes," he said with an eye roll. "But it's stupid."

"Tell him," Livy pushed.

Vic sighed. "She's smiling."

"Exactly. And what the fuck does she have to smile about?" Livy moved back into the center of the kitchen. "That's not normal behavior."

Shen shrugged. "Maybe she's just happy."

"What honey badger do you know who's fucking happy?"

"Well—"

"None! That's who. Not unless liquor and snake poison's involved. But her . . .?" Livy finally admitted what everyone in the Yang family already knew. "She's completely sober right now, which tells me one thing."

Vic gazed down at her. "Which is?"

"She's a serial killer."

"Because she . . . smiles?"

"*Yes.*"

With her hair in a top knot and the ends scrunched a few times to help the curls form, Charlie washed her hands, dried them, and groped for her glasses. She knew she'd left them on the counter, but now she wasn't quite sure where they were.

The blur placed them into her hand and she put them on. Then she faced the blur and . . .

"Oh . . . my."

A brow arched. "Something wrong?"

Nope. Nothing was wrong. Everything was kind of . . . perfect.

He was *so* pretty.

Square jaw. Brown hair with gold highlights. And dark brown eyes. And that perfect head sat comfortably on a thick neck attached to giant shoulders that were joined to a frighteningly large body.

Not a fat body. An overwhelmingly *muscular* body.

How did he find clothes for that physique? The dark blue T-shirt he currently had on seemed to barely contain all those muscles.

Charlie realized she was staring . . . she might even be drooling.

"What was the question?" she asked.

"Is something wrong?"

"Wrong? What could be wrong?"

"People are trying to kill you?"

"Well, yeah, there's that," she admitted. "That's definitely a problem. But, ya know . . . sadly not the first time."

"So all three of you are on the run?"

Charlie sighed. "Very. I thought we could at least stay here a couple of days but now . . ."

"I think I can help." He pointed a finger at her. "I might know a place you can stay. You'll be safe. *Really* safe."

Dropping her hands on her waist, Charlie said, "Dude—"

"Berg."

"Whatever. I can't ask you to do any more than you've already done. I mean, you've been amazing. I owe my life to you. I already can't pay that back."

"You don't have to pay back anything, and you're still not safe."

"That's not your problem. That's *my* problem because being the daughter of Freddy MacKilligan means safety and security are just not part of my vocabulary."

"You need a place to re-group. Figure out what you're going to do next. And I think we both know you can't do that here. I don't know Livy well, but she makes it clear when she doesn't like someone. And she does *not* like your sister. But I think I can get you a place where you'll have a little time to breathe."

Charlie hated bothering this man again. But, as always, her father had put her in a situation where she was left with few—if any—options.

How could anyone be *that* big a fuck up? How could one man cause so much damage to so many without putting in that much effort to begin with? He was known for ridiculous schemes that managed to destroy entire banking systems. Deals that went so bad, his partners either ended up in prison or dead. Poorly planned plots and cons that blew up, but somehow didn't affect Freddy MacKilligan at all, yet had his daughters running for their lives . . . again.

Her father, as always, was the *king* of the fuck up.

Until now, though. Because, finally, he was sitting in cold storage, and Charlie couldn't wait to bury him. To be done with him. To pretend someone so idiotic had never existed.

"Want me to make the call?" her handsome savior asked when her silence went on and on.

"I . . ."

"I really don't mind. In fact, I *want* to do this for you."

"Why? I mean . . . are you really that good a person?"

He shrugged and said, "Yes. I am. But I'm a bear, so we're naturally loving and giving."

"Really? Because when I hear about bears, they're either going through people's garbage or attacking people in Alaska who were out on a jog."

"Because we were startled. Don't startle us, we don't attack."

"Unless you're really hungry."

He gave an excruciatingly sweet grin. "Unless we're really hungry."

Charlie laughed and decided to bite the bullet.

"Okay. Your help would be greatly appreciated." She glanced at the front of her phone and checked the time. "Uh . . ."

"What?"

"I'm just wondering if Livy would let us stash our stuff here for a couple more hours before we bail."

"Securing the place shouldn't take that long."

"Oh, it's not that. We're just here in the city to identify our father's body and we were supposed to be at the morgue, like, an hour ago."

"Wait a minute." He held up his hand, palm out, his head cocking to the side before he asked, "Your father's dead?"

Crossing the middle and forefingers on both hands, Charlie raised them and said with a big smile she truly felt, "Here's hoping!"

Chapter Six

William MacKilligan sat down on the steps behind his house and stared at the kennels where the dogs were kept.

They were usually barking. They barked all the time. Vicious beasts used for protection and, as Will liked to call it, "persuasion" when necessary. A bloke would reveal all with one of the MacKilligan dogs growling at them.

But those same noisy dogs were quiet. Because they knew, instinctually, if they made one noise, Will was likely to kill every last one of them.

To say he was angry would be a *gross* understatement. Since he was a teen, he'd been putting up with this bullshit, and he was done.

For more than fifty years he'd had to deal with the American side of the MacKilligan family, caused by his father's insatiable libido, and it was mostly not that big an issue. He had two half-sisters in the United States that he could tolerate on a good day and another half-brother he never saw. But that idiot. That fucking idiot.

Freddy MacKilligan.

That idiot Will wouldn't put up with any more. Not for a second longer.

But trying to find him would be the challenge. Like the snakes they all loved to eat, the bastard was wily. Could hide in plain sight sometimes. Or so it seemed.

But Will was done playing this game with him. Especially now. Especially after what that bastard had done to him. Had done to the family.

He didn't even bother contacting his other half-siblings in the States. He doubted they would care any more than his own brothers and half-brothers here at home did. Not when it came to Freddy MacKilligan. And business-wise, they had no connections. The Scottish MacKilligan finances never mixed with the Americans. That's how their father had set it up and that's how it stayed.

His eldest son sat down beside him on the step.

"The uncles are calling," he said calmly.

"Let 'em call." Will shook his head. "I can't believe Freddy did this."

"I can't believe he's *smart* enough to do this. The man's an idiot."

"A wily idiot. He's maneuvered his way out of more shite than you know."

"We have our people in the States looking for him but—"

"But he could be anywhere," Will finished for Dougie.

"Maybe his sisters know where he is. I know he keeps in touch with them."

"They ain't that close. They hate him." He thought a moment. "What about Freddy's girls?"

"The daughters?" Dougie snorted. "They hate him more than you do. They wouldn't help him. Besides, they got their own problems right now."

"What are you talking about?"

"Someone's trying to get the youngest again."

"What? Another drug dealer looking for designer meth?"

"No idea, but I can find out."

Dougie made the offer, Will was sure, without really thinking about it. It was just his way to always get his father the information he might need as quickly as possible.

But instead of dismissing the suggestion, Will looked at his son and said, "Yeah. Find out."

Surprised, Dougie asked, "Really? You sure?"

"I'm sure. Find out. Find out everything."

"And then what?"

"Then we see what we can do with that information. See how we can make it work for us."

"Even if it involves the girls?"

Will nodded. "Their father doesn't care about them, but if there's one thing the man does fear . . . it's that oldest girl."

"Charlie." Dougie stood. "I'll see what I can find out."

Will stood as well, already feeling a little better. Still angry, but now with some hope. "And, if we're lucky, and all this gets fixed . . . I'll be able to kill me brother with me bare hands."

Dougie patted Will on the shoulder. "We're all hoping for that, Da. We're all hoping for that."

Max glanced over her shoulder, cringed when a corpse hit the glass window, followed by a desperate scream of rage.

"So," the detective standing next to her said, "I'm guessing that was *not* your father?"

Max ducked before the leg torn off another John Doe corpse could hit her in the head. "Yeah. That's not our dad . . . unfortunately."

"Then you'd better get your sister out of here before I have to arrest her for desecration of a corpse. Or multiple corpses."

Max reached out to pat the shifter cop on the shoulder as a thank-you, but he jerked away from her so violently, she decided not to push it. She knew that sometimes honey badgers made other shifters nervous.

Besides, it was one of those days, wasn't it? When everybody was just a little more sensitive than usual.

"Put that torso down right this second, Charlie MacKilligan!" Stevie yelled, pointing her finger at their outraged sister and using her own body to protect the poor morgue attendant. "Right this second!"

Berg walked into the room, cell phone in hand, eyes on Charlie.

She stood in the middle of Vic and Livy's living room, staring blankly at the far wall. The three sisters had just returned to the apartment, but he honestly didn't know what was going on.

Stevie rushed in from the kitchen with a glass of what looked like scotch on the rocks in her hand.

"Drink this, Charlie. It'll help."

Charlie's blank gaze focused on the glass of scotch and she locked on it for several long seconds.

Everyone in the room watched her watching the scotch. Berg had remained at Livy's place because he'd found the sisters a place to stay and needed to take them there. Coop, however, refused to return to his own New York apartment because he wanted to "see what happens next!" His exact words. Dag and Shen were still hanging around because neither had anywhere interesting to go anyway. And Vic and Livy lived here.

They all watched Charlie, the room silent. Until she suddenly barked, "I need to bake."

Her sisters quickly moved out of her way and she disappeared into the kitchen.

"There's nothing in there," Livy called out to Charlie, "that anyone can use to bake." She glanced at the others. "What? I don't shop a lot."

"This is bad," Stevie said softly. "When she starts baking . . ."

"So," Coop guessed, "it was your dad? I'm so sorr—"

"Oh, no," Max cut him off, her arm swinging out toward the big picture windows. "He's still out there somewhere. Alive. Fucking up our lives."

"Your father's *not* dead?" Vic asked. Max and Stevie shook their heads. "And your sister's upset because . . ."

"He's *not* dead."

Vic leaned back in his couch. "Didn't see that coming."

Charlie suddenly walked back out of the kitchen, a bag of unopened flour in her hands. "Do you all realize—"

"Uh-oh," Stevie said softly, her head dropping.

"—that the only reason we're all here is because of my father?" She pointed at Coop. "You had to cancel the rest of your world tour because of my father." She pointed at Berg. "You were shot and stabbed because of my father."

"I'm not sure we can blame him specifically—"

She pointed at Livy. "You got in a fight with your cousin because of my father." Pointed at Vic. "Strangers in your apartment because of my father." She gestured between her and Max and Stevie. "Recent attempts on our lives, most likely because of our idiot father."

"We don't know," Stevie interrupted, "that Daddy had anything to do with any of this."

Her sisters suddenly turned to her and stared. For a really long time. Until Stevie finally admitted, "It was *probably* him, but we don't *know* it was him. That's all I'm saying."

Making a sound of disgust, Charlie turned on her heel and walked back into the kitchen.

"Where did she find the flour?" Livy asked Vic. "We have flour?"

"I don't know why you're all mad at me!" Stevie argued. "He is still our father!"

"I'm not angry at you," Dag suddenly announced, thoughtfully gazing across the room. "But I don't know you. So I don't have any reason to be angry at you."

A "beep" sound from the kitchen had Livy frowning. "We have a microwave oven?" she asked Vic. "When did we get a microwave oven?"

A moment later Charlie returned from the kitchen. Now she held a stainless steel mixing bowl in the crook of her left arm and a wooden spoon in her right hand. And whatever she had in that bowl was taking a hell of a beating from that spoon.

"No one is angry at you, Stevie," Charlie stated, still mixing. "I don't blame you for how you feel about that idiot."

"I call him Dad," Stevie said to the others.

"But we have a serious problem here. We're not safe while he's alive."

"I could track him down," Max said. "Kill him." She glanced at Stevie. "Cry a little about doing that if it will make *you* feel better."

Stevie's eyes narrowed. "It wouldn't."

"No, no." Charlie shook her head, still mixing. "I can't ask you to do that. If there's one thing our father knows how to do, it's hide. You'll never find him, and you'll just get frustrated."

"Because her frustration is everyone's main concern in this particular conversation," Vic muttered.

"We need a safe place to hide," Charlie reasoned, her mixing arm never stopping. "With Dad still alive and the ones trying to kill us still out there, we have to find a safe house. We may have to leave New York."

"I don't think they're trying to kill all of us," Max

suddenly announced to Charlie. "Just you and me. I think they want Stevie alive."

Charlie briefly stopped mixing. "What makes you think that?"

"Well, you know when we—" Max abruptly cut off her own words and looked around the room. "Uh . . . you know . . . when we were in the *Mercedes* near where we picked up Stevie?" she asked vaguely.

"Yeah," Charlie said.

"That time, they didn't try to blow us all away. They tried to negotiate, which only makes sense . . ."

"If they wanted Stevie." Charlie began mixing again. "Unbelievable," she snapped. "He sold her again."

Vic's head snapped up. "Wait . . . what?"

But the sisters ignored him.

"We've got to get out of here," Charlie told her sisters.

"Wait," Berg said before they could leave. "I have a place for you guys. A safe place."

Charlie gave him a very small smile. "I don't feel right getting you involved. You know . . . again."

"It's already set up. I promise, you can't find a safer place."

Max snorted. "Like we haven't heard that before."

"If my brother says it's safe," Dag cut in, "it's safe."

"Okay." Charlie smiled even while Max appeared not to believe a word Berg was saying. But Berg didn't care if the honey badger believed him or not.

"Just give me ten minutes to finish the cookies and we'll go."

She disappeared back into the kitchen and Max pointed at Berg. "You better be right about this. Or I'm going to get cranky."

"You can't find a safer place than this one," he promised, meaning every word.

The pair stared at each other, Max sizing him up,

making sure he was telling the truth until Livy threw up her hands and demanded, "Is no one else concerned about what the fuck she's using to make those cookies?"

After Charlie put a plate of the most amazing honey-lemon sugar cookies Berg had ever tasted in Livy's hands—"*Where in the unholy fuck did you find stuff to decorate these cookies with?*"—Berg took the three women to Grand Central Station, where they caught the Long Island Rail Road.

None of them spoke as they headed out to Queens. Stevie pulled out a reader from her bag, giving her access to thousands of digital books. She read the entire trip and didn't say a word. Max, with a small smile on her lips, gazed at random people on the train until they got up and moved.

Charlie simply stared out the window.

When they arrived at the Jamaica station, they got off and Berg led them to the garage where he kept his SUV.

The three women silently put their bags in the back of his vehicle and piled inside.

On the drive, Stevie continued to read, Max continued to smile, Charlie continued to stare.

Coop had wanted to come along on this trip but Berg had a feeling that the sisters didn't really want to be bothered with anyone at the moment. The fact that they had to be bothered with Berg was probably a tad more than they could stand. Adding a nosey jackal would no doubt push one or all three of them over the edge. So Dag took the maestro home and Berg was here.

Berg turned onto his street. He loved this Queens neighborhood and had been grateful when he'd found it. Living in the City wasn't really his thing. He'd been raised in Washington, after all, and with his parents, he was used to a much more . . . relaxed way of life.

He got out of his SUV and went to the back. He pulled out their bags just as his phone went off.

Berg looked at the screen and cringed. His sister's text was in all caps. That was never good.

"Uh, I'll be right back, ladies," he said, pointing at the house he'd secured for them. "Why don't you guys have a look around the yard."

Berg started across the street until he got another all cap text . . . then he ran.

Charlie stood by her sisters, the three of them staring out over the Queens street that Berg had taken them to before running away like he was on fire.

She briefly wondered if he'd actually come back. Considering the day she'd already had . . . she wouldn't be surprised to find out that this was all an elaborate setup to kill her and Max and take Stevie, and the sweet bear was the great mastermind behind it all.

It would be her luck, wouldn't it?

"I guess this could be less safe," Max commented, her gaze examining everything quickly and closely.

Charlie glanced down one side of the street and then the other. "What does that mean? What's wrong with it?"

Max watched her for a moment before asking, "We need to get your allergy meds, sweetie." She briefly glanced at Stevie, who was staring up at the sky. "And this one needs to be less oblivious."

"Why? What am I missing?" Charlie asked before she sniffed the air. But she couldn't detect anything. She really needed her meds. "What am I not smelling?"

"Don't sweat it." Max sighed. "It's not like we have a lot of choices."

Because, once again, their father had made choices impossible for his daughters.

"It's very nice, though," Stevie remarked. "You know . . . for Queens."

Max glanced at her sister. "What do you know about Queens?"

"I know about lots of places. Been to lots of places. You're not the only one who travels a lot, Maxie MacKilligan."

"You travel from lab to lab and mental hospital to mental hospital. Not exactly like you're taking in the scenery on your way to and from."

"How do you know what I do or don't do? You're never around."

"Because I know *you*. You're the only person I've ever met who didn't have time to notice the Eiffel Tower while *in* Paris."

"I was busy! And I'll have you know I've seen it since."

"You three the sisters?" a gruff voice asked from behind them.

Max instantly went for one of the knives she kept on her body at all times, forcing Charlie to grab her hand before she could pull one free. A skill she'd taught herself very early in life so that she could keep her middle sister out of juvenile detention and then, when Max was older, prison.

Stevie, also startled, screamed like she'd been stabbed, her back arching, before she flipped herself onto the nearest tree trunk, her claws digging in. With a warning hiss, she scrambled backward up into the branches, disappearing among the leaves.

The gruff man who'd been standing behind them stared at the tree, wide eyes wider. "Uhhhhh . . ."

Stepping in front of her middle sister—so if Max tried to stab anyone, she'd have to take Charlie out first—she held out her hand.

"Charlie MacKilligan," she said, introducing herself. "This is my sister, Max, and in the tree is Stevie."

Big brown eyes focused on Charlie. "Why do you all have boy names?" he asked, now appearing nervous. Not that Charlie blamed him.

"My father always wanted boys. But, like Henry the Eighth, he only got girls."

"Actually," Stevie explained from her hiding place in the tree, "Henry had a son and he was crowned king after his father's death, but he was sickly. Didn't last long. That's when Bloody Mary—"

"Why is that one up in a tree?" the gruff man asked.

"She's a genius. So she's weird."

"Is she always so . . . jumpy? We don't like jumpy around here."

Charlie tried to think of a good answer that wouldn't lose them their temporary home before they even saw it. But before she could say a word, a bee flew by, briefly lurking around Max's face. And just like that, her sister was off.

"Where are you going?" Charlie demanded.

"Bees," was the only response she got back. But it was really all Charlie needed.

"She's going to be a problem," the gruff man said.

"I know it seems that way—"

"We don't like her kind here."

Charlie blinked, shocked. "What did you just say to me?"

"You heard me."

Stevie's head stuck out from the leaves and she accused, "You *racist!*"

The gruff man frowned. "Huh?"

"You heard me! You're a racist. And when Max gets back, she's going to kick your ass for it!"

Berg walked out from behind a house across the street and jogged over.

"Sorry about that," he said, coming closer. "My sister . . . had some issues." He smiled. "So how are we getting along?"

"You didn't tell me what they were," the gruff man said.

"Yeah." Charlie couldn't help but sneer. "Two women of color must be terrifying for you."

The two men looked at each other and back at Charlie.

"What are you talking about?" Berg asked.

"Apparently only Stevie can stay here in your precious neighborhood. She seems to be white enough."

"And you, sir," Stevie yelled from the tree, "will not make me feel horrible for what *you* said. I will not take the mantle of white guilt on my shoulders, thank you very much!"

Berg shook his head. "Tiny doesn't care that you're black. Or that your sister's Asian. That's probably the last thing he cares about."

"It really is," the gruff man sighed.

"*His* name is Tiny?" Charlie asked, staring *up* at the man. He was taller than Berg. And wider.

"Family nickname," he growled.

"All Tiny cares about is that you guys are honey badgers," Berg went on.

"*That's* going to be a problem with my neighbors," Tiny admitted. "Especially the ones with hives."

"Why would that matter?" Charlie asked. She was confused until she realized Max had taken that particular moment to return to her side. A dripping honeycomb was in her hand and hundreds of angry bees were hanging from her face like some bizarre tribal mask.

"Jesus!" Charlie snapped, quickly stepping away from her sister and waving more angry bees from her own face.

Max gazed blankly at her, ignoring the other bees that were still attacking her like the horde they were.

"What?" Max asked.

Deciding it was a waste of her time to have this discussion now, Charlie returned her attention to the men and guessed, "I see. You're *all* bears. This neighborhood is all bears!" She grinned, proud of herself for finally figuring that out without her ability to smell.

The two men glanced at each other again. "You didn't know that?"

"Allergies," she reminded Berg.

"You couldn't tell just by looking at Tiny?" Berg asked.

"There are big full-humans everywhere. Most of them are on steroids, but still . . ."

"Look," Tiny said, "it's nothing personal. But"—he pointed at Max—"she's already stealing from hives. That one"—he pointed at Stevie—"is way too jumpy. And you . . ." He stared at Max a moment before ending with, "You smell weird."

"I had a shower and my clothes are clean."

Berg shook his head. "He doesn't mean you smell bad. You just don't smell like a breed or species he's dealt with before."

"Which means you're a hybrid. And not a bear hybrid either. We only deal with bear hybrids."

"Racism!" Stevie yelled from the safety of the tree.

"It's not racism," Tiny grumbled.

"But it is bigotry," Berg told him. "And you know how my sister feels about that." The bear gave Tiny a strange, knowing smile, and Charlie briefly wondered what it meant. "I really would hate to tell her about this. You know how she loves to lecture—"

"All right," Tiny cut in. "All right. But if they turn into a problem, it's on you."

"Fine."

"No, no." Charlie grabbed Berg's arm and pulled him away. "Excuse us." She dragged him across the yard until they reached the fence. "Dude, you do *not* want to be responsible for anything that me and my sisters—especially Max—do." She leaned in to Berg and whispered, "Trust me on this."

He leaned down and whispered back, "I appreciate your concern, but Tiny is a difficult bear. If he thinks the hives are at risk he will not let you and your sisters—especially Max—stay." He straightened up, smiled. "It'll be fine."

"It won't be fine. My sisters and I attract trouble."

"I've noticed that."

"So why would you want to be part of it? Do you have poor decision-making skills? I bet you do."

"I don't think—"

"Look, I'll take care of this," she said, patting his chest. "Trust me."

Charlie walked back until she stood right in front of Tiny. "Listen up, I'll take full responsibility for my sisters. Any damage done, any hives invaded, any bears startled into panic, it'll be all on me. I'll fix, repay, replenish, or apologize as needed. You have my word on it."

She held her hand out and, after staring at it for a long moment, Tiny took it, his freakishly large fingers swallowing her hand whole.

"I trust you," Tiny said to Charlie. But then he locked his gaze on Max. "But this one I don't trust."

Max shrugged, her mouth filled with stolen honeycomb. "That's probably wise."

Charlie waited until Tiny and Berg turned away before cuffing her sister on the back of the head. "Idiot!" she quietly snapped. She started to follow the two men, but stopped long enough to bark at Max, "And get those goddamn bees off your face!"

* * *

When Tiny led them into the unoccupied house, Berg grimaced a little. It had been ages since Tiny had had tenants here and he'd not kept the place up. Even worse, he'd clearly been using it as some sort of hoarder's extra storage.

"So what do you think?" Tiny asked.

"Ummmm . . ." Charlie began.

"You also hoarding pets here?" Max flatly asked. "Maybe some dead bodies?"

Charlie grabbed her sister by the neck of her T-shirt and shoved her toward an open doorway. "Go check out the kitchen, please, and let me handle this."

Her sister shrugged and walked off, and Tiny led Charlie on a tour of the house. Berg trailed behind, still cringing at every new sign of how bad this house actually was. He was suddenly glad his sister wasn't here. Britta would be all on his back over this.

"How could you let Tiny show her such a shitty house? What were you thinking?" His sister had little tolerance for what she called "The Obliviousness of Berg and Dag."

An obliviousness she prided herself on *not* having. "Daddy and I are the only ones who keep this family alive," she would remind her brothers. "You do realize that, don't you?"

They ended up back in the living room and Tiny began, "So what do you—"

"All right," Charlie cut in, "here's the deal. Take five hundred off the rent—it was way too high anyway—and we'll get this place cleaned up for you. So clean, you'll actually be able to rent it for what you're trying to squeeze out of us."

"Uh—"

"Plus, no thirty days' notice. When we leave, we

leave. *But*, before you complain, we'll give you three months up front and in cash. And if we leave before the three months, you get to keep the extra. Deal?"

Tiny gazed at Charlie until he shrugged and said, "Uh . . . deal?"

Berg had no idea why Tiny had made that sound like a question but . . . okay.

With a smile, Charlie shook Tiny's hand again, turned her head, and yelled out, "Max!"

Max came in from the kitchen. She'd finished the honeycomb and had cleaned off the honey and dead bees from her face. Now she had bright red, angry sting marks all over her skin. If it bothered her, she didn't let on.

"What?" she asked her sister.

She jerked her thumb at Tiny. "Money."

With a nod, Max suddenly pulled off her T-shirt and both Berg and Tiny backed up, hands raised.

"Now wait a second—" Tiny said, trying to halt her. He had a sow mate who'd tear his balls off if he even entertained the idea of taking out rent in trade.

But Max shook her head. "Get over yourself," she said before digging into her bra and taking out chunks of cash. She'd managed to place the bills in a way that made them look like actual breasts. She handed the big chunks to her sister and put her T-shirt back on.

Charlie quickly counted out the cash and handed it to Tiny.

"Okay. Well." Tiny blew out a breath. "Um . . . if you need anything, I'm down the street. Berg knows where."

"Thanks."

"And remember, Tiny," Berg added as the bear lumbered toward the front door, "they're not here. If anyone that's not from the neighborhood asks about them, let me know."

With a grunt, Tiny walked out, and Berg offered, "You know, we've got extra bedding you can borrow over at my house. And me and my siblings can come by tomorrow to help you clean up the place. I'm sure this is all really daunting."

"Sure." She smiled at him. "And I can't tell you how much I appreciate everything you've done. After the day I've had . . . you were my only bright spot. Thank you."

"No problem." Now. He should ask her out now. Mostly because he didn't know when she'd leave. She'd paid for three months, but he got the feeling she'd only done that because she didn't expect to be here three months and she didn't want any complaining from Tiny. "Um . . . sooooo—"

Sensing he was being watched, Berg glanced down and to his left. Max stood right next to him, gazing up at him. He then looked to his right and down. Stevie watched him, eyes narrow in distrust. But when she realized he was staring back, she forced a smile that just made him feel terribly uncomfortable.

Maybe this wasn't the best time to ask Charlie out. Yeah. Probably not.

"Okay, well . . . see ya tomorrow."

Charlie watched the bear walk out of their temporary home, the front door closing behind him.

Alone with her sisters, she let out a breath and looked around the room.

"You said we'd clean this place?" Max asked.

With an eye roll, Charlie snapped, "Don't worry. I wasn't including you. I know how much you hate to . . . you know . . . help."

"As long as we're clear."

"I can help," Stevie said, grabbing the first thing she

saw. "I can organize or . . . uh . . . put stuff in a pile. Or I can—"

"Or," Charlie quickly cut in, "you can relax. Let me handle this."

"Charlie, this is a lot of stuff, and you have to be as tired as—"

"Let me handle it. I'll give you guys things to do . . . later."

"Sure you will." Max snorted and disappeared up the stairs. Stevie just shook her head and went toward the kitchen.

Once they were gone, Charlie let out a relieved sigh. Now she could see what needed to be done and handle it. It wasn't that she didn't trust her sisters or Berg to help her; it was just that people tended to get in her way when they thought they were helping. And everyone always needed some kind of direction. It was just easier for her to take care of it herself.

What Charlie didn't understand was why everyone insisted on acting like that very sound reasoning was somehow wrong!

The house was way bigger than Max had realized. Old but very nice. It just needed to be cleaned. Something she was sure her sister could easily handle. Charlie wasn't one for sitting around, doing nothing.

Max picked a room with a window seat. She sat down and stared out at the quiet Queens street. The big bear who she felt positive really liked Charlie came by with fresh bedding and towels, handing it off to Stevie.

Sadly, though, Max couldn't concentrate on much, like the bears and all the hives they had around this street. She shook her head. Her father wasn't dead. How could she concentrate enough on anything when people were still after them? And now they were on a street filled with bears. For their safety.

Charlie would try to fix this on her own, but nope. They needed backup. They needed friends.

Pulling her phone from her back pocket, Max hit speed dial and waited for the other side to connect.

"Is he dead?" a low voice asked without even a hello.

Max smiled. "Sadly, no. And we're in trouble."

The low chuckle she knew so well. "Of course you are. I'm across country . . . but I'm on my way. And there's one other thing I heard about your father that I think I should tell you . . ."

Max closed her eyes . . . and sighed.

Chapter Seven

The front door slammed open and Berg dropped his head so he could focus exclusively on his breakfast. Dag tried to do the same thing, but his plate was already empty. So he tried to make a run for it, but their triplet was already in the kitchen doorway, snarling like an angry sow. Which was exactly what she was at the moment.

"That woman," she snapped, pushing Dag back into the kitchen. "That obsessive, crazy woman!"

He knew she meant Coop's oldest sister, Toni Jean-Louis Parker Reed. A jackal that he now realized made a grizzly sow look like a crack-addicted mom, she was so protective of her siblings.

Britta dropped her travel bag and purse to the floor. "She was on my ass from the time I met her at the airport in Milan through dealing with local authorities about the attack, until I was finally able to shake her at JFK. And the whole time she's freaking out on me!" She pointed an accusing finger at Berg. "And you left me with her!"

"You said you could handle her," Berg reminded her "We all know I think highly of myself and think very little of everyone else. But this time I didn't realize the depths of her crazy!"

She pulled out a chair and dropped hard into the seat. She looked around at the table and reached over to snatch bacon off his plate. He growled in warning.

"*Don't even start with me!*" she bellowed.

They ate in silence, and Dag made more bacon and toast for their sister and Berg. After several cups of coffee and the food, his sister's entire demeanor changed.

Britta relaxed back in her chair, one foot resting on the opposite thigh. "So what are we up to today?"

Amazing what a little food and coffee could do for a grizzly female.

"I'm going over to help out Charlie and her sisters."

Britta rubbed her nose with the back of her fist. "Who's Charlie?"

Dag, still eating, poured honey onto a slice of wheat toast. "The woman who almost got him killed."

"You met her again? How?" Britta leaned forward. "Was she still naked?"

"Sadly, no," Dag said with a grin.

"Why is she here?" Britta asked. "Did you track her down and bring her here?"

Insulted by even the suggestion, "Of course not!"

"But he did get Tiny to give her the old house across the street so he can easily stalk her."

Berg glared at his triplet. "Why are you talking?"

Dag wrapped his big hands around an oversized coffee mug. "I just find it fascinating what you're doing for this woman. It's so unlike you."

"I'm helpful," Berg argued. "I help where I can. I'm beloved."

Dag and Britta quickly looked away from each other and Berg knew they were trying not to *openly* laugh in his face. Something he did appreciate.

A sound at the kitchen doorway attracted their attention. They watched as their two-hundred-pound Caucasian Bear dog or Caucasian shepherd—depending on who you asked—stretched and yawned before briefly sitting so he could use his back paw to scratch his neck and jaw.

When he was done, he moved beside Britta, placed his paws on the table, and leaned over until he could grab the entire pile of bacon Dag had made. Then he disappeared into the other room to eat in peace.

The siblings refocused on each other and Britta asked Berg, "You know, you said this woman was a shifter, but you never told me what she is."

"She's a hybrid," he said, trying to keep it simple.

"Hybrid what?"

Berg spun his answer carefully. "She said her mother was wolf."

"Echhhh." The entire left side of Britta's face twisted in annoyance and disgust. Like most bears, she had little tolerance for wolves. Something that should distract his sister for quite a—

"But her father is honey badger," Dag volunteered.

Britta threw up her hands. "Really?" she asked Berg.

Berg, at the same time, threw up his hands. "*Really?*" he asked Dag.

Charlie opened the front door and three very large people who looked almost exactly alike stood on her porch. She briefly wondered how that would be. Having siblings who actually *looked* like each other. She and her sisters each resembled their mothers. Thankfully. Charlie disliked her father so much, she would not like to see his mug staring back at her from the bathroom mirror every day.

"Hi," she said with a smile. It surprised her that not only was she *not* unhappy to see Berg, but she was actually glad to see him.

"Hey." Berg held up a bucket filled with cleaning supplies. "We've come to help."

"Sure. Come on in." She stepped back and let the trio into her home. The males had to duck to clear the doorway. The female didn't, but her brown and gold hair nearly got snagged on the doorframe.

Berg walked farthest into the house, pausing in the living room. He stopped. He stared. Then disappeared through the hallway to the kitchen. A few moments later, he came back in and gawked at Charlie.

"What?" she finally asked.

"Where is it?"

"What?"

"The mess. The hoarder mess that Tiny left you with."

"Oh. That. I cleaned it up. Started yesterday. Worked late into the night. Slept a couple of hours, then got up around three or so and finished. Looks pretty good, too, right? I put all his junk in the garage so he can pick through it at his leisure."

Max walked into the room, holding a jar of honey. She used a spoon to ladle big gobs into her mouth.

"I don't understand," Berg said. "How did you three get this all done so quickly?"

Max gave a short laugh and said around the spoon in her mouth, "Three? This is all her. We didn't do anything."

"Not true," Charlie reminded her. "You two cleaned your bedrooms."

"So we could go to sleep before you did."

"So, you cleaned this house by yourself?" Berg asked Charlie.

"Well—"

"But I told you we'd be back today to help. Why didn't you wait?"

"Uh . . ."

"Yeah, Sis," Max taunted. "Explain to him why you didn't wait."

"Shut up," Charlie told Max. She didn't need to yell it. She knew Max understood without yelling. She focused on Berg. "It was just easier—"

"To do it by yourself? Really?"

"I could just get in there and get it done. Easy-peasy."

"I get it," the woman said. "If you do it yourself, you get it done the way you want without having to constantly explain or give direction."

"Yes! Thank you!"

"Because you're the only one who can do it perfectly. Everyone else is a fuckup."

"Yes! Wait . . . no."

Berg shook his head. "Fell into my sister's trap. This is Britta, by the way. And you remember Dag?"

Feeling stupid, Charlie admitted, "It's not my fault that people can't take *basic* direction. I can tell them. I can write shit out. I can give them diagrams, and they still do it wrong! It's just easier for me to do it myself. So I do. It's nothing personal."

"It's not?"

"It's not personal!"

"Did you get to the outside?" Berg asked, probably trying to head off an argument.

"What's outside?" she asked.

"Trees. Plants. Right now it looks like you live in Grey Gardens."

"Oh. Uh . . . yeah, you can do that." Because Charlie didn't care about what was outside. She'd only said she'd take care of the inside. The outside, in her opinion, was not her problem. "Thank you."

Chuckling and still sort of shaking his head, Berg walked off through the house, his siblings following after him.

Max, leaning against a wall, her jar of honey nearly finished, began counting, "Five, four, three, two—"

A panicked, hysterical scream, followed by bear growls. Stevie ran into the living room and dove under one of the couches. Where she would stay for . . . most likely a while.

"There are bears!" she screamed from under the couch. "There are bears in our house! *Why are there bears in our house?*"

Charlie scratched her forehead and faced Max. "Any word on Dad?"

"Not yet."

"Why do I feel like you're hiding something from me?"

Max shrugged. "Because I probably am."

"Is what you're hiding going to give me a migraine?"

"Yes."

"Then keep it to yourself for now."

"That was my plan."

"*Does no one care that there are bears in our house?*" Stevie screeched.

Max glanced out one of the windows; Berg walked by on the other side. "How long are we going to stay here anyway?"

"Until we at least know what's going on. Why? You don't like it here?"

Max shrugged. "I'd rather be in the city. This is . . . the 'burbs."

"It'll be nice. We can live like normal people for once."

Stevie poked her head out. "Did you hear that? Chittering. There are squirrels in this neighborhood. *Squirrels!*" She went deeper under the couch.

Max licked the back of her spoon. "Yep. Just like normal people."

Berg slapped at the hand rubbing his head from the tree limb above him. "Stop messing around and get back to work."

"I have been working. For hours! And now I'm tired," Dag complained. "And hungry." He patted Berg's head again.

Fed up, Berg grabbed his brother's arm and yanked him from the tree, slamming him to the ground. He was about to lay into him when Charlie called out, "You guys hungry?"

Berg ran over his brother's chest to get to the metal table on the patio right outside the back of the house. There was a plastic, red-checkered tablecloth spread out and fresh food in big aluminum trays. A lot of food.

Berg had almost reached the table when Britta stepped in front of him and shoved him back with her shoulder.

"Me first," she said, smiling.

"Sit," Charlie offered, her hand indicating the metal chairs.

"Did you make all this?" Britta asked.

"I made the call that brought all this food here. That's kind of the same, right?"

Britta, a consummate food orderer herself, laughed and sat down.

Max brought out another platter of food and Charlie glanced back at her, tossing over her shoulder, "You guys go ahead and get start—"

She stopped talking when she saw that the Dunn Bears had already started. Food was piled on their plates, mouths already full, chewing having already commenced.

"Oh." She blinked a few times. "All right."

"Sorry," Berg said around his food.

"No need to apologize." Charlie sat down on the bench opposite them. "You've done so much work, I'm not surprised you're hungry."

"The place looks great," Max said, straddling the bench. "I had no idea we had a pool."

"All bear homes have a pool. Or a hot tub. Some have both. Most of us really like water."

"This is a bear home?" She gave a small frown. "You barely cleared the doorways."

"The house was originally built for black bears. You'll find a few fox homes down the block . . . I practically have to crawl through their doorways."

"Where's Stevie?" Charlie asked.

Max, reaching for a premade honey salmon sandwich, shrugged.

Charlie forced a smile. "Excuse me a moment."

She went inside and, for a few seconds, there was nothing but silence. Then yelling. Lots of yelling.

Three minutes later, Charlie returned. She had her arms around her sister's waist and was carrying her like a panicked cat she was trying to take to the vet. Stevie's arms and legs stuck straight out. And there was hissing.

"Put me down!" Stevie demanded.

"You need to eat."

"It's not my diet I'm worried about!"

"You're being overdramatic. Stop it."

"I will not stay out here!" Stevie screeched, legs and arms now swinging wildly. *"I will not be eaten! My brain is too important for future societies to allow it to be eaten!"*

If Max noticed any of what was going on, she didn't show it, focusing instead on her sandwich and the bag of honey barbecue chips she'd opened. But Berg and his siblings were fascinated.

"Look," Charlie ordered her sister, aiming the woman at the Dunns. "They already have food. There is no reason to eat you."

"Are you insane? *They're bears!*"

"J'accuse!" Max suddenly announced; then she laughed. Berg got the feeling she was having her own conversation in her head.

"Stevie, I would never let anyone hurt you," Charlie calmly reminded her sister. "Not now. Not ever. So please. Eat something. You haven't eaten all day, and I really don't want to do that intravenous thing again, do you?"

"You sure she took her meds?" Max asked, not even glancing at either sister.

"Stop acting like I hear voices," Stevie said.

"You don't?"

"I have a panic disorder, not schizophrenia."

"Then act like you've got some sense and sit down." Max slid down the bench and Charlie placed Stevie in the open spot.

She was a cute little thing. Not like her sisters at all. Max was petite but powerfully built. And there was something about her that screamed "sex!" He wasn't sure why. Berg wasn't attracted to her. To be honest, she scared him a little. The way that she looked at the world . . . it was like watching those full lions on the Serengeti. Like she was an apex predator and the rest of the world was just her available prey.

And Charlie . . . she really seemed less shifter than any of them. If Berg couldn't smell it on her and hadn't seen her in action in Milan, he'd never guess that was what she was. She was too calm. Too reasonable. And definitely gorgeous. All those soft brown curls framing her perfectly proportioned face; those dark eyes that looked at everything with curiosity and warmth; and that strong but soft body that he *knew* could handle all sorts of things . . .

Nope. Nope. He had to stop thinking about all the things her body could possibly do. Especially with his sister and brother sitting on either side of him.

But Stevie wasn't like either sister. Medium height but so thin. He had the feeling her sisters often had to force her to eat. Was she one of those sad women who worried about their weight constantly? Who flipped out when they ate a whole muffin or counted every calorie, not for health reasons but because, God forbid, they should gain a pound in a world of "thigh gaps" and giant asses that had to be medically enhanced because those women didn't eat enough to get an ass like that on their own.

Her blond hair reached past her shoulders but she clearly dyed it that color, because the roots were returning to their natural brown, white, and . . . wait, orange? Did she naturally have orange hair? The only breed he knew who had that color hair if they were particularly unlucky were tigers.

Was she part tiger?

Tiger and honey badger together? What did that mean about little Stevie? Frail-looking, easily panicked, but surprisingly sharp-eyed Stevie.

"Want me to ladle out your food for you?" Max asked Stevie.

"I can get my own food, thank you very much."

"You sure, sweetie?" Max gently patted her sister on the back and Berg could tell it did nothing but irritate Stevie. "I can spoon-feed you, if you'd like. Make plane sounds and everything!"

"I have hated you since I met you!" Stevie screamed in her sister's face.

"You have no idea what true hate is!"

While the pair screamed, Charlie took it upon herself to put small amounts of food on a paper plate and place it in front of Stevie. The youngest of the sisters began eating while still yelling at Max, unaware that Charlie had put together her meal for her.

"Drinks!" Charlie said, realizing what she'd forgotten. She pointed at a cooler. "I bought a bunch of stuff since I didn't know what you guys would want. There's iced tea, bottled water, soda, beer, and wine."

Dag jumped up and went to the cooler. "Beer!"

"Wine," Britta said, holding out her hands for Dag to toss her a bottle.

Berg was in the middle of swallowing a big bite of his sandwich, so he didn't answer right away, assuming he could just get what he wanted once he was sure he wouldn't choke on the food.

"Don't you want something to drink?" Charlie pushed, appearing concerned. Did she think he was like her sister and needed someone to put food on his plate? "If there's nothing you like in there, I can get something else. We have other stuff in the kitchen. Or I can order more stuff. If you want."

Berg, still chewing, gazed at her. He'd never met a fellow shifter so . . . helpful before. It was as if she couldn't stop herself.

"Well?" she pushed again when he didn't answer.

Berg pointed at his mouth, chewed a few more times, and finally swallowed. "Water's fine."

She smiled, almost in relief. "I have water. Sparkling and flat."

"Uhhhh . . ."

Dag slammed a bottle of water in front of Berg's plate before sitting down in his own spot and getting back to his food.

Berg pointed at the bottle. "This is fine."

"Okay. Great."

"Are you going to sit down and eat?" Britta asked, taking her wine opener off her keyring and pulling the cork from the bottle.

"Of course."

"Then do it," Berg said. "I want to see you sit down and eat."

"What? You don't think I can?"

"No," the Dunns replied as one.

Max and Stevie had stopped fighting, and now watched their sister, their expressions curious.

Charlie looked from one to the other until she'd examined the entire table. "None of you think I can just sit down and enjoy a meal?"

"No," they all said. Even her sisters.

She glanced over her shoulder and Berg was guessing she had planned to go back into the house and do something else once she got everybody eating and drinking.

Giving them all one more look, she slowly—oh, so slowly—sat down on the bench beside Stevie.

"Need us to make a plate for you, dear?" Stevie asked.

Narrowed eyes glared. "I can get my own food, thanks."

They silently watched as Charlie put food on her plate and got up so she could grab a beer from the cooler. She used her bare hand to remove the beer cap and took a swig. But it wasn't until she took a bite of her steak sandwich that they all went back to eating their own food.

As Charlie predicted—to herself anyway—Stevie finally relaxed around the bears once she got to know them. Contributing to the conversation just like a person who had an average IQ.

Of course, that's what Charlie always loved about Stevie. She might be one of the smartest humans in the known universe, but around "the normals" as Max called everyone else, she didn't act superior. She seemed like anyone else who had a panic disorder and the occasional bout of deep depression that required additional medications.

But Stevie hadn't had a bout of that depression in quite a while. Thankfully.

"Okay," Britta said, nursing her third glass of wine. "You're half wolf and half honey badger. And you're half tiger and half honey badger?" Stevie nodded. "Really? Because you don't seem like either."

"Pray you keep thinking that way," Max muttered and Charlie looped her arm behind Stevie and smacked their middle sister in the back of the head.

"I think of myself as kind of a liger," Stevie explained. "Even though ligers are composed of two of the strongest apex predators in the world, they are surprisingly gentle and sweet natured. Despite their enormous size."

"So the badger and tiger cancel each other out?"

"Mostly," she replied, which made Max snort.

Again, Charlie slapped her sister in the back of the head.

"But not you?" Britta asked Charlie.

"But not me what?"

"Did your two sides cancel each other out?"

"I wouldn't say that. It's more like they found a way to work together."

"Like uranium and Oppenheimer!" Max crowed.

Stevie pointed her bottle of water at Max, eyes narrowing. "What's *that* supposed to mean?"

"Do I really have to explain it? To *you*, I mean."

"So you're all bears," Charlie quickly interjected before her sisters could expand their bickering to a full-blown knife fight with the plastic cutlery.

Britta smirked because she understood exactly what Charlie was doing, but the two males frowned at her.

"Uh . . . yeah. We're bears," Berg said.

"And triplets. That's rare, isn't it?"

"For bears . . . or people?"

Charlie thought a moment before replying, "Both, I guess."

"Triplets are very rare for both," Stevie said while eating her salad. "Unless your mother had in vitro fertilization."

The triplets shook their heads.

"Then, yes," Stevie went on. "Very rare. In fact, statistically—"

"I don't want to hear statistics," Max rudely cut in.

Stevie's right eye twitched. "Maybe everyone else does."

"They don't."

And boom. They started yelling at each other again, but it was so hysterical and stupid that Charlie couldn't even make out what they were saying.

"Any sign of your father?" Berg suddenly asked when there was a brief pause in the yelling, and Charlie wanted to kiss him. Because if anything could waylay a Stevie-Max fight, it was their idiot father.

Charlie shook her head and went to the cooler to get another beer. "Unfortunately, no."

"He's a true weasel," Max stated. "I've never met anyone who can weasel their way out of more bad situations than our father."

"I couldn't believe he wasn't in that morgue," Charlie said, sitting back down in her spot. "I was so disappointed."

Stevie let out a small sigh. "Me, too."

"Is he really that bad?"

"Britta," Berg said low, shaking his head at his sister.

"What? It was just a question. I'm curious."

"Don't be. It's none of our business."

"Charlie doesn't mind talking shit about our father." Max opened a jar of honey-covered peanuts. "It's like a pastime for her."

"I don't go out of my way to talk about him." She closed her eyes as that angry feeling washed over her. "But he makes me so crazy!" She pointed her finger at the three bears. "And I refuse to live a codependent existence with that man."

Max snorted. "She learned that word in ninth grade and she hasn't let it go since."

"I haven't let it go because it perfectly explains *why* he is the way he is. Everyone has a codependent relationship with that idiot and that's how he keeps starting shit. And getting into shit. And *I* refuse to be a party to that. And I'm not letting you two be a party to that. And the way to avoid it is honesty. People ask me what my dad's like, and I tell them, 'He's a scumbag.'"

"We all have issues with our parents. Don't get me started on my mother—"

"Please don't," Berg suddenly begged, both he and Dag imploring Britta with their eyes.

Britta nodded. "Fine. But what terrible thing, *exactly,* has your father done to you guys?"

"Everything," the sisters said in unison.

"Oh, come on. You've gotta be more specific than that."

"*Britta,*" Berg growled as Dag reached over and took the wine bottle away from her.

"I wasn't done with that," she complained.

"Yes, you are," Berg muttered.

"You want to know what my father's done?" Charlie asked.

Berg shook his head. "You don't have to say—"

But she didn't let him finish, instead flipping her hand over, palm up, and gesturing to Stevie.

Her baby sister shrugged. "He ruined my credit by the time I was six."

Britta cringed. "Oh. Okay that's—"

"When my mom died," Charlie explained, "she left each of us some insurance money. Mine was for college. Dad asked to borrow it . . . I never went to college. Not even community."

"Well—"

"He used my baby picture," Max announced, "to sell nonexistent Asian babies to infertile couples desperate to adopt."

"Oh!" Britta's expression became even more horrified. "Oh, my God!"

"He's the reason Max's mom is in prison," Charlie tossed in.

Stevie took another sip of water. "As my legal guardian—"

"Which he wasn't," Charlie added.

"—he sold all the rights to my early music. Music that is now worth millions and *millions* of dollars. I haven't seen a cent from any of it."

Max popped more peanuts into her mouth before noting, "You hear her music in expensive car commercials all the time."

"And he sold it for . . . what was it, Charlie?"

"Fifty grand."

"Right. Fifty grand. Fifty grand that I never saw a cent from."

"Because he was going to pay it back to you after he got his business off the ground," Charlie reminded her.

"Oh, yes. The can't-fail business that turned out to be a pyramid scheme that also bilked the elderly out of a few million."

"None of which he managed to make any money from," Charlie added.

"But he also managed not to get any prison time." Max chuckled. "Everybody else went to jail *but* him."

"Yeah," Britta finally agreed. "That is definitely the worst—"

"And remember that time he 'accidentally' "—Max asked her sisters, making air quotes with her fingers— "sold me into domestic slavery?"

"How the fuck did he do that accidentally?" Dag demanded.

"How did he put it again, Charlie?"

"Uh . . . that he thought he was just hiring you out as a playmate for their children."

"Yeah, like they were fourteenth-century Russian princes," Stevie replied.

"But," Max continued, "as soon as he dropped me off at the family's house, they handed me an iron, a basket full of clothes, and told me to get to work."

"You poor thing." Britta shook her head. "How long before someone got you?"

"No one came to get me."

"Wait." Charlie raised her hand. "Let's be clear here . . . we didn't have *time* to get you."

"That's true," Max admitted with a smile. "As soon as they handed me that iron, I beat the husband with it, and then proceeded to tear the wife's face off with my claws. I left them crying, screaming, and bleeding with the kids trying to call the cops."

Berg and his siblings stared at Max until Berg asked, "How old were you?"

"Twelve. Right?"

"Eleven," corrected Stevie, the keeper of all specifics. Not hard with her brain.

"I went through puberty a little early," Max added to explain an eleven-year-old shifter with claws.

"What happened after you got away?"

Max shrugged. "No idea. Dad took off with the thirty grand he got for me and I walked back to the Pack house in Wisconsin."

"Where was this family?"

"Utah."

"You walked back by yourself?" Britta asked.

"It wasn't the first time."

But Charlie didn't want to talk about that long-ago incident. That was one story the three sisters didn't really discuss with anyone but each other. The story about her mom's death. Not now. Not ever. It was too close to their hearts.

"And yet," Charlie pointed out to change the subject, "our father is the only con I know who never makes any money from his cons."

"How is that possible?" Berg asked.

"Because he's an idiot. I thought we made that clear."

"But what about the money he stole from you guys?"

"Well, that thirty grand he got for me only lasted him about a week," Max said. "I think he blew it at the grey-hound track in Florida. And probably on some hookers."

"He does love prostitutes," Charlie sighed.

"And the money he got for the adoption scam . . . dear old Freddy got scammed out of that by the woman he was working with." Max sighed. "Because he is that stupid."

"Plus, because of that particular scam, he's no longer allowed in Florida," Charlie said, trying to remember.

"You can be banned from a state?" Britta asked.

"Don't know. But when you have enough warrants for your arrest and enough loan sharks desperate to see you dead . . . I'd say you're not allowed back into a particular state."

"He's also not allowed in Budapest, or France, or Germany," Stevie added.

"God, Budapest." Max shook her head. "That turned into an international incident."

"And, yet," Charlie said, throwing her hands up, "he still managed *not* to make any money."

Max and Stevie eventually wandered off and Dag and Britta went back to bagging the rest of the dead plants and clippings from the yard.

Berg stayed behind and helped Charlie clear off the picnic table and put the few extras left in the refrigerator.

"I thought there'd be more left," she said, gazing at the near-empty containers on her kitchen table.

"You just fed bears. You're lucky you have your arms."

She smiled. "I know you're teasing, but you may want to keep those jokes to yourself when Stevie's around."

"Is she really afraid of us?"

"My Stevie's afraid of all sorts of things. She can't help it. She's been through a lot."

"What kind of music did she write?"

"Music?"

"She said something about your father selling her music."

"Oh. Yeah. She was a music prodigy when she was young. Taught herself piano by the time she was . . . three, I think. Wrote a full symphony by the time she was six and conducted the St. Petersburg Orchestra by the time she was seven."

"That's amazing. That's why Coop knew her."

"Yeah. But she gave it all up a long time ago."

"Because of her father?"

"Surprisingly, no. Too much pressure," Charlie said, taking the leftovers he handed her and placing them in the refrigerator. "All that performing. All those demands. She lost her love of music. So she went into something a little . . . easier."

"What's that?"

"Physics and math. Turns out she's a prodigy in that, too. I, however, barely passed algebra and Max's biology teacher threw one of those dead dissection frogs at her."

Berg opened his mouth to ask why her teacher would do that, but what came out was, "Wanna go out sometime?"

Frowning, Charlie turned from the refrigerator and faced him. "Huh?"

"You know . . . a date. Dinner. Maybe a movie. Without our siblings."

Charlie's frown deepened and she asked, "Why?"

Now it was Berg's turn to frown. "You don't seem . . . insecure."

"I'm not."

"Then why are you asking why?"

"If we didn't know each other, I would totally get why you'd ask me out. I mean, there's a definite spark between us. On some weird level, we do get each other. But you *do* know me."

"Yeah . . . and?"

"And why would you want to get involved with me? I'm cursed."

Berg straightened up. "Pardon?"

"I'm cursed. Some think the whole family is cursed, but I'm sure it's just my father. And his curse was passed down to his daughters."

Berg chuckled. "You don't really believe that." She stared at him, so he guessed, "You do really believe that."

"It explains everything. We're basically nice people—

well . . . me and Stevie—and yet, you met me when I
was running for my life. And, just so we're clear, I've
run for my life more than once."

"But it sounds like maybe that's all your father's
fault. That doesn't mean you're cursed."

"Doesn't it?" She pressed her hand against his arm.
"Look, you are such a sweet guy, and your siblings are
awesome. There's no way I'd infect you with the family
curse."

"So, you don't date?"

"Oh, I date. But only men I can barely stand. That
way if bad things happen to them, I won't care. You . . .
I'd care. And I wouldn't want to risk triplets becoming
twins because you have questionable taste in women."

Not knowing how to respond to that, Berg just stood
there. Staring at a closed refrigerator. He didn't even
realize that Charlie had gone until the cabinet over the
refrigerator opened up and Stevie waved at him.

"What are you doing?" he asked.

"I was trying to nap."

"A bed was not an option?"

"That's for when I sleep. Not nap."

Berg blew out a breath. "I don't know how to respond to that either."

"She shot you down, huh?" Stevie asked, even though
they both knew the answer.

"Like an allied plane over Germany."

"I know it's hard to believe, but it just means she
really likes you. No, seriously," she insisted when Berg
snorted.

"What's serious?" Max asked, walking into the room
with her face again covered in bees and honey.

"I thought Tiny said no stealing from hives," Berg
reminded her.

"Who said I stole anything?"

"Charlie shot him down," Stevie whispered. Loudly.

"I saw that coming." Max slapped her face, killing several bees in the process. "She doesn't want to pass on the curse."

"There is no curse," Berg insisted.

"It's really hard to look at our lives and not think there's a curse."

"I'm not saying you guys haven't had some hard luck, but curses? Seriously? It's more like your father is just an asshole."

"He's definitely an asshole." Max walked to the sink and washed the bees off her face. "But our sister also believes she's cursed, and no one is going to change her mind just by telling her she's not being logical. She's never logical when it comes to our father."

Max dried off her face with a paper towel but when she turned around, Berg had to look away.

"Don't worry," she promised. "The swelling goes down in no time."

"Good to know."

"Look," Max said, "our sister has a lot going on. And that's been her life since birth. She takes care of everybody. That's what she does. But we want her to know what it's like to be normal."

"Because she's too involved in your lives?"

"Oh, God no. We thank every deity that exists for each other. Charlie's the reason I'm not doing hard time in a federal prison."

"And I'm not making meth because of her." Berg looked up into the cabinet Stevie was still ensconced in, and she explained, "My father once sold me to a Peruvian drug lord because, and I'm quoting, 'You're good with science.' But thankfully Charlie didn't let that happen."

"And somewhere there's a Peruvian drug lord who wishes he still had two hands," Max muttered; then she laughed. When Berg didn't join in, she went on. "We just want the best for our sister. She clearly likes you because she doesn't want you cursed—"

"There is *no* curse," Berg said again.

"And you seem refreshingly normal. You have siblings that haven't actively tried to have you killed. Your sister complains about her mom in that cute, *normal* way. Without malice or the desire to track her down and kill her. You could be really good for her."

"And she'll be the *best* thing that's ever come into your life," Stevie told him plainly.

"But you guys make me sound so boring."

"Yes," Max said flatly. "Very boring is a man who can shift to a fifteen-hundred-pound bear."

"It's only a thousand pounds. Polar bears shift to fifteen hundred."

Max gazed at him a long moment before stating, "Well, that proves your point."

"Normal is not dull," Stevie said. "I've had *whole* days that were normal. I go to work, I come home, I order in some Chinese . . . normal." She closed her eyes and let out a big sigh. "It's awesome."

"Yeah," Max said. "I really don't have normal. But I've come to accept that I won't. But my sister . . . she wants us to have normal. To be happy. To not be in prison."

"To not be serving any drug lords."

"And she's sacrificed a lot to help us with that. So I think you should spend some time with her and find out if you really like her."

"But she clearly told me no, she wasn't going to date me."

"Date?" Max sneered. "Dude, you're a shifter. You don't date. You just hang around until before you know it, you're part of her life and she can't bring herself to get rid of you."

"You mean like a stray dog?"

"Or a stray cat. Either one would do us fine. If it turns out you spend some time with her and she's not really for you, or vice versa . . . you walk away. Like normal people do. Not like my dad, who has set a house or two on fire when he's been kicked out on his ass." Max walked around the kitchen table until she stood next to Berg. "But if you do like our sister, then you dig in there, Fido."

"I am not a dog."

"No," Stevie noted, "but dogs and bears are very similar genetically."

Berg faced the badger-tiger mix, his arms crossed. He was tall enough that he didn't even have to look up at her. He stared her right in the eyes.

After a full minute, she reached out and grabbed the cabinet door and slowly closed it.

"Just give it a shot," Max said.

"Well . . ."

Charlie walked into the kitchen and held her phone up. "Why is Aunt Bernice calling me?"

Max shook her head. "I have no idea." She paused. "Unless she knows . . ."

"Unless she knows what?"

"Nothing."

Charlie sighed. "What did he do?"

"Charlie—"

"Just tell me," Charlie ordered, her hand gesturing. "Do it. Just tell me what he did."

Max let out a breath, then announced, "Our father hacked into our uncle's bank account and stole a hundred million British sterling."

Charlie gazed at her sister as long as Berg had stared at Stevie. Finally, she asked, "Which uncle?"

"Charlie—"

"Which. Uncle?"

"Will."

"He stole from Uncle Will?"

"Yes."

Charlie's shoulders slumped and her head dropped. For a long moment, Berg thought maybe she was crying.

Until Charlie's head snapped up and she bellowed, "*Everybody out! I need to bake!*"

Stevie scrambled out of the cabinet, climbing on Berg's shoulders and down his back so she could run out the back door. Max simply sauntered out. She acted like she had all the time in the world, but she still *left*. And without saying a word or making a joke.

That just left Charlie and Berg.

"Why are you still here?" she asked him.

"I just wanted to let you know I'm here if you need me."

"Oh, really," she said with a huge amount of sarcasm. "You just happen to have a hundred million British sterling lying around your house somewhere so I can pay back my psychotic uncle who's a gangster? Is that what you mean?"

"Um . . . no. But I really like baked goods, and I'm willing to test your food for you."

Charlie blinked, appearing stunned, before one side of her mouth curled the tiniest bit.

"I'll keep that in mind," she promised before motioning him away with her hands.

"And I'm always hungry," he teasingly added before walking out the back door. He smiled a little when he heard her give a small chuckle.

But as soon as he stepped around the side of the house, Stevie jumped in front of him. He took a step back, startled by her sudden appearance.

"Did . . ." She glanced at the house and back at Berg. "Did I just hear my sister . . . laugh?"

"Yeah. A little one."

"Laugh? Now? After hearing what my father did?

And knowing how bad this is going to be? And you made her laugh?"

"It wasn't a guffaw or anything. It was more a light chuckle, but . . . yeah. I guess. Why?"

Stevie abruptly grabbed Berg's T-shirt and brutally ordered, "You stray-dog this, Berg. *You stray-dog this!*"

"Uhhhhh . . . okay."

Then she was gone . . . into a nearby tree. Because that was normal.

Britta moved over to his side. "Everything all right?" she asked.

"Weird but . . . all right." Then Berg felt the need to add, "Although that just applies to us. For them . . . it's weird and bad."

"How bad?"

"A hundred million British sterling bad."

Britta's mouth dropped open. "How is that even possible?"

"Apparently their father has a way." He motioned toward their house with a jerk of his head. "Do me a favor, Sis . . . look into it."

Chapter Eight

Max gazed down at the kitchen table, which was covered in all sorts of baked goods. From simple sugar cookies to complicated breads and desserts. Her sister had been up all night making this food. Stevie tried meditation and yoga to relax. Max got into fights with bees. And Charlie baked.

"What are we supposed to do with all this?" Max asked Stevie. "I mean, I can pack it away, but even *I* can't eat this much before it all goes bad."

"I'm half Siberian tiger and I can't eat all this."

"What would normal people do with this much food?"

Stevie thought a moment. "Give it to friends and family."

"We don't speak to our family and we have very few friends."

Charlie walked into the kitchen and held up her phone. "I'm going in!" she announced.

Max rolled her eyes. "Just 'cause that old bitch called doesn't mean you need to call her back."

"We need to know what she knows."

"I doubt she knows much of anything. It's not like the

two sides of the family are chatty. Uncle Will is probably blaming the American side for what Freddy did."

"Our state-side kin would have never helped him. Any more than we would."

"Maybe she just wants information since Will won't tell her anything."

"Which is kind of rude," Stevie complained, "coming to us for information when she didn't even invite us to her daughter's wedding."

Charlie frowned. "Who's getting married?"

"Uh . . . the youngest one. Carrie, I think. They're in New York for the whole event right now. The future hubby is apparently very rich."

Charlie smiled. "Then I'm sure Bernice wouldn't want anything to fuck with her daughter's perfect society wedding."

"You mean like Dad showing up to start shit?" Max asked.

"That's exactly what I mean."

Charlie placed the phone on the table and hit redial, turning on the speaker. Then they all leaned in . . . and waited.

"So is your father dead or not?" their aunt asked without any preamble. Not even a hello.

"Nope," Charlie replied. "Not dead. Very much alive from what we can tell."

"Just great!" Bernice snarled. Max imagined her aunt pacing one of the grand rooms in her Rhode Island home. The wedding might be in Manhattan, but Bernice was one of the Rhode Island wealthy due to a very advantageous marriage in her youth. And that was the only way Max could visualize her. "Do you know where he is? Is he still in New York?"

"No idea," Charlie said. Then, after glancing at her sisters, she added, "He could jump out at any time with one of his crazy schemes. Asking all your rich friends for money. When he's not picking their pockets or stealing their jewelry off their necks in front of cameras. It will be fabulous! Is the *New York Times* going to report on it all for you? I'm sure they have access to Dad's last sixteen mugshots from around the world."

There was silence, then a muffled scream from the other end of the phone and, silently, Max and Stevie laughed hysterically. Stevie slid down the refrigerator until she sat on the floor, arms around her middle. Max leaned over the kitchen table, her head resting on the wood. Charlie, of course, stayed focused on the phone.

"He needs to be found," her aunt finally stated.

"And I need smaller tits," Charlie told her, "but we don't always get what we want."

"Do you know what's going on right now, little miss?"

Charlie leaned in a little and said, "No. What could be going on right now?"

"My daughter is getting married—"

"Oh. A *family* wedding? But that can't be . . . because *we* weren't invited. And we *are* family. Right?"

Now Max was still on the table but on her back, her legs kicking out like a crazy toddler's. She couldn't help it. This was the best! Her sister was the absolute best!

"It was nothing personal," Bernice lied. "We just don't like any of you."

Now all three sisters were laughing out loud. No longer bothering to hide it anymore. Because, although it was true that Bernice didn't like any of them, they were also the only ones she could truly be herself with. The socialites never saw the *true* Bernice MacKilligan Andersen-Cummings.

Clearing her throat to stop the laughter, Charlie told her aunt, "My sisters and I are well aware of your feelings about us, so . . . good luck with my dad." She reached down to disconnect the call.

"Don't hang up!" Bernice ordered. Then, softly, she added, "Please."

Charlie pulled her hand back and rested both arms on the table. "Yes?"

"Your father needs to be found. I can't afford for him to just . . . show up at my daughter's wedding. This is too important."

"And what do you want from us?"

"For you to find him. For you to *manage* him."

"We are not our father's keeper," Charlie stated with absolute conviction. "You'll have to manage him on your own."

"I don't have time for that. Things here are a little bit . . . overwhelming at the moment. Adding your useless father to this situation . . ."

"Plus there's the other problem."

There was a long pause before Bernice asked, "*What* other problem?"

So Bernice *didn't* know.

"Dad stole money from Uncle Will."

"Christ on a cross! How much money?"

Charlie scratched her forehead with her thumbnail. "A hundred million pounds."

Bernice was silent for so long, Max was sure she'd disconnected the phone or passed out. But she hadn't.

"He can't be that stupid," she said, her voice like a whisper.

"We both know he can be. He *is* that stupid."

"And to steal from Will . . . what was he thinking?"

Charlie rolled her eyes. "I'm guessing he wasn't."

"They'll be coming for you," Bernice told Charlie.

"For what?" Charlie scoffed. "I don't have a million pounds just lying around to fix my father's fuckup.

And Dad has never given a shit about his daughters, so threatening us won't work either."

"But you're the only one, Charlie, who has ever been able to manage the stupid fuck. The Scots know that. They'll use it. They'll use your sisters."

Charlie began to rub her forehead. "Can't you talk to them?" she asked between clenched teeth. Charlie hated asking any of the family for anything. So she didn't. Until now.

"Me? That won't help you. Will and I are not exactly close. But if I were in your shoes, I'd let Will and all your Scottish uncles know, in very clear terms, that you and your sisters are not to be put into the mix when it comes to dealing with your father."

Charlie exchanged confused glances with Max and Stevie.

"I'm not sure I know what that means," Charlie finally admitted.

"Figure it out. We are on an open phone line. Until then, how about we meet for tea?"

Charlie hated tea. "Tea? Why?"

They could hear pages being flipped. "I have some time on Tuesday. Three o'clock. At the Kingston Arms. I'll meet you at the front desk. Just you. And please . . . dress appropriately."

The call ended and Charlie straightened up.

"You gonna go?" Max asked.

"Yeah." Charlie began to pace the room and Max watched her closely.

"What are you thinking?" she asked her sister.

"I'm thinking about what she said. About dealing with Uncle Will." Charlie abruptly stopped and focused on Max. "What do you think Uncle Will is planning, to get back his money, I mean?"

"Honestly?"

"Honestly."

Max rubbed her nose. "I think he's sent over a bunch of guys to kill one of us and take the other two hostage, hoping that'll bring Dad out of the woodwork and get his money back, while showing the rest of the family that they risk their children when they fuck with him."

"But Dad won't care. He won't care if Will kills all three of us."

"I know."

Charlie thought a moment. "Do you think Will was behind the attacks in Milan and Switzerland?"

"No."

"Why?"

"That chopper. In Switzerland."

"Are you going on again about that helicopter?"

"It was military grade," Max insisted. "Uncle Will is not paying for that. The fucker's too cheap. That's why I know that with a hundred million in play, he's gonna do something. Personally, I agree with Bernice. He's gonna make a move."

"Of course you agree with Bernice. Because she said we should strike first."

"No, she said we should let Uncle Will and the others know that we're not to be fucked with because of our father. I say we set up . . . an opportunity."

"An opportunity to what? Fuck us over?"

"Can I make a suggestion?" Stevie asked.

Charlie let out a long sigh, but it didn't relieve the tension in her shoulders. The strain on her face. "Of course," she said to Stevie.

Their baby sister stood, smoothing down the front of her too-big sundress. "I say you call him up. Uncle Will. And tell him we want to talk to him. Some place private in the City."

"And then?" Charlie asked.

Stevie shrugged her shoulders and lifted her hands, palms up. "If Uncle Will truly just wants to talk, then we talk, tell him we don't know what Dad's up to, and everybody goes their separate ways. But if Uncle Will intends to use us to get at Dad . . . then we do what we do. I mean, if they're going to use us as an object lesson . . . maybe it's time we make a lesson of them."

Charlie studied her sister a moment. "It'll get messy."

"Anything involving Daddy gets messy. Call Uncle Will, Max," she suggested while reaching into her oversized backpack, which was jammed with her notebooks, pencils, and pens. "Or his eldest son, Dougie. Pick an abandoned building and tell them we want to meet on Monday. Give it a sense of urgency so they don't think we're planning anything." Stevie pulled out the SSRI antidepressants and antianxiety meds that she used to manage her panic disorder and placed them on the table. "You keep these for now. I'll go back on them later."

"Are you sure—"

"I'm sure." Stevie nodded. "If they really want to hold our father against us . . . we'll show them all—the entire family—what they're really risking when they challenge the MacKilligan girls."

Charlie reached over and pulled Stevie close, kissing her on the top of her head.

Max placed the meds in a drawer for quick and easy access while Charlie examined the table filled with all her baking. "God, what are we going to do with all this food?"

Stevie leaned her head back and said, "I have an idea for that too."

This time Charlie's eyes narrowed. "What idea?"

Charlie picked up the plate with the honey-pineapple cake she'd baked and headed out toward Berg's place. She wanted to let him and his siblings know how much she appreciated their recent help, and according to Stevie, they'd probably finish off the rest of the baked goods, too.

Besides, getting out of the house might ease Charlie's anxiety. Her baby sister might have a panic disorder, freaking out at the slightest weird sound or fast-moving squirrel, but Charlie was all about what could *possibly* happen. That was what kept her up nights. Worrying about things she didn't really have any control over, but knowing that didn't mean she could stop worrying. Actually, she worried more.

But maybe she could distract herself. At least for a little while. That's what the actual act of baking did for her. Distracted her. Calmed her. Now she was going to try doing the same thing by sharing her food with near-strangers. It was, to be honest, the first time she could think of when she'd known people not related by blood or Pack well enough to feel comfortable to offer them food.

Charlie came down the porch steps and reached the front gate. She'd just stepped through, closing it behind her, when the rumbling of a souped-up car had her turning. The car pulled into a spot not too far from her, and she waited to see who came out while sliding her hand around to grab the butt of the gun stuck into the back of her jeans under her T-shirt.

The driver door opened and she watched the man who stepped out, her eyes briefly closing. How could Max do it? Of all the people she could have called . . . why him?

And to bring him here? A bear-only neighborhood? Had she lost her mind?

When he saw her, he smiled and Charlie's grip tightened on her gun. She could just drop him here. She really could. But she knew Max would never forgive her for that. It could be the one thing that would possibly break the bond between them. Or at the very least damage it so that it would take decades to repair.

He stopped just as he reached the trunk of his car. "Don't shoot," he said, still smiling. "I know you want to, but that'll just bring out my sister and cousins . . . and I'm sure you remember what happened to the last girl that hurt my tender feelings."

Using all her internal fortitude, Charlie released her gun and dropped her arm to her side.

He laughed and came over to her.

"Don't—"

But it was too late. She was already enveloped in big arms and pressed against an excruciatingly large chest.

She held the plate with the cake away from her body, but she could already hear him sniffing, his body leaning over to take a ruthless bite.

"Touch that cake," she warned, "and I'm taking your dick."

Dutch Alexander pulled back. He was just six feet, but wide as a house. And all of it muscle and power.

"You never like to share, MacKilligan."

"Not with weasels."

"I think of you as a sister."

"Shut up."

"Is everything all right, Charlie?"

Their landlord, Tiny, stood behind her, eyeing Dutch.

"I'm fine." She tried to pull away, but Dutch held her tightly. Why? Because he enjoyed irritating her. Always had. "Do you mind?"

"Can't I show affection to my best friend's beloved older sister?"

Charlie placed her hand underneath his jaw and unleashed her claws, making sure the middle one pressed against his jugular.

"I'll take that as a no." Dutch released her and stepped back, which was impressive because Dutch usually had no concept of personal space. He was a touchy-feely guy who loved hugs and affection, which many found surprising when they realized what he was. What he *truly* was.

But just in case Dutch tried to hug her again, Charlie took a step back as well, which was when Tiny took a big step forward. The six-foot-nine man thought to use his natural strength and size to intimidate the smaller but equally wide foe.

Before Tiny could even flex his muscles, though, Dutch was next to him. Against him. He sniffed his way up Tiny's chest, looked at him, then abruptly huffed. Twice.

Shocked, Tiny took a startled step back and Dutch huffed again, moving closer. Huffed again, moved closer. Then he unleashed his fangs.

Fangs that could crush nearly anything.

The bear unleashed his claws, but Charlie quickly stepped between the two huffing males and snarled, "I am *trying* to be a good neighbor. I'm not sure how one does that, but I'm almost positive bloodshed is not involved!" She pointed her finger at Tiny. "So put those claws away." She glared at Dutch. "And don't you even *think* about doing anything involving your anal glands."

Dutch grinned, his fangs still out. "Sweet talker."

"Here, Tiny." She handed Tiny the cake she'd been planning to give to the Dunns. "It's honey-pineapple."

"Oh. Uh . . . thanks."

Tiny took the cake and turned to walk away, but he stopped, looked back at Dutch.

"Honey badger?" he guessed.

"Hardly," Dutch said, his voice full of that ridiculous pride, his fang-filled grin widening even more. "Wolverine."

Frowning, Tiny focused on Charlie. "I didn't know you'd be bringing wolverines here."

"Racist."

Charlie slapped her hand over Dutch's face, knowing that would do little to keep his big mouth shut, but she had to try.

"He's just here to see my sister. I promise he won't cause any trouble."

Tiny grunted and again started toward his house a few doors down. But as he walked away, he muttered, "And I'm not racist. Wolverine is not a race. Honey badger is not a race. It's a species."

Dutch retracted his fangs and asked Charlie, "You're blaming me for this, aren't you?"

In answer, Charlie reached up and slapped the back of Dutch's head. Just like she did to her sister. Just like she'd been doing to both of them since the first day Max had brought the little shit to the Pack house. The wolves had not been happy, but the pair had only been twelve and the adults were just glad Max actually had a friend. Any friend. But, as always, it had fallen on Charlie to keep the pair in line. A job she did *not* enjoy.

The front door to their rental house opened and Max stepped onto the porch.

She threw her arms up and cheered, "Dutchy!"

"Maxie!"

Max ran down the steps and Dutch leaped over the gate. They met somewhere in the middle, the pair ramming into each other, before air-kissing and twirling around each other with their arms spread wide.

It was quite the display. But nothing Charlie hadn't seen before. Over and over and over again. But at least Max had friends. Annoying friends, but friends.

Charlie turned to go back to the house and get something else she could give to the Dunns. Maybe the cinnamon rolls would be a good choice. But a banging door had her looking over her shoulder to see the Dunns' front screen door on the ground and a wet, small bear charging across the street.

A few seconds later, Berg Dunn came running after it, his arms and T-shirt dripping wet and covered with soapsuds.

"Get back here! Bastard!"

The bear leaped over Charlie's low fence and disappeared around the back of the house. Berg stumbled to a stop beside Charlie.

"It's legal to have full-blood bears in this town?" she asked.

Berg's head cocked to the side, brows pulling low in confusion. "That wasn't a bear. That's my dog."

"That thing was a dog?"

"Yes," he replied, sounding indignant. "A Caucasian Shepherd Dog. My parents breed them."

"Never heard of them."

"They're from Russia. They're trained to protect livestock from bears, wolves, and jackals." After a moment of silence, he added, "He doesn't like getting a bath. But he smelled."

"Now you both do."

Berg nodded toward a laughing Max and Dutch. "Who's the dude?"

"That's Dutch. Max's friend."

He sniffed the air. Sniffed it again. Leaned in and sniffed again.

"He's a wolverine," she told him when she couldn't stand that noise another second.

"Oh." Berg blinked. "Wow. Really? I've never met one."

"They mostly live their lives among full-humans. Fewer fights. Speaking of which, I was going to bring you a cake."

"You *were*?"

"I had to give it to Tiny. He was about to get into a fight with Dutch, and that wouldn't have ended well for either of them."

"Well . . . thanks anyway."

"I have some other stuff. You want to check it out?"

"Sure."

"We better get you in there before Dutch sees it." She opened the front gate. "He can put away more food than seems humanly possible. He's like a vacuum."

The front door to the house slammed open and, screaming, Stevie ran down the porch stairs, across the yard, and over the fence without even a pause.

Shocked, Charlie yelled after her, "*It was just a dog!*" But her reasoning didn't stop an already panicked Stevie. She focused on Max. "Well, go get her!"

"Why do I always have to—oh, fuck it!"

Max charged off after their sister and Charlie headed into the house with Berg behind her.

"Let's get your dog and . . ." Charlie stopped, her gaze locked on the living room window. "Isn't that your dog?" she asked, pointing at the enormous animal wiggling on his back in the middle of the grass.

"It is."

But if her sister had seen the dog in the yard, she wouldn't have run out of the house, leaving the safety of closed doors. So Stevie had reacted to something *inside* the house.

Charlie reached under the coffee table and grabbed the .45 Max had holstered under there, putting a round in the chamber. Berg's "Whoa!" barely registered before she went through the house, her weapon clasped in both hands, her elbows out at her sides. She never held the gun far from her body. That would make it easy for someone to knock it out of her hands when she went around a blind corner.

She stopped a few feet from the kitchen and glanced back at Berg. "What are those sounds?"

He paused a moment, then rolled his eyes. He walked over to the swinging door and pushed it open. With the gun still in front of her, Charlie moved closer but immediately lowered the weapon when she saw a group of what she assumed were her neighbors sitting at her kitchen table or leaning against the counter and devouring her food.

"I see your mistake," Berg explained, moving into the kitchen. The neighbors barely noticed him. "You left the window open."

"We smelled all this a block away," a sow said between bites of lemon cookies.

"Did Tiny give you the right garbage cans?" a male bear asked, remnants of raspberry Danish in the corners of his mouth.

"The *right* garbage cans?"

"Yeah," Berg explained. "Bear proof."

Charlie felt her left eye twitch. "I need bear-proof garbage cans?"

"Some of us get hungry at night when we're roaming around," another sow explained. "But we're usually too lazy to shift back to human to get the garbage cans open."

"When we do get the garbage cans open, most of us are quite neat about it," the first sow explained as she reached for the ginger cookies. "We put back in the cans what we don't eat. But *some* people—"

"Like the Hendersons, three doors down."

"—aren't so polite. But if you bear-proof, you'll be fine."

Charlie nodded a silent thank-you to the intruders before glancing at Berg and growling, "Can I speak to you outside?"

* * *

Berg followed Charlie into the backyard, but he was a little surprised when she suddenly spun toward him, an angry finger pointing at his chest.

"You said we'd be safe here!"

"You are."

"How can you"—she stepped back to allow a hysterically screaming Stevie to run past her; a snarling Max followed close behind with Berg's ridiculously happy dog after both of them—"say that when there are bears in my kitchen?"

Berg didn't answer her right away. He was too busy watching Stevie leap up and over the two-car garage behind the house. Max and the dog, sadly, had to run around the garage to get to her.

"Wow. She cleared that easy."

"Pay attention to me!" she ordered. And when she had his attention, she said again, "There are *bears in my kitchen!*"

"Yeah . . . so?"

She threw up her hands. "*In what world is that safe?*"

"Let's start with . . . how about no yelling? And you couldn't be safer than with bears in your kitchen."

"Explain that to me," she managed to say without raising her voice.

"You're worried about strange guys coming into your house, killing you and Max, and kidnapping Stevie, right?"

"That would be the most likely scenario."

"How are they going to get past a bunch of hungry bears in your kitchen?"

She opened her mouth to reply, closed it, opened it, then demanded, "What?"

"We scented that weasel long before he ever hit our street. My sister had binoculars on him as soon as his car rumbled around the corner. We are very protective of our neighborhood. We have to be. We've got a huge lion pride that way"—he pointed south, then east—"and three wolf Packs that way."

Charlie suddenly glanced off. "I *did* hear roaring last night. I thought I was just really tired."

"That was Craig. Old lion male. Retired Navy man. Super cranky. He roars every night to let us all know where his territory begins and ends. And when the full moon comes, you get the howling. Unless the wolves have had tequila. Tequila nights are noisy nights."

Charlie folded her arms across her chest and asked, "You don't find that . . . weird?"

"Find what weird?"

"Being surrounded by lions and wolves and . . . bears in my kitchen. That seems really weird to me."

"Not to me, but I grew up in an all-bear neighborhood in Seattle. Lots of hippy bears. Lots of honey and pot." He motioned to her. "You weren't raised by badgers at all? Because they usually keep close to their own."

She snorted. "We're not considered 'their own.' After my mom died, we lived with my grandfather's Pack. They protected us, but they didn't really"—she briefly struggled for the right words—"teach us. That's not right either. They taught us stuff . . . just not shifter stuff."

"What did they teach you?"

"They taught me and Max how to drive . . . of course, that was so we could chauffer Stevie around to all her college classes and private lessons."

"Oh."

"The shifter stuff they taught their pups, but they didn't consider us their pups. They just made sure we were fed and kept alive. And my grandfather was busy running the Pack. I think he thought his Packmates were helping us more . . . but they really weren't. Still, they didn't try to kill us either or chase us off before we were eighteen, so I considered that a win."

"I guess. So, in other words, you don't spend a lot of time around other shifters."

"I don't. And Stevie doesn't. Max has a bunch of friends through—"

"The weasel?"

She smirked. "He's the brawniest member of the badger family. I would suggest you not fuck with him."

Berg suddenly heard crunching sounds behind him and turned to see that the weasel was standing behind him, biting off chunks of meat and bone from a frozen-solid leg of lamb.

"Hope you don't mind," he said around his food. "The bears ate almost all the sweet stuff and I was really hungry."

He took another bite, his wolverine jaw easily decimating what most humans and several breeds of shifters would have to thaw first.

Charlie stared at the weasel with a definite look of distaste before ordering, "Go away. Over there."

Without question and still eating, he moved away from them.

Berg was glad to see she didn't like Max's friend. Especially when the first thing Britta had said about him behind her binoculars was, "Nice ass on that short guy."

"Well, now that you're here," Berg suggested, "we can teach you about shifter stuff."

"What do I need to know?"

"Can you scent the difference between a polar bear and a grizzly?"

"Don't all bears smell alike?"

Berg looked off for a moment and took a deep breath. He especially didn't like the weasel's knowing laugh.

"*No*," he finally replied. "We do *not* all smell alike."

"Okay. Okay. Don't get moody."

"But see? It's insults like that I . . . we . . . can help you avoid."

"If you think it's necessary."

Before Berg could tell Charlie exactly how necessary it was—especially if she was going to live in this neighborhood without broken bones—Clark McKlintock walked around the garage, through the back gate in the fence, and over to the pair.

"Hey, Clark."

"Berg."

"Charlie, this is Clark McKlintock. He lives on the next block. He's a polar."

She stared at Clark for a few seconds, then asked, "Should I smell him?"

"I wouldn't." Berg shook his head and again focused on Clark. "So what's up, Clark?"

"Was wondering if this is yours?"

"If what's mine?"

Clark turned around and showed them his back, where the quivering, sobbing mess that was Charlie's baby sister had attached herself. She was still human, but claws on both her hands and feet were buried deep into poor Clark's flesh.

"Oh, shit!" Charlie immediately grabbed her sister around the waist. "Let him go!"

"Safe bear," Stevie said. "Safe bear. It petted dog. So he is safe bear."

Well . . . that was logic. Not necessarily good or sound logic though.

Charlie attempted to drag her sister off Clark's back but she simply dug her claws in deeper.

Clark looked over his shoulder at Berg. "Could you get this mutt off me, please?"

Berg almost thumped the polar in the back of the head. "Mutt" was a rude way to talk about hybrids, but Charlie didn't seem to notice. Mostly, he was sure, because she was busy trying to deal with her sister. But also because she didn't know better. She didn't know she'd just been insulted.

But he did. And it pissed him off *for* her.

Pulling Charlie's hands away from her sister, Berg said, "You know what? Let's make this a learning opportunity."

Charlie frowned at him but, after a moment, she took a step back.

"Now," Berg said, using his best professorial voice, "this may *appear* bad. And it is. But your sister still managed to choose well in this instance."

Now completely confused, Charlie looked over at the weasel. At this point, he only had a hunk of frozen bone left, and he was gnawing on it like a chicken bone.

He grinned around his meal at Charlie's questioning look and nodded.

With a shrug, Charlie said, "Is that a fact? Please explain."

"First, polar bear is always a good choice. It never occurs to them to react to anything. They just lope along."

"You do know that what she's doing to me now hurts, right?" Clark asked.

"Whereas," Berg continued, "grizzlies are fast to react. Chances are if she had done this to my sister, Britta would have shifted to her grizzly form and dropped back-first onto the ground. But a polar . . . ? I'm surprised he even noticed. They're so slow . . . and dull-witted."

"Hey," Clark complained. "Wait a minute—"

"They're also slow moving physically. Compared to grizzlies, I mean. And almost every other shifter . . . ever. You and your sisters could easily outrun them. And you can easily out-think them. Without much trouble. Because they're that fucking stupid."

Clark jerked around and pushed him, which pissed

Berg off, so he shoved the polar back and let the muscle between his shoulder blades grow, making his shoulders larger.

But before he could go after the big idiot, Charlie stupidly jumped between them, her arms spread wide to keep them apart. Had she lost her mind? She couldn't be that clueless to the shifter life, could she? Then again, he and Dag had gotten in the middle of a badger fight—so who was he to talk?

"Hey! *Hey! Gentlemen!*" She looked at both of them. "Stop it right now!"

With her arms still outstretched, she pointed one finger at Berg. "And I don't need you to protect me from big, slow-moving assholes."

"I'm not slow," Clark said. And when they stared at him, he added, "Mind or body . . . owwwww!" Eyes wide, he stared at Charlie. "I think her claws are getting longer."

"They're totally getting longer," she said with no obvious sense of urgency. "In fact, they can get so long that they can sever your spine in at least ten places." She stepped in close to Clark, gazing up at him without any fear. "Because me and my sister are *mutts* and that's what we do. We are freaks of nature and we can erase you. So be nice to us . . . or I'll show you exactly what I can do to you." She stepped around him, stopping by his side, and adding, "And you won't even have time to scream."

Moving away from the stunned polar, she barked, "Let him go, Stevie!"

Stevie suddenly hit the ground, her ridiculously long claws covered in blood and gore.

The poor girl was panting and sweating and completely freaked out.

With her gaze locked on Clark, Charlie ordered the weasel, "Take her inside, Dutch."

"With the bears?" he asked.

Charlie scrunched up her nose, annoyed. "Shit."

"No, no," Stevie ground out. "I'll be fine." Pressing her fists against the ground, she forced herself up. "I can be around the bears."

Charlie sighed. "Sweetie—"

"I can be around the bears!"

That slightly hysterical bellow had both Berg and Clark taking a big step back, *away* from the thin hybrid. Her sister, though, moved closer. And she laughed a little.

"Brave woman," Clark muttered low to Berg.

"You sure?" Charlie asked her sister. "I'm sure the idiot wouldn't mind taking you out for ice cream."

"The idiot you love," the weasel corrected. And Berg wanted to slap him. Just once. Back of the head.

"There's a great place a few blocks over. Sammy's Ice Cream Palace. Only a few minutes away," Berg told her. But when Charlie raised an eyebrow, he quickly added, "A full-human place. Lots of full-humans. You can find the address on your phone. But I'd suggest using any water hose at any house to wash off her hands and feet—since full-humans usually freak out at the sight of young women covered in gore."

"Excellent." The weasel pushed himself away from the house and came toward Stevie.

From around the corner, Max came running in, panting, with Berg's dog beside her. He seemed happy and entertained. She, however, did not.

She started to speak but the panting kept her from anything more than harsh breathing sounds.

Max rested her hand against her hip and bent over at the waist.

Laughing, the weasel went to his friend. He turned away from her and, with some sort of unspoken offer and acceptance, Max climbed onto his back. She rested her arms on his shoulders and he held her with his hands under her legs.

He started off, and Stevie fell in beside them. She seemed much calmer now, but who knew how long that would last.

"Is she going to be okay?" Berg asked Charlie. "This is New York. There are a lot of bears in New York. And Jersey."

"She'll be fine once she's back on her meds."

"Why would she be off her meds?"

Charlie didn't answer him, just walked back into the house.

"You know you don't have a chance with her, right?" Clark asked about Charlie.

Unable to resist any longer, Berg slapped the back of the polar's head. He probably put more force behind it than was necessary, but Clark was getting a little of the residual anger Berg felt toward the weasel too.

Clark spun around, fist pulled back, but all Berg had to say was, "Don't make me get my sister."

Lowering his arm and sneering, Clark headed back toward his street.

"Just keep those honey-stealing badgers off our territory," he warned before disappearing around the garage.

Although Berg wasn't really as worried about the MacKilligans' honey-stealing ways as he was about what would make a very careful Charlie suddenly allow her panic-riddled sister to go off her much-needed medication.

Chapter Nine

The waitress placed a giant Viking boat in front of her sister filled with what was called a banana split but, to Max, looked like a wide bowl of useless calories. And Stevie dove into it like she hadn't eaten in days.

"Is this why you're so thin?" Max asked. "Because you're eating all this crap instead of real food? You haven't gone vegan, have you?"

Mouth full of ice cream, banana, nuts, chocolate, and caramel, Stevie gazed at Max. "Really?" she finally asked, chocolate and caramel already smeared on her chin and upper lip.

"Let her enjoy her ice cream," Dutch said between sips of his strawberry shake. "And since ice cream is filled with dairy, doubt she's become a vegan."

"I wouldn't put it past her to become some hippy freak just to get under my skin."

Stevie said something but her mouth was full of banana split, so Max leaned forward and asked, "What?"

She swallowed and said, "Fuck you."

Dutch laughed loud, causing the Ice Palace patrons to look over at them.

"The best part," Dutch explained while still laughing, "was that you leaned forward to get that."

"Shut up," Max said. Then she laughed too.

This was why she kept Dutch around. With all the shit that went on in her life, it was nice to have someone who saw the humor is goddamn *everything*. And she adored his family. They'd let her stay at their house any time she'd wanted. She'd hang with Dutch and his loud, ridiculous sisters, and their parents had been fine with it.

Even Stevie would sometimes go to Dutch's house and spend time with the wolverines. She never found them threatening for some reason. She didn't jump into their hardcore play, but instead would sit somewhere, working in her notebooks and watching the family interactions. They didn't pressure her to be part of anything, so she felt welcome and comfortable.

There had been only one problem over the years . . .

"So Charlie *still* hates me."

"Yes," both Max and Stevie said together.

"Why?" Dutch asked. "I'm charming. Adorable. Everybody loves me."

Stevie swallowed her ice cream before replying. "She thinks you're a bad influence on Max."

Max and Dutch laughed at that . . . but they stopped when Stevie continued to eat her banana split and stare at them.

"You're serious?" Dutch asked.

"Very. She doesn't trust you. She thinks you'll be the one who will put Max in prison."

Max blinked in surprise, and she wasn't easily surprised. "When did she tell you that?"

Stevie thought a moment. "Three years ago. Over rabbit. At a French restaurant in the Alps. We went on a little vacation when I had a slight breakdown. I went after one of my colleagues with a fountain pen."

"Why?" Dutch asked.

"I was under a lot of stress. And his tone, when he

was telling me something about some tests we had run, bothered me. So, you know . . . fountain pen."

Dutch started to ask more questions about what Max knew he'd now call "the fountain pen incident," but she bumped his elbow with her own. She knew that Stevie would never be able to explain her reaction to Dutch's satisfaction. In those nice, straight lines of everyday storytelling. Her mind didn't work that way when she had her "moments."

Instead, Max and Charlie tried to keep Stevie out of those situations where she might feel overwhelmed. She could handle a lot more than normal people, but when she did crack . . . she cracked big.

"So what should I do?" Dutch asked. "To get your sister to like me?"

"Absolutely nothing," Max told him.

"She'll eat you alive." Stevie dropped her spoon into her dish and sat back. She'd finished the entire thing.

Max shook her head. "You're getting another one, aren't you?"

"It's so good." She motioned to the waitress and ordered another, but this time with, "Extra chocolate syrup, extra caramel, and extra nuts."

When the waitress walked away, Max asked her sister, "You're not going to throw this all up later, are you?"

"Are you asking me if I have an eating disorder?"

"Yes."

"No. I don't have an eating disorder. I have a panic disorder and bouts of depression. I do worry I might start hoarding at some point, but it hasn't happened yet. And, of course, when one needs a sense of control in one's life it can definitely lead to an eating disorder or hoarding. But, personally, I'm more worried about the hoarding. Mostly because I do enjoy food and I *don't* enjoy vomiting. Now if you're wondering *why* I'm so thin these days, it's because my metabolism has kicked up again. I've had to adjust my meds accordingly, taking them four times a day, which is unpleasant, but necessary because my system grinds through them so quickly. Thankfully, my doctors have really been on it, but they're in Germany, so I guess I need doctors here. At least until we can head back. Not that I necessarily want to go back. I mean, don't get me wrong, working at CERN has been amazing, but I don't know. I don't know if it's still right for me but I could just be under a lot of stress right now and it's probably not a good time to make those kinds of decisions." She glanced off, looked back at Max and Dutch. "Does it seem like I'm talking a lot? I feel like I'm talking a lot. I can't wait to get back on my meds. Tomorrow can't come soon enough."

"What's happening tomorrow?" Dutch asked.

Max silenced her rambling sister with one raised finger. "Not a word."

"Oh, come on." Dutch smiled. "You're not going to tell me?"

"No. Because you'll want to help and you can't."

"I'm very helpful."

"This is on us. And you can't be there." Max's phone vibrated in her back pocket and she slid out of the booth. "I can't be responsible for protecting you."

Dutch reared back like she'd slapped him. "When have you *ever* had to protect me?"

Max pulled her phone out of her pocket and answered it. "Hold on." She lowered it and said to her best friend, "Trust me on this."

Another mountain of ice cream, bananas, syrup, and nuts was placed in front of Stevie and she'd already dug in before Dutch attempted to woo information out of her.

"Sooo—" he began.

"Nope," Stevie cut him off before putting a spoonful of ice cream and banana into her mouth.

He dropped back in his seat. "Come on! Tell me!" He began to wiggle around like he was still a teenager with what she was sure had been a form of shifter-ADHD. "Tell me!"

"You never did listen to my advice about taking Ritalin, did you?"

"I don't need Ritalin. I have laser-like focus . . . hello," he said to a pretty young woman walking by. "Beautiful day."

Stevie rolled her eyes. Men, in general, were disgusting. She knew that. That's why she had very little tolerance for them.

"Why were you never afraid of me?" Dutch suddenly asked.

"Pardon?"

"You were completely freaked out by those bears—and we won't discuss why you ladies are currently living in an all-bear neighborhood—but you've never been afraid of me or my family."

"Bears eat people," she said plainly. "Their paws can crush heads like I can crush a cracker in my fist."

"But I'm a wolverine," he announced, as if that explained . . . everything.

Stevie reached across the table and pinched his cheek. "And such a cute little wolverine you are too!"

He gazed at her. "The worst part of that statement was your weird little girl voice."

"If it makes you feel better, I have always worried that one day I would have to testify in court because someone was rude to me and my sisters in front of you. 'No, your honor, I have no idea how that man's head got separated from his body. I blacked out. Dutch

wasn't even there. I have mental issues, you know.' "
She grinned and Dutch laughed.

"I appreciate that you'd lie for me."

"Of course. You're like family, which should be obvious because Charlie doesn't like you."

Dutch shook his head. "I still don't get that. I am *adorable*."

"Of course you are."

He gazed at her banana split until Stevie said, "Just get one already."

"I am starving."

"When was the last time you ate?"

"Like . . . two hours ago."

Stevie smirked. "That's nearly forever for you."

"I know. It really is." He motioned to the waitress and pointed at Stevie's banana split. "Two of these, please."

"You sure Max will—"

"Oh. Max. Make it three!" he called out.

Stevie went back to her split and, in between bites, said, "You know what you *can* do for us?" Dutch, flirting with another woman across the shop, missed her question so Stevie snapped her fingers in front of his face to get his attention back. "You *can* do something for us."

"Oh! Cool. What?"

"Get us a clean car. One that you don't really need to return to anyone."

"A getaway car."

She hated using that term but . . . "Basically."

"Consider it done."

"Excellent."

"I can also drive for you guys."

Stevie started to argue that but she had ice cream in her mouth.

"Don't worry," he quickly added. "I promise not to get out of the car. I'm just better at getting rid of cars than Max is."

Stevie shrugged. "Fine," she said. "But Charlie's not going to like it."

"Crazy." He suddenly looked at her. "But you like me, right?"

"I tolerate you."

"Which for you is good."

"It's very good. Although the guy I went after with a fountain pen . . . I tolerated him, too."

"Good to know."

Max came back into the shop and dropped into the booth next to Dutch. "We're all set for tomorrow's meeting."

"I'm driving," Dutch told her, sounding smug.

But Max snorted. "Don't act like Stevie told you everything. She didn't. She just hates when I drive."

Stevie pointed her spoon at Max. "Because you drive like a maniac. We're safer with the crazed wolverine."

Dutch winked at her. "See? You do like me."

"Nope," Max corrected. "She tolerates you. And that does not stop her from hurting you with a fountain pen."

Stevie sneered, "I barely touched that whiny baby."

"I heard you nearly took his eye out."

"He shouldn't have made me mad."

Dutch put his arm around Max's shoulders, smiled at them both. "God, I missed you guys."

"See? He's just proving my point," Stevie pointed out to her sister. "Crazed wolverine."

Dee-Ann Smith, wearing a Tennessee Titans T-shirt and her daddy's old trucker cap, sat on the floor and warded off the blows from the plastic knife with her bare hands.

"Good," she encouraged. "Keep going."

Her mate walked into the kitchen. "Dee-Ann, we have comp—no!" He reached down and took the plastic knife from the small hand gripping it. "We have had this discussion," he told Dee-Ann and the ball of energy glaring at him.

He cleared his throat. "Knives are not toys or weapons. They are for cooking and eating."

"That's not what granddaddy says."

Ulrich Van Holtz sighed and tossed the plastic blade into the recycle bin. "We've got to stop sending you to Tennessee every summer."

"Do that and I'll walk there on my own." Lizzy-Ann Van Holtz Smith stared up at her father a few seconds to get her point across before turning and walking away from him.

Ric glared down at Dee-Ann.

"What are you lookin' at me like that for?"

"You know why." He pointed at their six-year-old daughter and whispered, "She's your fault."

"I was never that arrogant. That's a Van Holtz trait."

"Did you forget we're waiting?" a voice yelled from the front door of their Manhattan apartment.

"That's because you don't matter," Dee-Ann retorted while getting to her feet and ignoring another glare from her mate.

Growling a little, he went to walk their guests into the kitchen. Why, she didn't know. They'd been here enough. They knew the layout of the apartment. Did they really have to keep all these airs and graces for a cat and a bear?

Dee-Ann looked over and saw that her daughter had put out plates, napkins, and utensils on the island in the middle of their kitchen.

"What are you doin'?" Dee-Ann asked.

"Being a good host."

The refrigerator door opened and closed. A few seconds later, her baby girl attempted to climb onto one of the stools while holding a platter with a sizable hunk of angel's food cake on it. When Dee-Ann tried to assist her, she pulled her little arms away. "I've got it," her daughter practically hissed at her.

"Watch that tone, missy. I ain't ya daddy."

"Obviously."

Unable to get her ass up on the seat of the stool, Lizzy braced her legs on one of the stool rungs and the base of the island. Using all her strength, she lifted the plate of cake.

Cringing, Dee-Ann quickly placed her instep against the outside of the stool so it didn't slip and, making sure her daughter didn't see her, she placed one forefinger under the plate and kept it balanced as Lizzy pushed it onto the island's marble top.

Once it was in place, Lizzy dropped to the floor and looked up at her mother with those cold blue eyes.

"Told you I had it."

Dee-Ann flashed her fangs, accompanied with an appropriate growl of warning. Lizzy hissed back. There were no fangs but she got her point across. As had once been pointed out by Lizzy's extremely frustrated teacher . . . until she'd looked up into Dee's yellow-eyed gaze.

After that, Ric went to all parent-teacher conferences.

"Is that my favorite girl?" a voice rang out.

Lizzy grinned and went around the island. "Auntie Cella!"

Marcella Malone crouched low and opened her arms. "Come here, brat."

Lizzy-Ann ran into her godmother's open arms, giggling when Cella kissed her on the neck and hugged her tight.

"What are you up to, brat?"

"Risking a good scruff-yankin'," Dee-Ann volunteered.

Lizzy ignored her mother and took Malone's hand. "I have the table all set for you, ma'am."

Malone bit her lip to stop from laughing. "Why, thank you."

"This way." Lizzy led her to the island and pointed at a specific chair. "You sit here."

Malone sat down as her mate and Ric came into the kitchen.

"Uncle Crush." She took Lou Crushek's hand and led him to another stool before she climbed up on the island, resting on her knees.

"Cake?" she asked, using her best "restaurant voice."

"Yes, please," replied Crush, one of Lizzy's *many* unofficial "uncles." Already Dee-Ann feared for any boy who came sniffing around her little girl. It would not end well for hopeful suitors.

Lizzy held her hand out. "Knife, Daddy."

"Nope." He went to one of the drawers and pulled out a cake server, placing the handle in his daughter's pudgy hand. "This will do to cut a cake."

Lizzy stared at the cake cutter and back at her father. "You don't think I could use this as a weapon?"

Ric went pale and Crush's mouth dropped open, but Malone's hand flew to her mouth, trying to stifle the laughter and failing.

"Are you here for a reason, Malone?" Dee-Ann quickly asked in the hopes of preventing one of those long lectures Ric insisted on concerning their daughter.

Because, honestly, it wasn't like Dee-Ann hadn't warned him *before* she'd gotten pregnant. Then Lizzy's lineage had been confirmed when the first thing their daughter did, her second day on this earth, was to bite down on the doctor's hand. The shifter doctor didn't even try to pretend that what Lizzy was doing was remotely normal. Especially when she stared at him with those intense blue eyes while she bit down harder. It was all gum and terror.

Of course, the situation didn't improve when Dee-Ann's daddy took the baby from the doctor and said, "She don't like you, cat . . . get out."

Malone didn't respond to Dee's question right away. Too busy trying to keep that laughter quiet. Eventually, she cleared her throat and said, "You free tomorrow?"

"Yep."

"We got a call. Someone wants us to take a look at something."

That was . . . vague. Malone wasn't really good at vague.

"Somethin' messy?" Dee-Ann asked.

"Not for us. We're just to observe and report."

"Report to who?"

Ric, in theory, was her boss. Orders usually came from him or his Uncle Van. They'd been working together for the simply named Group since a few months after Dee-Ann had been discharged from the Marine Corps. A US-only protection team for shifters. All shifters, including the ones Dee-Ann's daddy called "the mutts and the freaks."

Malone's international team, however, only protected the felines. Katzenhaus not being big on the canine or ursus love.

More and more often, though, they were forced to work together to protect everyone, but usually Dee-Ann's orders came from Ric or his boss, Niles Van Holtz. But before Dee-Ann could point that out to the feline in her home, her daughter said, "It's whom."

Dee-Ann gazed at her daughter, carefully cutting big wedges of cake and placing each one on a plate for their "guests."

"What?" Dee-Ann asked.

"It's whom. 'Report to whom?' Not who."

It took Dee-Ann a few seconds to realize her six-year-old was correcting her grammar. She handled that with a smirk and a sharp, "Shut up."

"Dee!" Ric chastised, shocked.

Malone, however, burst out laughing, unable to hold it in anymore.

And Crushek just ate his cake.

"It's all right, Daddy," Lizzy replied, pushing a plate toward her father. "She just knows I'm right."

Dee-Ann reached over and took the plate of cake Lizzy had cut for her father, knowing full well it would annoy the hell out of her.

"I still say we drop her off at the pound," Dee-Ann told her mate after a few bites of her cake. Again, just to annoy her child. "She's still small. Someone will take her."

"Yeah," Crush said around his own cake, "but they'll only bring her back."

Lizzy narrowed her blue eyes on Crush and, staring at him, reached over and placed one pudgy forefinger on his cake plate. Then, without breaking eye contact, pulled the plate away from him.

At that point, Malone ran from the room, her laughter filling the apartment. And Dee-Ann followed, because she couldn't stop laughing either.

Charlie was grateful when her sisters returned to the rental house with their next-day plans locked in tight and a seventy-inch flat-screen television in the trunk of Dutch's car. While Max and Dutch set it up, Stevie told Charlie that their route was already mapped and they'd even stopped by the location to make sure everything they needed was in place, which wasn't a lot. Just a few extra weapons and emergency clothes.

What irritated Charlie, though, was that Dutch was there for the entire discussion, which meant to Charlie he was now officially involved.

Charlie didn't want Dutch involved but he'd promised to stay in the car and out of their way, if that was what she wanted. And it was. As far as Charlie was concerned, Dutch's presence would only make things worse. And Max would be distracted because she'd be busy trying to protect him.

So it was better this way.

Also better, at least at the moment, was the new TV. Charlie was so glad Max had gotten it for them. It not only cut down on the arguing between her sisters—especially once they'd gotten the cable set up and found the horror channel—but it gave Charlie a chance to leave the house without her sisters noticing or worrying.

Charlie sat down on the top step and tried her best to enjoy the summer night. There was just one problem. She had the worst migraine ever. So bad she couldn't even look up at the streetlight because it felt like looking into the sun.

She removed her glasses and pressed the palms of her hands against her eyes. Then she wondered if her brain was *literally* rolling around inside her skull. Because, at the moment, that's exactly how it felt.

So Charlie wasn't exactly surprised when she started hearing weird noises. Puffing. Air puffing. Why the hell was she hearing air puffing? What was puffing air around her?

Charlie lowered her hands, opened her eyes and saw the bear sitting right by her stairs. An actual bear shifter in his bear form.

Such an interesting world she currently lived in.

"Hi, Berg. How are you?" Berg puffed in reply and, unable to help herself, Charlie placed her hand on his head and stroked the fur. It wasn't soft like a dog's but it was still cool to be petting a bear that she didn't worry would rip her arm off.

Now . . . if she could just keep herself from throwing up because of the migraine, her night wouldn't be so bad.

Berg and his brother walked home from the bodega three blocks over. The sloth bear who ran it was "madly in love" with their sister so they'd been forced to stand there while the sixty-year-old asked questions about her dating habits. Questions neither of her brothers were willing to answer. But he always asked just before he rang up everything, making what should be a twenty-minute outing into a forty-five-minute drag.

Now Berg just wanted to get home, break open a beer, and put his feet up. But as he neared his house, he had to stop and stare at Charlie petting the head of another bear.

"What's going on over there?" Dag asked.

"I really don't know."

"She thinks it's you, doesn't she?"

"Probably."

"It's a juvenile black bear. Todd's not even fifteen."

Sighing, Berg handed the grocery bag over to his brother. "I'll handle it."

"You better," Dag said, continuing on toward their house. "Because in two more minutes, we both know Todd's gonna roll over on his back."

"Dirty little perv."

Charlie put her free hand to her forehead and closed her eyes tight. She should go to bed, but she knew as soon as her sisters saw her crawling up the stairs, they'd be all over her trying to help. But there was no help for migraines. There was medication, vomiting, and sleep. Oh, and carbs. She always needed carbs after she had one of her bad migraines.

She knew what had brought this on, too. Everything. Her life right now was stressful, but this had been the first time in days when she'd been able to relax. When she'd felt remotely safe. Despite the bears wandering around her house, eating her baked goods, and terrorizing her baby sister. And because she was able to relax . . . her adrenaline had gone down and whatever caused her migraines had gone up.

Now she was in complete misery with her migraine meds somewhere in goddamn Milan.

"Hi, Charlie."

Charlie opened her eyes and squinted up. She recognized that blur, but she put her glasses back on anyway.

She gazed up at Berg and asked, "If you're there . . . who is that?" She looked down at the bear she was still petting.

"That's Todd. He lives down the street with his parents."

"So he's a child."

"Pretty much."

Sighing, Charlie pulled her hand away.

"Go away," Berg ordered the kid, but apparently feeling a little sassy, the young bear rose to his hind legs and gave a short roar, which did not help Charlie's migraine.

Berg's chin dropped and his eyes narrowed. He glanced at Charlie. "Excuse me a minute, would you?"

She shrugged and watched Berg suddenly walk around to the other side of the house. Once he was gone, the kid dropped back to all fours and placed his big bear head on her leg.

"You *must* be kidding," she snarled at the little bastard.

But the kid wouldn't move and Charlie wasn't sure she was in the mood to get in a fight with a bear.

But then Berg returned. Only now he had shifted. And he was *huge*. So huge her mouth dropped open as she watched him stomp his way around her house. He, too, was puffing and growling a little, but he wasn't running. He didn't have to.

The kid stepped away from Charlie and went up on his hind legs again. But so did Berg and he was at least a foot or more taller.

Then Berg roared and Charlie winced, her brain making it very clear that it hated the sound by sending a searing pain to a spot right behind her eyes.

The kid took off running and Berg went after him. Neither made it far, though, because Berg swung out his front leg, slapping the kid against the side and sending him flying into the middle of the street, where he hit the ground hard, bounced up in the air, and landed on the other sidewalk.

Charlie had to admit, she found it kind of entertaining.

The kid, unharmed—although Charlie was guessing his ego was badly bruised—scrambled back to his feet and ran off, but Berg turned around and trotted back to Charlie's house.

He briefly stopped in front of her and rubbed his snout against her leg.

"Dude. You're drooling on my leg." She scrunched up her nose. "Ew."

Berg went back around the house and a few minutes later, returned. Human and fully dressed. He sat down next to her on the step.

He pointed to where the kid had been standing. "Black bear." He pointed at himself. "Grizzly or brown bear. Huge difference."

"I see that now." She laughed but immediately regretted it. Her head was screaming.

She put her fingertips to her forehead and began rubbing, shutting her eyes. "Owwww."

"Hey, what's wrong?"

"Migraine."

"You don't have anything for it?" He was silent for a moment, then asked, "Does *Stevie* have anything for it?"

"Stevie doesn't get migraines. She gets average headaches. Generic aspirin works for her. And I kind of hate her because of that."

"My sister has over-the-counter migraine meds. I can get you that. And some Coke."

Charlie stared at him and he was momentarily confused before he finally said, "Coca-*Cola*. Not cocaine. We don't do that because it would probably make our hearts explode. And it's illegal."

Charlie thought a moment. Shrugged. "Actually, anything that could possibly help this would be greatly appreciated."

Berg grinned. "I'll be right back."

She watched him jog off toward his house, and only one thought made it through the pain in her head . . .

"He's got a great ass."

Berg returned to a wounded-looking Charlie, still sitting on her stoop. His sister had handed over an entire bottle of meds and a freezing cold bottle of Coke as well as her "recipe" for managing her own migraines.

"Okay," he said when he stood in front of her, "take four of these and then drink the Coke. The entire bottle."

Charlie opened her eyes and held her hand out. He put the pills in her palm and she popped all four into her mouth. He gave her the Coke and she drank half the bottle. Took a breath and drank down the rest.

"Now give it a few minutes."

He took the bottle from her and sat down beside her.

"You don't have to stay," she told him.

"I know." He put the bottle aside and rested his elbows on his knees. "But I'm gonna."

"Good," she sighed, resting her head on his shoulder. "I could use the company."

"I'm sorry about your head."

"I'm sorry I thought that little bear was you."

"You have so much to learn, my child," he teased, pleased to hear her chuckle. "Do your sisters know you've got a migraine?"

"No. And please don't tell them. They worry about me and when they're worried about me, they argue more."

Now Berg chuckled. "That's Dag and Britta. And me and Dag when we're worried about Britta. And Britta and me when we're worried about Dag. So I get it."

"You do get it, don't you? It makes talking to you easier."

"What do you mean?"

"I've been with a few people—friends, boyfriends—who don't quite understand why I drop everything to rush to Stevie's side. Or why I can't go on a last minute getaway because the money I have is set aside in case I have to bail Max out of jail or, if she's in prison, bribe gang members not to kill her. If you don't have the kind of relationship I have with my sisters, you don't understand. But you seem to get it."

"I was trapped in a very tight space with two other people for nine months. When that nightmare is over, you either love each other or hate each other. We're lucky. We actually get along. We protected a set of quadruplets once who were actively trying to kill each other. Now they all have restraining orders, which just seems sad."

"Very." Charlie looked up at him. "Do you three all own the house?"

"We do. Together we had enough for the down payment. Separately, we could only afford human-sized condos. We checked a few out. We couldn't clear the doorways, our beds and couches wouldn't fit. And the showers were absolutely impossible for any of us to fit in. This made more sense."

She smiled. "I think it's cool. The question for me is how long will Max and Stevie be able to stay in the same house without killing each other."

"As long as you're here, they should be fine."

"Oh, really?" she asked, her smile growing a bit.

"You may not realize it, but you have a lot of control on those two."

"I learned the hard way. Trial by fire."

Berg studied her face. Noticed the deep frown had eased. "Feel better?"

"Actually . . . I do. Thank you. And Britta."

"No problem. She loves helping migraine sufferers."

"We're a very loyal group. Our suffering is kind of unique. It bonds us."

She glanced back at her house. "I should get inside. Make sure Dutch hasn't filmed my sisters beating the shit out of each other and sold it online."

"Oh, is the weasel here?" Berg sneered, unable to help himself.

"Don't worry. Now that I'm feeling better, I'm throwing him out in ten minutes."

"Good. So . . . breakfast tomorrow?"

She smirked. "I thought I said no date?"

"Not a date. Breakfast. *Meeting* for breakfast. It's something you do with your mother. Or an old aunt."

Charlie laughed. "Sorry. I can't. Have plans tomorrow morning." She glanced at her phone. "Or today. I've lost track of time."

"Maybe lunch then. I'm free all day."

Charlie patted his shoulder " 'Night, Berg."

"Goodnight, Charlie."

She stood, then disappeared into her house. Berg grabbed the empty Coke bottle and walked back to his house. When he went inside, his sister and brother sat at their kitchen table.

"Did it work?" Britta asked.

"It did. Thank you." He dropped the Coke bottle into the recycle bin.

"You like her, don't you?" Britta asked.

Berg faced his siblings. "I really do."

"You do know her sisters are kind of nuts, right? She's great, but . . . she's not alone."

"You mean as opposed to me?"

"We may be with you until the end of time, brother, but we're normal," Britta argued.

Berg walked over to the kitchen table and reached into the wild beehive his siblings had placed on a piece of wax paper before tearing into it. He tore off a honey comb, ignoring the angry killer bees stinging his hand and put it into his mouth. It was still warm and delicious.

"You were saying?" Berg asked before he slapped at the bees now attacking his face.

Chapter Ten

Right after the sun came up, Charlie and her sisters piled into the "clean" car Dutch had found and headed toward the Bronx with Dutch driving.

This whole thing was not exactly what Charlie would call a "good idea," but it was really all they had. Because if her aunt was right, this would be their only chance to let their Scottish kin know that they should never involve Freddy MacKilligan's daughters in Freddy MacKilligan's bullshit.

If he'd really stolen money from his brothers—and Charlie was sure he had—then they should deal with Freddy directly. Not try to use his daughters to get revenge. Freddy's American half-siblings already knew that, but not the Scottish ones it seemed.

Although there was still a small, sadly hopeful part of Charlie that wanted her assumptions to be wrong. That hoped this would just be a normal meeting between relatives and not a grand plot for something else.

They reached the abandoned building in the Bronx, and while her sisters got out of the backseat, Charlie crouched in the open passenger doorway. "Drive down the street like you're leaving us here and then loop back after a couple of miles. Okay? Meet us on the other side of the building."

Dutch nodded. "Got it." She started to stand but he leaned in a bit and said, "Whatever you guys are doing . . . be careful. And be lucky."

Pushing her glasses back up on her nose, Charlie couldn't help but snort. "Luck is not something we MacKilligan girls ever really have. But thanks, Dutch."

She stood and closed the door, walking toward the boarded-up building.

Looking down both sides of the street and across it, Charlie nodded at Max, and her sister yanked off a few of the boards so they could get into the building in a different way than her sister had the day before. No one else would know they'd already been in the building to prepare for what was happening right now. Max went in first and Charlie helped Stevie through.

Once they were all inside, Charlie took the lead, heading up to the tenth floor of the building on the shaky stairs since the elevators no longer worked.

This had once been a school of some kind and there were still desks and chairs in the classrooms. It reminded Charlie a little bit of her high school days, when she used to spend most of her time protecting her sisters. Max had been a year behind and Stevie was about to start taking college prep classes because she'd quickly advanced out of middle school.

They reached the tenth floor and entered a very large room that was once a science lab. The large, long tables and cabinets were still in place but the equipment had been stolen or damaged by squatters over the years.

One of their cousins stood at the opposite end of the room in a tailored dark suit. His black-and-white hair freshly cut. His black leather shoes expensive. He looked a lot like their dad and, despite herself, Charlie held that against the men of the MacKilligan Clan. She couldn't help it.

"Cousin Charlie," Dougie MacKilligan greeted with that lilting accent. He was part of the Scottish side of the family. And, like their American kin, they barely acknowledged that Charlie and her sisters were related by blood unless they needed something from them.

Charlie used to think that their family acted this way because of racial prejudice. But no. It was because they were Freddy's offspring. It was Freddy they wanted to pretend didn't exist. Freddy they wished wasn't blood. And, by extension, his three daughters.

"Long time, Dougie," she replied.

He motioned them into the room. "Come. Come. Let's talk."

The three of them entered the lab, and as soon as they reached the middle of the room, they were surrounded. Not by more MacKilligans, unfortunately, but by military types. Like the ones who'd already come after them.

"This seems a little harsh," Charlie said to her cousin. "Letting them kill us."

"Now, now," Dougie quickly corrected. "That's not what's happening here. We've worked out a lovely deal for you three."

Max snorted. "Really?"

"Yes, cousin. Really." He held up a finger. "One thing, though."

Two men quickly checked Charlie and Max for weapons, and Charlie was really impressed. Max didn't kill even one of them.

The guy checking Charlie stepped away from her after a few seconds, but the one checking Max was still finding weapons.

Dougie rolled his eyes. "You haven't changed, Maxine."

"It's Max. Just Max."

Once a small pile of knives of varying sizes sat on a lab table, Dougie continued explaining the "lovely deal" his father and uncles had come up with for Freddy MacKilligan's girls.

"Now, we know you lot have no say in the shite your father does. And we also know that threatening any of you with death . . . well, to be honest . . ."

"He's not going to care," Charlie reminded him.

Dougie smiled. "Exactly. But, dear cousin Charlie, we know how persuasive you can be with your father. So this is the deal. These gentlemen will take your baby sister"—one of the men grabbed Stevie's arm and pulled her close; all the men in the room ignoring how Stevie's eyes widened and her body went completely rigid—"*but,* and this is an important 'but,' they're not going to kill you and they will *never* hurt her. In fact, you'll even be able to get her back." His eyes locked on Charlie's. "Once me Da gets his money and she helps out our associate."

He spread his arms, palms up, smile wide. "That seems fair, don't you think?"

"You really think you can trust these men?" Charlie asked, a little disgusted by her cousin.

"They want one thing. They want Stevie."

"*Me?*" Stevie demanded, her panicked voice hitting new notes that had the wolf in Charlie nearly howling. "What did I do? *Why do you want to kill me?*" she screamed hysterically.

Dougie's eyes crossed and he raised his hand toward Stevie. "No one wants to kill you! *You* are safe. You cooperate and your sisters cooperate, everyone will be fine."

"Do you really believe that?" Charlie asked her cousin.

"Not everyone's like your father. I made the deal, it's solid. Just don't do anything stupid."

"But . . . we're MacKilligans. All we do is stupid things. And I can't let them take my sister."

The door leading to the lab suddenly closed and one of the men stood in front of it.

Charlie smirked. "Do you really want to play it this way, gentlemen?"

"Charlie," her cousin said, his voice calm. "Don't do this." He stepped closer and whispered, "These men may be full-human but even a honey badger can't handle a shot to the head. And once they get over the shock of your shifting . . . that's exactly what they'll do. Shoot you in the head—and they'll *still* take your sister."

"I don't shift," Charlie whispered to her cousin before moving away and saying loudly, "But I will say that my sweet baby sister has been off her meds for almost . . . twenty-four hours now." Unable to help herself, Charlie smiled. "And. Stevie. Is. *Anxious*."

They both had their rifles aimed at the building across the street, using their scopes to see what was happening inside the old lab classroom.

They'd been sitting here since before dawn, to make sure they didn't miss anything, but they didn't plan to kill anyone unless necessary. Their task was to observe and report to their bosses.

The problem for Dee-Ann, though, was that she didn't rightly know what the fuck she was observing.

"This just went bad," Dee-Ann said to Malone. "I don't like that they've locked them girls in with them."

"Me neither."

"Then let's start picking them off."

"No," Malone said coldly. "Observe and report. That's it. We're just here to see what they do."

"Don't seem right. They're outnumbered. Out-gunned."

"I know but they're not our problem. Badgers say they take care of their own. We should believe them."

"Then why are we here?"

"For something new, so could you just calm the fuck down, hillbilly?"

"Their deaths will be on your head," Dee-Ann muttered before returning her gaze to the scope.

Dougie moved from in front of the window. He wouldn't put it past his crazy American cousins to have someone on another building with a rifle and a scope, ready to start shooting them all.

And to think he'd volunteered for this job. Wanting to help his father and to keep things from spiraling out of control. But could anything that involved Freddy MacKilligan *not* spiral out of control? It didn't seem so.

Still, he didn't think these three little honey badgers would be that much of a problem. They had no weapons and although they could shift and start tearing into these men, they'd only end up getting shot in the head and that would be that.

He couldn't see the oldest one taking such a risk. She was so protective of the other two. Everyone in the family knew that about Freddy's girls.

But even though Dougie waited, his cousins didn't shift. The oldest two did nothing but stand there, watchful but seemingly unafraid. The youngest, though, was panting and desperately trying to wiggle out of her captor's hold.

Max pointed at the man holding her sister and warned, "I'd let her go if I were you."

The man only smirked as he slammed a syringe in the girl's neck and pressed the plunger down.

That had been stupid. The human men in this room didn't understand that to drug a honey badger was a wasted effort. It might knock that thin little thing out for about twenty seconds but beyond that . . .

Stevie didn't even stagger, though.

Instead, screaming, she slapped at the man's hand. Problem was, he still had the syringe buried in her neck. The needle broke off and stayed imbedded in her flesh. Not that she felt it. Not as crazy as she was acting.

Dougie had heard Stevie was the high-strung one, but her distraught screaming and the way she yanked herself free from the man stunned him and everyone else in the room . . . except her sisters, it seemed.

"You're trying to kill me!" Stevie hysterically accused the man. *"You're trying to kill me!"*

Had no one taught this girl anything? Did she not listen? Not only could some bullshit drug *not* hurt a honey badger, but she was the one they wanted alive. The last thing they were trying to do was kill her. One would think she'd be more concerned about her sisters, but she seemed overly involved with herself.

Bent over at the waist, one hand on her upper chest, Stevie panted out, "I can't breathe! I can't breathe! My lungs are shutting down!"

Dougie gestured to a bland-faced Charlie. "Are you going to do something about this? Or just let the poor girl give herself a heart attack for nothing?"

"All right," Charlie said, rubbing her nose. "I'll do something." She glanced at her sister. "Max."

Max grabbed the arm of the man closest to her. She yanked it out straight and shoved her free hand—palm up—forward, breaking the man's forearm into two pieces.

That man's scream had the others scrambling to take the safeties off their weapons; clearly their earlier agreement no longer in effect. Not that Dougie blamed them. The two girls would die because their judgment was just as bad as their soon-to-be-dead father's and hysterical baby sister's.

Charlie scrambled over one of the lab tables but bullets slammed into her back, sending her flipping forward. With a grunt of pain, she disappeared on the other side of the table and Max grabbed a blade from one of the men's leg holster. She cut the inside of the man's thighs, then his throat, before diving behind a nearby pillar; bullets tore into the concrete seconds after she disappeared.

Stevie's breathing was so hard now Dougie was sure she was truly going to give herself a stroke. And, sadly, she'd witnessed Charlie getting shot in the back. So now she was screaming, "Charlie! Oh, my God! They killed Charlie! *We're all going to die!*"

Shrieking and crying, she shoved past two men trying to grab hold of her and dove face first behind a lab table.

As one sister disappeared, another reappeared.

Max and her stolen blade came up behind another man. She cut his throat and slammed the blade into the neck of the man standing beside him.

A new attacker grabbed her from behind, big arms pinning hers to her body. She rammed her foot hard on his instep. Twice. Then bent her knee and brought her foot back against the man's knee, breaking it.

Another aimed a gun at her and began firing. Max turned hard, bringing the one holding her along for the ride, so his back became her shield. By the time he hit the floor, he was dead from friendly fire.

Dougie sighed and reached for his phone. He quickly texted his father, "It's all gone to shite, Da." Something his father would not like, but what could Dougie do?

Bullets flashed past Dougie, but he only moved his head slightly to the left to avoid getting shot.

His phone vibrated, letting him know his father had texted him back, but as he was about to read the message, Charlie appeared behind one of the men blindly shooting at the room, trying to kill Max, who'd managed to brutally knife six more men so far.

Charlie grabbed the man from behind, trying to get his gun. But one of the man's cohorts came to his rescue, putting a gun to her forehead. She grabbed that gun, though, with both hands, and turned her body into the man's. Then she pulled the trigger for him, shooting the first man twice in the head. She aimed and shot another and another.

Slamming her foot into the instep of the man she was struggling with, she pulled out of his grip with his gun still in her hand. She shot him twice. In the head.

She dropped the empty magazine, reached down and took another mag from the man she'd just killed. Shoved the full mag into the gun, put a round in the chamber, and turned to find a .45 aimed at her.

As the shooter pulled the trigger, Max came from underneath him, shoving his arms up so the shot went wild; then she finished him with a blade across the throat.

That's when they all froze. Even his two cousins, which was what made Dougie a tad concerned. Nothing had phased them so far. So . . . what *would* exactly?

It started out like a low grumble. Then it became a roar. A big cat roar.

Orange, white, and black striped paws the size of massive platters landed on the lab table, crushing the thick slab of granite under the weight of each paw. Like someone putting their hands in snow. Then the biggest honey badger head Dougie had ever seen appeared.

"Oh . . . fuck," Dougie whispered.

While they all stared, Stevie's shifted form began

to rise . . . and rise . . . and rise. Until her head nearly reached the ceiling . . . and even then, Dougie got the distinct feeling that she wasn't standing completely straight yet. That she was still bent over.

Staring down at the remaining men, Stevie suddenly leaned forward and roared, shattering the windows throughout the room and, Dougie was sure, the entire building based on the screams he could hear from outside.

No longer thinking about the women kicking their asses, the men aimed their guns at the thing baring rows of massive fangs at them. Honey badger fangs that were quadrupled in size.

Then Stevie did something Dougie didn't expect from any badger or cat because they weren't physically capable. She charged up the wall and onto the ceiling. All twenty or so feet of her hung from the ceiling tiles.

Her long tail snapped down and wrapped around the neck of one of the men, tossing him across the room and out the shattered window.

"Kill it!" one of the men bellowed, and the rest began firing.

Stevie skittered across the ceiling until she reached the man who'd given the order. She landed on him, grabbing the wailing man in her maw and dragging him off to the far corner of the lab, ignoring the bullets and screams of the other men.

And while Stevie had their full attention, her sisters, without shifting or unleashing their claws, went around killing. Max stuck with the blade, but now she had two. One in each hand. She moved fast and quiet. With no mercy she killed.

Her sister stayed with the .45, moving through the remaining men with the weapon held in both hands, raised to eye level, but held close to her body. Each of her victims got a head shot unless the male tried to move on her first, in which case she shot twice in the chest and then in the head.

As for Stevie . . . all Dougie could hear were screams. All he could see was her back arching each time she pulled more flesh from bone.

Some men managed to make it out the door, climbing over each other. No longer were they a smart, elite unit of killers. Not after meeting the MacKilligan sisters.

Dougie heard sirens and glanced out the window next to him.

"Cops!" he yelled at Charlie.

She shot another head before she looked at him and nodded.

"Go," she told him, not even out of breath. No fear or panic or even anger in her dark brown eyes. "And tell Uncle Will we said hi."

Max started to go after the men who'd managed to get out the door, but Charlie called her back.

"We have to get Stevie!"

Max glanced around at the carnage. "Where the fuck is she?"

Charlie pointed up and . . . yep, that's where their baby sister was. Again hanging from the ceiling but now with part of some guy hanging from one of her fangs. A part she was not going to want to give up.

Shifted-Stevie tended to "play" with her prey. And guard it territorially. Like most house cats.

"Dude," Max told her sister, "we don't have time to calm her down."

"I've got it." Charlie moved closer to her sister but not right under her because she didn't want any more blood dripping on her.

"All right, you," she said, pointing a finger at her sister. "You get down here right now. Right now, Stevie MacKilligan. This instant!"

Stevie lowered her eyes and made a little mewling sound. She took a step back—still on the ceiling—not wanting to give up her prize.

"Don't you dare run away from me, Stevie! You come down here right now! *This minute!*"

Stevie released her grip on the ceiling and came crashing to the floor.

"Spit it," Charlie ordered her baby sister. "Spit it!"

Annoyed, Stevie spit the torso out of her mouth.

"Shift back to human. Right now!"

With just a thought, Stevie returned to her human form. Now naked and covered in blood, she stood there, eyes downcast. It wasn't shame, though. Charlie knew that. It was more like contrition. Like a little girl caught tearing the head off her sister's favorite doll.

"Cops are securing the building . . . and coming up the stairs," Max announced after checking the windows.

"Let's move."

The three of them ran out of the lab and up the stairs until they reached the roof. There was a long summer dress already waiting on the ledge of the building. Max tossed it to Stevie and she slipped it on while Charlie went from corner to corner, trying to figure out where the cops had set up.

She found that they hadn't made it to the back of the building yet, so she motioned her sisters over.

"Go," she ordered Stevie.

"Have you lost your mind?" Stevie asked, already beginning the panic process all over again. "When you consider the physics of—"

Pressing her hand against Stevie's chest, Max shoved her sister off the roof. Screaming, Stevie fell but as she neared the ground, she suddenly turned over and landed on all fours.

"Always with the drama," Max announced before following her sister over. Sadly, she didn't have any cat in her, so she landed hard, the concrete under her cracking from the impact.

But the honey badger still got to her feet and shook it off.

Charlie got on the ledge and was preparing to jump when she felt eyes on her. She spun around, gaze searching all the nearby buildings. She saw the scopes, the rifles. The women holding them.

She bared her fangs in rage, and in answer the dark-haired one bared her fangs back.

Well . . . at least they were shifters.

"Charlie!" Max yelled. "Move your ass!"

She knew she couldn't deal with this right now, but she mentally filed it away for later. Because she had a fear it would come flying back at her at some point.

Charlie jumped, aiming for an abandoned car. Her shoulder hit the roof and she immediately rolled down and off the car.

She tried to shake her shoulder out, but it was too damaged.

"Move!" Max barked.

Charlie started running, ignoring the, "Stop! Police!" behind her.

She dove into the open front door and Dutch hit the gas.

His turn was so wild, the passenger door closed on its own and he was moving.

The way the car handled, Charlie knew Dutch had picked it just for this sort of thing. Getaways. Proving, once again, that he was no good for her sister. He was useful, no doubt about it. But he was also trouble.

Grateful for the man's driving skills, Charlie held on as Dutch got them away from the cops before they could dispatch a helicopter to follow them. A good thing since Charlie wouldn't put it past Max to handle a police helicopter the same way she'd handled the chopper in Switzerland.

"Do you know you've been shot?" Max said from the backseat.

Charlie spun around, resting on her knees to stare at her baby sister. "Stevie, you've been shot?"

Stevie blinked at her. "She was talking to you."

Frowning, Charlie looked down at herself, but saw nothing except her wounded shoulder. And she just needed to get Max to yank that back into place for her.

Max leaned forward, reached around her and when she sat back, she held up two fingers covered in blood. "Oh. Guess I was shot."

After a moment, she dismissed it with a wave of her hand. "It's a scratch. I'll be fine."

Charlie settled back in her seat and looked at Dutch. "We need to get rid of this car."

"Already on it, sweetness."

She gritted her teeth. "Don't call me that."

"Honey pie? Lady divine? Pretty ass?"

Charlie glared at him. "You're taking advantage of the fact that I owe you, aren't you?"

Dutch laughed. "Of course I am!"

Chapter Eleven

John Mitchell disconnected the call and stared, shocked, at the closed door leading to the cockpit of the private jet.

Being in this business for as long as he had, he'd heard all sorts of things. *Seen* all sorts of things. But this . . .

He looked over his shoulder at the luxury jet. His clients were all the way in the back, spending time in their personal tanning beds. Apparently they didn't worry too much about skin cancer.

John headed through the roomy jet. He hadn't been in a jet this luxurious since his military days when he was lucky enough to work on Air Force One. His clients had serious money and were not afraid to use it. For anything.

The two ladies were already out of the tanning beds, both wrapped in white terrycloth robes, their personal staff giving them pedicures and manicures, while others massaged their shoulders.

"Excuse me, ladies," he said, stepping into the cabin. "I have word . . ."

One looked up from her copy of Italian *Vogue* and

he realized they both had green mud smeared all over their faces. It was not attractive. "They have her?" she asked with that Italian accent he was starting to find less sexy and more irritating.

"They killed everyone," he said plainly, "except their cousin and about three of my men who managed to escape."

"How is that possible?" She threw her magazine, frustrated. "Why does this keep happening?"

"Calm," the other ordered. And to John, she asked, "Now what happened?"

"I'm not . . . quite sure. My man talked about fangs and claws and giant tigers."

Both women laughed. "What?"

"I think they must have drugged the men," he reasoned. "Some hallucinogenic. That made it easier to shoot and stab them all."

"So we do not have the youngest?" one asked.

"No, ma'am. We don't."

The pair stared at each other through all that mud until one shooed away their staff and the other took out a slim gold case. She opened it and pulled out a cigarette, lit it, and focused on him.

"You failed. Again. You and the people you've hired. That makes us unhappy. You don't want to keep making us unhappy . . . do you?"

"Of course not."

"Then you," she said, pointing her cigarette at him, "will arrange a jailbreak for us."

"A jailbreak?"

"I think that is the term, yes? We will be hiring someone who understands the MacKilligans better than you do. And, I'm guessing, hate them as much as we do." She took a drag off her cigarette before asking, "Think you can handle that, Mr. Mitchell?"

"I can handle that."

"Good," she said, relaxing back with a sigh. "I'd hate to kill you, too."

Berg sat on his front stoop, attempting to pry his sister's favorite towel from his dog's mouth.

"Give it to me! Now!"

His sister had been right. Taking the dog his mother had given her triplets had been a bad idea. Not that he didn't like dogs. He did. Sort of. And he'd grown up around them. His mother dabbled sometimes in breeding the enormous canines so that local bears could have the extra protection. But these dogs were strong willed and, to be blunt, bitchy! They were often used in Russian prisons to keep the convicts in line.

"She's going to kick both of our asses if you don't give me this towel!"

"Hi, Berg."

Berg looked up from the tugging dog to see Charlie's sister standing in front of him. "Hi, Stevie. What happened to your neck?"

"Oh, nothing. It's already healing. But I was wondering if you have a first aid kit."

"Sure." He leaned back and yelled through the screen door, "Dag! Get the first aid kit!"

"Which one?" Dag called back.

Berg focused on Stevie again. "What do you need it for? A sprain? A cut? Your neck?"

"Gunshot wound," she replied casually.

So casually that Berg didn't realize he was yelling, "Gunshot wound!" to his brother until his brother yelled back, *"Who the fuck was shot?"*

"Char—" was all she got out before Berg dropped the towel and charged over to what the rest of the neighborhood was now calling, "the badger house."

He ran inside and bellowed, *"Charlie!"*

She appeared in the hallway wearing nothing but her blood-soaked jeans and bra; her shoulder appeared weirdly fucked up.

"What are you yelling for?" she asked calmly, frowning.

"You were shot?"

She waved it off. "Oh, that. Yeah. I'm fine."

"You're covered in blood."

" 'Covered' is a bit of an exaggeration, wouldn't you say?"

"No!"

She came close and whispered, "If you're going to get hysterical—"

"I'm not hysterical. You've been shot."

"You were shot in Milan. You didn't get hysterical."

"I'm a *bear.*"

"Uh-huh."

"Which means a .45 isn't going to do anything to me except piss me off."

"What about bear spray? Does bear spray work?"

"Why are you asking?"

"Why aren't you telling?"

Dag ran into the house, a giant metal white box gripped in his big hands. He froze when he saw Charlie.

"Oh, my God!" he gasped. "You're dying!"

Charlie's eyes crossed. "Can we all calm down? There's no need to be hysterical."

"How are we hysterical?" Berg asked.

"By running in, *assuming* I'm dying—"

"You are *drenched* in blood," Berg reminded her.

"And your shoulder looks really weird," Dag flatly added.

"That just needs to be yanked back into place." She scratched her chin. "And a little duct tape on the gunshot wounds will stop the bleeding."

"You're not a headlight on an old Chevy," Berg told her.

She rolled her eyes but before she said anything, she suddenly sniffed the air. "I got a pie in the oven. Wait here."

Charlie walked away and Berg looked at his brother. Together, they headed toward the kitchen behind Charlie, but Berg's dog ran in first, his sister's towel still caught in his mouth. He stopped in front of Berg and stood there. Being annoying.

"You are killing me."

"Is that Britta's Restoration Hardware towel?" Dag shook his head. "She's gonna kick your ass."

"Good!" Stevie said from behind them . . . and loudly. "You have the kit."

To be honest, Berg had forgotten about Charlie's little sister. Looking at her now, he saw something different about her.

First, she was speaking to them without either of her sisters being there. Second, her eyes were open really wide. Like she was perpetually stunned by something. Third . . . back to the talking. She was talking . . . a lot. And fast.

"Thanks for loaning us this first aid kit," she said, taking the kit from Dag, "we really appreciate it but, wow is it big, I'm really surprised how big it is, do you guys get injured that much that you need such a big case, we do, of course, but that's not surprising, I mean just today Charlie got shot but that was before what happened, not that I blame them, it was either them or us and so her and Max had to kill all those men, I mean if they hadn't, no matter what our cousin said, they probably would have held me for a long time, and killed both my sisters, so, yeah, Charlie and Max totally had to kill them all, sorry if I'm talking fast, I sense I'm talking fast, but I just took my meds, and they haven't kicked in yet, but when they do, I'll be way calmer, but at least I'm not afraid of you guys right now, but I always feel better after I shift, the problem is that no one else feels better after I shift, right?" Then she laughed, patted Berg on the arm, and reminded him, "Stray dog it!" before disappearing down the hallway toward the kitchen.

Stunned, the brothers stood there. Silent.

Because, really, what was there to say?

Ignoring the excruciating pain in her shoulder, Charlie quickly put her glasses back on before she bent down and, with oven mitts on, pulled the lemon custard pie out of the oven and placed it on the counter to cool.

She smiled at its perfection.

"Bear in the kitchen," Max said and Charlie turned around expecting to see the Dunn brothers behind her. But no. It was that dog.

"He's going to eat my pie, isn't he?" she asked Max.

"If you leave it on that counter, he will."

Charlie moved the pie to the open window, pretty sure the dog couldn't lean that far over to reach it. But that's when Max reminded her, "You're gonna attract bears again."

"Dammit!"

Holding the pie in her hands, she studied the kitchen.

Max looked up from the newspaper she was weirdly reading. Weirdly, because it was an actual newspaper. Made of actual paper. Charlie had only seen her use her phone the last ten years to read anything. Books. Magazines. Anything.

Charlie didn't even know where her sister had found a newspaper.

"You could just get rid of the dog," Max said.

"I'm not killing a dog."

Max quickly looked up, eyes blinking. "I meant throw him out; not kill him."

"Awwwww, I'm glad that's what you meant," she happily replied.

Max glared at her before going back to the paper. That's when Stevie walked into the kitchen.

"Who's killing a dog?" Stevie looked down at Max. "Why are you killing a dog?"

"I'm not—" Max suddenly stopped talking and stared at Stevie. "Were you outside talking to those bears?"

"No."

"Good. And I'm not killing any—"

"I was *inside* talking to those bears."

Max closed her eyes and Charlie asked her baby sister, "What did you say to them?"

"I don't really remember because I was talking so fast, and you know what happens when I'm off my meds and start talking, I just go and go and go, and I kinda just kept going without really stopping because you know how I get when I'm not on my meds but I've panic-shifted. And I may have told them nothing, but then again I may have told them everything I'm really not sure but—"

With pie still in hand, Charlie ran out of the kitchen and returned to the living room to find both bears just standing there . . . staring at each other.

"Pie!" she announced, shoving it under their noses. "Lemon custard. Bet you two like that! Want it? You can have it! *Take it!*"

Berg gazed at the pie and then her before asking, "So how many people did you kill?"

Charlie cringed. They should have locked Stevie in

her room, but she could claw her way out if she was anxious enough.

"It's not what you think," she promised.

"So, you *didn't* kill a bunch of people?"

"Not like that. Like we went on a murder spree. They were trying to take our sister. And they weren't afraid to get rid of me and Max to make it happen. What did you want us to do?"

"It's not what you did, Charlie. I don't know what you did or why you did it. What I do know is that you've probably attracted a new problem to you and your sisters."

"A new problem? What kind of new problem?"

The two look-alike males simultaneously blew out a breath and looked away from her gaze . . .

"All right, bitches! We have a problem!" she yelled toward the kitchen.

"I thought we killed our problem!" Max yelled back.

"Apparently that wasn't effective."

"Is it Stevie's fault?"

Charlie frowned at Max's question. "No."

"So I can't hit her? Because I feel like hitting her."

"Don't hit Stevie!"

Charlie looked back at the two bears and asked, "So what do we do now?"

Berg held up a finger because Dag was on the phone. He grunted a few times and disconnected.

"They're heading this way," he said to his brother.

"Who's heading this way?" Charlie asked, but the bears ignored her.

"Who did they send?" Berg asked Dag.

Dag scowled. "A Smith."

Berg took an abrupt step back, like he'd been struck. "We have to get them out of here."

"And take them *where*?"

"Someplace with a lot of people. Smiths don't like to strike with an audience."

Knowing the brothers were so busy talking to each other, they were completely ignoring her, Charlie headed back into the kitchen. Max had poor Stevie in a chokehold and was telling her, "Sleep. Just go to sleep. Shhhhhh."

Charlie walked across the kitchen and placed the pie she was still holding onto the windowsill.

"We have to get out of here," she told her sisters.

"Why?" Max asked, still choking a pissed-off Stevie. But despite Stevie's very narrow frame, she was really hard to choke out. Like most honey badgers. The way she was clawing at Max's arms, though . . . that was all cat.

"Apparently we've gotten some attention from . . . I don't know. The bears, maybe. They didn't specify, but somebody."

"Did they give you a name?"

"All they said was, 'A Smith,' which I found quite vague."

"There are two sets of Smiths in this world," Max said.

Charlie frowned. "I'm sure there are more than two—"

"One set are wolverines," she went on, "but they'd never come after us because of Dutch. And then there's the Smith Pack that, I believe, is crazy enough to come after us."

"Smith Pack?" Charlie thought for a moment. "Didn't Gramps mention them once?"

Max nodded. "He said we were never to date or have pups with them or he would, without a doubt, disown us."

"Disown us from what? He got nothin'."

"Just his love."

"Oh, shut up." She looked at her still-bleeding shoulder. "I need a clean T-shirt and jeans and *would you let her go!*"

Max released Stevie, who spun around on her knees and began slapping at her giggling sister.

"You are such a bitch!"

"Stevie!" Charlie barked, pulling on a fresh pair of jeans and a navy blue T-shirt. "We don't have time for this."

Stevie got to her feet, pointing her forefinger at Max. "I hate you."

"I'm trying to help you."

"Shut up!" She faced Charlie. "What's happening now?"

"Find your backpack. We're getting out of here."

"Okay." When it came to being on the run, Stevie had learned over time to simply follow orders.

She pointed at Max. "And you can bandage up my gun shot wounds on the drive out of here."

The bears walked into the kitchen as Max reached under the kitchen table and pulled out a sawed-off shotgun she'd stashed there. Along with many other weapons she had under the kitchen table. In the cabinets. Under and around the beds. Beneath the dining room table. The living room couch. The end tables.

Max didn't leave what she called "basic home defense" to chance.

The bears froze in the doorway.

"That's not legal," Dag noted.

"You're so cute," Max said with a smile, pushing past both males.

"We have a place you can go," Berg said to Charlie.

She shrugged. "What's the point if they're just going to chase us down? Better to face them here."

"You don't want to face down a Smith."

"I don't know what that means."

"And my goal," he went on, "is to work out an agreement that will allow you to stay here safely. Without worry. But I can't do that if you're having a gunfight on the street with the Smiths."

Max walked back into the kitchen with a box of shells, although the shotgun was already loaded. Max just wanted to make sure she had extra. "We could win a gunfight."

Berg glared down at her. "That's not helping."

Max grinned and looked at her sister. "What do you think?"

Charlie dug her hands into her hair and said to Berg, "I hate dragging you deeper into this."

Berg patted her shoulder. "That's sweet, Charlie, but who gives a shit right now? You've got a Smith on your ass."

"Is it really that big a deal?"

Dag leaned over his brother's shoulder. "It's *that* big a deal."

Stevie, her backpack securely on, her eyes wide, pointed at the window behind Charlie. "Someone just took your pie."

Charlie glanced back and saw that, yeah. Her pie was gone. "The dog?" she asked.

"Nah." Max pointed. "He's under the table. After he opened the fridge, took out leftover steaks from yesterday, and dragged the entire pan under the table to eat."

Berg crouched and snarled, "Get home!"

The entire table moved a few feet when the dog stood up while still under it, lifting it off the ground with his back. Stevie grabbed and held it, allowing the dog to keep going.

"What's his name?" Max asked Berg.

"Who?"

"The *dog's*."

"Oh. Uh . . ."

"You didn't name your dog?" Charlie demanded.

"Can we please go?" Berg asked. "*Before* the gun-fight?"

Shaking her head, Charlie took a 9mm out from under the kitchen table and tucked it into the back of her jeans. She pulled on a light denim jacket to hide it and, tsk-tsking the entire time, walked past the two bears. Her sisters following her.

"You're welcome," Berg said from behind her.

"I didn't thank you yet," she reminded him. "And keep that attitude going, I may never."

The women walked out of the kitchen and Berg scratched his head. That's when he saw his brother staring at him.

"What?"

"What the fuck have you gotten us into?" Dag asked.

"What are you talking about?"

"There has to be an easier way to get a date."

"That's not what this is about. We're being helpful."

"Do they need help? Because they don't really seem like they do."

"With Smiths coming here? Of course they need our help."

The sisters suddenly walked back in, Charlie still leading the way.

"Car just pulled up in front of the house," Charlie said. "Dutch is gone. We'll need to steal a car."

"I can do that," Max announced, marching by.

Berg grabbed the shotgun she still held, quickly aiming it toward the ceiling. Once he was sure no one would accidentally get shot, he calmly asked, "Can you grab something a little less . . . conspicuous?"

"Oh sure!" she said with a big, friendly smile. She released her grip on the shotgun and moved to the kitchen table. She reached under and came out with a .45.

"A Desert Eagle is less conspicuous?"

"Than a shotgun? Yeah!"

Berg continued to stare at her until she rolled her eyes and said, "Fine." She dropped the gun on the table and went to the cabinet under the sink. She pulled out a strap with several holsters on it. Each holster held a knife. Stevie lifted up her sister's T-shirt and Max strapped the knives around her torso. Then she tacked a few more holstered knives to her jeans and Stevie let the T-shirt drop.

"Okay!" Max said with that pretty smile. "Let's go! I've got a car to steal."

"Or we can just borrow Mrs. Fitzbaer's car. Nice elderly sow who lives one street over, and she lets me and Dag borrow it all the time."

Max's smile faded away. "Fine. But just so we're clear . . . I find that really boring."

"Sorry."

"It's all right. I'm just letting you know."

Max walked out the back door, leaving the brothers with Stevie. She gave them a small half-smile.

"Sorry about earlier," she said. "But my medication has finally kicked in. I'm calmer. And I amped up the dosage a little bit . . . so I don't find you nearly as terrifying."

"Great, Stevie."

She cleared her throat. "But . . . should you suddenly decide you have to eat me, I have bear spray in my backpack. A proprietary mixture of my own that will burn the eyes from your head." She patted Berg's arm. "I'm not saying I'll use it. I'm just saying it's there. In case you have any . . . terrifying ideas. Involving me. Okay?"

Berg nodded. "Okay."

"Excellent. Very good!" She turned and rushed after her sisters, her overstuffed backpack so heavy and Stevie so thin, it looked as if she should topple over. But she didn't. Because none of the MacKilligan sisters were quite what they appeared.

Berg didn't bother to look at his brother. What was the point? He didn't need to see him to hear him clearly.

"I'm telling Britta what an idiot you are."

Chapter Twelve

Dee-Ann came down the stairs of the large house and went into the kitchen where Malone was.

"Looks like they're gone."

Malone grinned. "You're gonna love this." She suddenly tipped the kitchen table onto its side. Holstered guns and knives were duct taped to the underside.

"That seems like . . . a lot."

"Ya think?" Malone laughed. "These are your kind of girls, Smith. They've got weapons"—she raised her hands, forefingers up, and made a circle in the air—"all over this house. In cabinets, behind doors, under beds, next to beds . . . *in* beds. I'm trying to figure out where they got all this shit."

"We need to find these girls."

Malone lifted her nose, sniffed the air, then opened her mouth wide, pulled back her lips, and stuck out her tongue.

She'd done it before when they were tracking. She called it a "flehmen response," but Dee-Ann just called it nasty. Because that's what it was. Just nasty!

Malone closed her mouth and made a smacking sound. "There were bears here," she announced.

"There are bears everywhere. It's a bear neighborhood, genius."

"I mean there were bears *here*. In this space. And one of them was hot for one of those girls."

"How do know that?"

"Pheromones." She made that tongue sucking against the roof of her mouth sound again. "I can taste it in the back of my throat."

Dee-Ann held up her hand and told Malone, "You cats are just plain nasty."

Malone walked across the room and stared out the window. "If he likes her, he'll want to protect her."

"None of those girls need nobody protecting them."

"You know how guys are, though. Especially bears." She looked at Dee-Ann over her shoulder. "And there are two places they'd probably think of taking them. But one of those places, they can't risk yet. So that leaves the other." She nodded. "Yeah, I think I know where they took the girls."

Malone was so cocky, Dee-Ann couldn't help but ask, "What, Malone? You fuck a bear on the regular and you think you know what all other bears will do?"

Malone thought a moment before replying, "Yes. Yes, I do. And do you know why, Air Bud? Because I am *awesome*." She giggled. "God, I love me. Don't you love me?"

"No."

"Go," Berg said to Charlie from the front seat of Mrs. Fitzbaer's Hummer. "We'll park the car and be right in. Don't talk to anybody or go anywhere. Just stay in the lobby. Okay?"

"Okay."

Charlie opened the back door and climbed out of the

enormous vehicle. Of course, after seeing the "elderly" sow who owned this behemoth, she understood why the woman needed it. She had to be nearly seven feet tall. Charlie had made the assumption she was a lonely old maid, but nope. She was a widow whose polar bear husband had been nearly eight feet tall, and together they'd had six giant children who were scattered all over the world trying to help with global warming to assist the full-blood polar bears trapped on melting ice caps.

She was really starting to find this shifter life interesting. Living with a Pack that barely noticed her, was terrified by Max, and a little freaked-out by Stevie hadn't really shown Charlie the entire shifter world that existed out there. All this was new to her.

They made their way into the Sport Center's main lobby. Kids with basketballs or ice skates pushed past Charlie and her sisters, all rushing to their practices. There were sports stores of all kinds and restaurants on the first floor. The ice rink was also on this floor, but the basketball courts, gymnastic practice rooms, and some admin offices were up on floors two through eighteen.

There was also a state-of-the-art, high-end gym that probably cost a small fortune to join, and a bunch of sports physicians and surgeons who probably only worked on Olympic athletes and pro ballers.

"Wow," Stevie gasped, her gaze raised to the high ceiling. "All this for sports."

"Sports is big business," Charlie noted. "And this is what big business buys."

"All this money, but scientists still have to beg for funds in the search to end cancer." She shook her head, lips pursed. "Disgusting."

Now that Stevie was back on her meds, she was once-again rational, if a little nervous.

Thankfully, Charlie wasn't so easily spooked. She

didn't have time, always too busy keeping her sisters safe or stopping them from doing something stupid.

A group of laughing girls walked by, roller skates hanging from the bag one of them held.

"Hey, look," Max pointed out. "Derby girls."

"You want to play derby?" Charlie asked, surprised. Max was not exactly a team player.

"Oh, God, no. But I do love watching them beat the shit out of each other." She began to follow. "Come on. Let's see if we can find out if there are any bouts coming up."

"We're supposed to wait for the guys," Stevie reminded her.

"We'll be gone two minutes. Come on!"

They followed the fast-moving women expertly cutting through the crowd until they disappeared into a stairwell guarded by two security guards.

"Okay, we're done," Charlie said, grabbing Max's arm and holding her back.

"Why?"

"Whatever is going on back there, I don't want to know."

Max pulled her arm away. "Don't be such a drag."

"How are we supposed to get past security?" Stevie asked.

"Leave it to me," Max said with way more confidence than either of her sisters felt for her.

She sauntered up to the two guards and smiled. "Hey."

The two men looked at her with no real expression. The nose of one twitched and he suddenly opened the door, holding it for them.

Max walked in and Charlie ran after her. Stevie slipped in right behind.

"What was that?" Charlie demanded, catching her sister's arm.

"Apparently I'm *really* good at being sultry."

Charlie stopped her sister and pulled her around to face her. "But, honey . . . you're *not* good at being sultry."

"She's right," Stevie agreed. "Actually, your sultry is almost threatening."

"Gee . . . thanks," Max muttered. She shook her head. "Look, let's just go explore a little. It'll take forever for the guys to find a parking spot around here. Five minutes."

"I'm concerned the stairs only go down," Stevie pointed out. "Are we going to a morgue?"

"Why would there be a morgue in a sports center?" Charlie asked.

"Because Soylent Green is people?"

"I am *so* sorry I let you see that movie," Charlie sighed.

"Come on, come on." Max started down the stairs and they followed.

"Aren't you a little concerned," Charlie asked, "that there was security at the door?"

"Why would I be? They were shifters."

"They were?"

Max stopped and faced her. "I thought you got your allergy meds."

"I did. And Stevie introduced me to a new nasal spray sent from those German doctors. So far it's *really* good."

"And yet you couldn't smell—"

"I don't go around smelling people, Max. Sometimes they smell funky."

"You don't go around smelling. It's just . . . you just . . ."

Stevie walked past them and headed toward the door on the next floor. "She doesn't get it, Maxie. I don't know why you go on so about it."

"But we're shifters!"

"Would you stop screaming that," Charlie snapped. "We don't know who's around here."

"Hey, guys?" Stevie called out. She now stood in front of the open door, staring out at something. "You may want to check this out."

Charlie went down the stairs and stopped behind Stevie. She was taller than her sister, so she could look over her head. It was another lobby. Like the one on the first floor. There were restaurants, stores, and people dressed for the sport of their choice.

But there was a distinct difference between this lobby and the one on the floor above. It was the energy. And it took a moment for her to understand what this all reminded her of, but then it hit her. Like a lightning bolt.

A watering hole in Africa. One where all the local animals had to go to get a drink. Lions, gazelles, giraffes, wild dogs. Predator and prey all meeting in the same place because they had no choice. And although these were all predators, many of them had their cubs and pups with them. The way the mothers watched out for their offspring—keeping them close; gazes darting around, searching out any danger, any risk; ready to attack at a second's notice—reminded Charlie of going to the mall with her mother.

"They're all shifters," Stevie said, fascinated, her mouth slightly open. "All of them."

"I've heard about places like this," Max explained. "Been invited to a few, but never went."

"Why?"

She shrugged. "Seems weird. Being around a bunch of people where the only thing you have in common is that you can shift into an animal."

"I get the appeal," Charlie said. "Kind of like that time I went with Gramps to that family reunion. Being around people who connect with you on a very specific level can be nice. Seeing all those different shades of brown in one place was very comforting, and none of them were shifters because it was my great grandmother's side of the family. But I still felt . . . connected."

"I go to Chinatown," Max stated flatly, "and I don't feel connected."

"Awww, sweetie." Charlie put her arm around Max's shoulders. "That's because you're you."

"Excuse me," a low voice said from behind them.

Charlie and Max separated and three very large men walked by. One of them smiled at Charlie. "Hey, beautiful."

"Hi," she replied, unable to stop a surprised chuckle.

Max rolled her eyes. "Oh, my God. Really?"

"You can't let me have that? Cute guys notice me and you can't let me enjoy the moment?"

"Cute guys notice you all the time."

"No. Short guys notice me. And guys who like big tits. Neither ever look me in the eye or call me beautiful. He did."

"He's seven feet tall. You could give him a blow job without getting on your knees."

"The point is," Stevie cut in, "that you already have a tall guy who thinks you're beautiful." Then she smiled. Weirdly.

Charlie stared at her baby sister. "What are you talking about?"

"You know." Stevie fluttered her eyes . . . which was, again, weird.

"Sweetie, you don't do coquettish well, so stop that."

"Come on." Max moved around them and out the doorway. "Let's check this out."

"We have to meet Berg and Dag," Charlie reminded her.

"Five minutes."

"No. Let's just get back upstairs and—"

"There's a Starbucks."

"Ooh." Charlie stepped past the doorway. "Coffee."

Max pushed Charlie toward the very large Starbucks. "Go get us coffee and something with honey."

"Cinnamon for me," Stevie corrected.

Realizing she'd never get her sisters out of here anytime soon, Charlie went into the Starbucks and got in line. Might as well get herself a cup of coffee to soothe her nerves before she went to track down Berg and Dag. She didn't want them to worry.

As it was, she couldn't believe how amazing the Dunns were being. Going out of their way—constantly—to help her and her sisters. How was she ever going to pay them back? How was she ever going to pay back Berg? She'd never known a guy like him. He was just so . . . nice! And she really liked that. She liked how nice and responsible he was. Only her grandfather had ever been that responsible, but he was also grumpy. Sometimes very grumpy.

Not Berg, though. He was just a really nice guy. Who also happened to be *really* hot.

Charlie rubbed her forehead. She had to stop thinking about Berg that way. He deserved better than MacKilligan crazy in his life. He was too nice for her. What was she going to do with a nice guy but ruin his life?

The line grew even as she moved forward and it didn't take her long to realize that the woman standing behind her was sniffing her.

Not enjoying that one bit, Charlie looked over her shoulder and asked, "Can I help you with something?"

The woman was black, long and lean, in a designer dress that looked perfect on her. She was beautiful but Charlie found her bright gold eyes disconcerting. Especially the way they were locked on her. And the way her nostrils flared as she leaned in to take another sniff did nothing but make Charlie want to slap the holy hell out of her.

"You're bleeding," the woman finally said.

"I've got my period," she lied, hoping that would end the conversation. It didn't.

"I'd believe that if I didn't smell the gunpowder. When were you shot?"

Charlie glanced around but no one seemed to be paying much attention to their conversation.

"Don't worry about it," she insisted. "I got it handled."

"Doubt it." The woman suddenly grabbed her upper arm, and it took everything Charlie had in her not to pull her gun and shoot the female directly in the head. "Come on."

"Look, lady—"

"I'm a doctor. We'll get it cleaned out and wrapped up in a few minutes and you won't get the fever."

"I don't get the fever." Charlie knew about the fever. She'd been hearing about it ever since she'd moved in with the Pack. The fever that allowed shifters to heal themselves in about twenty-four hours. A fever that Charlie and her sisters didn't get. Instead, they healed in their own . . . unique, individual ways. Ways she was not in the mood to discuss with this beautiful, lean woman who was making her insecure about her own looks.

"Sure you don't." The woman pulled and, gritting her teeth, Charlie let the stranger take her out of line. What was wrong with her? If this had happened among full-humans, Charlie would have just handled it. Like she handled everything else. Quickly. Brutally. And with no remorse. But she wasn't doing that here. Maybe because a fellow shifter wouldn't be so easily put off. She couldn't scare this woman with a silent stare or a low-volume growl. And it wasn't until this moment that Charlie realized how frustrating that was.

As the woman led her through the crowded lobby toward a set of elevators, Charlie glanced back in the hopes of spotting her sisters, but nope. They'd wandered off as she'd known they would. Like two exploring bear cubs wandering away from the mama bear. She expected no different from Max, but she often forgot Stevie's problems with crowds . . . in that she had no problems with crowds. Her panic disorder reared up when she felt trapped and alone. But Stevie didn't feel alone in crowds. In her mind, she could call for help and someone would come running to her aid. That's what allowed her to play in front of vast crowds, to lead entire orchestras, to wander around Paris in the springtime while ignoring the beauty and the danger of the city all around her.

Once, Charlie and her sisters had been separated at a peace rally in England that turned violent. When the three sisters met again, Max had a bruised face and swollen knuckles. Charlie had a bruised throat and broken ribs. And Stevie was singing "Give peace a chance" with a bunch of hippies. Untouched. Unbruised. Happy as hell.

But one bear in the yard and Stevie was up a tree, screaming, and unable to breathe. Weird.

They stepped into the elevator and went down a few floors. The woman still had a grip on Charlie's arm while she held her phone in her free hand and read emails.

"Look," Charlie tried, "I appreciate—"

"Nope."

"Nope what?"

"Just nope," the woman said, not even looking up from her phone. "Whatever bullshit you're about to tell me. Nope."

The doors opened and they were moving again. Only this time, as they walked, people greeted the woman.

"Hey, doc."

"Lookin' good, doc."

"Marry me!"

"I'll be by around two, doc. My leg is acting up again."

The woman nodded and smiled as shifters of varying sizes greeted her, but she never stopped and she never eased her hold on Charlie's arm.

Well . . . at least she was a doctor. Of some kind.

The woman dragged Charlie into a very active medical facility, filled to the brim with shifters of varying sizes.

"Hey, doc," the receptionist said. "Your one o'clock is here."

"Ask them to wait, would you, Sal? I've got an emergency."

"Yeah, but—"

The doctor didn't wait for the receptionist to finish. She simply took Charlie into a room and over to an exam table.

She briefly left and returned a minute or two later wearing a lab coat with a stethoscope in the pocket and a blank chart. A nurse followed in behind her.

"Okay, hon," the doc said, opening up the chart and beginning to fill it out. "Let's get that stuff off and see what we're dealing with."

"I really can't afford health care"—at least not health care here—"so I can just—"

"Move from that spot, and I'll have Nurse Konami put you in a headlock that will make your eyes bleed."

Charlie glanced over at the nurse. She wasn't a particularly tall or brawny woman. Nothing too threatening.

"Uh-uh," the doctor said, still not looking at her. "Nurse Konami may be full-human, but she is married to an Asian black bear and she deals with football and hockey players all day, every day. Men and women two to three times your size are terrified of her and for good reason. So if I were you, I'd take off your clothes, put on a gown, and shut up."

Charlie knew she could still fight her way out of here. If nothing else, she was armed. But Berg had brought her here. He must have some connection to the place and she wasn't about to embarrass him. So, as much as she didn't want to, she'd suck it up for the very nice bear who'd been helping her and her sisters.

She pulled off her light jacket, T-shirt, and bra and sat there. Refusing to put on the robe. Partly because she hated those things, but also because she'd been busy putting her gun under her jacket so the two females wouldn't see it.

"By the way, my name is Dr. Davis. And let's get a look at—" She'd finally looked up from her paperwork and stopped when she saw Charlie sitting there, topless.

"So, you're not shy," she guessed.

"No."

"Excellent."

She walked over and carefully pulled off the gauze that Charlie had stuffed in and around the wounds on her back.

"Huh," she heard the doctor say and Charlie looked at her over her shoulder.

The doctor's expression changed a bit, her brow pulling down in concern and confusion. She wanted to step away and Charlie didn't blame her.

"You really don't have to do anything," Charlie explained while the doctor stared. Or gawked. "It'll work itself out."

"My dear girl, *this* is not going to work itself out."

"Actually, it will. You just have to wait a little bit. It's in the final stages."

"The final stages before your death?"

That made Charlie chuckle. "As if my life could ever be that simple." She looked around the room. "Got a magazine I can look at while we're waiting?"

Max put a baseball cap on Stevie's head and stepped back.

"Perfect."

Not really. The hat was way too big—it was apparently "bear sized"—and covered half of Stevie's face. Embroidered on the hat was "The Carnivores," which seemed really bold to Max. Just putting out there that they were all meat-eating predators and everything.

It was true that Max had had more interaction with shifters outside the Pack than Charlie or Stevie, but those shifters were Dutch and his family and their few friends. Wolverines. Like the honey badgers, the wolverines weren't involved with the "shifter nation" as they called it. They preferred to be around full-humans or, even better, no one. They could be quite introverted. Not unpleasant, rarely rude, but introverted.

So seeing all these shifters in one place, hanging out, pretty much getting along was . . . unusual. Interesting, though.

"I can't see," Stevie complained.

"But you look adorable." She took a picture with her phone and texted it to Charlie seconds before Stevie slapped the hat off her head.

Laughing, Max showed the picture to Stevie. "Adorable."

"Do you ever get tired of mocking me?"

"No."

"I'm going to look for a bookstore."

"Why?"

Stevie patted her shoulder. "You make me sad. Do me a favor and keep an eye out for Charlie. If we go missing, she will flip out on us."

"I know, I know."

Max went through the sports store and found a few shirts and caps she wanted to buy, but it had been a while and she thought it was best to go track down Charlie before Charlie had to track down her and Stevie. Their big sister's anxiety went through the roof when she couldn't find them, and Max didn't want to be responsible for the ulcer she was sure Charlie was going to get if she didn't relax a little.

Max walked back to where she'd last seen her sister. She stood outside the Starbucks and, going up on her toes, she tried to look over the heads inside the open café. So many tall people.

Frowning when she didn't see her sister, Max decided to go inside for a closer look. But as she began to move, she heard a screeched, "*Livy!*" And then something landed on her back.

Without thought, only instinct trained into her since the death of her adopted mother, Max reached behind her, grabbed hold of whatever had her, lifted up and over, and slammed the person onto the floor.

She rammed her foot against a chest to pin her prey to the ground and pulled out the blade holstered at the back of her jeans. She raised the blade over her head, about to drop onto the prey beneath her to keep it pinned in place. But a hand grabbed her wrist, halting the blade mid-attack and yanking her back and away.

The grip on her wrist was firm. So firm, Max knew she couldn't break it. So she turned her body, dislocating her shoulder. She ignored the pain and unleashed the claws on her free hand, burying them deep into someone's side.

She heard a grunt of pain and finally looked up—and holy shit! Up!—until she was gazing into bright blue eyes surrounded by white hair.

Max hissed, unleashing her fangs. In return, the man unleashed his own.

And when his two eyeteeth continued to grow until they reached past his square jaw, like a pair of tusks, Max decided . . . she was out. Fuck that shifter shit with their honorable "fang to fang, claw to claw" code that Dutch had always told her about.

Max yanked out her claws, causing blood to arc out of the male's side and splatter several onlookers. She spun again, the pain in her shoulder very close to making her pass out. But she clenched her jaw, and when she faced the man again, she quickly sized him up before kicking him mid-chest. Shocked by the power of the blow, he finally released her, sending Max reeling. She hit the ground, rolled backward, and stood. By then she had blades in both hands. Her wounded shoulder couldn't move much, but she could still have his eyes out and his throat cut before the pain got so bad she'd wish that someone would just kill her already.

She cracked her neck and started forward, but two adorable bookend bears slid to a stop in front of her, both with their big arms out, matching eyes wide in panic.

"No, Max!" Berg said. "Don't do it."

Max narrowed her eyes. Not because she was plotting something but because her shoulder was killing her. But the two males misinterpreted.

"You can't do this," Berg begged. "Please. Just walk away."

"Max?"

Max looked away from the two bears and saw her cousin standing a few feet away.

"What the fuck are you doing?" Livy walked closer, shoving the two bears out of the way. "Starting shit again?" She growled before yelling, "*Again?*"

"It wasn't me! It was—" Max started to point at the man who was behind the bears, bleeding from his side. He'd done the damage to her shoulder, but he hadn't actually started anything.

Max looked over the crowd, finally pointing at a black woman in roller skates. "It was *her.*"

Livy turned and Max saw her cousin's entire body go tense. "What did she do?"

"She hugged me from behind."

Livy rested her hands on her hips. "I thought we talked about that sort of thing, Blayne."

"Okay, this looks bad," the woman called Blayne said, skating forward, focused on Livy. "But I thought it was you."

Max stepped up beside her cousin. "Is *that* your excuse? That we all look alike?"

"What?" Blayne's eyes widened in horror. "No! Of course not!"

"Really, Blayne?" Livy asked. "Because it sounds like you're saying we all look alike."

Of course, they were cousins and Blayne hadn't actually seen Max from the front. She was just going on body size and the short hair. But that didn't matter . . . because this chick was just too easy to fuck with. Hell! Max could do this all day!

"Because we're *Asian*?" Max asked.

"Of course not! I mean, my husb—"

"What?" Max pushed. "You about to tell me that some of your best friends are Asian?"

"Actually, my best friend is . . . um . . . look, I'm

just saying that . . . um . . ." Her brown eyes narrowed. "You two are fucking with me, aren't you?"

Max started laughing. She couldn't help it. Who was this little weirdo?

The big guy who'd gotten between Max's blade and Blayne's sternum stepped up beside Blayne and glowered down at Max.

"You tell 'em, honey," Blayne said. "My *husband*."

Max knew she was looking at a fellow half-Asian, so she was kind of expecting a "talking to" as Charlie liked to call her lectures. To be honest, looking at the size of the guy and seeing the blood dripping onto the floor from the side she'd ripped open with her claws, she'd gladly welcome a "talking to" rather than a "beating on."

Still glowering, Blayne's husband demanded, "Do you skate?"

"Yeah!" Blayne agreed. "Do you . . ." She turned to her husband. "Does she *skate*?"

"We need a new enforcer. And she's mean."

Max grinned. "I *am* mean!"

"I think she's a serial killer," Livy added . . . for some reason. "Look at that smile," she said flatly, pointing at Max. "That sick, disturbing smile."

Max tilted her head to the side and tapped Livy on the elbow. "Thanks so much, cousin," she said with as much sweetness as she could possibly manage.

Frowning, Livy stepped away from her. "See what I mean?"

"She was going to kill me," Blayne accurately pointed out to her husband.

"She wouldn't be the first."

"Where's your sister?" Berg asked Max.

"Which one?"

"Don't play word games."

"Excuse me, Britta," Blayne's husband interrupted, glaring at Berg. "I'm trying to have a conversation."

Berg's eyes briefly closed and he gave a short shake of his head while Dag smiled a little and looked away.

"I am *not* Britta, you Cro-Magnon. I'm Berg. That's Dag."

"Is there really a difference?"

"Yes!" Berg insisted. "Yes, there is."

The man shrugged. "I don't see it."

Berg's jaw tightened in frustration and Max wondered how many times he'd had this conversation with the tusk guy. Clearly more than once.

"Let's get your sisters and go," Berg finally said, focusing on Max.

Max shrugged. "I have no idea where they are. Go find them."

"Max—"

"Yeah," Blayne's husband said, "go find them." He reached out and grabbed Max's wrist. "She'll be at the training rink."

"I can't believe this!" Blayne nearly shouted. "She tried to kill me and now you're going to test her out to be your enforcer?" Her big brown eyes welled with tears. "I am the *mother* of your children."

He faced her, but still didn't release Max. "I don't understand the connection."

"I should be more important to you than hockey."

He looked off, blew out a breath. "You *should* . . ."

Max bit the inside of her cheek to stop from laughing.

Blayne stomped one skate-covered foot before skating off, a group of derby girls following her.

The giant glowered down at Max, but now she saw a hint of a smile around his eyes and at the corners of his mouth. "I'm going to pay for that later."

Berg watched Max follow Bo "The Marauder" Novikov.

"Does he really not know that we *aren't* Britta?" Dag asked. Again.

"If it doesn't involve hockey or that one woman who tolerates him . . . I don't think he notices anything."

Livy tapped Berg's arm. "So what has my cousin and her sisters gotten you two involved in? Are you in danger? Did you lose any money? Are you being followed by foreign interests?"

Berg frowned. "What are you talking about?"

"Look, as someone I don't necessarily want wiped from the face of the planet—"

"Awwww. Thanks, Liv."

Berg stared at his brother. "What's wrong with you?"

"—be careful that you don't get too involved with the MacKilligan sisters."

"Why?"

"Well, according to my mother and aunts, they're cursed."

"Cursed," Berg repeated. "Uh-huh."

"By ghosts."

Scratching his forehead, Berg gave himself a brief moment before asking Livy, "You believe they're cursed by ghosts?"

"No. I don't believe in ghosts."

"So you just think they're cursed in general?"

"Yeah. I definitely think they're cursed. It's their father's fault, though. I think he pissed off a witch or something."

"You don't believe in ghosts . . . but you believe in witches?"

"Witches exist."

Berg nodded. "Okay. I'm walking away now."

He did, and Dag followed behind him.

"If I were you," Livy called out, "I'd find the little sister before you go looking for the big one. If you don't have the little one, the big one is going to flip the fuck out."

Berg stopped walking and let out a sigh.

"Livy's right, isn't she?" Dag asked.

"Yeah."

"But Stevie could be anywhere here."

"Well . . . let's try to think like her."

Dag folded his arms over his chest and said in all seriousness, "So where would a former child prodigy and genius with an extreme panic disorder who is being hunted by all sorts of people go when in a shifter-filled sports center?"

Berg began scratching his forehead again. First with one hand, then the other. Until he finally just buried his face in both hands and let out a very large, very pained sigh.

There was a food court! And a shockingly large and well-stocked bookstore! She even found an entire store devoted just to honey! Honey! She'd gone in there, despite the large grizzly sow behind the counter who wouldn't stop glowering at her. She'd started to panic a little but she swallowed it and put in a large order to be sent to the house for her sisters—she was actually not a fan of honey. Too sweet for her taste. But once the order was in the sow went from glowering to glowing. Suddenly she was more than happy to help Stevie even without knowing what the hell Stevie was. She kept sniffing. At one point, when Stevie was looking at a large display of chocolate-covered honeycombs—Max *loved* honeycombs—she felt the sow standing right behind her. And Stevie was almost positive that she sniffed the back of her neck.

Thankfully, her meds were working well and Stevie, after years of group and individual therapy, was able to "deep breathe" her way through the oncoming panic until the sow moved away from her.

After leaving that store, Stevie bought a large order of very crispy french fries, a large bottle of water, and asked for extra ketchup. Then she found a bench in the middle of a high-traffic area where she could comfortably people watch.

Everyone was going somewhere or coming from somewhere and didn't notice her at all. She loved it.

Watching the movement of people, hearing their voices rise and fall, listening to the noises coming from the nearby food court made her think of music. Made her think of what she could do with these sounds. She could easily see trained dancers moving to what was playing in her head.

She smiled a little. It had been years since she'd had the time, energy, and emotional fortitude to allow herself to think about her own music. To let her easily stressed-out mind wander down those roads of emotion and art.

To this day, she still got emails from fans. Her work was still discussed in music schools and prestigious university music programs. Some classical orchestras still attempted to play her beloved but most-complicated symphonies to sold-out audiences. At one time, she had been the one conducting those orchestras even though she'd only been about seven and had to have a specially made podium in order to see and be seen by the orchestra and audience. She was ten when she'd walked away from all of it. She'd hit a creative and emotional wall that had her—literally—hanging from the ceiling by her newly formed claws, unable to breathe, unable to think, unable to do anything but cry and hyperventilate until they started her on medication.

Medication, though, hadn't been an easy fix for Stevie. The first reason was because she was a shifter. Shifters had very amped up internal systems that allowed them to heal quickly without medication, which was great for physical ailments but a real problem when one had mental issues. Then add in that Stevie was also half honey badger. Medications and poisons were easily absorbed and then pissed out by honey badger shifters. Sixteen-year-old Max had once tried vodka infused with the venom of the black mamba snake. She was in a coma for an entire day before she snapped awake, hungry and smiling. Smiling until a livid Charlie punched Max in the face, breaking their sister's nose and cheekbone as she screamed, *"Never do anything that goddamn stupid again!"*

And even though Stevie and Charlie were only half badger, with what Charlie insisted on calling "our dad's fucked up genes," they still had to manage their medications differently from nearly everyone else in the world. So it took years before Stevie and her team of psychiatrists and therapists and German physicians found the right combination of talk therapy and meds. In that time, she'd not only walked away from her brilliant music career, she'd run. Screaming.

Most of the prodigies Stevie had known when she was growing up had parents who would have *never* let them quit what had been a substantial, worldwide career. Especially considering the money she'd brought in. But Stevie's mother had abandoned her to Charlie's mom for reasons still unknown to her. When Charlie's mom had been killed and the three of them had gone to live with the Pack in Wisconsin, the Pack left decisions about Max and Stevie up to Charlie's grandfather and, eventually, Charlie.

When Stevie said she didn't want to write, play, or even think about music anymore, Charlie had only asked, "Then what *are* you going to do? Because you'll need to do something, and we both know it."

As always, Charlie had been right. If Stevie didn't occupy her mind, things would get bad for everyone.

So . . . Stevie focused on physics and math. She liked equations and science and behind it all, she'd always found a certain level of music. Of art. It turned out she'd been a prodigy in that, too, which meant all her scholastic financial needs were met by other people. Important since financially her father had eventually ruined what was left of her music career. Universities, labs, and some rich people liked being a benefactor to a child who tested out of high school by the time she was eleven.

The thing was . . . life wasn't exactly great now. They were being hunted. So what made Stevie feel comfortable bringing music back into her life? Why did she feel calmer than she had in a long while?

It could have been shifting to her animal form earlier in the day. She didn't do that often, which wasn't surprising. She kind of terrified everyone when she became a giant, tiger-striped honey badger bigger than even the polar bears and grizzlies.

Yet Stevie was starting to think it was being around her sisters that was doing her the most good. Yeah, Charlie's anxiety and obsessive baking could be trying, and Max never stopped fucking with Stevie, no matter how many times Stevie punched her in the throat. But at the end of the day, knowing they were there for her . . .

"Hello."

Stevie heard the voice. Someone was talking to her. Crunching on a french fry, she looked up. The handsome man appeared vaguely familiar but . . .

"Still don't remember me, huh?" he guessed with a smile.

"Should I?"

"We saw each other at Livy Kowalski's apartment . . . you were hanging from the ceiling before passing out from lithium. I'm Cooper."

Stevie picked up another fry, put it in her mouth, chewed . . . and stared.

"Still nothing?" When she continued to silently stare and eat, he said. "Maybe you remember my sister." But Stevie doubted it.

He turned, called out, "Cherise! Come here."

A pretty young woman walked over and Stevie sized her up instantly. This woman did not like being out in public. She did not like being around crowds. Stevie was guessing that if she had even one more minor trauma, she'd end up going full agoraphobic if her family didn't keep an eye on her. But other than that unsolicited psychological diagnosis . . . nope. Stevie had no idea who this woman was either.

"Wow. Stevie. Look at you!" Cherise said. "You look amazing."

"Thanks . . . *you*."

"She doesn't remember you. Or me. Or anyone."

"It's nothing personal."

"Really?" the male called Cooper said. "Because it feels personal."

"I have a *lot* of knowledge in my head. If something isn't important, I just get rid of it."

"How is that not personal?" Cherise softly asked.

"I get rid of a lot people in my head. I don't do it to be vicious. Or because I hate you. You're just not important to me. It's like clearing off a hard drive. All those songs you never listen to or out-of-focus pictures that are useless . . . you just wipe it off the drive. I mean, why would you keep that stuff?"

"Again, not seeing how this isn't personal."

"Well, to be blunt—"

The male raised a brow. "You mean you weren't being blunt before?"

"—my brain is important. I refuse to fill it up with meaningless crap. I really don't know what else to . . .

oh, my God." Stevie put her fries aside and stood. "Kyle?" she asked the tall young man walking toward their small group, smiling at her. "Oh, my God! *Kyle!*"

Stevie ran into the open arms of Kyle Jean-Louis Parker, hugging him tightly. Behind her, she heard, "*Him,* you remember?"

"Of course, I remember Kyle," she said, keeping one arm around his waist while Kyle's arm curled around her shoulder. "He's Kyle."

Kyle nodded. "Exactly. But you *do* remember these guys, Stevie." He pointed at Cooper. "Mr. Needy." Cherise. "Pathologically shy." He gestured to the young woman walking up behind them. "Genetic freak."

"Ohhhhh! Of course! Your siblings!"

"Seriously?" Cooper demanded.

"I'm leaving," Cherise quietly announced, before doing just that.

And, "Fuck you," from the sister that Stevie now remembered was a prima ballerina in an important ballet company . . . somewhere in America.

"See?" Kyle pointed out. "The genetic freak is sad because her brain can only do so much."

"That's it. I'm out." The genetic freak walked away, her middle finger held high in the air.

"Wait," Cooper called out. "Toni is coming to meet us here with . . . okay, well, she's gone."

"That restrictive diet sure does make her cranky," Kyle observed.

"Why do you do this?" his brother asked.

"You'll have to be much more specific." But before his brother could bother, he turned to Stevie. "So what are you doing in New York?"

"Running for my life."

"Oh, I'm sorry. Your father again?"

"Of course."

"Peruvian drug lords?"

"Who knows. My sisters are here, though."

"Oooh. The infamous Charlie and Max. I have been dying to meet them for years."

"Well, now you can. I told them all about you. So what are you doing in the City?"

"He was kicked out of another art school."

"I was not kicked out," Kyle argued. "I was asked to leave because some people can't handle criticism. Or the suggestion that they might have a borderline personality disorder that should get treated."

"Borderline or bipolar?" Stevie asked. "People often get those two confused."

"Definitely borderline. She came at me with a knife. Nearly took my eye out."

"That actually could have been anybody, with or without a disorder," Cooper muttered.

Kyle glanced at his brother before admitting to Stevie, "He's so jealous of me, he doesn't know what to do with himself."

"Jealous?" Cooper asked. "Of *you*?"

"You wish you had as much talent as me and my dear sweet Stevie."

"I do have as much talent as your dear sweet Stevie. And God knows, I'm better than you."

"See?" Kyle said to Stevie. "How he lives in his sad fantasy world?"

"Although Stevie doesn't remember it and it was at different times, we were both trained by the same maestro. We even played together at one point."

"But did you ever conduct the St. Petersburg Orchestra in a symphony you wrote . . . when you were nine? Didn't think so," Kyle said before his brother could reply.

"Hey, Coop."

Cooper turned and waved at a woman walking toward them, with a large male behind her.

As soon as Stevie saw him, she recognized that mane of hair. Stevie immediately moved behind Kyle, using his tall frame to block her.

It had been so long ago. And she'd been so young. Too young. Not even seventeen. He'd come into her life, trying to get her back into music. Trying to drag her back to a world she'd willingly left. But she'd listened to his pitch because he was a cat shifter and Stevie had stupidly thought he was like her. Would understand her. She'd assumed that it had all been about money for him, and to a point it was.

But that day he'd backed her into a corner in her lab, saying things to her that made her uncomfortable, but making her feel like she couldn't leave. That she had to listen. That she somehow owed him something.

Of course, those had been the days when her sisters had kept a much closer eye on her. They couldn't afford to go to college themselves, but they liked hanging out at her campus.

So, when her sisters had walked in to Stevie's lab, things had spiraled out of control quickly. After that there were cops and lawsuits and more threats—until it all disappeared. Stevie still didn't know how or why; she'd just been grateful.

But seeing him again. Even after all these years. All these changes in her life . . .

Stevie turned her back and prayed neither of her sisters suddenly appeared.

Coop saw Stevie move away as soon as Toni walked up with that lion male she was considering as an agent for Cherise and Oriana. He apparently specialized in representing artists and was known for making them very profitable deals. But the way Stevie reacted to the sight of the man . . .

Kyle, who rarely cared about anyone but himself, moved in front of her, helping to block her from the cat's sight.

Stevie was older than Kyle by a few years, but Kyle always got along better with adults than kids his own age. He didn't know how to talk to them. He did, however, know how to emotionally torture them, which was another reason he didn't spend a lot of time with kids his own age. Their parents wouldn't allow it.

Coop thought back and remembered some news, many years ago, about the possibility that Stevie MacKilligan would be reentering the music business. She'd apparently found an agent who'd convinced her that the world was at a loss without her music and passion. Then, just as suddenly as the rumor started, it stopped. There was no comeback. She stayed with science and moved through that difficult profession like a house on fire. But Coop also remembered reading a small story in a German paper about the "sisters of Maestro Stevie MacKilligan being investigated by American authorities" for a brutal assault. Since Coop hadn't really known Stevie's siblings, he hadn't paid much attention. He had his own psychotic siblings to worry about. He was just grateful none had ended up in the crime section of the paper . . . yet.

Now Coop studied the man with Toni. Another arrogant lion wearing a tailored suit—necessary for males that size—who couldn't seem to control his hair.

"Where are Cherise and Oriana?" Toni asked. "I told them to meet us here."

"Well . . . Kyle—"

"Okay. Enough said." Toni had been more on edge since Kyle had come back to the States. Add in the attack on Coop's hotel room and his sister was, to put it mildly, less patient than usual. "Any idea where they went?"

"I don't know about Cherise. But Oriana likes to watch the hockey players, and your mate's brother invited her to check out practice."

Toni's eyes narrowed. "Is she dating one of those idiots?"

"She hasn't told me anything. Kyle?"

"I don't care."

Coop sighed. "And Kyle doesn't care."

"We'll walk over to the practice rink. See if you can track down Cherise, please."

"If she hasn't already gone home. Why don't you just call Oriana? Or text her?"

Toni moved past Coop, lovingly bumping her shoulder against his as she went by. Letting him know her terseness had nothing to do with him. A gesture he appreciated at the moment.

"Apparently," she explained as she moved, the lion walking beside her, "she's blocked me on her phone. The little cow."

Coop smiled and waited for the pair to turn the corner before he walked past Kyle and stood in front of Stevie. She wouldn't look at him. The confident artist and scientist who couldn't be bothered to remember Coop's name suddenly appeared as painfully shy as Cherise.

It was clear she didn't want to talk about any of this, but he still had to know. He decided to go with the direct but non-invasive approach.

"If you had a little sister," he asked Stevie, "would you hire him?"

Kyle put his arm around Stevie's shoulders. A form of protection he didn't even bother to show his own sisters.

"If I had a little sister," Stevie said, her arms wrapped around her waist, "I'd keep her as far away from that fucker as humanly possible." She leaned against Kyle and added, "And he'd better pray that my sisters don't spot him."

Jai Davis watched, mesmerized, as the bullets that had been pumped into the hybrid female sitting on her examination table began to pop out of the wound on her shoulder.

According to Charlie MacKilligan, this was what her body did. The wound began to heal from the inside, without stitches, without surgery. At first, infected fluid poured from the wound while Charlie sat and read a three-year-old *Vogue*. So much fluid that Jai was surprised the girl didn't have a brutal, possibly fatal fever. Then, some blood.

At that point, Charlie said, "Almost done."

It was clear the hybrid was used to this. She didn't even have to look at the wound to know what stage it was in. She was still reading a magazine.

Jai and Ellen waited and thirty minutes later . . . bullets.

"That is fascinating."

"Is it?" Charlie asked.

"Not for you, I'm assuming. How often has this happened?"

"A few times over the years."

"You've been shot a *few* times?"

"Not just shot. There were a couple of knife fights, bar fights. Fight with a pit bull once, but she started it."

"Sure she did."

Pieces of the third bullet slid out and once out, the skin began to knit shut on its own.

"Amazing." Jai straightened up and walked around until she stood in front of Charlie. "Really amazing. When you shift, do you heal faster?"

"I don't shift."

Jai was surprised. She'd heard about a few shifters who refused to shift. Religious zealots from every branch who thought being a shifter was evil. Was this female one of those? "Is that a moral choice?"

Charlie looked at Jai, frowning. "Huh?"

"Is it a moral choice that you don't shift?"

"Why would that be a moral choice? There's nothing morally wrong with shifting." She leaned away slightly. "Are you one of those weird, crazy religious people?"

"No, no." Jai chuckled. "I'm actually a Buddhist. But you said you *don't* shift."

"Oh. Well, let me rephrase. I *can't* shift."

Jai folded her arms over her chest. "You can't?"

"Nope."

"Are you sure?"

"Positive. My sisters started shifting very early, but me? I just didn't. And my grandfather's entire Pack worked with me for years after I hit puberty. But other than claws and fangs . . ." She shrugged. "I don't shift."

"Are you . . . okay with that?"

"Well . . ." She thought a moment. "I heal really well. Have bones like iron. And my inability to shift is just more proof that my father can't get anything right. So I'm all good."

Jai laughed. She liked Charlie. She was . . . unusual. Although she'd never met a shifter who *couldn't* shift. She'd met a few who didn't know they were shifters. Who'd lived their lives as full-human and, when puberty hit, hadn't gone through that quintessential moment of shifting back and forth to human. It was rare, but it did happen.

But that wasn't Charlie's story at all. She had to be

the strangest hybrid Jai had ever met, and she'd met quite a few. There was a large and still-growing group of hybrids in the tri-state area, yet Charlie now stood out among them—and apart from them.

At least Charlie had a sense of humor about it. Nothing would be worse than if she was a whiny mess about herself. Jai hated people like that. The always-victim, she liked to call them.

Jai's cell phone vibrated in her coat and she took a quick glance. Slipping it back into her pocket, she moved forward and took another look at Charlie's wound. The scar was ugly but Jai couldn't see any lingering evidence of infection or internal damage.

"Get dressed," she ordered, "and I'll be right back."

Jai went down the hallway toward the large glass windows that separated the exam rooms from the waiting room. She saw her best friend standing among all the chairs. Sadly, though, Cella Malone was not by herself. She had that hillbilly hound dog with her.

Jai opened the thick glass door and went into the waiting room. "Hey, what's up?"

Cella jerked her head toward the exam rooms. "Do you have Charlie MacKilligan in there?"

It was true, Jai loved her best friend. She wasn't just a best friend. She was family. Their daughters—conceived before either was even seventeen—were like close cousins. But as much as Jai loved Marcella Malone, she didn't lie to herself about Marcella Malone.

"You know I can't tell you that," Jai replied. "Doctor-patient privilege."

"For shifters?"

"For everyone, dumb ass. You know that."

"Look," Cella went on, "I can't get into detail—"

"I don't want to hear it."

"—but we really need to—"

"Don't wanna hear it."

"—talk to the kid."

"Go away, Cella."

Jai heard the glass door close and she turned to see that some male had slipped past her into the exam room hallway.

"Cella, what have you done?"

"Trust me. Just give him five minutes."

Jai faced her friend, eyes wide. She was horrified. She knew what her friend did for a living. Had heard what her hound dog companion was *known* for. Knew the kind of people Cella hung around when she wasn't hanging around Jai and the Malone family.

Jai turned to run back into the exam room, to help her patient, but Cella grabbed her arm, held her in place.

"Five minutes," she said, calmly and coldly. Just the way Cella killed.

Chapter Thirteen

The helpful, full-human nurse had given Charlie a clean T-shirt to wear, and as she pulled it down— it was so big it reached her knees—she saw what was written on the front.

"The Carnivores," she read. "Subtle."

"It's the local pro hockey team," the nurse said with a smile, busy wiping away the remnants of Charlie's healing process. She had to admit, she was glad she didn't have to clean it up herself. What her body went through to heal was disgusting, but she was still grateful for it.

The nurse dumped unclean things in a special trash can, stripped off her latex gloves, and dumped those too.

"I'll be back in a moment."

"Okay."

The nurse left and Charlie looked down at her jeans to make sure they didn't have any gross stuff on them. They didn't, so she felt comfortable heading out into the world dressed in a weird black, silver, and white T-shirt with *Carnivore* written on it in giant letters.

It wasn't like the shirt was lying.

Reaching down, Charlie grabbed her burgundy Converse sneakers and placed them on the exam table. She was going for one when the door to the room opened and she lifted her head, expecting to see the nurse or the doctor, but it was neither.

Her frown grew deep, though, when she saw who was standing there.

"Dutch?" she asked, extremely surprised to see him. "What's wrong?" Her anxiety ramped up. "They didn't find the car, did they?"

"No, no. That's all done. I just need to talk to you, really quick."

"About what?"

"Um . . ." He looked off and Charlie let out a sigh.

"What did Max do?"

"What? Oh. Nothing. She didn't do anything."

"Then what did you do?"

"Well . . ."

"Look," she said, pulling on one of her sneakers, "I'll pay for Max's fuck-ups, but I'm not paying for yours. You've got family—ask them for money."

"I'm not asking you for money."

"Then what?"

He paused another moment before he just sort of spilled everything. "The people who came by your house earlier . . . they weren't there to hurt you, Charlie. They wanted to talk to you. Initially, they just wanted to talk to Max, but after seeing you, Stevie, and Max in . . . from what I understand . . . *rare* form up in the Bronx, they want to talk to all of you. About a job."

The second shoe forgotten, Charlie stood up straight; her mind churning, trying to make sense of what Dutch was telling her.

"You," she said, pointing her finger. "You sent those people to us. The people I saw on the roof. The ones watching us."

"They wanted to see Max in action and . . . well . . .

it just so happened, Max was in action. But so were you and Stevie. I mean, it really worked out well."

"Did it?"

"Yeah. They're really interested in you guys, and I have to tell you . . . it's an awesome job, Charlie. Excellent money. Benefits. Protection. I've been wanting to get Max hooked up with them for a while now, but . . ." He shrugged. "I knew you wouldn't be too happy about it."

"Really? Did you really know I wouldn't be too happy?"

"Look, Charlie, I know you haven't been crazy about me all these years. I'm not sure why. I'm amazing. But I think even you know that I wouldn't do anything to hurt Max or Stevie. I love you guys."

Charlie scratched the side of her mouth. She had a little itch there.

But then her fingers started to bother her and she curled one hand into a fist, placed the palm of the other over it, and cracked her knuckles. She did the same to the other hand.

"Now, Charlie," Dutch tried to soothe, "let's be calm about this. You know I adore you, but I'm not going to just let you flip out on me either. You understand what I'm telling you?"

"Yeah," she said calmly. "I understand."

Berg, after sending Dag off in the opposite direction, had continued his search for either of the two MacKilligan sisters. He knew where Max was, so he was intensely focused on finding Charlie or Stevie. Preferably both.

When he walked into the health center—where all the athletes went to get their "torn-artery repair"—he wasn't sure why he'd come. Maybe because it seemed logical Stevie might be here. She seemed remarkably comfortable with the medical profession.

But when he took a quick look around and his gaze locked with the yellow eyes of a Smith Pack female, he realized that he was probably right about finding at least one of the MacKilligan sisters here.

He also realized that they were in real trouble.

Berg smiled and fought the natural urge to let his grizzly hump grow. It added strength to his attacks, but he had to be careful when it came to members of the Smith Pack. They weren't like other wolves.

He slid his hand behind him, wrapping his fingers around the butt of his gun.

"Berg!" Cella Malone cheered. "I'm so glad you're here."

"Hey, Cella." He knew Cella Malone pretty well. And he liked her. But he never forgot who and what she was. "So, what's going on?"

"Pull that weapon out, son," the She-wolf drawled no longer looking at him, "and it'll be the last thing you ever do."

Cella frowned in confusion, her gaze darting back and forth between him and her Smith Pack associate.

"Wait," Cella said, walking away from Dr. Davis and over to him. She sniffed him. "It was *you* at their house. Hold on . . . do you think we want to *hurt* the MacKilligan sisters?"

Berg let his silence answer her question.

"Oh, God, no. No! That's not what's happening."

"Uh-huh."

"You don't believe me?"

"*I* don't believe you," Dr. Davis said from across the room.

"Jai . . . is this you helping?" Cella asked with false sweetness.

Dr. Davis didn't reply, so Cella refocused on him. "I can see how you might think we were . . . but we're not. That's the farthest thing from our minds. Just a conversation. That's all we want. So, if you could just—"

A crash from the exam rooms cut off Cella's next lies, and Berg moved past all the women, heading right to the glass door. He'd just opened it when the glass and blinds of one of the exam rooms exploded out—nurses, orderlies, and other doctors making a panicked run for it—and an annoying weasel landed hard on the hallway floor.

A few seconds later, Charlie followed Dutch out, glaring down at him.

"You're not being reasonable!" Dutch was saying just as Charlie reached down, wrapped her hand around Dutch's throat, and lifted the guy off the floor. With one hand.

Berg had to be honest. He hadn't realized how strong Charlie was. And, to be completely forthright, he found it kind of a huge turn on.

Shaking his head, Berg tried to get control of himself and the situation.

"Charlie, let him go!"

"He's a lying sack of shit," she growled out between clenched teeth. "And I'm gonna twist this motherfucker into a *pretzel*."

"Good Lord," the She-wolf sighed, pushing past Berg and sauntering into the hallway. Cella came in behind her. Berg tried to stop Cella, but she just pulled her arm away and kept going.

"Darlin'," the wolf said, standing beside Charlie and Dutch, "you need to put the boy down now. You don't want me to get nasty."

Charlie didn't even look at the wolf. She acted like she didn't notice her. How could she not notice her? Had her Packmates not warned her about the Smith Pack? He thought every shifter, *everywhere,* knew about the Smith Pack. And especially about Dee-Ann Smith.

Charlie's fingers tightened on Dutch's throat and the weasel began to turn a dangerous shade of blue.

Without Berg even really seeing it, Dee-Ann Smith had pulled a blade from somewhere and was swinging it toward Charlie's arm. Probably just to cut her. Probably just to snap her out of her homicidal rage.

But, still without looking away from Dutch, with her free hand, Charlie caught Dee-Ann's wrist in mid-swipe . . . and held it there.

Slowly, Charlie moved her gaze from the weasel to the wolf. Her eyes changed color behind her glasses. Dee-Ann didn't seem to like that and she unleashed her fangs while she tried to pull her arm away.

Charlie's lips pulled back over her teeth and slowly, rows and rows of large fangs descended from her gums. They weren't exactly wolf fangs. But they weren't all honey badger either. They were more like a bizarre combination of the two, and they were terrifying.

Then her jaw opened and it continued to open, yellow eyes bright, as she issued a growl-hiss that had Cella's fangs dropping.

Charlie had her back to the She-tiger, which was just the way Cella liked it. She jumped toward Charlie with nothing blocking her. Nothing there to stop her. Claws out and extended.

In that split second, Charlie turned to the right, flinging Dee-Ann into a shocked Cella, so that the two She-predators collided, slamming into the wall and falling to the floor.

He heard Jai gasp behind him, sensed the mountain lion starting to shift in order to help her friend.

"*No,*" he said to her. Because, that could only end badly.

Especially when he saw that Charlie still had her grip on Dutch.

"You lied to me," Charlie said, shoving Dutch against the wall, his feet not even touching the floor. "You've betrayed me and my sisters. And you know how I feel about traitors."

Dee-Ann managed to get to her feet, the blade still in her hand. She went for Charlie again.

Now Charlie dropped her prey, turned, and caught Dee-Ann's entire arm. She slammed the wolf into the wall, ramming her elbow into her throat, pinning her there. She brought her knee up and hammered it into Dee-Ann's lower abdomen.

Shaking her head, Cella scrambled to her feet and again attacked Charlie from behind.

With one elbow in Dee-Ann's throat, Charlie abruptly turned at the waist, bringing her other elbow back and directly into Cella's face, shattering her nose. Blood sprayed. Charlie slapped the flat of her hand against Cella's chest and shoved her, sending the She-cat flying back across the hall.

Charlie brought her free hand toward Dee-Ann's arm while tugging the arm forward. The two collided and Berg cringed when he heard bone break.

Dee-Ann howled from the pain and she dropped her blade.

"Charlie!" Berg called out when he was afraid she was about to focus on breaking Dee-Ann's neck. A move that would have the entire Smith Pack hunting the MacKilligan sisters down. Nothing would save them. Nothing.

Charlie froze but didn't look at him. He scrambled for something to get her attention. Not only to get it, but to keep it. It took him less than five seconds.

"I can't find Stevie. Max doesn't know where she is."

She looked at him and her yellow eyes returned to

brown. She released her grip on Dee-Ann's shattered arm and stepped away. But Dee-Ann, being a Smith, didn't drop to the ground. She didn't ask for help. She simply panted in pain and glowered at Charlie.

Charlie briefly paused to backhand Dee-Ann Smith, sending the She-wolf flipping down the hall.

She took a few more steps, then stopped again, this time next to the weasel. She kicked him three, okay, maybe five times.

After that, Charlie headed toward Berg. But, abruptly, she stopped again, raised a finger.

"Charlie, no—"

But she'd already run back into the exam room she'd just come out of. A few seconds later, she returned holding a sneaker. He hadn't realized until now that the whole time she'd been in the fight, she'd only been wearing one shoe.

She stopped by his side, lifted her leg, and tugged the sneaker on.

"Come on," she said when she was done. "I think I know where to find her."

Britta skated out onto the ice with her practice gear on. She'd been on the Carnivore practice team for two years now. She'd been offered a second-string position but with her schedule being so random, she couldn't commit to being available when the team needed her. And if she couldn't do it right, she didn't want to bother.

Besides, getting offered second string was a little insulting, but she expected no less from the bitchy head coach She-cat they had running the team.

Britta was halfway across the ice when she abruptly stopped and looked to her left.

"Huh."

She changed direction and skated over to the woman outfitted in hockey gear.

"Max?" she said, when she came to a stop. "What are you doing here?"

The badger shrugged. "No idea."

"Why are you wearing hockey gear?"

"No idea."

"Do you even know how to skate?"

"Well, I spent a few years in Wisconsin near a lake that used to freeze over. We'd go skating there with the other high school kids. So . . . I can skate forward . . . in a circle."

Britta winced. "You need to do more than that to play hockey."

"Yeah, that's what I thought. But this big guy put me in the hockey gear, and he didn't really listen to me. I sense he doesn't listen to anyone."

"Over seven feet? Looks like he actually *met* Genghis Khan?"

"Yeah. That's him."

"That's Bo Novikov. He became team captain last year. He's been out of control ever since. He's gone through, like, eight enforcers. I think two are still in rehab."

"Interesting. And what position is the enforcer?"

"It's not really a position. Not an official position. It's just the player that kicks the ass of anyone who plays dirty or fucks with team members who aren't as fight-y."

Max was quiet for a moment before she said, "I could do that."

"Except you still need to know how to skate." Max opened her mouth and Britta quickly added, "Backward and forward."

"Oh. Yeah. That's a problem."

"Do you want me to tell Novikov you can't do it? I'm one of the few people he listens to without walking away mid-sentence. And I'm not sure I want to hear my brother whine because you got hurt and Charlie's pissed about it."

"Are guns involved?"

"In ice hockey? No."

"Knives? Or bombs? Or Peruvian drug lords?"

"Not that I'm aware."

"Then Charlie won't care."

Bo Novikov skated over to the pair, stopped, looked back and forth between them.

"What are you two talking about?" he asked, looking a little paranoid.

"Just plotting your death," Max replied. Then she laughed. "Kidding!"

"Funny." Britta cleared her throat and said to Novikov. "She can't skate."

"She's standing. That's promising."

"Is it?"

Holding her broken arm against her chest, Dee-Ann asked a question she hadn't ever asked before, "Am I gettin' old?"

"Nah." Dutch, one of the few wolverines they had in the Group, forced himself into a sitting position, his arms around his ribs, blood pouring from his cheek, the side of his neck, and out of his mouth. That last was especially troubling. "She was just *really* pissed."

"You said she'd be reasonable," Malone accused, her voice muffled because of her broken nose. The cat doctor kneeling in front of her, trying to put the pieces back.

"For a MacKilligan . . . that was reasonable. Especially when it comes to Charlie MacKilligan and her sisters."

Dee-Ann glared at Dr. Davis. "Hey. Cat! Mind helpin' me? My arm's broken."

Davis barely glanced at Dee. "It'll heal."

"I gotta fix this." Dutch forced himself to his big feet.

"You better do somethin' or we're gonna have to put 'em down."

Dutch, despite the pain it caused to his ribs, crouched in front of Dee-Ann and said, "If you go near my friends with anything but a job offer and a smile, the last thing you'll have to worry about, Smith, are the MacKilligans."

"You threatenin' me?"

"Yeah," he replied casually. "I'm a wolverine. We're crazy." He grinned. "And you haven't even met the rest of my family and friends. You and the Group . . . stay away from the MacKilligans. I'll handle them."

He stood, groaning all the way, before slowly stumbling out.

Once he was gone, Dee-Ann looked at Malone. "Boy's gonna get a rude awakening."

"Is he?" Malone asked. "Just one of those bitches kicked our ass. And we're the best. The best!" Her eyes crossed. "Ow."

"Yeah," Davis said, "I'd suggest you not yell, sweetie."

"Is no one going to help me?"

Davis motioned someone over and a nurse crouched in front of Dee-Ann.

"Can't even get a doctor?" Dee-Ann complained.

The nurse, carefully examining Dee-Ann's arm, warned, "Don't make me get my staple gun."

"We also have another problem," Malone said, holding up her phone. "Just got a text. BPC is heading this way."

Bear Preservation Council. The international protection agency of the bear nation.

"Why?" Dee-Ann asked.

"Just a shot in the dark, but Berg was the one who got that crazy bitch out of here before she could finish either of us off. Maybe he's asked BPC to protect her and her sisters."

"BPC *hates* honey badgers and none of them girls are mixed with bear. So, they ain't hybrids the BPC would protect."

"Maybe he's got something to barter with. Or a family member high up in the BPC. Either way, we better call Ric."

Her mate? "What for?"

Malone stared at her from two eyes already purple and swelling. "Because, unlike you and me, Ric has never fought bears at a wedding."

"That wasn't our fault."

Malone sighed. "Sweetie, no one cares."

"I am not callin' Ric. I'll handle this. We'll get those girls to the Group offices and take it from there."

"How? We couldn't even get one of them to listen to a man she's known for over a decade. Just a conversation without even moving to a new location. What makes you think you can do better?"

Using her good arm, Dee-Ann retrieved her phone. "We have a bunch of people sittin' around who get paid to do what I tell them to."

"Excuse me if that doesn't put me at ease."

Dee-Ann got to her feet. "Get me a sling," she told the nurse. "And you just sit there with your kitty-cat friend, tryin' to look pretty."

Malone grinned despite the blood on her face and replied, "Unlike you, Fido, I don't have to try."

Chapter Fourteen

Cringing, Britta reached down and grabbed the honey badger's arm. She pulled Max to her feet.

"We should stop this," Britta said again.

"I'm okay."

"We haven't even touched you yet," Britta explained. "You can't skate even when no one is on you."

"Looks that way, doesn't it?"

The Marauder skated over to them. Stopped. "What?" Novikov asked.

Britta decided to step in. "She's done."

"We've barely started."

"And yet she's bleeding profusely."

Novikov frowned. "You're not even on the team. You're a practice player."

Britta skated in front of Novikov. "Your point?"

"My point is this has nothing to do with you."

"She's a friend. I'm helping her."

Max tapped her on the arm. "We're friends?" she asked.

"Quiet, tiny female."

"She's fine," he insisted.

"She's not fine. She can't skate."

"She can learn."

Reece Lee Reed—a wolf from the Smith Pack—skated around the trio and asked, "So are we practicing today? Or just gabbin' like girlfriends?"

Without taking his eyes off Britta, Novikov swung out his fist, sending poor Reece flying across the ice and into the opposite wall.

"Woooooow," Max softly let out.

"We cannot teach her to skate well enough to play hockey at the pro level. It's not possible. It's not like it's full-*human* hockey with those tiny little guys playing. Not one sow among them. This is just setting her up to get killed."

"You're annoying me."

"I'm sorry my rational logic goes against your hysterical plans to use a woman like a mad dog."

"I'm actually a honey badger."

"Shut. Up," Britta snarled.

And Max did, for a little bit. But then, while Britta and Novikov bickered, she abruptly moved between the pair and held up one leg to Novikov. "Get this skate off."

Without realizing what he was doing—he was so busy trying to rationalize his crazy scheme—Novikov quickly untied the skate. Then he untied the other when Max lifted it up. Once she had the skates off, she started walking off the ice, pulling off first her hockey shirt, then her elbow pads. Then her shoulder pads. When she dropped the shoulder pads to the ice, the small female suddenly took off.

Catching the move, Britta and Novikov stopped arguing and turned to watch.

Max charged across the ice toward the stairs that led to the bleachers.

"Uh-oh," Britta muttered when she realized that Coop's big sister was standing in those bleachers, talking to some lion. Her back was to Max, so she had no idea the crazed honey badger was headed right for her.

Britta started to skate over there, hoping to stop what she saw as the possible slaughter of Coop's sister. True, Toni Jean-Louis Parker got on her last nerve, but Britta didn't want her hurt either.

But before she could even get down the entire length of the rink, Max suddenly turned toward the protective glass wall that kept the audience safe from the play. Using her claws, she scrambled up and over. Once she touched down, she ran on the bleachers toward where Toni was standing. When she was about four bleachers or so below her, the badger launched herself up and over . . . and into the lion.

Startled, Toni jumped back as Max slammed the lion to the ground and began pummeling the cat with brutal fists.

Understanding that Toni wasn't the focus of the badger's rage, Britta slowed down. Maybe this was Max's old boyfriend. There were a few men in Britta's past that she'd love to slap around like chew toys.

It took the lion a bit to understand what was going on. But once he did, he began fighting back. First, he tried to push Max off and then punched her back. But if Max felt his blows, you couldn't tell.

She didn't scream or growl or say anything. She simply kept punching. Then, finally, she grabbed the lion's big head, her fingers digging into his mane, and slammed it against the floor two, three, five times.

When he seemed dazed, Britta watched Max slip her hand into her hockey pants and whip out a blade that had Britta, Novikov, and Reed bolting toward her.

Max swung her arm up over her head. The point glinted in the bright stadium lights seconds before it arced down toward the lion's chest.

They would never reach him. All three of them were fast, but not as fast as Max and her blade.

But Britta had to try. It was in her nature.

She pushed her body as hard as she could, trying to reach—

Inches from the lion's chest, Max's wrist was caught. Held. ·

Charlie yanked her sister up and away, pulling her to the stairs and keeping her there with nothing more than a glare.

The pair stared at each other, neither speaking. A silent conversation only siblings would understand.

Finally, Max smirked and slipped the blade back into her hockey pants . . . like they had been made to hold blades or something.

Max walked up the stairs, and that's when Britta saw Berg and Dag. Neither of her brothers was a big fan of hockey. So she knew they hadn't come here for her. They were here for something else.

For the MacKilligan sisters.

Charlie didn't move until Max was near the exit doors. The She-hybrid started to follow her sister, not realizing that the lion male had gotten to his feet and now stood behind her, bloody and bruised. He didn't seem to notice her, though; his gaze firmly locked on little Stevie, who stood beside Coop and his younger brother Kyle. The trio standing near the exit doors Max was about to walk through. When Stevie turned away, head down, Britta gave a small snarl. Now *she* wanted to hit the guy.

And maybe it was the sound Britta made. Or perhaps it was just sisterly instinct.

Whatever it was, Charlie turned toward the lion, her fingers curled into a fist, and that fist swung out and slammed into the male's face. Britta cringed. She could hear his jaw breaking from where she stood.

"She has gotta helluva punch," Reed muttered beside Britta.

The lion went down with a pathetic whimper, hitting the floor he'd just picked himself up from.

Charlie crouched down and spoke to him. Her voice so low, Britta couldn't understand what she was saying. But she could guess.

She could guess that Charlie was making it clear the beating he'd gotten from Max was nothing compared to the one he'd get from Charlie if he came sniffing around her sister again.

Britta had said something similar to Dionne Kapowski back in the ninth grade after she'd broken Dag's heart.

"Think we can teach that one to skate?" Novikov asked.

Britta let out a sigh. "*No.*"

"I thought we talked about this, Max. No killing other shifters with a knife or a gun, in front of witnesses. You know that." Standing outside the practice ice rink, Charlie grabbed Max's hand and held it up. "Next time use your claws."

"No, no," Berg quickly stated, stepping between the sisters. "Unless someone is physically attacking you, no killing. How about that? I saw you charge him, Max. He didn't attack you first."

"But I warned him," Max said. "I told him if I ever saw him again, I would beat him until he was dead."

Berg nodded. "I understand the logic, but I'm not sure in a court of law that would be an acceptable excuse for murder. Unreasonable, I know. But what can you do?"

Toni came out of the rink and walked over to Charlie. "Sooooo . . . I shouldn't have him around my sisters, should I?"

"No."

"Got it. Thanks." Then Toni left to track down the rest of her siblings.

"I'm—" Stevie began but Charlie cut her off by placing her hand over her baby sister's entire face.

"Do not say you're sorry. *You* didn't do anything wrong." Charlie moved her hand to her sister's shoulder and pulled her close, kissing her on the forehead. "I'm sorry you had to see him again."

"And that wasn't your fault either. Besides, I'm an adult. I'm not a kid anymore. I should be able to handle seeing him. I should be . . ." Her eyes suddenly grew wide as she stared behind Max. "Oh, my God. Dutch!"

Max looked over her shoulder and immediately started laughing. "Dude, what the fuck happened to your face?"

Holding onto his ribs, he glared at Charlie. "Wanna tell them?"

Charlie rolled her eyes, pursed her lips; her left eyebrow raised, but she said nothing. Her expression made Berg grin. She could be such a rude badass when she wanted to be.

"Charlie did this to you?" Max asked. She looked him over. "Why? What did you do?"

"What did *I* do?"

"Charlie's not me or Stevie. If she beat the shit out of you, it's because she thought you deserved it." Max paused, then asked, "Is this about those people you work for?"

Charlie slapped her hand against Dutch's damaged chest and, ignoring his pained whimpering, she pushed him out of the way so that she stood right in front of Max.

"What do you know about the people he works for?"

"Not much. Every time he tried to tell me, I changed

the subject because I couldn't have *been* more bored by the topic. And I'm definitely not taking a job where I answer to anyone. I like being my own boss."

Stevie stepped up beside her sister and, staring straight at her, asked, "What is it you *do* exactly?"

"You didn't have to beat Dutch up," Max continued, her hand landing on her baby sister's shoulder. With one healthy push she sent the slight female about twenty feet away until she hit the wall beside the rink doors. "I wasn't going to take any job."

"Dumb ass, they didn't want to offer you a job; they wanted to kill us. They saw us in the Bronx."

"Actually," Dutch interrupted, moving close to the pair again, "*no*. That was not the plan."

"So you say."

"So I know. I really just wanted them to see Max's skill. But, not surprisingly, they're now interested in all of you."

"Interested in all of us to do what?" Stevie asked before she looked at Max and hissed at her . . . like a house cat. Entire face pulling back, small fangs erupting from her gums.

To be really honest, Berg couldn't understand what the Group would want with Stevie. Unless they had a science lab he was unaware of.

"It doesn't matter," Charlie told her sisters. "It's all a lie. They want us dead."

Dutch's hands curled into fists. "Do you really think," he growled, "that I'd let anything happen to you guys? That I'd be involved in any way with people that would harm you guys simply for being who you are?"

It was the silence Berg noticed first. It was never silent in the Sports Center unless it was closed for the night. But here it was early evening and the place was dead silent.

He looked up and saw that their small group was surrounded by armed men and women. Shifters of different species and breeds. Dee-Ann Smith, bloody and bruised, her arm in a sling, standing behind them.

And, as soon as Berg noticed it, the sisters, Dag, and Dutch noticed it, too.

Dutch raised one finger and offered, "I know this looks bad . . ."

Charlie laughed. She couldn't help it. "I know this looks bad?" Yes! This looked bad. Very bad.

But she wasn't exactly surprised.

Whether it was what Stevie shifted into, Max's ability to decimate with a blade, or her own skills with guns, the MacKilligan sisters were more often seen as a liability than an asset. Unless, of course, one needed a brilliant scientist to create designer meth—then people were happy to overlook Stevie's issues.

Berg gazed at her and Charlie wondered if he was worried that she'd lost her mind. Her ill-timed laughs often caused that sort of concern. But ludicrous things would always be funny to her.

Berg raised a brow and now she understood that he was asking her what she wanted to do. He was ready to back her play despite the risk to him and his brother.

Before Charlie could make a move, however, Dutch focused on the wolf whose ass Charlie had kicked.

"What are you doing, Dee-Ann?" he asked. His voice was calm but Charlie had known Dutch since the idiot was a kid. He was a "calm before the storm" kind of wolverine.

"I think we all need to go to our offices and have us a nice, civilized little talk. Y'all wouldn't mind that, would ya?"

Charlie cringed. That accent. Oy!

"That wasn't the deal, Dee-Ann," Dutch reminded her.

"I think you need to mind yours, little man." Mind his what?

"Dee—"

The wolf pushed past the others and stepped in front of Dutch. "Don't test me, boy."

That's when Max moved. All Charlie could see was a flash of steel and, a moment later, a blade was pressed against the wolf's throat . . . and another blade was pressed against Max's.

The wolf and the badger eyed each other, both appearing impressed by the other's knife skill while each was ready to kill at a moment's notice.

Charlie said, "Step back, Max."

Max looked at her over her shoulder.

"Now," Charlie pushed. Then she jerked her head toward the Dunn brothers.

"Wait," Berg said before Max could move. "You're worried about *me*?"

"I can't fight them and look out for you, too. Or your brother."

The two bears glanced at each other and back at Charlie.

"You're kidding, right?" Dag asked.

"No. You two are used to military rules of engagement. We're MacKilligans. The only rule for us is to leave no witnesses." Charlie moved her attention to the She-wolf. "We'll go with you," she said, shrugging. "It's just as easy to leave no witnesses there as here."

With Max's blade still pressed against her jugular, the wolf's eyes narrowed on Charlie.

Her expression told Charlie the She-wolf was remembering how the three MacKilligan sisters had wiped out that room full of armed men. What thin, compact little

Stevie shifted into. What Max had pulled. What Charlie had done just five minutes ago.

And now the She-wolf was debating whether she should have them all killed right here. Right now.

"Berg Dunn?" a female voice called out. "Is Berg Dunn here?"

Frowning, Berg looked over the heads of the shifters surrounding him and raised his hand. "Yes?"

"Hi! I'm Tanya. Bayla Ben-Zeev sent me."

Charlie had no idea who that was but she saw Berg's shoulders relax a little.

"Your request has been approved," Tanya went on. "Just let us know if you need anything else."

Tanya, busy looking at her phone, began to walk away but Berg's, "Uh . . . actually . . ." stopped her.

"Uh-huh?" she asked, glancing up at him.

He gestured to the armed shifters surrounding them.

"Oh. Right. Sorry." She motioned to someone Charlie couldn't see. "Over here, ladies."

Charlie heard a growl and realized it had come from the She-wolf. A growl of annoyance.

Laughing and chatting, a number of super tall—and some very wide—women surrounded the group gathered around Charlie and the others. These women were armed but none of them had pulled their weapons yet. Instead, they just kept talking among themselves.

Stevie whimpered and she suddenly crept behind Charlie and buried her head against her back. She was panting.

All these women . . . they weren't just shifters. They were bear sows. Something that seemed to concern even the She-wolf.

But she wasn't giving up the MacKilligans without a fight.

"Excuse me, Tanya," the She-wolf practically snarled,

"but these ladies are under our . . . um . . . protection at the moment. So we'd appreciate if y'all would—"

"Sorry!" another female voice called out, as a six-foot-nine female rushed up to the group. "So sorry. I had to get the kids from skating practice." And the kids were with her. Three of them. One in hockey gear, the other in a skating dress, and the third, so small she was hanging from her armed mother's big shoulders.

The mother sow happily looked around the group before cheerily asking, "So what are we doing?"

That's when the She-wolf's compatriots lowered their weapons and one of them said, "Sorry, Dee-Ann. We're out."

Not clear on how disgusted she should be, Charlie softly asked Berg, "Did your bear friends just use that woman's children as shields?"

"Not at all. I know Stephanie. She's a big multitasker. She brought her kids because she's trying to do a lot of things at once. The beauty is . . . the other breeds instinctively know not to startle or upset a sow with cubs. None of them would be left standing and they know it." He winked at her before focusing back on the action.

The She-wolf stepped away from Max, both eyeing each other as they slipped their blades back into the holsters.

Without another word, the She-wolf walked off; those who'd come with her long gone.

"Tell Bayla," Berg said to Tanya, "thank you."

"Sure, sure," she replied, texting into her phone. "Just keep in mind, they're only under bear protection for as long as they're living on Carthage Street. Understand?"

"I understand."

"Okay. Great. Uh . . . Bayla will inform the other organizations." Still focused on her phone, she started to walk back the way she'd come. "The others will get you to your car since that Smith is not to be trusted. Okay? Great. Thanks!"

She walked into one of the sows, who pushed her away with a good amount of force. But Tanya didn't stumble or let the shove tear her attention away from her phone. Apparently, nothing could do that.

Berg smiled down at Charlie, but then frowned. "Charlie . . . are you okay?"

"Yeah. Why?"

"You look like you're in pain."

"Oh." She motioned behind her. "Stevie's attached herself to my back. Her claws are digging."

"Should I pry her—"

"No." Charlie shook her head. "If you do that, there will be tearing and ripping. So let's just pretend that we're all normal. That this weird situation—my sister attached to me like a spider monkey and all of us surrounded by the players of the WNBA—is completely commonplace."

She clapped her hands together. "Okay. Let's go!"

The group started off toward the exit but Max grabbed Dutch's T-shirt and pulled him back.

"That was the group you were trying to get me to work for?"

"Yeah. Why?"

"Sweetie," she said, laughing. "Seriously?"

"So you scare them, Max. You scare everybody."

"That's not what I'm talking about. That She-wolf . . . ?"

"Dee-Ann Smith?"

"You ever watch those dog trainers on TV who handle pit bulls?"

"Sometimes."

"They always say don't put two male pit bulls together. Don't put two female pit bulls together." She gestured between where the She-wolf had been standing and herself. "Her and me? Two female pit bulls. You put us in the same cage, Dutch . . . one of us is not coming out."

Chapter Fifteen

Ric Van Holtz was no longer surprised when his wife entered a room covered in bruises. Dee-Ann performed a very dangerous job and that meant, over the years, he'd sewn up knife cuts, cleared out bullet holes, and packed more ice than he could think of on bruised and battered body parts.

Yet he wasn't sure how offering three women a job had led to . . . this.

Her arm in a sling, Dee-Ann sat in a chair across from his desk.

With a painful limp and a brutalized face, Cella Malone made her way across his office and sat in the other chair.

The pair sat and didn't say a word, which was unusual. Not for Dee-Ann. She'd never been chatty. But usually, when the pair came in together, they were already in the middle of an argument about something.

Yet here they were. Silent and severely damaged.

"Should I assume we don't have any new employees?" Ric guessed.

Dee-Ann slumped down in her chair. Cella began studying something on the corner of his pristine desk.

Normally he'd ask, "How bad is this?" but he already
kind of knew. It wasn't every day one received a call
from the head of the BPC herself to tell him, "Stay
away from the MacKilligan sisters. They're under *our*
protection now."

"Did the bears do this to you?" he finally asked.

But then something shocking happened. Dee-Ann
slumped farther down in her chair, her gaze moving
across the room until it focused on the wall behind his
head. Cella suddenly became fascinated with the metal
band of her watch.

Now Ric was completely confused. He took a moment to study their wounds and realized there was nothing bearlike about them. No giant claw marks across
their throats. No obvious signs of head trauma from
claws or teeth. They had all their eyes. And nothing had
been ripped off them. Like their arms or legs or lips.

No, when Ric *studied* the damage done to both
women, what he saw was a beating. A harsh, you-
pissed-me-off beating.

"Are you telling me the MacKilligan sisters did this
to you?"

Cella cleared her throat, fussed with her watch band
a little more, before finally admitting, "Well . . . one of
them."

Ric's entire body jerked a little before he attempted
to clarify that statement with, "While the other two
held you down?"

The pair exchanged glances and Dee-Ann suddenly
shot up out of her chair and began to pace. Cella, however, dropped back in hers and blew out a large breath.
But neither spoke.

"Oh," Ric said. "I see."

* * *

"First there's Katzenhaus Securities," the weasel explained to Charlie and her sisters while Berg drove them home. "They protect the cat nation."

"There's a *nation* of cats?" Max asked.

"So many of them are solitary or have small families. They don't have big Packs or Prides, so they have no choice but to consider themselves a nation of cats. And then there's the Group."

"That's who you betrayed us for?" Charlie asked Dutch and Berg smirked, glancing at his brother in the passenger seat to see the identical smirk on his triplet's face.

"Okay," the weasel sighed in frustration, "one more time, with feeling, for the backseat . . . I didn't betray you! I was trying to get you bitches a job. Well, at least one bitch. And that job has an employer-match IRA and artery care. You won't find those kinds of benefits in Silicon Valley.

"Anyway," he continued on, "the Group protects *all* shifters, including hybrids, honey badgers, and wolverines."

"Honey badgers don't want your help," Max reminded her friend.

"The Group is aware of how the badgers feel, but they've still decided to include you, as well as my kind, despite those feelings. And the bears have the BPC. Bear Preservation Council."

"That sounds like a nonprofit charity."

"I think I gave them money once," Stevie said.

"You?"

"One of my coworkers is a big supporter. She was selling cookies or something to raise money. And you know how much I love a good chocolate cookie. But she's not a bear."

"BPC *is* a charity. They're all about the preservation and protection of bears worldwide."

"And they're the ones protecting *us*." Charlie suddenly leaned forward, her head between Berg and Dunn. "And my question is why? Why are they protecting us? Are you paying them?"

"No."

"Because we're not bears. I'm barely badger. Stevie's more cat. Max is irritating."

"Hey!"

"So why are they helping us?"

"Because I asked them to." Berg shrugged when Charlie kept staring at him. "I don't know what you want me to say."

"The truth. Have you given them your lives? Do you now owe them a blood debt? Do you have to kill for this?"

"Wow," Dag finally said. "You are really not used to people helping you."

"Because they don't unless they're getting something out of it. And I don't want to put you guys at any more risk."

"You haven't put us at risk," Berg insisted.

"You've been shot and stabbed."

"Not because of you."

"No, because of my father. I have brought his curse into your life."

"Maybe the bear just likes being helpful," the weasel suggested, but Charlie immediately pointed a damning finger at him.

"I don't talk to traitors."

"He's not a traitor," Max said. "He's just a pathetic, *pathetic* friend."

"And thank *you* very much!"

"Well, dude, what did you expect? You had to know once Charlie found out, she was going to be pissed. You're just lucky she only beat the shit out of you." She paused, then added, "You're lucky you still have your arms."

"Ungrateful. You're all ungrateful!"

"You tried to *capture* them?"

"Well, if you're gonna make it sound wrong," Dee-Ann complained.

"Dee-Ann, these aren't wild lions we're bringing in from Africa. These are human beings who have clearly been trained to kill when necessary. Why didn't you just talk to them?"

"We tried that. They'd already run. And we can't let that one girl out in the world runnin' around."

"You mean Stevie MacKilligan? You're worried about her? She's managed to go twenty-four years without rampaging in downtown Tokyo. I don't see why you couldn't have trusted her to hold on for a little bit longer."

"Don't get that tone with me."

"Well, when you're being irrational—"

"Irrational? Me?"

"What do you call it when you try to round up shifters you, and I'm quoting, 'Don't much like the look of'?"

"You didn't see her once she shifted."

"I didn't have to. I've seen Novikov. He has tusks. Like a goddamn walrus."

"She's bigger than he is shifted. She's gotta be at least twenty feet long. Maybe longer. That ain't right. That's—"

"Please don't say unholy."

"—unholy."

Ric briefly placed his head on his desk. "I love how your Christianity only comes into play when you don't have a rational argument for something you don't like."

"I know what I know. And I know what I saw."

Ric sat up straight again, focused on the head coach of the hockey team he owned. "Cella? Your thoughts?"

"I'm wondering if the two oldest can learn how to ice skate." She nodded. "They've both got mighty fighting skills and the middle one . . . she's dumb enough to be an enforcer for Novikov."

Ric placed his elbows on his desk and rested his chin in the palms of his hands.

"So, let me sum up—we've got one vote for total annihilation and one vote for forcing them to join the hockey team. Am I correct?"

"Yes," both females replied.

As soon as Berg turned onto the street, Charlie knew something was wrong.

"Why are all those bears standing in front of our house?" Stevie asked, panic in her voice rising. *"They've come to eat us, haven't they?"*

"Oh, my God!" Max exploded. "No one wants to eat your scrawny ass!"

"I have a high metabolism!"

Charlie snapped her fingers. "Stop it," she ordered.

"How do you do that?" Berg asked when both younger sisters immediately fell silent.

"Years of training and abuse, my friend. Years of training and abuse."

"You're like one of those Russian bear trainers."

"Yeah. It's great until they suddenly turn on you on live TV and rip your scalp off."

"You do know we're *right* here?" Max asked.

"Shut up." Berg stopped the car and Charlie got out, ordering her sisters to, "Stay here until I—"

But Max was already out of the car and walking toward the crowd of bears. Stevie had also gotten out and had climbed the closest big tree, where she nonsensically hissed at no one in particular.

Sighing, Charlie closed the car door and rushed to catch up with Max.

"What's going on, Tiny?" she asked when she saw their landlord.

"Something is in your . . . what happened to your face?"

"It's nothing. I just got in a fight with a wolf and . . . what was the other one?"

"Siberian tiger," Max replied

"Yeah. Siberian tiger. Oh . . . and him." She pointed at Dutch.

Tiny stared at Dutch and back at Charlie several times before informing Dutch, "She kicked your ass."

"I am aware!" Dutch snapped. "Can we now get back to what you were saying?"

"Something is in your house." He screwed his nose up. "It tried to cloak its scent. I mostly smell bear spray but . . . who puts bear spray on just to sneak into our neighborhood? I can't imagine anyone that stupid."

But Charlie could.

She looked at Max, and her sister's expression told her she thought the same thing.

"Where's your dog, Berg?" Charlie asked.

Berg whistled, then called out, "Hey! Shithead!"

Charlie growled a little. "You need to give that dog a proper name."

"How is that not a proper name?"

"Don't—" She stopped herself. Now was not the time.

Berg's dog came around from the back of his house and took his time trotting across the street to reach the group.

Once he stood next to them, Charlie bent over slightly to stare in the dog's eyes—even on all fours, the dog was goddamn huge—and then whispered into his ear.

With a bark, he ran toward the house and leaped into an open window that Charlie knew for a fact she'd left closed and locked.

"What did you say to him?" Dag asked.

"That's between canines." She smirked. "You wouldn't understand."

They heard a huge yelp from the upstairs. Then came the sounds of things crashing, running, more crashing, some screaming, a few barks of pain that did not come from a dog until finally her father crashed through an upstairs window, rolled down the shingled roof, fell off the roof, and landed in such a way that should have killed even him. His neck hit the ground first, legs bent up and over his head.

And although the bears gasped in shock, neither Charlie nor her sister were remotely phased when Freddy MacKilligan unrolled himself and got to his feet, seemingly unharmed.

"You," the asshole said, pointing an accusing finger at Charlie, "sent that vicious bitch up to attack me."

Charlie answered that accusation by slamming her fist into her father's face. Max slammed her fist into the other side of his face.

That's when Stevie moved from the safety of the tree.

"No, no, *no!*" She scrambled down the trunk and ran over to the group. She had to grit her teeth to make her way through the crowd of bears, but she still did it. And she did it for *him*.

Stevie planted herself in front of the whining idiot who was busy trying to put his jaw back into place. Not surprisingly, this was not—and would not be— the last time someone punched their father's jaw out of its socket. It had happened so much in the past, he didn't even need a doctor anymore. He just had to jerk

it back into place. The bears cringed when they heard
the *snap!*

"Ungrateful bitches!" he barked when he could
speak again.

Max hissed in warning before unleashing the blade-
like claws on each hand. She wanted to bathe in their
father's blood when she took his life.

"What the fuck are you doing here?" Charlie demanded.

"A little respect please. I am your father."

"Fuck your respect, bitch. Do you know what you've
done? Do you even care?"

"See?" her father asked . . . no one. "This is why I
need a son. You're useless to me. You don't even know
what I've been through and already you are accusing me."

"I'm accusing you because you're an idiot. And you
don't have a son because your DNA is as fucked up and
as impotent as you are!"

It was a low blow. One meant to wound and hurt. But
no child wanted to hear that even the father they hated
had never wanted them. Simply because they were born
with vaginas.

The missile she'd sent over his bow found its mark;
her father grabbed her by her T-shirt, curling his fist in
the cotton material and yanking her close.

Charlie wasn't scared. She'd stopped fearing her father decades ago. Plus, she had Max there. Those claws
were flying back, readying a strike so brutal the bastard
would easily lose his arm. But before Max could finish
the attack, Berg Dunn's big body was between Charlie
and her father. Dag on the other side.

And the other bears . . . ? Ready to move. His neighbor grizzlies had allowed their grizzly humps to pop.
There were fangs. Claws. All unleashed and at the
ready.

Somewhere behind their father, Stevie whimpered and Charlie knew her poor sister was using all her energy not to run screaming from the street, the neighborhood, the state, the country . . .

With utter calm, his gaze lowered, Berg growled, "Sir, I'd strongly suggest you move your hand away from your daughter. And I mean do it *now*."

Stupid but always a survivor, Freddy MacKilligan examined what was happening around him with fresh eyes. Stevie and Max might be the smallest ones there, but they were also the least in danger. All those bear eyes were focused on Freddy. And he knew it.

He let Charlie's T-shirt go and raised both hands, palms out, showing those surrounding them that he was not a danger.

"Now if you'd step back a few feet," Berg suggested/ordered, his gaze still not on Freddy, although Charlie didn't know why.

When her father didn't move quickly enough, Berg's dog reappeared, putting his big body between Freddy and Berg, snarling and snapping until her father stumbled back.

Then the dog came around Berg, nosed Dag out of the way, and sat down beside Charlie.

She reached over and patted the dog's giant head.

"You need to go," Max said to their father. "Now."

"I need a place to stay."

He'd barely gotten that last word out before Max and Charlie started laughing. The big, loud, *mean* laugh they only used when it came to their father.

"Fuck you . . . go!" Charlie said, still laughing.

"You're just going to throw me out on the street?"

"Yes," Charlie and Max said together.

He went for the weak link. "Stevie?" He tried for a sad expression. "You wouldn't throw your daddy out, would you, sweetie?"

Stevie took off her backpack and dug her wallet out. She yanked out several bills. "Take this. Go."

"Stevie!"

"You need to go. I can only protect you for so long. And even I am running out of patience here."

"But I'm your father."

"I know," Stevie said on a sigh, tugging the straps of her pack back onto her shoulders. "I double-checked my DNA. You're definitely my father." And she couldn't have sounded more defeated by this information. "But all my therapists say that I need to cut myself off from toxic relationships. And Daddy . . . you're toxic."

"This is *their* fault, isn't it?" he said, his accusing glare lashing over at Charlie and Max. "They've turned you against me."

Stevie shook her head. "It's like you don't even try to listen to me."

"I'm not going to let these two evil females come between us. I love you, Stevie. You're my favorite daughter."

With a cringe, Stevie asked, "How is that a good thing to say? For *any* reason." She motioned him away when he tried to hug her. "Daddy, just go."

Fed up, Charlie pulled her cell phone from the back pocket of her jeans.

"What are you doing?" her father demanded.

"I'm calling Uncle Will and telling him exactly where you are at this very moment."

"You wouldn't dare."

Charlie briefly held up her phone. "I have an international plan. And he knows you stole his money."

"I did not!"

Charlie paused to let her shoulders slump in exhaustion. "Really, Dad? Seriously? Of course you stole that man's money. And I hope he cuts your throat for it."

Freddy slapped her phone out of her hands and Charlie had her gun pulled and pointed at her father's head, but before she could squeeze the trigger Berg had picked her up and moved her away. Dag had one hand around Freddy's throat, moving the much smaller badger back, ignoring his thrashing and curses.

"Get her out of here," Max said to Berg, tossing him Charlie's phone. "Otherwise, she's going to kill him."

He took Max's direction and carried Charlie toward his house. But unable to keep her rage in check, she screamed, *"This isn't over, old man! I will hunt you down and kill you! I'm calling Will and telling him exactly where you are! I will have all the MacKilligans looking for your dumb ass! And when he cuts your heart out, I will dine on it with a good Scottish ale, you worthless son of a bitch!"*

Berg carried her inside his house and into his living room. He placed her on the couch and sat down beside her, taking the gun from her. He cleared the chamber and dropped the mag, placing all the pieces on the coffee table in front of them.

Done with that, he relaxed back on the couch, his arm touching her shoulder.

For several long minutes they sat like that, in silence until he finally repeated, "With a good *Scottish* ale."

Charlie laughed and couldn't immediately stop. Only her father could make her this . . . psychotic. With every other part of her life she was reasonable, calm, rational. But with her idiot father . . .

She rested against Berg's big arm, tears of laughter streaming down her face.

"It was so specific," Berg noted, his laughter joining hers.

"I'm sorry," she said.

"For what?"

"Bringing my family's crazy to your nice, quiet street."

"Don't even worry about it. Bears love this shit."

She wiped her tears, gazed at him. "They do?"

"We say we hate it, but we're all so nosey . . ." He shrugged. "We really love watching when it's not happening to us. Sorry."

"As long as my father's crazy isn't putting you in a bad situation with your neighbors, I don't care if they watch every second of the drama. It's the least we can do for you guys. You know, entertain."

"You sure it's okay to leave Max with your dad? She looked about as ready to kill him as you did."

"She reacts to me. If I'm not there, she should be fine. Besides, she wouldn't upset Stevie by killing him. She knows she'd never hear the end of it. We could be in an old age home, Max on her death bed, and Stevie would find a way to bring that shit up and make her feel guilty all over again."

"Wow, she's good."

Charlie smiled, proud of her sisters for completely different reasons. "Stevie can learn anything from a book. And when it comes to psychiatry, she's read them all. So she wields guilt like a master swordsman. And Max isn't nearly as much of a psychopath as the social worker said because otherwise, she wouldn't feel any guilt at all. At least that's what I tell myself. All the time."

Grabbing her father by the back of the neck, Max dragged his dumb ass into the house, with Stevie leading the way because she was too afraid to remain behind with the bears.

Dag took it upon himself to get the neighbors to disperse, although Max heard a few of them ask if Charlie was upset enough to start baking again.

Once in the kitchen, Max shoved their father away. He spun around, fist pulled back. But all Max had to do was cock her head to the side and stare at him. He quickly changed his approach.

He lowered his fist, smiled, and opened his arms wide. "Honey!"

She held up her hand. "Don't even bother. Just get your shit and go."

"I have nowhere to go. They're out to kill me."

"Because you stole from your own brother."

"That's not—"

"*Dad.*"

"It was an accident."

Max glanced over at Stevie, but her little sister just sadly shook her head before dropping into one of the kitchen chairs.

"Okay, well, not an accident," her father corrected. "But—"

"Where's the money, Dad?" When her father did nothing but stare at her, Max guessed, "Someone stole it from you, didn't they?"

"It's not my fault!" he cried. It was the man's refrain. According to their aunt, he'd been using it since he could talk. It was his first full sentence. "But Will is blaming me anyway. He's always been out to get me. You have to help me."

"No," Stevie said before Max could. "No, Daddy, we don't."

"You'd throw me back out there?" he cried, arm sweeping wide.

"We don't have to," Stevie reasoned. "The bears will do it for us."

She looked behind Freddy, and Max moved so she could see as well. Dag stood outside the open kitchen window, brown eyes watching their father closely.

"Everything all right?" the bear asked. "You guys need anything?"

"Not yet, Dag," Max said. "But don't go anywhere."

Freddy's head dropped, realizing he couldn't manipulate his way into a place to stay. Not even with Stevie.

"Fine," he said. "I'll go. But do you think I can get a little more—"

"Cash?" Max asked, and when her father simply gazed at her, she finally snapped. "How the fuck do you steal over a hundred million and *still have no goddamn money*?"

Chapter Sixteen

Charlie stood. "I better go back over there."

"That sounds like a really bad idea to me."

She nodded. "It is. I can't lie, but—"

Berg gripped her arm and she thought he was about to pull her back onto the couch, but he stood and led her to his kitchen. He stopped and grabbed two beers from the refrigerator, then continued to lead her out the back door.

He stopped on the porch, closing the screen door and dropping to the top step. Still holding onto her arm, he guided Charlie until she sat on the step beneath him. He handed her a beer and held onto his own.

Charlie honestly didn't know what she'd expected after that, but she was totally unprepared for what he did do.

Which was absolutely nothing.

She kept waiting for something. One of those "dude moves" as Max called them. A stroke on the back of her neck. A kiss to her cheek. A massage for her shoulders. But nope. He just drank his beer. Quietly.

Charlie became so anxious, she finally asked, "What are you doing?"

"Me? Nothing."

"Yeah. Why are you doing nothing?"

"Do you want me to do something?"

"No."

"Then . . . okay."

"I guess I'm just used to guys making the move."

"What guys?"

"Just guys."

"Full-human guys?"

Charlie sipped her beer. "Yeah. Mostly."

"Well, most shifter guys aren't making the move."

"Why not?"

"We like our faces attached to us rather than on the floor . . . in front of us."

"You think I'd hurt you?"

"Not on purpose. My sister didn't mean to nearly tear her high school boyfriend's arm off when he snuck up behind her and tried to cover her eyes. That was an uncomfortable conversation for my dad with the kid's parents."

"So you're just cautious . . . in general."

"Yes. I don't want my arms ripped off."

Charlie chuckled a little. "I don't think I *could* tear those arms off."

"I've seen you in a fight. Yes, you could."

Britta came around the side of the house carrying a big duffle bag and her hockey stick, several other players with her.

"What's going on?" she asked. "People are milling. I know there's drama afoot when people are milling."

"It's not a big thing," Berg said, attempting to protect Charlie from what he couldn't. The walking embarrassment that was her old man. "Just go to practice."

Charlie frowned. "I thought you guys *were* at practice."

"That was practice with Novikov. Then we come

here, get a little snack, and go to the rink a couple of streets over so there's no sobbing."

"I couldn't help it!" one of the players announced, pacing away. *"He was really mean to me."*

"See?" Britta asked. "Now what's going on here?"

"Britta."

"My father's here," Charlie announced, refusing to pretend anything when it came to Freddy MacKilligan. "Being an asshole!"

"Why did he come here?" Britta asked. "Didn't he steal, like, a hundred mil from his own brother?"

"Britta!"

"What, Berg? Is that a secret?"

"It's nothing to be announced."

Charlie shrugged. "Announce away."

Charlie began stretching out her neck, tensing up at the thought of another confrontation with the idiot.

"I should go over there," she said again, but even she knew there was no real commitment behind the statement.

"He's still over there?" Britta demanded.

"My sisters will try to get rid of him, but Stevie's too nice and I don't want to see Max in prison, so . . ."

Britta dropped her bag and sticks. "Come on, guys," she said to the other players before marching off.

Charlie jumped up to block the sow, but Berg placed his hand against her hip and advised, "You'll never stop her."

"But she doesn't have to—"

"It's not about 'have to' for Britta. It's about her infinite will."

Getting blindingly frustrated by her father, Stevie was relieved when she heard the doorbell. She rushed to the front door and yanked it open.

"Yes?" she asked the young man standing there.

He sighed, shook his head. "You *still* don't remember me?"

"I should?"

"You just saw me a few hours ago. I'm Cooper." When she continued to silently stare, he added, "Mr. Needy?"

"Oh! Kyle's brother." His gaze rolled up and he took several deep breaths. "Do you need something?" she pushed. "Or do you just want my autograph?"

"At first I felt bad about this, but now . . ."

Gazing directly at her, he reached his arm out and yanked something over.

Kyle.

"Do you mind if he stays with you for a while?"

"Well—"

"Great!" Kyle's brother shoved Kyle into the house, ignoring the fact that his brother tripped and nearly fell to the floor before he got control of his long legs. "I think the family needs a break from him, and you seemed like a better option than the Motel 6 near La-Guardia."

Disgusted, Stevie shook her head and chastised, "I don't believe you people. Kyle Jean-Louis Parker is a *genius*. And as a fellow genius, I think all of you should treat him much better than you—"

"I can't!" the overrated pianist yelled out dramatically before stomping back to his waiting limo. "I can't!" he screamed again before getting in and disappearing down the street.

"Wow," Stevie said to poor Kyle as she started to close the door. "Your brother has issues. Has he had any psychological tests?"

"Of course not. Although I've highly recommended them."

Stevie nearly had the front door closed when something pushed it open again.

"Hey, Stevie."

It was casually said. But it was casually said by a bear standing with several other bears and some dogs and cats.

Without thinking, only instinct, Stevie arched her back and jumped back about ten feet. Then she scrambled over a wingback chair and pressed her body into the corner.

Britta gawked at her before stating, "I don't know what the hell that was. But we'll not discuss it. I'm here for your father."

Stevie gasped. "Are you going to eat him?"

Britta started to answer, stopped, headed into the house instead; her friends followed behind her.

"Outstanding specimens," Kyle noted. "Think they'll sit for me?"

"Aren't you worried they'll eat you?"

"No."

"Lucky."

Before Stevie could warn her father about the bears, there was another knock at her front door and a, "Hello?"

"Yes?" she called out, afraid to move.

The Asian male slowly walked inside, looking around.

"What are you doing here?" Kyle asked the man with contempt.

The male grinned when he saw Kyle. "Your sister ordered me here. I'm to stay by your side as long as you're away from your family. In case anyone tries to kill you. Since you're just so important."

"I *am* important, peasant."

"Keep calling people peasants, you probably will get killed."

"Whatever. I'm hungry." Kyle sniffed the air, and headed toward the kitchen.

"Hi," the male said, giving Stevie a little wave. "Sorry about this."

"Kyle should be protected. His brain is very important."

"If you say so."

Stevie came around the chair and walked over to the man, holding out her hand. "Stevie MacKilligan."

"Shen Li. We met. At Livy's apartment? When your sister tried to kill her cousin and the grizzly."

"Oh. I do think I remember you."

Pulling her hand away, she asked, "Are you a bear?"

"Yes. Giant panda."

"You know"—she put her hand to her chest—"I'm not afraid of you at all."

"You shouldn't be." He grinned. "I'm very nice."

"And so cute!" She grabbed his cheeks with both hands and twisted. "Like a big stuffed toy!"

"Uh . . ."

"Hey," Max said from behind her, "Dad's getting in an argument with some bears. I'm really hoping they kick his—Stevie! What the fuck are you doing?"

"Isn't he *cute*?" Stevie demanded, her fingers still on Shen's face. But then her sister was next to her, slapping her hands down.

Max didn't know what her idiot sister was thinking! Not only did the giant panda look confused and irritated, but he was armed. A holstered Sig Sauer attached to his jeans, just barely covered by a light jacket.

He wasn't as big as the grizzlies and cats that had just stormed into their house. Only six feet or so, but his shoulders were wide as hell and there was nothing but muscles under that black T-shirt and jeans. And unlike Max herself, he didn't dye his black hair one color, instead letting those black stripes cut through his thick, white strands with pride. Sharp cheekbones accented the black eyes currently staring at Stevie.

"But look at him!" Stevie practically squealed. "He's just so damn adorable!"

Max didn't know what her sister was looking at. The man *she* saw was probably military trained and would have no qualms about hurting people that got too close to those he was trying to protect. But Stevie was acting like he was one of those giant stuffed pandas at the front of a big toy store.

Grabbing her sister's hands away from the poor guy's face, she yanked her across the room. She was about to start yelling when Britta came stomping through the house. She had their father caught by his hair, bending him over at the waist so he couldn't put up a fight. She kept him in front of her, pushing him while her friends backed her up by merely being there.

"Your daughter wants you out, so you're out," Britta said to him calmly. "And if you come back, we'll rip the skin from your bones."

She led him out of the house, and her friends disappeared with her. The door slammed shut and Max let out a sigh. She didn't know how Charlie did this on a daily basis. Maintain order. Honestly, it would have been easier just to make a run for it or lay waste to everyone in a five-mile radius. Illegal but easier.

Oh, and . . . yeah . . . *morally* wrong.

Moving away from Max and Stevie, the panda said, "I'll be staying here to keep an eye on the kid. Hope you guys don't mind."

"Wait . . . that kid's staying?"

"Just for the night, I'm sure. There was some family drama apparently."

Well, Max completely understood that.

"He's my friend," Stevie said, yanking her arms away from Max. "Kyle can stay for as long as he wants."

"How old is that kid?"

"Seventeen."

Max raised an eyebrow and Stevie gasped. "We're not *that* kind of friends!"

"You better not be. I'm sure Charlie wouldn't like that one bit." She started to return to the kitchen, but she realized that Stevie was heading toward the unsuspecting panda, who had turned away as he put his bag down on the couch.

Terrified at what she might do next, Max rushed over and grabbed her sister around the waist. She lifted her up and carried her out of the living room and into the kitchen down the hall.

Max dropped her and spun Stevie around to face her. "I'm going to say this once: Stay away from the panda."

Stevie clapped her hands together and crowed, *"But he's just so cute!"*

About fifteen minutes later, Britta returned, looking quite proud of herself.

"All done."

"Thanks."

"And just so you can relax, I paid three of the Mueller boys down the street to drive him to Philly. They'll drop him in the middle of the Southside; he'll have to fend for himself there."

Shocked laughter exploded out of Charlie. "You . . ." She gave herself a moment to regain control. "You didn't have to do that."

"I spent two minutes with that man. Trust me . . . it was a pleasure."

She retrieved her bag and sticks. "You should stay for a while. I'll bring dinner back."

"I don't want to put you guys out."

"You're not. But I know from personal experience,

sometimes you need a break from your family. Even the ones you love. Besides, some smart-ass kid is at your house now. You probably don't want to go back tonight."

"What smart-ass kid?"

"No idea, but he said he was a genius." She rolled her eyes. "What. Ever."

"Name's Kyle," one of the other players volunteered.

"Oh." Charlie nodded. "Yeah. He actually is a genius. But from what my sister tells me, he is a lot of work."

"See? You don't want to go home. Stay here. Relax. Watch TV. I'll bring dinner back." She motioned to the players. "Come on, bitches."

Charlie waited until they were all gone before informing Berg, "I love your sister."

"She has a way. Speaking of which, you don't have to stay if you don't want to."

Looking over her shoulder, she asked the bear, "And if I want to stay?"

"Then you are more than welcome."

"I don't want to put you guys out, though."

"You won't."

The screen door opened and closed and Dag stood on the porch, scratching his head and staring at a sheet of paper.

"Where have you been?" his brother asked.

"Taking orders."

"Who was giving you orders?"

"Uh . . . everybody." He took a step forward, still staring at the paper. "Charlie, if you are feeling moody and need to bake, there are, um, requests here."

"Requests?"

"Yes. Mrs. Franklin would like your cinnamon rolls. Mr. Gronbech would like your honey cake with white icing. But Tiny wants your honey-pineapple cake." Poor

Dag scratched his head in frustration. "I can't read my handwriting here."

"Dag," she said, patting his leg. "It's okay. I'm not in the mood to bake. I've had a long day. I just want to do . . . nothing."

"Oh, okay. Good." Letting out a relieved breath, he leaned against the railing surrounding most of the porch and stayed there.

Charlie didn't really think about it until Berg cleared his throat.

"What?" Dag asked his brother.

"Go away."

Dag's gaze slowly bounced between Berg and Charlie. "Oh!" he finally said, grinning. "Right. Got stuff to do." He went back into the house.

"Yeah," Berg muttered, "lots to do. Like look at porn online."

"Don't judge. Sometimes one needs to check out bad homemade porn to feel alive."

"Big porn fan, are you?"

"Not particularly. Except the Japanese animation stuff."

"Seriously?" Berg asked, laughing.

"Yeah. If I watch that stuff then I'm not worrying 'what do her parents think?' Why don't I worry? Because the girl getting hardcore fucked while still managing to keep her nurse's hat on—an actual video by the way—is just animation."

"That's amazing logic."

"Isn't it, though?"

As promised, Britta brought dinner back but, thankfully, not her fellow players. Those she'd sent off, so it was just the four of them.

Charlie had checked in on her sisters by texting them

and the reply she got back must have been satisfactory because she didn't run over there to see what might be happening. Instead, she relaxed and hung out. She read the newspaper while Berg fought with his idiot brother about what to watch on TV.

After dinner, she read the current events magazines Britta kept on the coffee table so they looked like they were thoughtful bears while Berg continued to fight with his idiot brother as well as now his obnoxious sister about what to watch on TV.

The fact that the three of them still disagreed and fought like they used to when they were cubs didn't seem to bother Charlie, and Berg appreciated that. Then again, considering what went on around her at any given time, dealing with the Dunn triplets must have been like a vacation in comparison.

Around midnight, Dag went out after getting a text from a She-cat a few streets over and Britta took her laptop—and whoever she was direct messaging—up to her room. When the door closed behind her, Berg knew she was in for the night.

That left him and Charlie sitting on opposite ends of the couch.

He was just about to move over to be closer to her when the dog suddenly sauntered into the room, climbed over the coffee table, and into the middle of the couch. He stretched out fully so that his back feet nearly touched Berg's leg. His big head dropped into Charlie's lap and she immediately began petting him while still reading her magazine.

Berg wouldn't have been so pissed, though, if his dog hadn't looked over at him and given what Berg could only guess was a dog smile. Or leer. The bastard was mocking him!

Eventually, Charlie tossed the magazine aside and walked out. He heard the door to the first-floor bathroom close and that's when Berg tapped the dog on his hind leg and motioned to the floor.

Ignored, Berg tapped the dog again and added, "Get down."

Now the animal growled at him.

Fed up, Berg went ahead and pushed the dog off the couch. He hit the floor with a heavy thud, but he got up in seconds, turned, and threw himself at Berg.

The two wrestled on the couch until they rolled off and slammed to the floor, their big bodies shoving the coffee table halfway across the room.

"Ahem."

Berg cringed and glared down at the dog he'd finally pinned to the ground. And there went that rude, toothy dog grin again.

"If you're going to wrestle him on the floor," Charlie said, standing over them, "you should really name him."

"He started it. He wouldn't move."

"He's a two-hundred-pound dog. He doesn't *have* to move."

Getting to his feet, Berg faced Charlie. "You're not leaving, are you?"

"I have a meeting tomorrow with my bitchy aunt. For tea." She stuck her tongue out. "I hate tea. Then again, I hate my aunt." She rubbed her forehead. "But I know Stevie's going to be up all night with Kyle . . . talking about . . . genius shit."

"You can stay here for the night," Berg offered and without moving anything else, Charlie lifted her left eyebrow. "On . . . on the couch. Appropriately."

"You don't mind?"

"Not at all. Actually, I'll take the couch and you can take my—"

"I'm not taking your bed," she cut in. "Although I appreciate the offer."

"Actually," Berg said, trying hard not to outwardly

cringe, "we have extra bedrooms, so you can have one of those."

Charlie pushed a loose curl off her forehead before asking with a smile, "You offered me the couch and *your* bed before one of your extra bedrooms?"

He cleared his throat. "I forgot we had them."

"You forgot you had extra bedrooms? I didn't know I was so distracting."

"Well, ya are," he snapped back, embarrassed.

Laughing, she said, "I'll take the couch."

He frowned. No longer embarrassed but confused. "Why? You're more than welcome to—"

"Oh, I know." She placed her hand on his forearm and her fingers were warm and dry and he liked how they felt against his flesh. "But if someone breaks in, I can shoot them . . . legally."

"You're talking about your dad, aren't you?"

"When am I *not* talking about my dad?" she asked, clearly disgusted. "But, honestly, I wouldn't put it past him to drag his ass back here and start some shit. And I'd like to ensure he's greeted properly. So the couch is good."

With a shrug, Berg went to get Charlie a new tooth-brush and toothpaste. While she returned to the bath-room, he went upstairs and grabbed extra pillows and blankets from the closet. He returned to the living room and proceeded to make up her "bed."

"Blankets?" she asked when she walked back in. "It's, like, 80 degrees outside."

"Trust me. In about an hour, Britta will turn the air up. She's a grizzly and hates the heat."

"Okay," Charlie said on a chuckle.

Berg finished and motioned to the couch. "Madam."

"Thank you. For everything. I really mean it."

"Any time."

Charlie stepped close and her arms slipped around

his chest. She was hugging him and Berg hugged her back, holding her tight against his body. And for once—for him—it wasn't an awkward thing because of height differences and not knowing fully what kind of relationship he really had with Charlie. There was no fumbling. No leaning down or stretching up. It was the most comfortable hug Berg had ever experienced with a woman who wasn't a close relative. And to his bearlike way of thinking, it was because Charlie fit perfectly into his life.

She just didn't know it yet.

Charlie pulled away first, giving him a wink and smile before dropping onto his couch. She kicked off her sneakers and stretched out, letting out a big yawn as she relaxed into the cushions.

With a nod, Berg forced himself to walk away from her, leaving Charlie alone on that couch. He turned off all the other lights in the living room, letting her handle the one by her head. He was about to go down the hallway to the stairs when he heard Charlie giggle a little.

He looked back and saw that his stupid dog had gotten on the couch with her. He was by her feet now, letting her rest them on his big head.

"Psst." Berg motioned to the dog to come, but he wouldn't move. *"Psssst."*

"He's not bothering me," Charlie said, her back to the room. "You can leave him."

But Berg didn't want to leave the bastard! He wanted to be the one that Charlie was putting her feet on. He wanted to be curled up with her on the couch for the night.

Who knew he'd ever see that damn dog as a romantic rival? But here they were!

"Okay, well . . . if he gets on your nerves, feel free to *kick him off*," he spit out the last part between clenched teeth, his gaze locked with the dog's.

"Will do. 'Night, Berg."

" 'Night, Charlie."

Berg made his way up to his room, sat on his bed, and stared at absolutely nothing until his sister walked in. She wore one of the team hockey shirts, which reached down to her knees.

Smirking, she said, "You dumbass. You left her with the *dog*?"

Groaning, Berg fell back onto his bed, his sister's laughter giving him a headache.

Chapter Seventeen

They suddenly decided to move her in the middle of the night. Men in body armor and shielded helmets, so that she couldn't see their faces.

They burst into her cell but seemed thrown off to find her awake and sitting on her bed, feet on the floor, elbows on her knees, and hands clasped in front of her. She'd been waiting and they knew it.

The group paused for a brief second before moving on. Someone grabbed her by the back of the neck and shoved her to the ground on her face. They pinned her there before cuffing her arms and legs and then adding the chains. They blindfolded her and put a leather bit in her mouth to keep her from biting.

Once done, they lifted her up and proceeded to carry her out. There were no catcalls from other cells. No sounds at all. But she could hear the increased heartbeats. The panicked breathing. The scent of fear. All those men around her waiting for her to do something.

Yes. She was in the men's prison. A decision made after the third body was found. They couldn't pin the murders on her, but they wanted to. Of course, it didn't help that the bodies stopped dropping in the women's cells once she was gone.

Mairi MacKilligan was not taken to another part of the prison as she expected. The "crazy ward" they all quietly called it, where they put the worst of the worst. They had put her there once before . . . but it had not ended well. She'd dig holes through the concrete and into the other cells around hers, and then she'd have some fun. Get back to her cell, hide the hole, and wait until the guards came by to do a cell check. She'd smile when she'd hear the gasps of shock. Or the screaming. She loved when there was screaming.

They'd put her back in the regular cells not because they had no evidence she'd done anything—they never had evidence—but because she and the "gov" had come to an agreement. She'd stop killing and he'd let her stay in the regular cells. She'd agreed . . . with a smile. He'd cried after she'd left his office. She didn't know why. She'd kept her promise. She hadn't killed anyone. Why bother with all the mess when she could get them to do the job to themselves?

But no. They didn't take her anywhere else in the prison. Instead, they carried her out altogether and threw her into the back of what she suspected was a van.

Men came in with her, the back door closed, the engine started, and they were moving.

No one spoke around her. They'd learned not to. She remembered voices. Remembered conversations. And then she used them against those people just because she could. She didn't need a reason. She had always bored easy.

They drove for hours. She could sense the sun had come up when the van finally stopped. The doors were opened, several gloved hands picked her up . . . and threw her out of the van.

The doors quickly closed and she heard the squeal of tires as they drove off and left her. Not that it mattered. She could get out of her chains anytime she wanted. She'd just never bothered. Where was the fun in that?

She gave herself five minutes as she was always big on testing her skills. The last chain hit the ground and she'd reached up to take off her blindfold when she heard, "That was impressive."

Mairi smiled around her bit and dropped the blindfold. She blinked against the light until she could see the men standing in front of her. American men, heavily armed. Except for the one she guessed was the leader. He was older, wore jeans and a thick blue sweater, but still had that military haircut. That military bearing.

"You going to kill me here . . . um . . . ?" she asked.

"John Mitchell. And that would really piss off my clients. They're very interested in meeting you."

"Meeting me for what?"

He crouched down in front of her and said, "They need your help. Your help to hurt people. They've heard you're good at that."

"Very good."

"And a chance to get even with your family. To get even with the ones who left you to rot in prison."

Mairi felt it snake up her back. Like an electric current. Making her fingers tingle and her nipples hard. The excitement. How she felt when she stole jewels or broke a bloke's arm or cut someone's throat in the dark . . . when they never knew she was even in the room.

She got to her feet, cracked her neck. And waited.

The man motioned toward their vehicle and Mairi followed . . . smiling.

Chapter Eighteen

Berg walked out of the second-floor bathroom, freshly showered and shaved, a towel around his waist.

He was heading to his bedroom when he caught sight of his sister and brother staring into one of their extra bedrooms.

Berg walked over to them and looked into the bedroom. To his surprise, Charlie sat cross-legged on the mattress, her wrists resting on her knees, her eyes closed. He sensed she'd slept on the couch, but was using the bed to meditate. A strange decision, but she was doing it all quietly. Unobtrusively.

So what were his siblings doing? Why were they watching her like her head was spinning around?

He grabbed both by the back of their T-shirts and dragged them down the hall to his bedroom, shoving them inside.

"What are you doing?" he asked in a whisper.

"The question," Britta said, "is what is *she* doing?"

"She's meditating."

"Why?" his siblings asked.

"Get out," he ordered. "And leave her alone."

They left without a word, and Berg dried off and put his clothes on. He stuffed his wallet into his back pocket and walked out of his room. He was about to head to the stairs but couldn't help but go back to the bedroom and check on Charlie. She was still there, still meditating. But now that stupid dog had joined her. Big head resting against her hip, his wagging tail slapping against the bed.

He spotted Berg and leered at him again. Berg pointed at the dog, then used the same finger to draw a line across his throat.

It was childish, but he couldn't help it. Damn dog.

Shaking off his annoyance, he headed downstairs and went into the living room. That's where he found Stevie. She looked much calmer than she had the day before. Clearly her meds had kicked in, and Berg was surprised at how relieved that made him.

"Hi, Stevie. What's up?"

"Is Charlie still here?"

"Yes. She's upstairs—"

"Meditating," his sister answered for him, coming into the room. "Does she do that sort of thing often?" His sister made it sound like they'd caught Charlie smoking meth. It was meditating, for God's sake!

"She's meditating?" Stevie's smile was wide and bright. Very adorable. "I'm so happy! I gave her books on that a few years back but didn't know she was actually using the techniques."

"Why does a shifter need to meditate?" Britta asked.

"It's to help with her GAD."

Britta gripped Berg's forearm.

"Ow!"

"What is *that*?" his sister demanded, gawking at Stevie. "Is that something we can catch? Is my brother going to die?"

"It just means general anxiety disorder. My sister has had it for years. Probably since after our mom died." Stevie pressed her hand to her upper chest as if she were in front of an audience explaining the different kinds of disorders in the world. "I have panic personality disorder, which has elements of anxiety. But Charlie—not surprisingly—has anxiety disorder with some bouts of depression. The meds she takes help but one doctor told her, when she was about fifteen, that if she didn't get control of her anxiety, she'd have a hole in her gut the size of Texas. I don't want my big sister to have an ulcer, so we've been working on a way for her to manage her anxiety. She doesn't need meds like mine, though. Her issues are much less . . . complicated."

She held up a small plastic container with seven compartments. Each compartment had a letter representing the day of the week on it. "That's why I brought her meds over. They may not be as complicated as mine, but she can't just not take them. Especially the one for anxiety and the beta-blocker. The beta-blocker is to help with her racing heart issues."

She nodded. "I'll put them in the kitchen next to a glass of water. Along with her contacts, which just came in. That way she doesn't have to worry about her glasses so much. Just make sure she takes her pills before she goes out, please."

Stevie moved past them and out into the hall. She walked off, but a few seconds later, came back and went the other way. A minute after that, she ran back the other way.

"I found it!" she called out from the kitchen. "No need to help. I found it."

"Are they all on meds?" Britta asked, staring at the empty hallway.

"I'm not," Max said from behind them.

Berg and Britta turned to face Charlie's middle sister and, together, brother and sister screamed and stepped away from her.

"Dear God, Max! What happened to your face?"
Berg hysterically asked.

She shrugged, the quills in her face wiggling when she did. "A porcupine attacked me. Flung its quills at me." She glanced around, seemingly not bothered by the many—*many*—quills hanging from her face like some weird, horrifying mask. "Charlie around?"

"She's meditating."

"Oh. I'll wait. She knows how to get these out." She stood there for a moment before announcing, "I'm going into the kitchen for water . . . do you have straws?"

"In the cabinets somewhere."

"I'll find them."

She left the room and Berg and Britta counted down, "Three, two, one—"

"Max!" Stevie exploded from the kitchen. *"What the fuck?"*

"I was attacked. It flung its quills at me. It's not my fault."

Stevie appeared outside the living room, finger pointing at what they assumed was her sister. "You are such a liar, Max MacKilligan. Porcupines don't *fling* their quills. They back up into whatever is attacking them. That means your face was down near its ass when it got you! What is wrong with you? Who attacks a porcupine?"

"If you're going to make a big deal about it," Max said as she walked back into the living room, "I'll just leave."

Without meaning to, both Berg and Britta yelped and jumped away from her again. The sight of her face was just that horrifying.

"Sorry," Berg said when Max rolled her eyes. "But your face. It's freaking us the fuck out."

"Don't apologize to her," Stevie said. "She deserves what she got. Leave the porcupines alone, Max!"

"Are you done lecturing me, *Mom*?"

Eyes narrowing, Stevie gripped her sister's shoulder with one hand and took hold of about six quills with the other. Then she *yanked*.

Max howled in pain and jerked back. *"You bitch!"*

She pushed past Stevie and disappeared down the hallway, calling out, *"Charlie!"*

Stevie grinned, the quills—bloody at the tips—still gripped in her hand. Then they all jumped yet again when they heard Dag's startled roar of surprise.

A few seconds later, he stumbled into the living room. *"What the fuck was in her face?"*

It wasn't that Charlie had really learned to calm her brain when she meditated, but she appreciated having a few minutes to herself to just sit. True, her brain was still sifting through the thousands of things she had to do every day, but it was a start. And so far she'd staved off any ulcer-like pain in her stomach—an improvement since she was fifteen and a doctor wondered what she was doing to herself to cause such problems—so she considered that a plus.

Her ridiculously enhanced hearing—both badger and wolf hearing being what it was—told her as soon as her sisters made an appearance at the Dunn house. She was also not surprised when she heard chatter, screams of horror, arguing and, eventually, more screams of horror. The MacKilligan sisters didn't know how *not* to make an impression.

Still, she'd have preferred not to open her eyes and see Max standing in front of her with her entire face covered in porcupine quills.

"You're the only human being I know who *purposely* fucks with porcupines."

Max shrugged, the move making the quills wiggle. "He was under the beehive I was trying to get to."

"You're supposed to leave the beehives alone. We had this discussion."

"Well, if it makes you feel better, I didn't get anything."

"Yes," Charlie replied flatly. "I do so enjoy seeing my little sister used as a goddamn pin cushion." She pointed. "Bathroom. Now."

It took a lot of time to carefully extract the quills from Max's face. They had a way of locking themselves under the flesh and she had to cut off the top part first to let out the air and then slip the quill out. It was the only way she knew of to remove them so as not to damage Max's face more than it already was. The first time it had happened, when they were with the Pack, Charlie had found Max before any of the She-wolves. Before the She-wolves could discover what had happened, Charlie had ripped out most of the quills, causing damage to her sister's face and, unfortunately, allowing a few quill tips to travel deep into the flesh. The She-wolves ended up taking Max to the doctor to get out the rest. It had not been pretty.

After that, though, Charlie had taken it upon herself to find a local vet and ask him the best way to remove quills.

"From your dog?" he'd asked.

"Uh . . . sure. The dog. The *dog* will have quills in his or her face."

But no. Charlie had never met a dog that ended up in that situation. She knew it happened sometimes, but she'd never seen it. Her sister however . . .

After Charlie got all the quills out, she wiped Max's face down with an antiseptic and told her not to pick at it when it started to scab. If she did everything right, she should be completely healed in about forty-eight hours.

"What happened with Dad after I left?" Charlie asked, scrubbing her soapy hands under the bathroom faucet.

"Your She-bear protector tossed him out on his ass."

"Before Britta got there. Did you guys give him more money? Did he beg for you guys to protect him?"

"We didn't give him anything. Even Stevie. Except for the couple of bucks she gave him when we were all outside, she seemed pretty done with him. I might be able to kill him anytime now."

"Not if it's going to send you to prison."

"Who'd put me away for doing the world a favor?"

"Why do you smell like panda?" Britta asked Charlie's sister.

"Shen Li's at our house protecting the great sculptor prodigy Kyle Jean-Louis Parker."

"So? Why do you *smell* like him?"

Berg cringed. His sister really didn't know how not to be nosey. If she had a question she wanted answered, she didn't let a little thing like politeness and civility get in her way.

"I kept hugging him."

"You? You kept hugging a *bear*?"

"Yeah. The cutest bear ever! Unlike with you guys, I don't feel nervous around him at all. I never sense he's going to eat me or tear off my arms or whatever. I won't have to use my bear spray on him," she said with great certainty.

Britta turned toward Berg and asked low, "Should I tell her the truth?"

"No," Berg replied quickly. "Let her live in her happy world and we'll hope that she doesn't have to use her bear spray on you."

"Why?"

Berg shook his head, not willing to tell his sister the danger her eyes were in.

Charlie entered the living room with Max, and Berg was grateful to see the quills had been removed from Max's face. Of course, now she looked like she was suffering from chicken pox, but that was still better than the quills.

Anything was better than the quills.

Charlie looked at her watch, her eyes narrowing. She brought her wrist closer to her face.

"You forgot your glasses," Berg reminded her.

"Oh. Yeah." She brushed her hand against the front of her T-shirt, the outside of her jean pocket, the entire collar of her T-shirt, then she turned in a circle, looking around the room.

"Your head," he finally announced when he couldn't stand it another second.

She brought her hands to her hair but it was a mess of curls and she seemed to be having trouble finding them.

He moved over in front of her and carefully pulled the glasses off, trying not to snag her hair. Once he had them loose, he used the bottom of Charlie's T-shirt to give them a quick clean—something he'd seen her do often—before carefully placing them on her face. He made sure the frames fit perfectly on her nose and behind her ears before stepping back.

"We should get you one of those old lady chains so you can wear your glasses around your neck."

"That's never going to happen."

"You'd look adorable."

She grinned and Berg couldn't help but smile back. They kept staring at each other until they seemed to realize at the same time that they were being watched by the women in the room.

Charlie looked away first, snarling at her sisters to get out.

"Your contacts arrived," Stevie announced, sauntering by her sister. "I put them in the kitchen with your meds. I guess I could have mentioned that earlier . . . but then we wouldn't have seen the whole putting your glasses on for you thing."

"Such a gentleman," Max teased, following her baby sister out the door.

Britta, however, silently refused to leave until Berg roared in her face again and again; then she walked out in a mild huff.

He cleared his throat, burying his fists in the front pocket of his jeans. "Can I see you later?" he asked, getting right to his goal. Afraid if he didn't, he might never do it.

Charlie gave a little laugh. "Are you just a glutton for abuse? I can tell you right now, I'm not into leather and chains. So if you just like abuse—"

"I don't know what you're talking about. I just want to see you later."

"And if the curse travels?"

"I'll risk it."

"Foolish and a sign of poor decision making." She let out a breath. "But fine. I have to see my aunt today, but after that . . ."

"Do you need me to go with you?"

"Oh, God." Her eyes widened and she shook her head. "I couldn't do that to you. I couldn't do that to any person. Even an enemy. I'll handle my aunt. But I'll text you when I get back."

"Sounds good."

She looked around. "Where's your sister?"

"Probably in the kitchen being haughty. Why?"

Charlie stepped onto the wood coffee table so that

they were nearly eye level. Leaning in, she dropped her arms onto his shoulders and pressed her lips against his.

Berg smiled against her mouth, sliding his hands around her waist, pulling her in tighter. Her body pressed against his and he knew he'd been right last night. Charlie fit him perfectly.

He teased her mouth open with his tongue and for several minutes they simply stood there tasting each other, enjoying each other.

"Bitch, get off my coffee table," Britta said as she passed through the living room. "That shit is a Lock MacRyrie original and cost me a small fortune."

Laughing, Charlie pulled back, her arms still hanging over his shoulders. Staring down at the table she asked Berg, "Who?"

"We're coming with you," Charlie heard when she was scrunching gel into her hair with her fingers.

She was bent over at the waist, hair hanging down, so she waited until she straightened up before asking her sisters, who were standing in the bathroom doorway, "Why?"

"We just think it's for the best," Stevie said, attempting to make it seem like no big deal.

Charlie stared at her sisters before asking, "Is this because I punched her that time?"

"Of course not—"

"Yep."

Stevie cringed before snapping at Max, "Would it kill you to lie just a little?"

"But it *is* because she punched her. And now we're going to put them together in the same room, during the high-stress time of a wedding, to talk about Dad. If we're not there . . . we'll just be bailing Charlie out later."

Stevie's lips twisted, her gaze locked on a spot on the floor, before she finally admitted, "Max is right."

"Fine." Charlie studied her hair in the mirror, attempting to make her curls "act right," as her mom used to put it. "But if that bitch starts anything—"

"And *that's* why we have to go," Max said before walking away. "We all know she's going to start something."

Stevie reached over and slapped Charlie's arm.

"Ow."

"And would it kill *you* not to prove Max right all the time?"

Before Charlie could answer that—it would have been, "Yes, it would"—Stevie had stomped off.

Chapter Nineteen

Ric finished his presentation to his Uncle Van and Aunt Irene and faced them. "Well? Any questions?"

"She goes from five-foot-six to about twenty feet when she shifts?" Irene glanced off and added, "That's fascinating. I'd love to get my hands on the woman's blood."

Uncle Van glared at his full-human mate. "Is that really your only concern here?"

"I don't have a concern. I don't see the problem."

"Dee-Ann wants to put her down," Ric explained. "And her sisters. But I think that's because the oldest basically kicked her ass."

Van struggled not to smile. "Dee-Ann *Smith*, daughter of Eggie Smith, got her ass kicked by the oldest *honey badger*?"

"Don't laugh," Ric warned his favorite family member in the universe. "Just don't."

"Uh-huh."

"I really don't believe in killing people because one is petty," Aunt Irene stated, coldly analyzing the situation as she often did. She was, after all, one of the greatest minds in science despite what her enemies and critics might say. And she had a lot of enemies and critics. "If I operated that way, I would have killed . . . well . . . everyone."

"That's my feeling," Ric agreed. "The problem is we really can't expect the honey badgers to step in and self-manage this situation."

"We can't?" Van asked. "Why not?"

"Well, first off they're honey badgers, which means they're automatically difficult. But the biggest issue is that even among the honey badgers, the MacKilligan family is not exactly welcome. It's as if most of the badgers are torn between hating and fearing them while also finding some of them laughably pathetic."

"Wait," Irene said, sitting up a little straighter. "The MacKilligans? These women are named MacKilligan?"

"Yes."

"And the one that turns into a T. rex that you called Stevie—"

"She's not quite a T. rex, Aunt Irene."

"—is actually Dr. Stevie Stasiuk-MacKilligan? *That's* the Stevie you were talking about?"

"Yes. Why?"

She suddenly laughed. A sound she rarely made, which only worried Ric more.

"Oh, gentlemen, you have much more to worry about than the apparent fact that Stevie MacKilligan can shift to something that's twenty feet tall."

"And what is that exactly?"

"Well," Irene leaned back in the office chair, "with a few household products and some gum, she could destroy all of Texas." Irene thought a moment. "In fact . . . she nearly did." She thought a little longer and amended with one forefinger raised, "No, no. Sorry. That's incorrect." She nodded knowingly. "It was Nevada. She almost destroyed Nevada. And from what I understand, the only thing that stopped her at the time—because she was apparently suffering from some major bout of depression—was the intervention of her sisters. So unless you are positive you can wipe them all out at the same time, I'm not sure it would be wise to try."

Ric and his uncle stared at Irene until Van turned to him and said, "Why don't you go talk to the oldest? It seems like she's the one in charge."

"I'm not sure that's the best idea," Ric admitted. "With the bears now protecting her and her sisters."

"Don't forget who you have in your corner, Ulric," Van reminded him with a warm smile. "You've always had your own bear connections, you know."

Dag was standing on a tree limb, reaching to get the bee hive high up among the leaves. Normally, he would have left the bees alone much longer so that the hive could be even bigger, but he was worried about Max MacKilligan. She'd already raided the hives of three different bear homes.

Just that morning, Mr. Walton had found her hanging from one of his trees. He'd actually thought she was dead, because she was draped stomach down over a low limb under the hives, arms hanging listlessly, porcupine quills covering her face, angry African bees attacking the back of her head.

But when he got closer, he heard the snoring. She'd just been sleeping. Happily.

Walton had come to their house raging, but Britta had calmed him down and taken care of it in her way. Keeping the situation from escalating beyond the three of them.

Dag's brother really liked Charlie MacKilligan. A lot. There wouldn't be much she could do at this point to piss him off, which meant the hives on their property were not safe from Max MacKilligan.

Dag heard a low whistle. A whistle his siblings used when they wanted to get his attention.

He stopped reaching for the hive and peered out past the leaves to see his sister pointing at a spot on the ground. He looked down.

A young male was standing beneath the tree, staring up at him.

"Uhhh . . . can I help you?" Dag asked, assuming maybe the kid was lost.

"No."

By now Britta had reached them and asked, "Kyle, what are you doing?"

Finally tearing his gaze away from Dag and moving it to Britta, the kid blinked several times before he said, "You didn't tell me you were a twin."

"I'm actually a triplet, but I didn't have to tell you that. I don't know you."

"I need you three to pose naked for me."

"Okay." Britta clapped her hands together. "You need to go."

"Are you embarrassed? You shouldn't be. Just because you're not like some stick model doesn't mean you don't have your own form of perfection."

"You think that's a compliment, but it's not. So I need you to go."

"Do you know who I am?"

"I know I don't care who you—"

"I am an artist. People beg to sit for me. And I'm asking *you*. Bears. You should feel honored."

"And yet I just want to punch you in the face."

Dag dropped from the lowest branch and moved to his sister's side.

"We appreciate the offer," he said, "but go away."

"I know you're uptight suburbanites, trapped in your tiny little vision of the world—"

"I'm going to crack his jackal bones like kindle," Britta warned Dag.

"—but imagine being part of something greater."

"You mean you?" Dag asked the kid.

"Of course that's what I mean." He took his phone from the back pocket of his long shorts. He studied the screen a few seconds before holding it up in front of Britta.

Britta's expression of annoyance quickly turned to surprise and then awe. "You did that? *You?*"

"Told you. I'm amazing."

"Wow. You're like that Michelangelo guy."

"Oh, please." Kyle lowered his phone. "I'm *better* than Michelangelo."

"Wowwwwww," Britta sighed, gawking at the kid. "Seriously?"

Kyle stared back. "Yeah. Seriously."

The Kingston Arms.

Charlie had heard about the hotel chain for years. Not from shifters. From everyone else. It was an extremely expensive hotel that had just opened its newest location in Dubai.

She had always known that it was shifter owned and operated but that was all Charlie knew. Her mother and definitely her grandfather's Pack could never afford a place like this, and none of them would ever waste the money when a Holiday Inn Express would do just as well.

"This place is awesome," Max sighed beside her.

And they were only in the lobby. Just the walk to the front desk seemed about a mile long. There were also stores and major restaurants with more of the same on the floors below. A few restaurants on the higher floors.

Full-humans mingled easily—and obliviously—with shifters of all breeds and species.

"I could live here," Charlie said.

"Who couldn't?" Max pointed at a ridiculously large map of the hotel with a listing of all the available services.

The three of them stood there, staring, trying to figure out where they were and where they needed to go.

"I say we wander around aimlessly until we find her."

Charlie smiled at Max. "Bernice would lose her mind. Besides, she said go to the front desk."

They made the long hike to the front desk, taking it all in. But Charlie knew they focused on different things.

For Stevie, it was about the people. The energy. Everything that surrounded them. She drew all that in and her brain organized and sifted until she had a story to tell through music or science. When they got home later, she'd jot notes into one of the precious notebooks she kept in her backpack for possible later use.

For Max, it was about finding trouble. She searched out the drama, the weakness, the open doors. Although she didn't do much stealing—that Charlie knew about—she still had a thief's eye. Just like her birth mother. She could size up a jewelry store or one of those brand-name places with all the expensive purses that people sat on a waiting list for, and she could come up with several ways in and out with thousands to hundreds of thousands of dollars' worth of merchandise.

But for Charlie, it was all about escape. Where were the exits? Who stood between her and her sisters and those exits? What could she use as a weapon? Were there cops nearby? Could she incapacitate and escape or would she have to take a life? These were the questions she asked herself every time she entered a building. To the point that she barely realized that's what she was doing. It was like breathing to her. Or finding water when she was thirsty.

As always, it was about protecting her sisters and herself.

They reached the front desk and without even doing that off-putting sniffing thing everyone had been doing to Charlie, she knew the woman helping them was a shifter. A cat shifter, based on her eyes and the snobby way she looked over the three of them.

"May I help you?" she asked after giving a plastic smile that revealed pointy eyeteeth.

Charlie placed her hands on the counter. "Yeah, we're looking for Bernice MacKilligan."

The employee typed into her computer and looked up. "I'm sorry, but we have no one by that name."

"Think she's at another hotel?" Stevie asked.

Max snorted. "Bet she's under her rich person name."

Charlie rolled her eyes. "Right. Forgot. I meant Bernice Andersen-Cummingzzzzzzzz," she said, turning the *s* into a long, drawn out *z* because she'd found out when she was younger that her aunt hated when she did that.

"Oh, of course." And there went that plastic smile. "We've loved having Mrs. Andersen-Cummings and her family here at Kingston Arms."

Max's laugh was loud and *long*, before she finally got out, "You are *such* a liar."

Berg sat on his front stoop, focusing on the car part in his grease-covered hands, trying to figure out exactly what his sister did when she got behind the wheel of a vehicle that could cause so much damage.

He used a rag to diligently remove excess oil, allowing the hands-on work to help the part of his mind not focused on the task to figure out what he was going to do later that night.

Berg didn't just want to drag Charlie over to his house for dinner and then merely get her into bed. It would be nice, he was sure, but he wanted to do something a little more special for her. She deserved better than what she'd been getting from life lately, but Berg had never been much of a wooer.

He simply didn't have the charming patter of the cats or the dogged persistence of the canines. The thought of just sticking around until she finally gave in like the wolves seemed to do bothered him on a visceral level. No matter what her sisters kept saying about "stray-dogging it."

Bears, unlike the other shifters, had a little something called self-respect. He wanted Charlie to be with him because she really liked him, not because, "Eh. I couldn't get rid of him anyway."

A big SUV pulled into a spot right in front of Berg's house but he didn't really take notice until the dog came out from under the porch, ran up to the white picket fence, and began barking.

The passenger door opened and a wolf stepped out. Berg recognized him right away. Ulrich Van Holtz. The head of the New York division of the Group. He was Dee-Ann Smith's boss.

He was dressed casually enough but very Manhattan in his black jeans, black T-shirt, and black work boots. But Berg wasn't fooled. The T-shirt and jeans were designer and probably cost a few hundred, easily. The boots, Berg was sure, had probably not been purchased at the Brooklyn Army Surplus where the Dunn triplets always got their work boots.

But this wolf was smart. He didn't come alone into bear-only territory. He brought a bear friend with him.

One that Berg recognized since he'd been forced to go shopping for overpriced furniture at his "gallery"— God forbid they should just call it a store.

Lock MacRyrie got out of the SUV and followed his friend over to their fence.

Now the dog was on his hind legs, front legs placed on top of the pickets, and continuing to bark at the two strangers coming too close to his territory.

Berg stared at the pair with one eye, the other closed against the sun.

"Yeah?" he pushed when they just stood there.

"Mr. Dunn, I'm—"

"I know who you are. And I know your mate. She had guns pointed at my friend and her sisters yesterday."

The wolf at least had the decency to look a little ashamed by that, but his friend seemed oblivious, studying Berg's picket fence.

"That's true. But when Dee-Ann attempted to speak to your friend, I was told she reacted a little more harshly than seemed necessary."

"I was there. Smith should have minded her own business and let Charlie pummel that little weasel. She didn't and so she ended up getting her ass kicked."

At this point, the dog was still barking, not caring that he was being annoying. Not caring that they were forced to raise their voices. Not out of anger but because that was the only way they could hear each other over all that racket.

"Look," the wolf began, "I understand that—"

The wolf's words stopped. The barking stopped. And all because the large grizzly standing with the wolf had somehow managed to yank one of the pickets off the fence. Not on purpose. Berg knew when he was being threatened. He'd been known to do some threatening of his own. But this wasn't threatening. This was just the usual bear curiosity that ended up causing a lot of damage.

Berg stared and the wolf cringed, and, finally, the dog slowly moved away from the grizzly in front of him. Apparently, he did see the torn fence as a threat.

"Oh, shit. Sorry." MacRyrie held the picket up. "I, uh . . . can put it back for you."

"That's okay. I can fix it."

"Anyway," the wolf continued in a lower volume now that the barking had stopped, "I was hoping to work something out with the MacKilligan sisters."

"Then what are you talking to me for?"

"It seemed smarter to discuss this with you first."

"Did it?"

Berg heard high-pitched yelping and looked behind him. His sister came around the corner, her grip tight on the back of a jackal's jeans, lifting the denim high and into the kid's ass crack.

"It's time for you to leave right now," Britta informed Kyle.

"You are being unreasonab—ow, ow, ow!"

Unlatching the fence gate, she shoved the jackal through as if that alone would keep him out. "When you're eighteen, you can come back here and ask us about posing naked . . . that way I can slap the shit out of you without any guilt. Or charges of abuse of a minor. Until then . . . stay out of our territory, skinny dog."

The wolf closed his eyes, took a breath, before asking the jackal, "Again with this, Kyle?"

The kid looked at the wolf but Berg wasn't sure that he recognized him until Kyle said, "You do seem to forget that I don't answer to you, Ulrich."

"I can always get Dee-Ann involved, if you'd like."

"Unlike the rest of the world," Kyle scoffed, "I don't fear the great Dee-Ann Smith. Mostly because she finds me"—air quotes—" 'off putting.' You ask a woman for specific details about all those she and her murderous father have killed throughout their terrifying lives so that you can praise their skills in a sculpted piece for the ages . . . and suddenly *I'm* the mentally disturbing one."

"Kyle—"

"Although I do wonder . . . what is it like to be married to an actual sociopath? Do you sleep at all? Or are you too afraid she'll wake up in the middle of the night and cut your throat for the hell of it? Do you fear for the safety of your child?"

"Okay, that's it!" Britta suddenly exploded, yanking the gate open and storming through. She grabbed the kid by the back of his jeans again and now his hair. She lifted him off his feet and carried him back to the honey badgers' house. "You are a horrible, *horrible* child and if you'd been my son, I'd have taken you directly to a military school!"

"Your sister is awesome," MacRyrie said.

"She does not tolerate bullshit from anyone. Especially other people's bratty kids."

"We really just wanted to talk to Charlie MacKilligan and her sisters about a job with us," Ric finally said.

"And now? What? You want to lock them up?"

"Lock up who?" Britta asked as she walked back, slapping her hands against each other like she'd just finished cleaning up a mess.

"Charlie and her sisters."

Britta stopped, crossing her arms, gaze locked on the wolf and bear interloper. "Lock them up for what? For being who they are? For being different? For being hybrids? I expected more of a Van Holtz. And if you think the bears are going to let you start doing that bullshit . . ."

There was silence after Britta let her words—and

warning—fade out. And that silence lasted until Lock MacRyrie suddenly faced his friend and announced, "Yeah, we're not going to let you get away with that."

Eyes crossing, Van Holtz suddenly gawked at the bear he'd brought to back him up and snarled, *"Lock!"*

"But we're not!"

Charlie and her sister walked into the giant hall that had been reserved for the wedding reception. Unlike most wedding venues, this gargantuan hall had been booked for an entire two weeks to get everything ready. Most events just needed a day to get a room set up. Maybe two. But her aunt wasn't taking any chances. It also meant that she'd been planning this wedding for at least two . . . maybe three years?

Who planned a wedding for that long? Human or shifter?

The venue was amazing, though. Elaborate crystal chandeliers throughout with a giant one in the middle of the room right over the dance floor. Round tables with chairs decorated with expensive-looking fabric.

The color scheme seemed to be white and red and gray. Standard color choices and hard to get wrong. Though if anyone could, it was Charlie's cousin.

As they entered the room, the three of them leaned to the side, so the flying vase of flowers missed Charlie's head by inches. But to be honest, she was mostly impressed at the reaction times of Max *and* Stevie. She'd trained them both well—by actually throwing things at their heads when they were growing up.

"I hate it!" Carrie MacKilligan Andersen-Cummings screamed at her one older sister and three younger ones, who stood around her, eyes in mid-roll. "I hate it! *I hate it all!*"

"I'm leaving," Stevie abruptly announced, turning on her heel. But Max grabbed the back of her neck and yanked her around.

"We don't desert each other," Max reprimanded. "Especially when it's this entertaining."

Bernice rushed to her daughter's side. She clasped her hands together as if she was praying . . . or trying to stop herself from choking the life out of her pain-in-the-ass child.

"What is it you want, sweetheart?"

"I don't want roses," Carrie spit out. "Everybody has roses! *I deserve better than roses!*"

Carrie's sisters, standing behind her, looked at each other, and Charlie wondered how long before one of them snapped and killed her in a fit of sibling-on-sibling rage.

"Make. It. Better. Mommy," Carrie ordered before stomping off in heels that had to be five inches high. Designer. Probably cost more than Charlie's entire wardrobe.

The oldest, Kenzie, nodded at Charlie and she nodded back. But that's when Carrie spotted them and screamed across the room, *"What the fuck are they doing here?"*

"Calm down," Bernice ordered her daughter. "They're here to see me."

She walked over to Charlie and said in a low voice, "I thought I told you to come alone?"

"I ignored you," Charlie admitted.

Bernice placed the tips of her fingers against her forehead, closed her eyes, and changed the subject. "So, any word on your father?"

"Yeah," Max answered, "we just saw him yesterday."

Brown eyes snapped open and Bernice gawked at them. "You *what*?"

"Just saw him yesterday."

"He doused himself in bear spray to sneak into our all-bear neighborhood," Stevie explained. "He smelled unpleasant."

"I knew it. I knew that he would ruin—"

"What are they doing here?" Carrie demanded, coming close. She looked at Charlie. "You guys are not invited."

Charlie nodded and said, "I see you got your nose fixed."

Finger pointing, Carrie stepped toward Charlie but her mother quickly pulled her back. "Sweetheart, let me handle this. Go over with your sisters."

"Fine." She glared at Charlie. *"Whore."*

"Your ass is still flat."

Bernice grabbed her daughter's arm and yanked her away before she could drag her claws down Charlie's face. A move Charlie did appreciate. Those claws could leave scars forever depending on how deep one cut.

"Wow," Stevie muttered, watching the mother and daughter moving away. She lowered her voice to a whisper, "Her ass *is* flat."

"She's never had a good ass."

"Personally," Max added, but not bothering to lower her voice, "I like that she made her nose so ridiculously small that she can barely breathe now." She studied her cousin for a moment and finished up with, "It's like she has all this face"—she held her hands about two feet apart—"but this"—she closed her hands until she made a tiny circle with her fingers and raised her voice several octaves—"tiny little nose."

Charlie and Stevie laughed loud until their aunt came over and took hold of Charlie's arm.

"With me, ladies. With me. Kenzie, you're in charge until I get back."

"I don't want to be."

"I don't care!"

Once out of the hall, Bernice stopped and faced the nieces she had barely acknowledged all of their lives.

"Time for tea?" Charlie asked.

Bernice let out an exhausted breath. "Fuck the tea. Let's hit the bar."

"It's not even noon yet," Stevie wisely pointed out, but Bernice wasn't having it.

"So you gonna make a big deal about it?" Bernice demanded, arms thrown wide, stepping up to Stevie.

Charlie and Max immediately moved in front of their baby sister to protect her from the raging, middle-aged She-badger.

"It's never too early for a good scotch," Charlie said gently, sweeping her arm forward. "Please, Aunt Bernice, lead the way."

Her aunt stalked off and Charlie started to follow until she heard Max chuckling beside her.

"What?"

"I am *so* entertained right now."

Stevie pushed past her sisters and followed their aunt, tossing over her shoulder, "That's probably because you have a high probability of being a psychotic."

Max grinned. "But I'm a happy psychotic!"

"I am not trying to destroy anyone or anything," Ric explained to the grizzlies glaring at him. "I'm just trying to fix this."

"Fix what?" Berg Dunn asked. "They clearly don't want a job and basically just want you to fuck off. So I don't know why you or anyone else needs to talk to them."

"They're making some people nervous."

"That's not the MacKilligan sisters' problem."

"It could become a problem if the Group and Katzenhaus decide they're too much of a danger."

Dunn stood, his sister coming to stand next to him. "If that happens, you'll have to deal with the BPC," the bear warned. "Is that what you want? *Really?*"

"Yeah?" Lock demanded next to Ric. *"Really?"*

Ric grabbed Lock's arm. "Could you excuse us a moment?" He pulled his best friend a few feet down the block before stopping and facing him. "What the fuck are you doing, man? You're *my* backup!"

"You just said come with me. So I went with you. But this conversation is making me uncomfortable. My mate is a hybrid. Our children are hybrids. And now I'm hearing that Dee-Ann is on a rampage to kill hybrids."

"She is *not* . . ." Ric took another breath. "Dee-Ann is only concerned that Stevie MacKilligan doesn't seem to have full control of her shifting, and she can shift into a twenty-foot-long, tiger-striped honey badger."

Lock suddenly laughed. "That's cool."

"Let me repeat," Ric snapped. "She doesn't have control."

"Oh." He thought a moment, nodded. "You're right. That is a concern."

"I know. So help me. Think you can do that?"

The old friends gazed at each other for a long moment until, eyes narrowing, they looked at what now stood beside them.

Dutch grinned at them. The bruises on his face and neck were . . . substantial. And Ric knew for a fact that the wolverine was quite the scrappy fighter. Still . . . one MacKilligan sister had kicked his ass with hand-to-hand combat. One.

Ric did notice, though, that Dutch didn't seem bowed by the damage. Despite the bruises and still-healing wounds, he appeared pretty chipper.

"So," the weasel boldly asked, "what are we talking about?"

Lock sneered and started back toward the other bears. But as he walked past Dutch, he swung his arm out, sending Dutch flying across the street, across the fence of the home opposite them, across that bear's yard, and into the defenseless porch swing.

Lock didn't actually put a lot of energy behind that move, either, but he'd never been much of a fan of wolverines and despite having retired from the hockey team, he still had that mighty boar strength.

Ric followed his friend and stood silently as Lock said to the Dunn siblings, "How about we all meet later today in the BPC offices? You can just bring the eldest sister—"

"Charlie."

Lock nodded. "You bring Charlie. All you guys come with her. And Katzenhaus can send someone and Ric can represent the Group. No one," he quickly added, "will bring Dee-Ann."

"Or her father," Britta said, adding when they all stared at her, "Everyone knows about her father. No Eggie Smith or no deal."

"He's wandering the hills of Tennessee in his wolf form," Ric replied. "He's not leaving that happy life except for a full-on emergency. It'll just be me and my Uncle Van representing the Group."

Britta looked to her brother.

Berg shrugged. "I'll talk to Charlie about it."

"Excellent." Lock held his hand out for a shake but that's when he realized he was still gripping the picket he'd pulled off the Dunns' fence. "Oh . . . I can still fix this."

Britta took the piece of wood. "That's okay. By the way," She smiled. "I love your work, Mr. MacRyrie. We have one of your coffee tables. I've been saving up for one of your couches. Maybe a dining table." Her nose crinkled up and she went from gruff and dangerous to delightful. "You're so talented!"

Lock, as was his way, blushed, buried his hands in the front pockets of his jeans and shrugged. "Uh . . . thanks. And you can call me Lock."

Growling in disgust, Berg suddenly stomped back to his porch, snarling, "Go away before I change my mind."

His sister, however, gave another delightful smile and a little wave. "It was so nice meeting you, Lock."

Ric walked back to the SUV and got into the passenger side; Lock was already starting the engine.

Once they were on the road, heading back toward Manhattan, Lock observed, "Well . . . that was a very pleasant visit."

Not in the mood, Ric automatically replied, "Shut up."

"And now it's a little *less* pleasant."

" 'You're so talented, Mr. MacRyrie,' " Berg mocked his sister in a high-pitched voice, watching as she waved at the SUV carrying the bear and wolf.

When the car turned the corner, the piece of wood his sister had been holding came flying at his head. He ducked, the wood flew past him and rammed into the head of poor Dag, who'd been coming around the corner of the house.

"Motherfucker!"

Britta cringed before blaming Berg. "See what you made me do?"

"Me?"

She rushed to Dag and wiped the blood from his head with her hand. "This is all Berg's fault," she told Dag.

"I know it is."

"Why is everyone blaming *me*?"

"Excuse me?" The weasel had picked himself up after being tossed across the street by Lock MacRyrie and was now standing outside their fence. Existing.

And his existing annoyed Berg.

Slowly, Berg and his siblings looked over at the weasel. Without saying a word, they focused on him . . . and waited.

Instead of getting the hint, he cheerfully asked, "Any idea when the girls will be back?"

They continued to silently stare, reminding Berg why he loved his siblings. Why he loved being part of triplets. For moments like these.

The weasel glanced around. "Uh . . . okay. Um . . . could you tell them I stopped by."

Staring.

"All right. I'll just, uh . . . I'll just text Max. Yeah." He nodded. "That's what I'll do. I'll text Max."

Finally, after the endless silence, he gave a wave and walked off.

When he was gone, Berg turned to those who'd shared a womb with him for nine months and—to their mother's great annoyance—three weeks and, as one, they smiled.

Will walked into his mother's house, where his brothers were waiting for him. He didn't know what he was going to tell them. "Our American niece is a giant, tiger-striped, honey badger" just was not a conversation he wanted to have with the MacKilligan boys.

But before he could say a word, his youngest brother, Jim, said, "We have a problem."

"You mean besides our lost money?"

"I got a call from a contact at Saughton."

Saughton Prison. Also known as Edinburgh Prison.

Considered the most dangerous prison in the British Isles. And most of that, at least lately, was due to one prisoner.

Mairi MacKilligan. His brother Samson's only girl.

And, like her father, she'd ended up in Saughton before she was even thirty. Maybe, also like her father, she'd ended up getting gutted late one night in her cell.

"And?"

"Mairi's out."

Will shook his head. "She's there at Her Majesty's pleasure. And trust me, after what she's done, Her Majesty won't be letting her out any time soon."

"They didn't let her out, Will. She escaped. And no one knows where she is."

"It's Scotland not Africa. How hard can it be to track her down on this tiny island?"

"That's the problem," Jim said, folding his arms over his chest. "They don't think she's in Scotland anymore. Or Europe. Instead she's loose out there. And pissed at us because we left her in Saughton. You remember how she is, brother. This is gonna get bad."

Will dropped into the closest chair, gazing up at his siblings. "Oh, fuck."

Chapter Twenty

As soon as they walked into one of the hotel's bars, the bartender immediately grabbed a bottle of forty-year-old scotch.

Bernice held up four fingers and beside the bottle on the bar top was placed four glasses. She grabbed the bottle, the glasses, and moved over to a booth in the far corner. She poured a couple of ounces in each glass before sitting down, keeping the bottle very close to her.

Charlie slid in across from Bernice, and Max sat beside their aunt. Stevie sat next to Charlie.

Grabbing one of the glasses, Bernice held it up and toasted with great sarcasm, "To family."

She was waiting, so Charlie and her sisters each grabbed a glass, repeated, "To family," and tapped their glasses against their aunt's.

Bernice drank her scotch in one gulp before slamming it down on the table and filling it up again.

Charlie took only a sip, knowing she shouldn't do any hardcore drinking due to the meds she was on for her anxiety.

Max sipped, curled her lip in distaste, and asked one of the waitresses for a bowl of honey roasted peanuts.

Stevie, however, took her scotch in one gulp and the rest of them gawked at her.

She dropped the glass on the table and, when she realized they were all staring, explained, "Seriously? You're surprised I know how to drink after spending more than a decade around scientists and engineers?"

Not having a response to that, Charlie focused on her aunt. "So, how's that wedding going?"

Bernice's eyes narrowed on Charlie and she socked back another gulp of scotch.

"I'm just going to put this out there," Bernice said, studying her now-empty glass. "I've raised a horrible child."

"I appreciate your honesty," Max replied.

"But this wedding has to go off without a hitch."

"Don't you have a wedding planner?" Stevie asked.

"Of course. The best in the business. A She-tiger who is, to say the least, *bitchy*. And that Irish whore has been working my last Scottish nerve. Yet, she has been doing an amazing job. There's just one"—she held up her forefinger—"little problem."

"The bride?" Max asked, her elbow on the table, her chin resting on her raised fist.

Bernice gave a short nod. "The bride."

Stevie, perhaps emboldened by the one drink she'd had, suddenly perked up and asked, "I'm sorry but . . . why are we here? We're not even invited to the wedding. So whether your daughter is being a prick or not . . . I don't see how that's our problem."

Keeping her fist raised, Max moved her face around until she could press the back of her fingers against her mouth, hiding her surprised smile.

Bernice polished off another round of scotch before admitting, "To be blunt, I didn't invite you two. I invited her." Charlie saw that finger pointing at her and she wanted to head right for the exit. "Everyone in the family knows about you, Charlie."

Charlie prepared herself to be insulted. "Knows what?" she asked, sounding defensive even to her own ears.

"That you get shit done. That *you* can shut down bullshit like no one else. I know you may not realize that because of the problems with your father, but trust me. No one could control that idiot of a man. And you have definitely done better than most."

"Um . . . thank you? But short of locking Carrie in a dungeon and only releasing her for the wedding so that we can drag her down the aisle by her hair, I'm not sure—"

"That's an option," Bernice cut in. "See? Already we're brainstorming."

Max sat up straight in her seat, eyes wide, her laughter moments from spilling out.

"An option that I'm not sure is, uh, legal," Charlie felt the need to point out. "I mean . . . does Carrie *want* to get married?"

"Yes! Definitely."

"Okay. That's good. But maybe I should clarify . . . does she want to get married to the guy who's showing up on Saturday?"

Bernice glanced off. "Ummmmm . . ."

"If that's a question you can't answer in the affirmative right away, then perhaps you should call of the wed—"

"*No*," Bernice said immediately, not even letting Charlie finish her sentence. "We are going through with this wedding." She waved her hands around. "Aliens and dragons could suddenly attack our entire planet, and I'd still make sure this fucking wedding happened."

"Look, Bernice . . ." Charlie cleared her throat. "It's not that I don't appreciate your sudden willingness to, uh . . . *acknowledge* that I exist. But Carrie has sisters and you and . . . unless you just didn't invite us to the funeral, I'm assuming your husband is still alive. So, you know, getting them to help is probably your best option. Especially since I'm not about to do anything illegal."

She let out an annoyed sigh. "And?"

"So why am I here?"

"So you can do what you do, Charlie MacKilligan. Remove obstacles. We've all watched you over the years. Someone gets in the way of Stevie receiving some fancy scholarship or funding . . . you handle it. When that Wisconsin high school wasn't going to let Max walk during graduation because of what she did to that cheerleader—"

Max's smile was almost sweet. "Bobby-Jean Hamilton." She nodded. "Head cheerleader. Voted most likely to succeed. And I beat the holy hell out of her in the cafeteria." She gave a little shrug. "You know . . . just because."

Bernice gestured to Max with both hands. "You see? The school had every right *not* to let her walk for graduation. But you fixed it. She walked. And I want you to do the same for my little girl. Get her to walk down that aisle before I kill her and have her stuffed and mounted in my home as a warning to the rest of her sisters."

Charlie focused directly on her aunt, knowing better than to look at Max. She could *not* look at Max or the laughter would never end.

She began, "Again, I appreciate what you're going through, but I don't think—"

"How much?" Stevie suddenly asked.

Charlie turned her body so she could look directly at her sister. "What are you doing?"

"What? She expects you to do this for free?"

"I don't care if she wants it for free or not. I'm not

doing anything. I'm not involving myself in this craziness. Instead, we're all going to head back to bear street, as I like to call it, and find me something to wear because I *think* I have a date tonight with a very handsome man who can shift into a thousand-pound beast." She looked back at Bernice. "So as much as I—"

"I'll give you fifty thousand."

Max blinked. "*Dollars? American* dollars?"

Charlie raised her forefinger. "I already told you, I'm not doing anything illegal. And I'm not killing anybody for you."

"If I wanted someone dead, I'd hire Max."

"Awww," Max said, gently touching Bernice's forearm. "That's sweet."

"Then what would you be giving me fifty grand for?"

"I need you to do what you do so well. Problem-solve. Find that problem. Deal with that problem. *Eliminate* that problem." And before Charlie could say anything, she quickly added, "Legally. I want you, Charlie, to do what you do so brilliantly. Fix the fucking problem. Not the wedding-specific stuff. I'm already paying that She-tiger whore a lot of money to make this wedding perfection. I need you to find out where the real problems are. The problems that are going to fuck my life. Find them and fix them."

"And if I can't?"

"You still get paid." When Charlie's eyes narrowed, Bernice went on, "I know you, Charlie. You're like your mother. When you commit to something, you don't walk away. I know if you promise to do your best on this, you will. If my daughter still manages to fuck it up . . . that's on me. As her mother. And I'll deal with that in my own way," she said in a tone that made Charlie worry for her younger cousin.

"What about expenses?" Stevie asked.

Charlie slapped the glass her sister had only drunk

from once, sending it flying across the bar. "No more liquor for you!"

"I'm not letting you get screwed over. We're getting you the best deal."

"You want to talk deal, Stevie?" Bernice leaned forward, looking directly at Charlie's baby sister. "I'll give her twenty-five K up front. Cover all expenses. And no matter what happens, on the day the wedding *should* take place, I'll give her the other twenty-five K." She held up her finger before Stevie could say anything. "But . . . if the wedding *does* happen. Meaning Carrie and Ronald P. Farmington the Fourth walk down that aisle, say their vows, and leave on their honeymoon at the end of the night, I'll give her a bonus of thirty-five thousand dollars on top of the fifty." She glanced at Max. "American dollars."

Bernice relaxed back in the seat, tossing her hands up before asking, "What ya gotta say now, bitches?"

Stevie nodded at Charlie. "Take it."

"What are you doing to me?"

"Getting you a job."

"Stevie, you know that once I'm in—"

"Yeah. You're committed. I get that. I also know this wedding is to take place *this* Saturday. Take the fucking money."

Charlie looked at Max, but she could already guess her sister's answer.

"Take the money, dude," Max said.

"All right. I'll do it. But you two are helping me," she said to her sisters.

"Why is this *our* problem?" Max asked.

"I'm not leaving you two with nothing to do in *Bear* Town. I'm going to keep you both busy. It's in everyone's best interest."

Stevie gave a sad sigh and said to Bernice, "She's right."

"By the way," Charlie added for her aunt, "I consider my sisters expenses."

"Whatever." Bernice looked at her watch. "All right. I've gotta get back to that demon beast I gave birth to."

Max slid from the booth, allowing her aunt to get out.

"Another thing," Bernice said before she walked away, "your father—"

"I'll work with the wedding planner and security about him. You do have security for this event, don't you? *Real* security?" When her aunt just stood there, gazing at her, eyes blinking, she said, "Don't worry about it. I got it."

She'd clearly been expecting more of a fight before Charlie would take this job, but what was the point of putting up a fight? For that kind of money, Charlie would deal with her father.

Once her aunt left, Stevie asked, "So what are we doing first?"

"Our first step . . . we find out what our bitchy little cousin is doing behind her mother's back."

Charlie's phone vibrated and she pulled it from her back pocket. "Yeah?"

"Hi. It's Berg."

She couldn't help but smile when she heard his voice, relaxing into the leather booth. "Hi. What's up?"

"Do you have some free time today?"

"Everything okay?"

"Yeah. The Group wants to meet with you, Katzenhaus, and the BPC. I can pick you up and take you there."

"Where?"

"BPC offices. And you can say no. I'll back you all the way."

"Hold on."

Charlie lowered her phone, "There's a meeting with the Group later today. Berg says he'll pick me up."

"Want me to come with you?" Max suggested. "I can kill everybody . . . get this all done."

"I could be wrong," Charlie replied calmly, "but that seems like it would not get this done as much as it would make everything worse."

Max shrugged. "You may have a point."

"Thank you. Now you two stay here, start sniffing around the bride. I'll deal with everything else. And no fucking fighting!"

"Should I call Dutch?" Max asked.

"The traitor?"

"Wow, you're really not lettin' that go."

"*Not* lettin' that go. And do what you want. I already kicked his ass. He knows where I stand." Charlie returned the phone to her ear. "Berg. Tell me where to meet you."

Chapter Twenty-one

Berg picked Charlie up at the corner, outside the hotel. He'd planned to come alone, but Britta and Dag insisted. They sat in the backseat, waving at Charlie when she looked at them.

"Everything okay?" he asked, pulling back into midday traffic.

"Yeah. I got a job."

"Really? Doing what?"

"Making sure my cousin goes through with her wedding. I'm supposed to remove all obstacles. Legally," she quickly added. Not that Berg doubted that. He didn't think Charlie would kill for anyone but her sisters and only to protect them.

"Obstacles?" Britta asked. "You mean, like, the priest not showing up? Or the cake not being delivered?"

"My aunt has a wedding planner for that, apparently. I'm guessing, based on what she told me about my cousin Carrie, it's a lack of love."

"Your cousin doesn't love the guy she's marrying?" Berg asked.

"I don't think so, but I don't think it matters to my aunt."

Britta leaned forward, her hand resting on the head-rest. "Who's the poor schlub she's marrying?"

"Uh . . . Ronald P . . ." She thought a moment. "Farmington. The Fourth."

"Oooooh," Britta said, leaning closer. "He's rich. Like he-could-have-a-gold-yacht rich."

"I assumed. My aunt was adamant she needed this wedding to go through. To the point that she's willing to pay me eighty-five grand."

"*American* money?" Britta asked.

Charlie shook her head. "What is it with you and my sister and this concern over me not getting American money? It's the strangest thing."

The SUV turned on a street and Charlie looked back at Britta. "How expensive are you guys?"

Britta frowned. "Pardon?"

"I meant as security."

"Oh! Oh. Oh, we're very expensive."

Charlie looked at Berg and he nodded. "We really are. We do it to weed out the reality TV people who just want big guys walking behind them, looking terrifying while they're throwing wine in some woman's face. Why?"

"You and Britta have seen my dad, and I was hoping you could come to the wedding as additional security to keep the idiot from coming in and making an already horrible day even worse. It's this Saturday. I can get you specific times later."

"We can do that," Berg said, pulling into a large building's parking structure. "We'll do it for free."

"No you will *not*." Charlie smirked. "But only because I won't be the one paying. My aunt is covering expenses and she wants my dad not to infiltrate. So I expect you to double what you normally charge."

"Well—"

Knowing Berg was too nice, she looked at his sister and said, "Double charge."

"Got it!" Britta's fingers flew across her phone and, after a few seconds, she added, "Booked."

Berg stopped the SUV at the security booth. A man that had to be at least seven-and-a-half-feet tall looked down at him.

"Berg."

"Garland."

The metal gate went up and Berg drove in, quickly finding a parking spot.

They all got out and walked to the elevator. The doors opened and Charlie stepped in, her mouth open as she looked around.

"This thing is huge."

"We don't like to feel trapped." Berg pressed a button for the top floor. "Now, if you don't feel comfortable at any time, if you feel unsafe, you just let us know, and we'll get you out."

"Okay."

The floors ticked by.

Berg faced her. "Are you armed?"

"To the teeth. Anyone even twitches wrong—"

"No, no, no." Berg shook his head. "I need you *not* to kill anyone today."

"But if they twitch—"

"No!"

"What Berg means," Britta explained, "is if there are any problems, we'll handle it."

"Exactly," he agreed, nodding.

"If, let's say, some feline from Katzenhaus gives you any trouble, *we'll* be the ones to rip his arms off and beat him to death with them!"

"No," Berg sighed, again shaking his head. "That is not what I meant either."

                              *   *   *

Max peeked around the corner, watching her cousin Carrie on her cell phone. She was pacing and crying, but keeping her voice low.

Carrie turned to pace in Max's direction, so she quickly moved back behind the wall.

"What's going on?" Stevie asked.

"She's on the phone and crying." Max looked at her sister. "Crying."

"People cry."

"Honey badgers don't cry. Honey badgers don't cry."

"I heard you the first time."

"But I felt it can't be said enough."

"Hey!" Dutch barked, coming down the hall and both Max and Stevie shushed him.

"What?" he whispered, dramatically slamming his back against the wall, his gaze bouncing from one end of the hall to the other. "Are we under fire?"

"We're spying," Stevie softly explained.

"Oh, I love spying."

"So we've heard," Max teased.

Dutch grimaced. "Okay, I walked into that one."

"Dumb ass."

"Your sister still hate me?"

"Yes," Max and Stevie said together.

"Seriously?"

"Well, she hated you before," Stevie explained. "Now her hate is just enhanced."

Max checked around the corner and saw that Carrie had gone in the back way to the big hall where her wedding was being set up.

"You know how Charlie is," Stevie was saying when Max leaned back.

"She's a Leo with a Taurus moon," Max explained. "You're lucky all she did was kick the crap out of you."

Stevie rolled her eyes, a sound of disgust coming from the back of her throat.

"What?"

"You still believe in that astrology crap?" she asked.

"You don't?"

"I believe in *tangible* things," Stevie announced in her haughtiest voice. "Not ludicrous things."

"What about Eastern astrology? I bounce back and forth between Eastern and Western, so do you believe in Eastern astrology?"

"*No.*"

"Where is Charlie anyway?" Dutch asked to stop the fight he probably knew was coming.

"Berg picked her up to take her to some meeting with the BPC, the cats, and your people."

Dutch's usual smiling, relaxed face fell. "What?"

"No one told you?"

"No."

Max studied him a moment. "Should I go there and kill everybody?"

"Why is that always your first suggestion?"

"It's the most expedient."

"Should we be freaking out?" Stevie demanded. "I feel like we should be freaking out."

"No. I'm sure it'll be fine. If you're worried, though, I could go. Protect Charlie."

Max looked at Stevie and even her baby sister rolled her eyes.

"Dude," Max felt the need to point out, "she's surrounded by three *grizzly* bears. I think our sister's safe."

"Is she armed?"

Stevie snorted. "To the teeth."

"She's crying?" Charlie suddenly said out loud while staring at her phone. "What does Max mean she's crying? Honey badgers don't cry. Honey badgers don't cry."

Berg walked back to her and tapped her arm. She lifted her head, frowning. "What?"

"Could we get this done?"

She looked around and seemed to suddenly remember that she was in the middle of the BPC hallway talking to herself and tapping on her phone.

"Sorry," she said. "Sorry." She walked quickly to catch up to Britta and Dag, and Berg followed behind her.

They were headed to the office at the very end of the hallway. Bayla Ben-Zeev's office. She was the head of the BPC.

Berg cut in front of her so he could walk into the office first. He wanted to look around, make sure everything was as it should be. It wasn't that he was so worried, it was mostly habit. Personal security was his business, after all.

Unfortunately, Britta and Dag had the same idea, so the three of them ended up briefly caught in the doorway until Britta pulled free first, reaching back with both arms to slap him and Dag on the shoulders.

The two Van Holtz wolf males immediately looked out the window. Bayla sighed and rubbed her temples from behind her desk, and the newest New York head of Katzenhaus, Mary-Ellen Kozlowski, a cute but vicious little lynx, just rolled her eyes and sneered as only a cat can.

"Sorry we're late," Britta said. "Traffic."

"No problem." Bayla motioned to several empty chairs around her desk. "Come in."

Dag stayed by the door and didn't sit. He just stood there . . . glaring at the non-bears in the room. Britta sat down by the wolves so she could practically face the cat. Britta really didn't like cats.

Berg turned to escort Charlie into the room, to let

the others know—in no uncertain terms—the level of
protection she had. But she was again focused on her
phone, her thumbs tapping away on the screen.

"Charlie," he said softly, trying to get her attention.
"Charlie," he said a little louder, but still . . .

"Charlie!"

She didn't jump at his bark, just muttered, "One
second."

He couldn't even bring himself to look at Bayla. Not
when he already knew she hated to be kept waiting.

"Okay." Charlie slipped her phone back into her
jeans. She stepped around him and fully into the room.
"So sorry. There's a wedding, and you know how crazy
those can be." She said it so smoothly that she sounded
like she was legitimately part of the wedding rather
than just spying on her cousin for cash. "I really appreciate all of you taking the time to meet with me like
this. I always get so worried about my family, but I'm
sure this will make me feel much better."

She said all that without sarcasm. Without any of the
viciousness that always seemed to taint the conversations of different breeds put together in one room.

Charlie sat down, her smile warm. "Um . . . I'm
Charlie MacKilligan, which I assume everyone here
knows. But I'm unclear on who's who." Out of everyone, she looked at the lynx first.

The cat in a tiny white designer dress and designer
heels, her designer white purse resting in the big chair
with her because she barely took up any room in the
bear-sized furniture, took a moment. She seemed
stunned. Probably because cats were considered so
rude that most of the other breeds purposely ignored
them just to get under their skin.

Charlie wasn't doing that.

Pale green eyes gawked at Charlie before replying,

"Uh . . . I'm, um . . ." She cleared her throat, quickly tossing on her mantle of not caring. "Mary-Ellen Kozlowski."

"Hi, Miss Kozlowski." Charlie got up again and
went across the room, her hand held out.

Kozłowski jerked back, the legs of her chair scrap-
ing against the floor. Then she realized that Charlie just
wanted a handshake.

Charlie patiently waited, smiling.

Glancing around, expecting an attack of some kind,
Kozlowski finally took Charlie's hand, shook it.

"Nice to meet you," Charlie said before pulling her
hand away.

Those pale green eyes narrowed, desperately searching for sarcasm. When she didn't find any, she nodded.
"You too."

Charlie moved over to the wolves.

"Charlie MacKilligan," she said to the younger Van
Holtz.

"Ulrich Van Holtz. You can call me Ric. And this is
my cousin, Niles Van Holtz."

"Call me Van."

"I thought he was your uncle," Britta asked, also
clearly uncomfortable with Charlie's ease and warmth
with everyone in the room.

"It's a respect thing, right?" Charlie said, moving
across the room to Bayla's desk. "We have a couple of
'uncles' like that," she laughed, reaching her hand out
to Bayla.

"Charlie."

"Bayla Ben-Zeev."

"Very nice to meet you. And I love your name.
Bayla's pretty."

"Uh . . . thank you?"

Charlie returned to her chair, sat down.

Immediately, Bayla opened her mouth to get the discussion rolling, to make sure that everyone there understood that Charlie and her sisters were under BPC protection, that she would not tolerate any of their bullshit.

Berg knew exactly what to expect from the head of the BPC and he also knew what to expect from the Van Holtzes—calm, rational, barely perceptible threats—and from the lynx—blatant, outright threats and viciousness.

But without letting Bayla get in a word, Charlie just began talking.

"I have to say that I *really* appreciate everyone coming here today to help us."

Surprised, Berg looked up; his sister already gazing at him, eyes wide.

"I usually have to deal with these kinds of problems on my own and I'm starting to get overwhelmed. I mean, my father stealing money from his own brother, his brother using me and my sisters in the hopes of getting the money back by basically selling us to whoever wants my baby sister. And, I mean, I'm not handing over my baby sister to *anyone,* but especially not full-human males. My uncle knows we don't have the money to pay him back and he also knows that no matter what might happen to me and my sisters, no matter how bad, how horrifying or brutal, it will mean *nothing* to my father. But my Uncle Will was hoping that *I* could get the money back from my father and he felt I would do that if someone had my sister. If her safety was threatened." She blew out a breath. "Once again, my father has forced me and my sisters into a situation that could get all of us killed."

There was a long silence until the elder Van Holtz asked, "Where's your father now?"

"He came to the house I'm renting in Queens. He

wanted money and someplace safe to stay. I . . . over-reacted a bit and now I don't know where he is."

"But he has the money?" Ric Van Holtz asked.

"He did. Max—my middle sister—talked to him after I left and she seems to believe that he's lost the money."

Kozlowski looked around the room before refocusing on Charlie. "I understood that your father took about a hundred million dollars."

"A hundred million British sterling, actually."

"How does one lose a hundred million of anything?"

"Oh, that's easy," she said with a casual air. "By being the biggest fucking idiot known to man or God."

Stevie wished she could say that such lowbrow activities were an insult to her amazing brain power and all her plans to change the world and humanity for good.

But she couldn't say that because she was enjoying herself *so much*.

Carrie had stormed away from her mother, screaming, "It all sucks! *I hate everything you've done! Why are you trying to ruin my wedding? This is my day!*"

It seemed to Stevie that Carrie had one level. Loud and hysterical screaming. She had no off switch.

Now, she stomped through the hotel like a linebacker in those ridiculous heels. She went straight for the exit and out on the streets.

Stevie, Max, and Dutch all followed, keeping in contact with Charlie through texts.

It was stupid but so much fun! Stevie rarely had fun like this. She was either working or in therapy. Only when she was around her sisters did she seem to have any fun.

Carrie suddenly darted into a bakery.

"She's binge eating!" Max announced as they stood across the street watching the store.

"What is your obsession with eating disorders?" Stevie asked. "Maybe she just wanted a bagel."

"It's a French bakery," Dutch felt the need to point out. "I doubt they have bagels." When Stevie faced him, he added, "Maybe she wanted a croissant?"

"Stop talking," Stevie said before she noticed that Carrie had come out the side door of the bakery and into the alley. And she wasn't alone.

The traffic had stopped, waiting for the light to change, so Stevie ran across the street after Max.

They went down the block on the right side of the bakery, going until they reached another alley entrance. Stevie followed right behind Max, only stopping when she ran into Max's back. Her sister didn't even budge, intent on peeking around the wall to watch what Carrie was up to.

Not wanting to risk touching the dirty alley floor, Stevie climbed up Max's back until she could look over her head and watch Carrie too.

Max leaned her head back to look at her. "Seriously?"

"Shhh."

Stevie cocked her head in an attempt to hear what the couple was saying. The man towering over Carrie was big. Not full-human big either, unless her cousin had decided to start hooking up with NBA players.

"What is he?" Stevie whispered.

"Polar, I think," Max whispered back.

The couple was whispering to each other—which made understanding what they were saying nearly impossible—and Carrie began crying at some point, which Stevie could tell shocked Max to her very honey badger core.

But weddings were stressful events. Right up there

with funerals and divorce, so Stevie was willing to give her cousin the benefit of the doubt. And, if you added in that she was clearly in love with someone besides her fiancé . . .

Well, yeah. That had to be stressful, too.

Then, things changed a little . . . and the making out started. It was like they were trying to swallow each other whole. But, after a few minutes, Carrie pulled away and rushed from the alley, forcing Stevie and Max to dive behind a Dumpster before their cousin could see them.

Once she was gone, Max used her phone to take a picture of their cousin's boyfriend before they made a quick escape as well.

"What do you think?" Stevie asked Max as they followed Carrie back to the hotel.

"I think she should stick with shorter guys. He was *way* too big for her. Watching them kiss was just . . . weird."

"That's all you have to say?"

"Yeah," Max replied, glancing at her as they walked. "Why?"

Berg opened the door and waited for Charlie to finish shaking the hands of everyone in the room, say her good-byes, and walk out. He followed, Britta and Dag bringing up the rear.

In silence, they made their way back to the elevator, waited for the doors to open, and got in. They went down all those floors to the parking structure. When the doors opened, Charlie stepped out first and they all followed. They reached his SUV and got in. He started it, then drove back onto the street.

Berg drove for about five minutes before he pulled over in a tow zone and stopped.

Staring straight ahead, he asked, "What the fuck just happened?"

Britta, who was now sitting in the front passenger seat, said, "A hybrid honey badger got three groups that detest working together to actually work together in order to find the person who has been trying to kidnap Stevie and shut him down."

Berg slowly nodded. "Yeah. That's what I thought happened." He glanced back at Charlie. She was again texting. "And how, exactly, did you do that?"

Charlie looked up, realized he was talking to her, and went back to texting while answering his question. "I didn't let it turn into a pit fight." When no one spoke, Charlie lowered her phone and explained, "If you let it turn into a pit fight, then it becomes all about winning. So you don't let it turn into a pit fight."

"We still don't know what that means," Britta pushed.

"Okay, I'll give you an example. When I was meeting with my aunt earlier, she brought up the fact that Max almost didn't walk for her graduation for beating up this girl. Most of the family believes Max just beat her up, you know . . . because. She is honey badger after all. But trust me, this chick had it coming. For years, since junior high, this girl kept picking on Max. She was the perfect cheerleader type. Looked really sweet, was really a bitch. And she hated Max. She made fun of her all the time, saying Max has shoulders like a man; she walks like a truck driver. And if the cheerleader got some beer in her, the ho became racist. Max and I were only one grade apart, so when I was in school, I managed to keep the pit fight from happening."

"How?"

"I already knew Max could destroy her, so I focused on Max rather than the drunk cheerleader. I simply reminded her that we didn't care what that girl said, that it didn't matter what that girl believed, that our only concern was protecting Stevie.

"And that worked . . . until I graduated. Stevie was already in college working on her masters. And that left Max alone with the cheerleader and her friends for an entire school year. Max held out, though, for longer than we thought she would. But about a week from graduating . . . pit fight. Why? Because none of the teachers or the administrators knew how to stop a pit fight before it starts. And once it starts . . . you end up with a bleeding, babbling cheerleader with no front teeth."

Britta cringed. She sometimes had nightmares about losing her front teeth.

"But then how did you get Max to still walk at graduation?" Dag suddenly asked.

"Oh, I knew the little bitch was going to be a serious problem and I knew that I'd graduate before Max, so I started keeping a file on the cheerleader. Basically, a dossier. I had enough information to bury her, and I made it clear to her extremely *indulgent* parents that if they didn't back me with the principal, her daughter could only use that early acceptance from Dartmouth to wipe her ass."

There was silence except for Charlie tapping away on her phone. Then, finally, Britta asked, "How old were *you* when you started keeping that dossier?"

"I guess I was about fourteen. Why?"

"Just wondering," Britta replied. She stared out the window and muttered again, "Juuuuust wondering."

Charlie met with her sisters back at the hotel. Britta and Dag had headed to Queens by then, but Berg had offered to come with her. She felt bad, though. He shouldn't have to be around the ridiculousness that was her cousin's wedding.

She found her sisters in some weird little coffee-house built into the lower floors of the Kingston Arms. She didn't understand why her sisters were there un-til she realized that this particular coffeehouse was all about honey. It wasn't bear owned, though. It was honey badger owned.

And the honey badger was ridiculously unpleas-ant . . . Max loved it.

A large paper cup of coffee was slammed down in front of Charlie and a plate with several honey buns was thrown in front of a startled Berg.

He roared when the plate hit the table, and Charlie didn't blame him one bit.

The badger sneered and walked back to his counter.

Grinning, Max asked, "Isn't this place great?"

"No!" they all replied.

"You haven't even tried the coffee."

Charlie stared at the innocent-looking cup. "He probably spit in it."

"I was watching him. Trust me. Try it."

She did. And as much as it irritated her to admit it, the coffee was fantastic.

"Try the honey bun," she pushed Berg.

He picked up the bun, sniffed it, studied it closely, sniffed it again—

"Oh, my God!" Max exploded. "Just eat it!"

Lip curling, Berg took a bite. He chewed, swallowed. Grudgingly smiled.

"Told ya."

"Could you stop being smug," Charlie asked, "and just tell me what's going on so I can get out of here?"

"We think she has a boyfriend," Max said before bit-ing into a giant lemon–poppy seed–honey muffin.

"The *bride*?" Berg asked, already on his third bun.

"It's gonna be messy," Stevie sighed.

"Her mother is going to flip out."

"If she doesn't love her fiancé," Berg asked, "then why is she marrying him?"

"Apparently he's a very rich full-human."

"We think he's a polar bear," Stevie said. "The boyfriend."

"She's screwing around with a polar bear when she's about to marry a full-human?" Berg frowned and glanced at Charlie. "You understand he could tear that man's legs off and do a little puppet dance with them, right?"

"Maybe you know him," Max said, pulling out her phone to show him the photo she'd taken.

"I don't know every bear, you know. So I'm not sure I can . . . This is your cousin's boyfriend?" Berg abruptly asked. "*Him?*"

Charlie cringed. "He's that bad?"

"He's definitely a problem." He motioned Max's phone away. "His name is Damian Miller. He owns a jewelry store on Forty-seventh Street, but his whole family is in the diamond business. And you don't get into the diamond business because you're a soft, friendly guy. His family has been in the industry since before the Russians sold Alaska to the States."

"Well, now we know what she sees in a man that's seven feet tall," Max remarked, dropping her phone on the table. "He's rich and probably buys her jewelry."

"He can still be a problem for your cousin," Berg said. "If he's territorial . . ."

"Why would he bother, though?" Max asked. "He's a rich jewelry guy who could probably get any woman. Why care about one honey badger? Enough, I mean, to want to ruin her wedding?"

Berg shrugged. "Because he's a bear. And he *can*."

"Then we should plan for the possibility that he'll

make an appearance just to cause problems," Charlie
said. "And we have to keep him out."

"Keep out a polar bear that wants in?" Berg nodded.
"Good luck with that."

"This is bad." Charlie admitted. "But I'm not dealing
with it right now. I'll talk to Bernice tomorrow." Charlie took another sip of her coffee before asking Berg,
"Are you still up for tonight?"

"Are you?"

"I am if you are."

"But you want to go, right?"

"Yeah . . . if you do."

"Oh, my God!" Max suddenly barked. "You two are
annoying the hell out of me."

"Shut up," Charlie snapped at her sister.

"You shut up."

Before Charlie could get into it with her sister—she
was in the mood to get into it with her sister—Dutch
suddenly ran into the coffeehouse and over to their
table.

"Hi!"

Berg growled a little and looked away. He was clearly
not a fan of wolverines. Or, at least, not this wolverine,
which she was fine with.

Dutch crouched next to her chair.

"I still hate you," she told him. "So why are you
bothering me?"

"I know you guys have had a long day, so I got you
into the hottest steakhouse in Manhattan and it's right
upstairs. Top floor of this hotel. People wait *months* to
get in and I got you a great table."

"Ooooh," Charlie mocked. "You got us into a fancy
restaurant. How exciting."

Berg leaned over and said low, "Uh . . . actually
it *is* a good restaurant. Shifter owned and run. They

just opened in the last few months, but they're already booked through the first of the year."

"So you're saying you want to go?"

"I wouldn't mind. Besides, if we leave now, we'll just be caught in traffic on the way back to Queens."

While Charlie pretended to debate the idea of taking Dutch up on his offer, Dutch began to beg.

"Please, Charlie! Please let me love you!"

It was so ridiculous that Charlie had to bite the inside of her cheek to stop from laughing.

The wolverine was *so* ridiculous.

"I don't want your love, idiot," she said when she could finally talk without laughing. "I will never forgive you."

"But I will give my life trying to make it up to you. My life. My soul. My underwear."

All Charlie could do was roll her eyes, but her sisters were laughing hysterically. Always so amused by their idiot friend.

Unlike Berg. He just motioned to the rude coffeehouse owner for more honey buns, his brown eyes glaring at the wolverine.

Dutch sat in a chair and grinned. "Charlie, let me plan your evening of love."

"Ew."

"I'll arrange everything. For both of you." He smiled at Berg and the bear's giant claw suddenly slashed at the wolverine's face, forcing Dutch to scramble back, falling out of his chair and landing on his ass. It wasn't a vicious attack. Just a bear-swipe of annoyance.

For the first time, they heard the coffeehouse owner chuckle before tossing another plate of honey buns in front of Berg.

"We'll take care of it," Max promised while she dragged Dutch off the floor by his hair.

"That's really not necessary," Berg argued.

But Charlie wasn't so quick to dismiss. "No. Let him do something right for once. You. Weasel. Go ahead. Do it. Create our night of love."

"Come on," Berg begged. "You're making me nauseous."

"But keep in mind," Charlie went on. "I won't forgive you. I'll still hate you. I will *always* hate you."

"There's a fine line between love and hate."

"Not for me."

Max pulled her friend toward the exit. "Give us twenty minutes."

Once they were gone, Berg asked, "Why do you put up with him?"

"Max likes him. She doesn't like a lot of people."

"Huh."

That was all he said. And yet Stevie slammed her hand down on the table, stood, grabbed her notebooks, her bag, and her cup of coffee, and went across the small room to another table, where she made herself at home. Alone.

Berg cringed. "Sorry. I didn't mean to upset her."

"I don't think you really did. She just wanted an excuse to leave." She glanced at her sister and smiled a little. "So she could work."

Another plate of honey buns along with some cinnamon rolls landed on the table in front of them, causing both Charlie and Berg to jump a little. The badger bared a fang before going back to his counter.

Charlie nodded at Berg's confusion. "He likes us," she insisted.

"I wouldn't want to see how he treats people he hates."

Chapter Twenty-two

B erg and Charlie hung out at the Rude Coffeehouse—
as they now called it—until Max returned without
Dutch and led them to an elevator that went express to
the top floor of the hotel.

As the elevator moved, Charlie reminded her sister,
"Don't forget to grab Stevie before you leave. Otherwise, she'll be sitting in that coffee shop all night. You
know how she gets when she starts working."

"Stop worrying. I'm on it."

"And we have to check in with Bernice tomorrow.
Give her a heads-up about what Carrie's up to."

"Okay."

"But don't tell her anything tonight. *I'll* deal with it."

"Okay."

"And have you heard again from Will?"

"Oh, my God!" Max exploded yet again. *"Would
you just fucking relax!"*

"Well, no need to yell at me."

"This is why you're going to get an ulcer."

The doors opened and they stepped into a large
restaurant. A *classy* restaurant. All Charlie could see
were designer dresses, designer bags, and expensive
jewelry.

She immediately looked down at what she wore. "Dude, we can't eat here."

"Calm down."

"I look like I just rolled up from a pickup basketball game at a local park."

Max hissed at Charlie through her teeth, one hand slashing through the air. Usually that was Charlie's move when she wanted Max to stop harassing someone.

Mortified, Charlie followed her sister through the thick crowd of people. Berg walked behind them. The entire place was packed. Every table filled. And mostly filled with shifters. Big tables in the middle of the room had whole wolf packs and lion prides. The groups roaring and snarling at their enemies as they ate.

A hostess smiled at Max when she pushed her way through the other shifters waiting to be seated.

"All set?" the woman asked.

"Yes. Here they are."

The woman grabbed two menus and a wine list. She motioned to them with a wave of her hand and started off. But Charlie couldn't get her feet to work. She had on a pair of her Converse sneakers. Bright purple! Jeans. A T-shirt with "I don't hear Mansplainin'" written on it. And tucked under that T-shirt . . . a Glock 9mm.

Not exactly a fancy-eatin' outfit.

Max pushed her from behind when Charlie didn't move. She was about to punch her sister, but Berg grabbed her hand and together they followed the hostess. She cut through the restaurant and Charlie assumed she was taking them to a table near the kitchen. Buried deep in the back. But they went past the kitchen, the soda machines, the bar, and kept on until they were going down a long hallway.

The hostess stopped in front of a door and opened it, gesturing with a sweep of her arm.

Charlie went in first and realized it was a private dining room.

An intimate space with a table already set for two people and wingback leather chairs. Big windows looked out over Manhattan, and the wood paneling made the room feel warm and intimate.

Berg came in after her. "This is awesome."

They sat down at the table and the hostess handed each of them a menu; a waiter stood beside her.

"This is Carl, your waiter for the evening. And Mr. Alexander wanted me to tell you both that tonight's meal is on him. Choose whatever you like from the menu and enjoy your evening."

"Whatever we want, huh?" Charlie smirked at Berg before telling the waiter, "I guess I'll have the most expensive thing on here."

"So, the surf and turf?"

"Sounds great."

"That's our whale blubber and zebra steaks—rare— with our world-famous peppercorn sauce."

Charlie's smirk turned to disgust and she again looked at Berg, who was studying his own menu. "Whale blubber?"

"The polars love that shit," Berg muttered.

"And zebra?"

"Lions. Although I've heard if it's cooked right . . . it's quite delicious."

"Ech." She shuddered. "No."

Charlie began to study her own menu, but all she saw was stuff she did not want. Bearded seals. Gazelle. Antelope. Beluga walrus. Giraffe.

"Giraffe?" she asked Berg.

"I heard it's gamey." Berg looked at the waiter and said, "I'll have the honey salmon with extra honey and the honey potatoes and the honey asparagus."

"Of course, sir."

The waiter turned to Charlie. "Would you like more time?"

"Can I just get a steak?"

"Of course. "

Relived, she smiled. "Great."

"What kind of steak? Bison, gazelle, elephant, crocodile, rhino—"

"Can I just get cow? Please."

"Absolutely. And sides?"

"Uhhhh." To be honest, she was afraid to look at the menu again. Who knew what they might offer as sides!

"May I suggest our potatoes au gratin?"

"It's just potatoes, right?

The waiter smiled. "Just potatoes and cheese."

"Weird cheese?"

"No, ma'am. French."

"That sounds perfect."

"And to drink?"

"Beer," Charlie and Berg said together.

The waiter pulled a two-sided laminated sheet out of his apron and held it out for Charlie and Berg to see.

"We have beer on tap as well as beer from around the world—"

"Oh, my God!"

"Two Heinekens please," Berg said quickly. "Bottled. Dark."

"Of course. I'll be right back with your drinks."

The waiter finally left, taking the menus with him, and Charlie let her head drop back. But she heard Berg laughing and she had to join him.

"Sweet, long-legged giraffes?" she asked. "And aren't rhinos endangered?"

"Out in the wild. We have our own . . . uh . . . ranches. For restaurants like this one. You've never been to a Van Holtz steakhouse?"

Charlie's eyes narrowed. "Van Holtz? Aren't they the guys who—"

"Yeah. We met them earlier. From the Group. Their Pack also owns and runs the biggest steakhouse chain in the States and Europe."

"But full-humans don't see that menu, do they?"

"No. Of course not. Those animal rights people would be all over their asses."

"Because they offer rhino!"

"Not wild. Shifters do not offer wild rhino or wild giraffes or anything that might remotely be struggling for survival on this planet. If you want wild, you have to go out hunting."

When Charlie frowned, he added, "As what you are . . . which means you could possibly get shot by human hunters. Something that has actually happened."

"You're kidding."

"Wish I was, but nope. There are quite a few of our kind, trapped in their animal form, stuffed, in some big game hunter's living room."

"That does not sound pleasant."

"There are also full-humans who know about us and take pleasure in hunting us down. The Group, Katzenhaus, and the BPC, just a few years back, tore apart a ring of hunters that specialized in shifters. Hunters are still out there, of course, but this particular gang of very rich assholes were . . . prolific."

"God, my grandfather really shielded me."

He rested his arms on the table and focused directly on her. "Why?"

"Well . . . my sisters and I had already been through a lot when we came to live with him and I guess he didn't want to freak us out."

"You mean what happened to your mom?"

"Yeah. We were . . . kinda there . . . when it went down. My father owed money . . . my mom didn't have the money . . ." She rubbed the back of her neck, desperate to change the subject. "Have you hunted as bear?"

"Yeah. But I grew up in Washington State, and we often vacationed in Alaska. We did the salmon run one year . . . but we got our asses kicked by the full-blood bears, so . . . yeah . . . we probably won't do that again."

The waiter returned with a busboy in tow. Beer was placed in front of them, water glasses filled, and warm bread, butter, and honey provided.

While they worked, the door to the room was left open and Charlie turned her head, pretty sure she'd seen something out of the corner of her eye. As she watched, something giggling ran by in the other direction. Charlie smiled when she realized it was a child. And hot on her heels was what she guessed was the child's giant-sized father.

The kid was fast, too, considering she didn't look much older than three or four. But she kept going, laughing the entire time. Shooting one way, then the other, until she was finally scooped up into her father's big arms right outside their open door.

With the girl hanging over his shoulder, the giant turned and blinked in surprise at Berg.

"Hey, Britta."

Berg closed his eyes, rubbed his forehead with one hand. "It's Berg. *I'm* Berg."

"If you say so." The giant walked into the room. Was his hair white . . . and gold? "You," he said, pointing at Charlie. "You punched out that lion at the practice rink yesterday."

"Yeah?"

"Do you know how to skate?"

Charlie didn't even bother to look at Berg anymore to make sure she was hearing what she *thought* she was hearing. "No."

"Do you wanna learn?"

"No."

"Are you sure?"

"Yes. I'm sure."

"What about your sister? Not the sickly one. The other one. With the blue hair."

"Go. Away."

"Fine." He waved at Berg. "See ya at practice, Britta."

Berg started to correct him again, but shook his head. "Why bother?"

"I ask myself that *all* the time."

They'd brought Mairi MacKilligan to the private air-strip that his clients owned. Their jet was on the tarmac and both women were inside, but they hadn't met with Mairi yet.

After a few hours, two of his men brought a bound and gagged male hostage into the hangar. They'd put a black bag over his head and dragged him kicking and screaming into the office with Mairi.

She sat at John's desk, her feet up on the metal, a fashion magazine open in her lap. She didn't even raise her head when they brought the man in. John briefly wondered if she were pretending not to care. Pretending not to be worried about being taken to a foreign country and held . . . for hours. With no idea about what was going on.

Then again . . . John's connections at Saughton couldn't get rid of Mairi fast enough. They took the money offered, but he had the feeling that they would have handed her over for free.

Standing by the side of the desk, John placed a .45 in front of the woman. She didn't even glance at it.

He started his speech. "You want to work for us? My client needs some proof that you're willing to do what they need." He gestured to the still screaming man. "This is your cousin. We grabbed him from your aunt's—"

John jumped at the shot at the same moment the bound man's head hit the wall from the power of the bullet and his entire body fell to the floor. The men outside the room scrambled to their feet, weapons drawn, ready to move, but all that activity was unnecessary.

Mairi dropped the gun back onto the desk and returned to her magazine.

Nothing about her changed. Nothing. No signs of stress. No signs of excitement either. Nothing but her one finger flipping the page of the magazine.

"That actually wasn't your cousin," John pointed out. "But I sense you really don't care one way or the other."

She finally glanced up, and John had known serial killers with warmer eyes.

"Is that it?" she asked. "Because . . . I'm bored. And the last thing you want me to be is bored."

John nodded, about to go out to the jet and get his clients, but the office door opened and one walked in, smiling at Mairi.

Moving quickly, John grabbed the gun, the barrel still hot, and tucked it into the holster attached to the back of his jeans.

Once he felt things were a little safer, he went to perform the introductions, but that was when he noticed Mairi doing something strange. Strange, even for her.

Gawking up at the client standing over her, Mairi leaned in and . . . well . . . she sniffed, sniffed her hard.

"My perfume, yes?" his client joked. "It is fabulous, I know."

Mairi continued to stare until she said, "You . . . feel so familiar."

Grin wide, his client stroked her hand through Mairi's

black and white hair and said, "Lovely girl, you have no idea . . ."

"Actually," Mairi said with a laugh, "I think *you* have no idea."

The food was awesome. The company perfect. And not once did Berg do anything stupid.

He didn't accidentally destroy the table. He didn't accidentally stand up and demolish the overhead lights. He didn't accidentally rip the door off the hinges by trying to open it. Part of all that was down to how the restaurant was designed. It was made for shifters, especially bears. So he ended up appearing almost normal to Charlie.

As they shared a chocolate soufflé that had Charlie's eyes rolling to the back of her head, there was a knock, and Ric Van Holtz peeked around the door.

"Can I come in?" he asked.

"No," Berg immediately said. He didn't want some model-handsome wolf ruining his night.

But Charlie cleared her throat and lifted a brow, silently reminding him that she had asked the Group for their help.

Sighing, Berg said, "All right."

Smiling—and did the bastard really have to be so pretty? And have such a freakishly normal height? How was that fair?—Van Holtz stepped into the room smelling like all the best kinds of food and asked, "Did you enjoy your meal?"

"It was great. Did you make it?" Charlie asked, probably noting his chef whites.

"I did. So I'm glad you enjoyed it. This is our newest restaurant and I just took over as head chef from one of my aunts."

"My salmon could have used more honey," Berg muttered.

The wolf's gaze lashed over to Berg and he growled out, "Then next time bring your own damn hive."

They snarled at each other until Charlie asked, "Any word on who is after me and my sisters?"

"We have one of our best investigators looking into it. She hopes to have something for you tomorrow morning."

"That would be great."

"My question, though," the wolf said, moving farther into the room, "is what do you and your sisters plan to do with this information?"

"Deal with the situation."

"And that's what concerns me," Van Holtz admitted, although he was working hard not to appear threatening. "What happened in the Bronx . . . we had to have our NYPD contacts handle things so that you and your sisters weren't tracked down and put in prison forever."

"It was self-defense."

"Of course it was." He smiled. "If you'd like, we could keep you informed about what's happening, but we— and I believe Katzenhaus and the BPC would agree— would prefer to handle the final outcome for you."

Charlie's eyes narrowed. "And what would we owe you? For such protection?"

Startled, Van Holtz began, "We wouldn't—"

"Because," Charlie cut in, forefinger raised, "my baby sister is not making designer meth. That is *not* where her science skills lie. And Max isn't going to become a hired killer for you or anybody else."

Van Holtz glanced at Berg again but the animosity was gone. Instead, he was just confused.

"It's a long story," Berg told him.

Van Holtz nodded, cleared his throat. "Uh, Ms. MacKilligan—"

"Charlie. Just call me Charlie."

"We—the Group—just want to protect ourselves. If you're found out . . . then we will all be found out. Trust me, no matter what one shifter breed might think of another, or how purebreds think of hybrids, at the end of the day, our real worry will always be the full-humans. The ones who have found out about us in the past have hunted us. For amusement. Like we're lions in a nature park." He took another step closer. "I understand you're used to working on your own, but now you don't have to. Now, to protect you and us, you have the full backing of three very powerful entities. The Group," he said, placing his hand on his chest. "Katzenhaus because of your, uh . . . non-meth-making youngest sister's tiger bloodline. And this is despite most cats' aversion to hybrids. And"—he looked over at Berg and smirked a little—"the BPC. We're all more than willing to help you. So let us."

Charlie studied the wolf for a long time. Almost an uncomfortable amount of time. But Berg was starting to understand how Charlie thought. How she worked. She was watching him to see if he looked away. If he showed any sign of weakness or lying. It was her instincts she trusted rather than anyone's words.

Finally, she said, "Get me the information . . . we can discuss it further then." She leaned in. "But if this turns out to be just a manipulation to get to my sisters"—her head dropped a bit but her eyes stared up at Van Holtz—"I will be *very* unhappy."

"Understood. I'll have my investigator come by your hotel room tomorrow morning."

"What hotel room? I'm staying in Queens, which you should know since you sent those two hulking broads to come get us there."

"One of those hulking broads was my mate, the other the coach for my hockey team. That being said, Dutch asked me to give this to you." The wolf placed a hotel keycard on the table. "He assumed you guys wouldn't want to drive back to Queens tonight."

Charlie stared down at the single keycard, but before she could complain about the assumptions being made, the wolf pointed out, "It's a Kingston Arms Premier suite. Completely paid for." He smirked at Berg. "Has two bedrooms."

Rude bastard.

Charlie picked up the gold card, held it between her hands. "That was a waste of Dutch's money," she muttered before looking over at Berg. "God knows, we only need the one bed."

And her gaze was so heated that Berg had to pick up the glass of water he'd ignored all through dinner and drink it down in one gulp.

Chapter Twenty-three

Berg pushed the double doors open and together they walked into the suite.

"Wowwwwwww," Charlie sighed.

"I didn't even have to duck," he noted, looking up to see that he still had headspace beneath the doorframe. "It's like how I imagine heaven."

Steps led down into the living room.

"I want to live here forever." Charlie did a little spin around. "Look at this place!"

Berg closed the doors. "Does this mean I need to be nice to the weasel?"

"Absolutely not!" She grinned before diving onto the couch. "Look at the size of this couch!" She ran from one end to the other. "It's as big as Nebraska!"

"It's bear-sized. So a polar can sleep on it comfortably."

"Or an elephant." With a laugh, she flopped onto the cushions. "Fabulous!"

Berg came around the couch and dropped down next to her. "Look. A basket."

"For us? Or do we have to pay for that shit like with a minibar?"

Not knowing the answer, Berg reached over and

grabbed the greeting card from the basket. "I'm guessing you'll need this," he read out loud. He took hold of the handle and moved the basket to the coffee table in front of them. The plastic wrap was a dark red so he couldn't see through it. He opened it and snorted.

"Love basket," he announced.

"Ugh," she said, rolling her eyes. "He is *such* an asshole."

Berg took a closer look before relaxing back into the couch. "Condoms. Oils. A couple of vibrators." He shook his head. "Subtle."

"The reason my sister likes Dutch so much is because he's as subtle as she is."

Now, right next to him, Charlie rested her head against his arm. He could see the exhaustion on her face, knew she'd had a long day and probably just wanted to go to bed. Alone. Without some big guy trying to sidle his way up to her so he could get laid. No matter what she might have said in the restaurant.

He pulled his arm out so he could put it around her shoulders and pull her in close.

"Get some sleep."

Her body relaxed. Her head now against his chest. "Okay."

After a few minutes, Berg thought Charlie was asleep until he heard her take in a deep breath.

"This new allergy med Stevie turned me on to is rocking my world."

Berg had to laugh. He'd never heard anyone talk about medications the way the MacKilligan sisters did.

"I can smell everything. It's like a new world has opened up to me."

"Now you can tell the difference between bears, I hope."

"Especially since you guys take it all so personally."

Charlie continued to sniff and Berg smiled, closing his eyes when he realized he was as tired as she was.

That was . . . until she suddenly turned her head into his body and began sniffing him.

She felt Berg jerk under her nose.

"Wha . . . what are you doing?"

"You smell awesome. But"—she took several more sniffs—"no cologne."

"I don't wear cologne. It bothers most of us . . . shifters I mean."

Charlie turned her body and took more sniffs, letting her nose lead her up to his neck, taking in Berg's scent.

When she pulled away, about to say again how awesome he smelled, she found his gaze locked on her face, jaw tight, brow pulled low. It should have frightened her, that particular expression, but nope.

Charlie leaned in, keeping her eyes locked on his, not wanting to lose the contact. Not wanting to lose him.

As she had earlier that morning—*Christ, had that only been* this *morning?*—Charlie pressed her lips against Berg's.

She really wasn't tired anymore. The thought of going to sleep now . . . no. She didn't want to do that.

She continued to kiss him, his body rigid beneath her.

Maybe he'd suggested getting some sleep because once he was alone with her, he wasn't really interested. Didn't really want to be bothered with a crazy female and her even crazier sisters and the psychotic family they belonged to despite the fact the family wanted nothing to do with Charlie and her siblings.

What sane male wanted to be part of all that?

Realizing she'd made a mistake, Charlie started to pull away, but he must have felt it. Must have felt her retreat because his big hands suddenly framed her face and he kissed her back. Hard and wonderfully overwhelming.

His tongue slid into her mouth, tangled with hers, while he pulled her onto his lap.

All sleepiness and doubt wiped from her mind, Charlie could only think about getting Berg Dunn's clothes off. She went for his T-shirt first, gripping the fabric with her hands and lifting, revealing abs and a chest that Charlie had assumed she'd only find in comic book hero movies.

Berg pulled back and lifted his arms so she could remove his shirt, then quickly returned, kissing her again, like he was trying to crawl inside her. Become one with her.

She should have been freaked out by his intensity. When guys she'd dated in the past, full-humans, attempted to come on to her like this, she couldn't get away fast enough. They'd made her uncomfortable, made her envision hard breakups that involved stalking.

But not Berg. She didn't get that vibe with him. So she let him overwhelm her. She let him grab her tight around the waist and pull her even closer, his lips never leaving hers.

His hands moved over her skin, fingertips sliding over scars and bumps, and he didn't seem to care. Scars weren't ugly to him, just reminders of what it meant to be the daughter of Freddy MacKilligan.

She didn't even know when he got her shirt off. Or her bra. She just knew her top half was naked and his mouth was on her breasts, sucking her nipples, his hands enjoying the weight before moving to her back, her waist.

Charlie gasped, his mouth on her nipples felt . . . different. Weird. Not bad, though. Not bad at all. More like outstanding. Yes. Outstanding. Like he had two mouths on one nipple.

Yeah. That was definitely weird. Weird she'd even thought of that.

But before she could try to figure out what was happening, he had her on her back, her jeans and panties down around her ankles.

She thought he'd take off her jeans completely but he didn't. He just lifted her legs, her knees bent, and pushed them practically over her head. It was like the jeans were ropes, keeping her legs trapped. Just the thought had her wet.

Then his face disappeared and his mouth was on her pussy.

Charlie gasped. She felt it again. Like there were two mouths on her rather than just the one. She didn't get it. Didn't understand it. But couldn't really even think about it too much. Not when he began to eat her out. His tongue was sliding inside her like he wanted to devour her. Lips playing with her clit. Twisting it this way and that. Owning it. Ruling it.

Reaching above her head, Charlie grasped the arm of the couch and held on for dear life. Twisting from one side to the other. It seemed like her body wanted to get away. That what it was feeling was just too intense. But no. She didn't want to get away. She wanted to stay here as long as she could, letting Berg Dunn twist her around his big fingers like the finest bread dough.

Her grip on the couch tightened. Her legs trembled. She heard roaring and realized it was in her ears. Like a tsunami crashing down on her.

Her back arched off the couch, but Berg—*thank God!*—held on. Kept her grounded to this moment as he made her come once . . . then again. One orgasm right after the other and she couldn't stop it. Not that she wanted to but it didn't matter.

She cried out at some point, but she didn't know when. She just knew that she was coming all over Berg's face and he didn't seem to care. He just kept licking and playing and holding her pinned to that giant couch that she wanted to take with her wherever she might move in the next ten thousand years.

When the second orgasm finally left her body, she realized she had Berg trapped between her thighs, unwilling to let him go.

She forced herself to release the man, panting harshly as she turned on her side.

Charlie gave herself a moment to calm down. She didn't want to say anything stupid. Do anything stupid that could ruin what had just happened. But she made the foolish mistake of looking up at the bear sitting beside her. His arms were stretched out across the back of the couch, his gaze focused straight ahead. Then his tongue lashed out and licked her juices from his face.

It was like he was licking the remnants of that honey bun they'd had earlier. Like he'd never tasted anything better.

And he was tasting her.

She shoved her jeans, panties, and sneakers off, then launched herself at the bear, shoving him down on the couch.

His eyes widened in shock.

"What's happening?" he demanded.

"Shut up," she ordered. She unzipped his jeans and yanked them down far enough to get his cock out. She grabbed a condom from Dutch's stupid—but helpful—love basket.

She had the condom on him, and that's when he decided to start talking.

"Charlie—"

She covered his face with her hand before grabbing his cock with the other and holding it steady so she could drop her pussy on it. She did and . . . holy shit.

Holy shit holy shit holy shit holy shit holy shit holy shit . . .

All his best intentions out the window.

He'd planned to do the whole taking his time, getting her to another orgasm thing. He'd planned on a good half hour for their first time. But then she'd attacked him. She'd come after him like a cheetah after a gazelle in one of those Animal Planet documentaries.

And God, he'd liked it. Loved it. Knowing she wanted him as much as he wanted her.

The problem now was that the bear in him wanted her. Not the man. The bear wanted her and Berg wasn't sure he could do much about it.

He decided to risk it. To take a chance that Charlie MacKilligan was really up for this ride.

He gripped her hips and in one move rolled them over—while keeping his cock inside her—putting her in the same position he'd had her when he'd given her head.

She gasped in surprise but she didn't try to push him off. She didn't seem pissed. Just curious.

He bent her knees and pushed her legs back so that when he leaned in, her ankles rested on his shoulders.

Placing his arms on either side of her, he loomed over her. And, again, she didn't seem to mind. He moved his hips a bit. This way. That. Until he heard her make a sound that was distinct. And he felt it. The way her pussy clenched hard. Knowing he'd hit the right spot, he plowed into her. Not taking his time. Not really thinking about much besides how good she felt.

He just fucked her. Hard. But he'd been smart, like most bears. Found the right spot so that, as he fucked her, his cock kept hitting it. Kept slamming into it.

Now her entire body clenched around him. Her hands reached up and grabbed hold of the couch arm again. He was grateful, too, because her claws came out, ripping into the leather rather than his flesh.

Her eyes were open wide and she stared right through him. Her breath shortening, her body beginning to shake. And he just kept going. The grizzly had taken over, claiming what was his, making Charlie his . . . at least as far as the bear was concerned.

She began to curse. The same phrase over and over. "Oh, shit. Oh, shit. Oh, shit." Until it was one, long word: "Ohshitohshitohshitohshitohshitohshitohshitohshit!"

Charlie exploded around him, her curses becoming a silent shout, her sweat mingling with Berg's, the couch arm devastated by those claws.

And he came right behind her. Unable to stop himself once he'd looked down into that beautiful face and saw such pleasure. Such happiness at what he was doing to her. Oblivious to what *she* was doing to *him*.

When the last spasm rolled through him, he collapsed on top of her, unable to move for at least two minutes. Then he was afraid he would crush her, so he moved them both onto their sides, staring at each other. Panting. Sweating. Smiling.

"This doesn't have to mean anything," she finally said, not hurting his feelings because he could hear the teasing in her voice.

"Oh, yeah?"

"Yeah. It could just be the haze of first time sex. I bet, if we try again . . . we'll find out it was a fluke."

To Berg's amazement, even before he registered

what she was really saying to him, his cock understood.
It twitched, still inside her. Still wearing the condom.

"We should definitely try again." He was still panting, but his body didn't care. He reached over her to the
basket, grabbed another condom. "You know . . . to be
sure."

Chapter Twenty-four

With her head buried in the mattress, blocking the scream she couldn't stop, the orgasm shot through Charlie's body. She couldn't really move, though. Berg had his hand on her back, keeping her pinned to the mattress, her ass in the air so he could fuck her from behind. His free hand teasing her clit. Managing to get yet another orgasm out of her.

She felt him stiffen above her and then he was coming, roaring. The goddamn windows shook a bit.

When he was wrung dry, he collapsed next to her, but he didn't relax until he'd pulled her into his body, holding her against his chest.

"Okay," she admitted, "maybe it's more than just a first-time sex haze."

"Yeah," he said, chuckling. "Maybe."

No longer wearing her watch because all her clothes were in the other room, Charlie asked, "What time is it?"

"No idea." He blindly grabbed the remote control by the bed and hit a button. The dark drapes flew back and they both screamed at the bright morning sun flooding their room.

"Close it!" she yelled at him. "Close it!"

The drapes quickly closed and they again collapsed onto the mattress.

"We've been fucking all night," she admitted out loud.

"Yes. We have been fucking all night."

"Awesome," she sighed, enjoying Berg's laugh as he hugged her tight.

They ordered breakfast from room service and nothing was more enjoyable than watching Charlie's reaction to the amount of waffles, bacon, and honey that was brought.

"Who is going to eat all this?" she demanded, staring at the *platters* of food.

Like Berg, she wore one of the hotel terrycloth robes, but this was a bear suite so it was a robe for someone Britta's size and Charlie was swimming in it. The back dragged behind her like some medieval train, and she looked like a queen to Berg.

"Is your brother coming?" she asked while Berg walked around the large table on the terrace.

"He is not coming and stop making me feel bad about how much food I eat. I'm a bear! I have an appetite."

"Uh-huh," she said, eyeing him when he ended up behind her and pulled out her chair. She jumped a bit. "What are you doing?"

"Being a gentleman. Enjoy it, this won't last."

She laughed. "That's probably a good thing. I'm not used to gentlemen."

Berg sat down in the chair next to her but leaned over to kiss her before he started to eat. She kissed him back, her mouth smiling against his; the palms of her hands pressed against the sides of his neck.

When he pulled back, his gaze focused on her lips, she pointed at him. "My stomach is growling. We're eating."

He grinned. Knowing she still wanted him, even after their long night, meant he could wait to get her back to bed.

They ate and talked, enjoying being on the terrace without anyone attempting to kill Charlie at that very moment. It was windy, but the walls on either side that separated them from the other terraces cut down on that problem considerably.

"Tell me about your mom," he said after a little time.

"My mom?"

"You talk about your father all the time. What about your mom?"

"She was amazing. And I'm not saying that simply because I lost her early." Her smile was so warm, so loving that Berg felt it in his chest. "She was the hardcore artist type, although she had no artistic skill whatsoever. She called herself a muse. She was there to inspire others to feats of greatness," she said while stretching her arms in the air, and Berg had the feeling that was a move her mother used to make. "Stevie's mom, although I never forgave her for just deserting her child, knew that there was no one better for Stevie than my mom. She knew how to get brilliance out of people without pressuring. Without pushing. You never want to push Stevie."

"How long has Stevie been . . ." He searched for the least insulting word.

"Nervous, high strung, and panicky?"

He shrugged. "Okay."

"Always. When you have an IQ as high as . . . possibly *anyone* . . . *ever*, it's hard not to also be kind of a mess. We're lucky she only has a panic disorder. She could have just as easily turned into the Unabomber."

Charlie lowered her voice. "And that nearly happened. But we managed it."

"And Max?"

She went back to her normal voice. "Max was the first to move in with us. Her mother called mine, asked her to babysit while she took on a job. Turned out the job was a jewelry heist that my father arranged. When things went bad . . . he ran, leaving her and the others behind. After that, Max just never left us."

"And what about your mother?" she asked, bringing the mug of coffee to her lips.

"My mother smokes pot."

He wasn't really surprised when her sip of coffee spewed across the table.

"Pardon?" Charlie asked, unable to stop her giggling.

"My mother has, as long as I've known her, been an aficionado of the leaf."

"Seriously?"

"Yeah. She's a very laid-back bear. Of course, now she's got the business."

"The business?"

"She used to make THC-infused honey for her and her friends, but now . . . she makes it for anyone willing to pay for it. Her business is getting huge . . . much to my sister's shame."

"Britta's not a fan?"

"My mother has always embarrassed her. She'd come to parent-teacher conferences in her tie-dye dresses with Bob Marley silk-screened on the front. She never smoked, though, when she was pregnant with us, which I appreciate."

"I thought she bred dogs."

"She did that, you know, legally."

"I am *loving* this story."

"You're making fun of me."

"No. Not at all. My mother wasn't exactly a saint, you know. She was just . . . awesome. And that sounds like your mom, too. I love awesome moms. And your dad?"

"Just a regular grizzly. If he could hibernate part of his life away in a cave . . . he would. Instead he just sleeps in his recliner, watches a lot of TV, and manages the hives my mother uses for her honey business. They're a good couple. At some point, I'm assuming, you'll meet her."

She swallowed her bacon, noticing that Berg was staring at her.

"Am I supposed to be freaked out because you mentioned meeting your parents?" Charlie asked, snorting when he gave a small, adorably embarrassed shrug. "I guess you forgot I'm half wolf. And we attach. I just spent all night fucking you. I wasn't planning on going anywhere anytime soon. And since you seem to have poor decision-making skills when it comes to choosing a woman, I'm going to assume that's not a problem for you."

"It's not," he said quickly, smiling.

"This doesn't mean we're married," she felt the need to amend. "It just means I'm not a one-night stand kind of girl. We just do what normal people do."

Berg looked off, thinking. And she knew he was trying to figure out what "normal people do."

"Date, dumb ass," she explained. "Get to know each other better. Keep having sex."

"Oh!" His smile returned. "Yeah, I can do that."

Charlie grabbed another strip of bacon and sighed out, "Bears."

* * *

Berg was having such a good time hanging out with Charlie—alone for once—that he was definitely annoyed when he heard a doorbell.

Frowning, they both stared at each other.

"Was that a doorbell?" Charlie finally asked.

"Yeah."

"This room has a doorbell? Like a house?"

"Apparently." He pushed back from the table, went inside, and across the room. He pulled open the door and blinked in surprise.

"Hi, Hannah."

Hannah Jameson was a bear hybrid and a close friend of Britta's. They'd played in the hockey minors together a few years back. Hannah went on to become Hannah "The Destroyer of Worlds" Jameson on the Carnivores team. A "power forward" that his bear friends who loved hockey worshipped. She was a high scorer or whatever and almost every time she was on the ice, she had two grinder foxes who protected her. The Gallo twins. At least one of his younger cousins had a poster of the three women on his bedroom ceiling. They were in full hockey gear except for their helmets and looked absolutely terrifying, but the kid loved them.

But Hannah also did investigative work for the Group. They'd rescued her years ago from a pit fighting operation somewhere up north and had paid for her room and board and education. She never did the "wet work" as guys in the Marines used to call that sort of thing.

At the same time, Hannah wasn't above taking on a challenge. Especially when she and Britta went to a bar and received less than respectful come-ons from drunk full-humans who thought it would be funny to "get a ride on the big girl!"

At six-three, Hannah never took that particular insult

very well. Neither did Britta. They'd bonded early on from their barroom brawls and the Group had always been nice enough to use its connections in the NYPD to get both out of jail in a timely manner and without any black marks on their records.

Still, he had no idea why Hannah was here now.

"Hi, uh . . . Daaaaa"—he frowned and she quickly changed it to—"aaaaBerg?"

"Da-Berg? Really?"

"I knew it was one of you."

He liked Hannah so he wouldn't hold it against her that after all these years she still couldn't tell him and Dag apart. Britta said she couldn't tell the Gallo twin foxes apart either. She just called each of them "Twin" and pointed.

"So what's up?" he asked.

"Is there a Charlie here?"

"Yeah. Why?"

"I found out some information about her recent problems. I usually just hand my research off to the agent in charge of the case, but I was told that would not happen because apparently she kicked that agent's ass." She smirked. "Brava, by the way."

Laughing, Berg stepped back. "Come on in."

Charlie stared at the remains of the bacon. The hotel had provided a platter full of two kinds of bacon. Crispy and chewy, each in its own separate pile. Berg liked crispy and Charlie had dug into the chewy. Perfect.

The problem was that when it came to bacon, Charlie didn't have an "off" switch like she did when she ate almost anything else. If there was a pound of bacon in front of her, she would eat that entire pound without even blinking an eye. So she only allowed herself to get bacon on holidays like Christmas or Thanksgiving morning. She was afraid if she ate it every day, her heart would explode from all the grease.

At the moment, there was a lot of bacon left and Charlie didn't want to finish it. Well . . . she *did* want to finish it, but she knew she shouldn't. Cholesterol could still be an issue with shifters. They weren't immune!

But her resistance was fading. Sitting on the terrace of a luxury hotel, with the hottest—and nicest!—guy she'd ever been with, wearing a fancy hotel robe, and feeling immensely relaxed from all that great sex . . . it seemed a perfect day for more bacon.

Her hand was over the platter when she heard Berg say, "Charlie, this is Hannah."

Charlie snatched her hand back and looked toward the open glass doors. Berg stood beside a tall, powerfully built, dark-haired woman with dark brown eyes and a pretty face. But there were scars on her neck and her bare arms. A lot of scars. Scars on top of scars.

"And Hannah, this is Charlie."

Hannah stepped closer and held her hand out. Charlie shook it and gestured to the table. "Hungry? We have a ton of food left."

"I haven't finished eating yet," Berg said, sitting down. "And you have to finish your bacon."

"I'm fine," Hannah said, pulling out one of the other chairs and sitting down. "Ric Van Holtz sent me over. I did research on the people who've been trying to take your sister Stevie? Plus, the, uh, stolen one hundred million from your Uncle Will?"

"Yes. Did you find out anything?" Charlie sighed. "It's a Peruvian drug lord again, isn't it? My father and his Peruvian drug lords."

"Um, actually . . . no." She opened her backpack.

There was a laptop in there but that wasn't what Hannah pulled out. Instead, she dug around until she grabbed a magazine. She placed it next to Charlie's plate.

"*Vanity Fair*?" Charlie asked. "You found the ones trying to kill me in *Vanity Fair* magazine?"

"I did. The pages are marked."

There was a pink Post-it in the middle of the magazine and Charlie quickly flipped to that page. Berg got up and crouched next to her.

Spread across the first two pages was a pictorial feature on what Charlie had to call the hottest women she'd ever seen. Dark-haired Italian beauties wearing gold bikinis that looked stunning against their golden brown skin, thin gold belly chains around their tight abs. On their feet they had Louboutins and on their wrists and necks, they had diamonds. Lots of diamonds.

Still, despite their obvious wealth, the whole thing looked a little lowbrow for *Vanity Fair* until Charlie read out loud, "The Twin Italian Invasion of Silicon Valley." She shrugged and looked at Hannah. "Who are they?"

"Caterina and Celestina Guerra. CEOs of a major software company out of the Lombardo region of Italy. Their mother was an aristocrat of Italian and Greek birth. Very wealthy. Very independent. And she needed that independence because she was disowned by her family when she had the twins."

"That's harsh."

"Well, she met a much older man. She was in her late twenties and he was in his late sixties—"

"Ew."

"—but she ignored her parents' concerns over the relationship. What she didn't know, unfortunately, was that her much-older lover was still married and that she was not the only mistress. When she found out, she didn't take it well. I think there were some rage issues.

Anyway, her parents cut her off. Her lover wouldn't help and cut off all contact. She was on her own with twin girls, but she was smart, vicious, and not afraid to get her hands bloody. She built a successful business and trained her daughters to take over, which they did when she got sick and died about a decade ago. From what I understand, the twins blame their biological father's absence for their mother's death. And they blame the father's family for his absence."

"That's surprisingly fascinating," Charlie said, "but I still don't know what this has to do with me and my sisters."

"Well"—she cleared her throat—"their father is . . . Colin MacKilligan. I believe your grandfather, which would make Caterina and Celestina . . . your . . . uh . . . aunts."

Charlie gazed at the woman called Hannah, then back at the magazine, where the women's matching smiles almost seemed to mock her. Unable to look anymore, she tossed the magazine onto the table and pushed her chair back, standing. She walked around the table and over to the railing. She stood there, her hands on the black metal, staring out over the city.

After a full minute of silence, Charlie suddenly screamed, *"I hate my familyyyyyyyyyyy!"*

Sitting outside on the front porch enjoying her breakfast of a couple of bananas, Max abruptly looked away from her morning paper and over the Queens street outside their rental home.

She glanced at Stevie sitting in the swing with the Dunns' dog, his giant head resting in her lap. The sisters locked eyes and Max began to ask, "Did we just hear . . ."

Her question died away and they gazed at each other

for a long moment before they said simultaneously, "Nahhhhhhh."

Berg cringed as Charlie's scream echoed out over the city, and he watched her begin to pace.

"What is wrong with these people?" Charlie demanded . . . of the air. "If I looked back into the MacKilligan lineage, would I only find assholes and scumbags? Are there any other kinds of MacKilligans? Am *I* a scumbag or asshole?"

"Of course not."

"Don't lie to me, Berg."

"I'm not lying. You can't be responsible for your asshole father, uncles, and grandfather."

"And aunts. I have asshole aunts, too."

"There is something else," Hannah said.

Charlie threw up her hands. "Oh, come on!"

"What is it, Hannah?" Berg pushed, hoping to get Charlie to focus and prevent Hannah from making a desperate run for it.

"From what I can tell . . . I don't think the twins know that shifters exist. I don't think they know they're not completely human."

Charlie stopped pacing, stared at the hybrid. "Is that even possible?"

"It's rare," Berg replied, "but it's been known to happen."

"How did they get through puberty and not know?" Charlie pushed. "Even though I can't shift, puberty was still hell on wheels."

Surprised, Berg asked, "You can't shift?"

"Nope. My father's fucked-up genes win again. I can just unleash claws and fangs, and it's really hard to kill me . . . which definitely *is* a plus."

"But think about it," Hannah said, pulling out her laptop and moving plates and platters so she could lay it on the table. "Instead of reveling in the success of their lives, they're busy trying to fuck over the people who they feel destroyed their mother. It's all that . . ."

"Honey badger rage?" Charlie asked.

"Without shifting, without even knowing what they are, they have no place for all that rage to go." Hannah began tapping away at the laptop keys.

"So what if they find out what they are? What if they learn to shift?"

Berg shook his head. "Being a shifter is kind of like being a hardcore drinker. It doesn't make you an ass-hole, it just enhances the asshole already within. These two females are not going to become lovely young ladies because they can let their honey badger out. I mean, do you think Max would be, deep in her soul, any different if she weren't a—"

"Okay. Okay," Charlie cut in. "I get your point."

Hannah turned the laptop around.

Charlie smirked. "You hacked into their private pic-tures?"

"Yeah. I'd strongly suggest you not look at the vid-eos." Hannah scrunched up her face, gave a short shake of her head. "Trust me."

"Oh, look . . . they hunt big game in Africa with rifles and crossbows. Nothing like standing over a dead elephant to make you feel one with nature." She flicked through a few more pics but then she ended up seeing her aunts naked.

Berg heard her squeak and watched her click away from those images as fast as her fingers would let her.

The real problem was when Charlie started to go through the twins' email.

Charlie seemed to be a speed-reader, zipping through

the information quickly until she abruptly stopped and shoved her chair back again. She stood and stalked off, back into the hotel suite.

Shocked, Berg leaned in to read the email that had upset Charlie. He saw the problem immediately.

His head dropped and he said to Hannah, "Charlie's father has been talking to the twins?"

"From what I can tell," Hannah admitted, "he stole his brother's money at their urging . . . and then the twins stole it from him. Not because they needed to, but more a 'why the fuck not' kind of thing. I'm guessing they think it's funny."

"And I'm guessing Charlie's father walked right into that shit."

Chapter Twenty-five

Berg had barely stopped the truck before Charlie was out of it and crossing the street to her rental house. She opened her front gate and stepped through, and Berg's dog ran around the side of the house to greet her. She petted him, but kept moving.

She walked into the house with the dog right behind her. She closed the door but had only taken a few steps when she heard a knock on it. She went back and found Berg standing there, appearing a bit disgruntled.

"What are you doing?" she demanded, in no mood. "Get in here."

"You closed the door in my face."

She headed toward the kitchen. "Not on purpose."

"That does not make me feel better. Especially when you made sure the dog got in."

Her sisters sat at the kitchen table. Max had her feet up, a magazine in her lap. Stevie was bent over a notebook, writing, her hand moving fast over the paper. She had a laptop open next to her work, but when she got really excited, she loved writing by hand.

Dutch was also there, his arms on the table, crossed. His head resting on his arms. He appeared to be sleeping. He could sleep anywhere, during anything, according to Max.

Not knowing how to start the conversation, Charlie tossed the *Vanity Fair* magazine in the middle of the table.

Max was the only one who reacted. She grabbed the magazine and quickly found the Post-it marked page. She held up the picture of the twin billionaires. "You want me to start dressing like this?"

"Yes. Including the gold belly chain."

She chuckled and studied the picture. "Who are they?" she finally asked.

Berg rested against the doorframe, arms crossed. He watched her but didn't say anything, which she appreciated. This was family business and one night of sex did not automatically make him family.

"Those billionaire twins are, apparently, our aunts."

Max frowned, confused. Stevie's head snapped up, eyes wide. And even Dutch stirred from his slumber, yawning and staring at the picture. He nodded. "Your aunts are hot."

"And have been trying to kill us."

Charlie went through the story quickly. Everything she'd learned from Hannah. As she spoke, she could feel her anger growing. Her father. Her idiot father.

True, he wasn't responsible for the angry twins, but he'd colluded with them. He'd gone against his own family for them. And he probably had no idea who they were. No idea whatsoever that the Guerra twins were actually his half-sisters. That they were only using him to get even with a family they hated for their own reasons.

Once again, his stupidity had put her in a situation where she had to do something she really didn't want to do.

When she was finished, she waited for her sisters to

react. To tell her what they thought, what they might want to do.

Stevie dropped back in her chair and said simply, "Those bitches."

But Max jumped up and came around the table to stand next to Charlie. She placed the magazine on the table and then proceeded to . . . pose? Yes, pose like the twins. It was . . . ridiculous.

"Dude"—Dutch shook his head—"no. Just . . . no."

"What? We can be as sexy as these two."

"No," Dutch said sadly. "No, you really can't." He reached across the table and grabbed the magazine. "How do you pronounce their last name?" he asked Charlie.

"Do I look Italian to you?"

"Wear-a," Stevie said, going back to her notebook. Charlie noticed it wasn't one of the college-ruled or graph paper notebooks she usually worked in, but a music notebook. Charlie couldn't remember the last time she'd seen her sister do anything related to writing music. It had been absolute years.

"Wear a what?" Dutch asked.

Stevie lifted just her eyes to Dutch. "Wear-aaaaa. That's how you pronounce it."

He pointed at the magazine. "But there's a *G*."

Fed up, Stevie snatched the magazine from him and threw it across the room. "*Don't* annoy me."

Charlie realized that Max was still standing beside her . . . still posing.

Her sisters weren't going to let their father fuck up their day yet again. Only Charlie ever did that. But not today. Not after her great night.

"We should get to work," she announced.

"On my modeling career?" Max asked. *Still* posing.

"Stalking our cousin the bride." She shoved Max, who flew toward Berg. He stepped aside and Max continued through the doorway.

"Not cool!"

Actually . . . Charlie thought it was very cool. Her new boyfriend could handle being around her family. For a MacKilligan girl . . . that was a win.

Britta disconnected the call just as Berg walked into the house.

"There's a job in California for a couple of days," she said, as he searched the side tables. "If you're interested—"

"I'm not. Where are your car keys?"

"Which car?"

"The SUV. And why do you have keys in multiple places?"

"It's in my bag and I'm not having this argument with you yet again." He picked up her small, black backpack, quickly located the SUV keys, and was gone.

She was about to yell at Dag, still asleep upstairs, to see if he wanted to go to California for a few days when Berg came back in the house and dropped into a chair across from the couch she was sitting on. He was smiling and seemed . . . satisfied.

"I thought you were going out," she said.

"I never said I was going out."

"Then why did you need my car?"

"Charlie and her sisters needed a car to go into the city."

Britta sat up, pointing a finger at her brother. "You gave those lunatics *my* car?"

"I need *my* car." He thought a moment, then added. "And they're not lunatics. They're . . ."

"They're . . . what?"

"Honey badgers. Mostly."

Britta was moments from yelling at her brother, but she heard someone come creeping down the stairs.

The cat shifter her brother had picked up the night before was wearing the clothes she'd been wearing when Britta saw her coming into their house with Dag.

She silently watched the puma walk by, heading toward the door. The twat smiled at Berg but didn't even acknowledge Britta, and it was her house too.

So Britta did what any sister would do, "I really wish you'd stop bringing your *whores* here, Dag!" she yelled at the cat's back

The cat stopped at the living room doorway, back muscles flexing. But after a few seconds, she headed out; the front door slammed shut.

Grinning, she looked at Berg. "What?" she asked when he shook his head at her.

"Do not do that when Charlie spends the night."

"I wouldn't do that to Charlie," she admitted, "because Charlie would rip my face off. Because she's a lunatic. *Which is why I can't believe you gave her my car!*"

"Lent. I *lent* her your car. She'll bring it back."

"Covered in bullet holes?"

Her brother shrugged. "There's every possibility."

They drove the Dunns' SUV into the city and parked in the structure across the street from the Kingston Arms.

"You find Carrie and keep an eye on her. I want to know exactly what she's up to."

Max nodded. "Okay. Dutch will be meeting up with us later."

"Why?"

"Honestly? I think he's having fun."

"I know I am!" Stevie suddenly piped in, her grin wide. "I feel like a spy."

"Whatever." Charlie motioned at her sisters. "Stay

on Carrie. I'll talk to Bernice." She sighed. "I guess she needs to know about her crazy half-sisters too."

"What makes you think she doesn't know already?" Max asked, so casually that Charlie began to worry. "Okay. Forget I said that. Forget I said anything."

Max sounded so concerned that Charlie asked, "What are you talking about?"

She ran her fingers over Charlie's forehead. "You've got the 'I'm freaking out' frown lines."

"Did you take your meds today?" Stevie abruptly asked Charlie. "I've got some Xanax in my bag."

"Why do you have—" Charlie took a step back— mentally and physically. "Nope. I'm not doing this. Do what I tell you to do, and I'll deal with Bernice. Okay? Great."

Charlie walked away, but Max's voice followed after her. "For someone who just got laid—"

Charlie turned fast, her arm raised, her fingers pointing like a gun. It felt good to see Max dodge behind the closest car, a move Charlie had trained her to do right after their mother had died. But she was worried that Stevie just stood there, staring, until Max grabbed her arm and yanked her behind the car, too.

"Hopeless!" Charlie yelled, heading off again. "So very fucking hopeless!"

"We love you, too!" Max yelled back.

Max was shocked to see their cousin up before noon. Even with her wedding day fast approaching, they never thought Carrie would drag her ass out of bed and face the day. Not when she had her mother and brides-maids handling most of the bullshit duties. But there she was . . . clearly sneaking out of her hotel room.

Knowing her cousins, Max assumed the others had gotten high on the hotel offerings of snake poison–

infused vodka and promptly passed out in a big pile of honey badger females, allowing Carrie to sneak away simply by stepping over her passed-out relatives.

Carrie eased the door closed and took a quick look around before running toward the elevators.

Max stepped back and pressed herself against the wall before her cousin passed the hallway she was hiding in with Stevie.

Once their cousin passed and they heard the ding of the elevator, they went after her, catching the next elevator. Max assumed that her cousin was going to the first floor. The fiancé was somewhere in the hotel with all his dude-bro groomsmen but Max doubted that's where Carrie was headed.

She stepped out of the elevator and went up on her toes, trying to see over the crowd of people in the perpetually busy hotel.

"There," Stevie said, pointing. They ran after their cousin, catching sight of her as she hurried outside and caught a cab.

Max stepped off the curb and raised her hand to hail her own cab. Stevie laughed behind her. "This is so cool. We're in hot pursuit!"

A cab stopped and Max pulled the door open with one hand and shoved her sister inside with the other.

"Dork," she muttered before ordering the driver to, "Follow that cab!" A statement that got almost hysterical laughter from her ridiculous baby sister.

Chapter Twenty-six

Charlie tracked down her aunt in the hotel bar, sitting with eldest daughter Kenzie. Charlie had to stop and look at her watch to make sure she'd read the time correctly.

It didn't seem as though her aunt was a raging alcoholic, but maybe the pressure of a wedding her daughter apparently didn't want was putting her under undue stress. A stress eased by forty-year-old scotch.

Charlie dropped into the booth next to Kenzie and across from her aunt.

"Well?" Bernice asked, her eyes so bloodshot, Charlie almost felt bad for her.

"It looks like she's been seeing some polar bear on the side. Named Damian Miller."

"A bear? Seriously?" Bernice demanded. "That girl!"

Kenzie relaxed back in the booth so that she was sitting at an angle, able to see both of them. "Are you really shocked by this? It's not like my sister makes good life choices."

"But she did. With Ron. The very rich Ron with wonderful connections."

Kenzie smirked at Charlie. "My mother's all about the love."

"Fuck love," Bernice snapped. "I'm talking about the financial future of this family."

"Resting on the giant shoulders of a spoiled brat." Kenzie gave her mother a thumb's up. "Good job, Ma."

"But she loves Ron. I know she does," Bernice insisted. "I see it in her eyes."

"In her cold, dead eyes," Kenzie muttered, making Charlie snort.

"Stop it." Bernice pressed her fingertips to her temples. "I'm not letting her ruin this. I'm not letting Carrie ruin what could be the love of her life. So I want you and your sisters to stay on her."

"We're not PIs," Charlie reminded her. "Other than finding out what we've already found out . . . I'm not sure what you want us to do."

"I want you to keep her out of trouble."

"Good luck with that."

Bernice slammed her hand on the table and barked at Kenzie, "Stop muttering shit under your breath!"

"Look," Charlie cut in, trying to keep the situation calm, "we have nothing confirmed yet. Max and Stevie are on her right now anyway; we'll just keep doing that. Monitoring the situation."

"Thank you."

"But there is something else."

"About Carrie?"

"No." Charlie let out a breath. "About your father."

Bernice frowned, glancing at Carrie. "What about him?"

Charlie reached into her messenger bag and pulled out the issue of *Vanity Fair*. She opened it up to the Guerra spread and laid it in front of her aunt. "Do you know them?"

She studied the picture of the twins before admitting, "Yes." She nodded. "They were in an ad for Versace a year or so back."

"Is that all you know about them?"

"What else is there to know about two vapid bitches from Italy?"

"That they're your half-sisters?"

Bloodshot eyes blinking wide, Bernice leaned forward to get a closer look at the picture; Kenzie did the same.

"They could be badgers, Ma. Look at those shoulders. Like linebackers. Big, Italian linebackers."

"He . . ." Bernice shook her head. "He couldn't have."

"Why are you so surprised?" Kenzie asked her mother. "He pretty much started a brand-new family over here without actually separating himself from the family he had in Scotland. And Italy is a hell of a lot closer."

Bernice raised her hands, palms out. "You know what? I can't deal with this right now. And I'm not sure why I should give a shit. Who knows how many pathetic women the old fucker impregnated in his *extremely* long life? I don't know how that's *my* problem."

"I didn't say it was your problem," Charlie explained. "But these are the two who have been trying to kill me and Max and grab Stevie. These broads are very rich, very determined, and very pissed off at the MacKilligans."

"No offense, Charlie, but you and your sisters are not exactly considered family."

"*Ma*," Kenzie said, glaring at her mother across the table.

"It's okay," Charlie told her cousin, appreciating that she was at least attempting to protect Charlie's feelings. "But you should know . . . that it seems they helped Freddy steal the hundred million pounds from Will."

That's when Bernice slammed her head down on the table and then rammed it there a few more times.

Charlie cringed a little and mouthed *Sorry* to her cousin.

Kenzie shrugged back seconds before her mother's head suddenly jerked up and Bernice growled, "Will there ever be a time when my brother does not find ways to *fuck up my life!*"

Charlie leaned away from that scream and admitted to her aunt, "Probably not."

Carrie met her seven-foot-tall polar boyfriend on 47th Street, where he led her to one of the many jewelry stores.

Stevie watched through the shop window as her cousin fingered a four-carat diamond set in a simple gold necklace.

"Is that a wedding gift?" Stevie asked Max.

"You got me."

Once he put the necklace around Carrie's throat, the polar led her through the store. They were arm-in-arm, and Carrie seemed to enjoy herself as the bear showed her all the sparkly jewels and the entire layout of his store.

So they wouldn't be seen, Stevie and Max moved away from the window and stood near a hot dog vendor where they had a clear view of the entrance.

"This is so not cool. What she's doing to her poor fiancé."

"Not everybody has the same opinion of love," Max said. "Maybe they have an arrangement."

"The arrangement should be either we're together or we're not together. Not 'I'll be getting jewelry from other guys before our wedding day' together."

"Maybe you're a little naive."

"Maybe you're an idiot."

Max punched her shoulder, so she punched her back.

They had headlocks on each other when the vendor finally pulled them apart. "Stop it! Both of you! Love is different for each couple! Now stop it!"

They separated, with the vendor pointing a warning finger at both of them before again focusing on his cart.

Max leaned close to Stevie and whispered, "We just got schooled by a hot dog vendor."

Stevie whispered back, "Are you saying that because you're putting down the hot dog vendor or because you really want a hot dog?"

She shrugged. "I really want a hot dog. And a pretzel."

They left the bar and Bernice went to the large room where the already-arriving gifts for the bride and groom were being stored. She left Charlie and Kenzie out in the hallway while she went inside and began making calls.

Charlie sat on the floor, her back against the wall, and waited. She could hear her aunt yelling. There was also some crying, but it was mostly yelling. Such hysterical yelling, Charlie really couldn't understand what was being said.

Kenzie sat down next to her. "I'm sorry about all this," she said, shocking Charlie.

"You didn't do anything. In fact . . ." Charlie thought a moment. "You have nothing to do with any of this."

"I know, but still . . ." She raised her knees and rested her elbows on them. "I might as well warn you now that I doubt any of my aunts and uncles will be much help. They will all be looking to protect themselves."

"I already know that. I just figured I should let Bernice know what was going on since I am taking her money."

"That's not true. You have a loyalty to family. Even this family. I'm just sorry we suck at returning it."

"Again, not your fault. You're the only cousin who's actually nice to us."

"Well, if I have a big family wedding, you and your sisters are definitely invited. But," she added, laughing a little, "not your dad."

"That is sound logic for a MacKilligan."

"I do try."

The door opened and Bernice came out. "Well, those bitches are definitely family."

"So Will knew?"

"He knew *of* them. But they never told us because they just considered the Guerra twins another one of our father's unfortunate mistakes." She gave a little sniff. "Kind of like me, I guess. Anyway, Freddy probably has no idea who these women are. Although I can only pray that all he did was let himself get led around by the nose rather than what he usually does."

"Based on what I read in that article and online, my father wouldn't have a chance with those two, which is good . . . because incest is the one thing I would like this family to *actively* avoid."

Bernice looked at the phone she had clutched in her hand. "There's something else. About my brother's daughter Mairi."

"Which Mary?" Charlie asked. "Mary Pat? Mary Christina? Mary Cecile?"

"No, no. Mairi spelled M-a-i-r-i."

"What about her?"

"She was doing hard time in Edinburgh Prison. But she's out."

"She was paroled?"

"Escaped and the family thinks she's headed to the States. They suggested we keep our eyes open. According to Will, she's . . . a little . . . unstable."

"Uncle Will who set his math teacher on fire when he was eight thinks that *Mairi* is unstable?" Charlie scratched her neck. "That's disturbing."

"Yeah." Bernice briefly closed her eyes. "This just keeps getting fucking worse."

"Ma," Kenzie warned, "your cursing is amping up and we have to have lunch with Ron's parents today."

"Fuck, I forgot. Fuck! I don't want to meet with those people."

"*Ma!*"

"All right, all right. I need to get ready to meet them." She pointed at Charlie. "I've made up my mind. You and your sisters need to get fitted."

Charlie glanced at Kenzie. "Fitted for what?"

"For your bridesmaid dresses. You won't walk down the aisle, of course, but you'll blend nicely with the wedding party so you can keep an eye on things."

Charlie got to her feet. "I've already hired additional security. There is absolutely no reason for me and my sisters to go to a loveless wedding."

"This isn't about security. This isn't about whether the waiters are serving from the right. This isn't even about managing any drunks during the dancing portion of the evening. This is about ensuring that nothing, and I mean absolutely *nothing,* ruins my daughter's day!"

"Does that include your own daughter planning to ruin her wedding?"

"I *especially* mean that!"

Charlie shook her head. "Look, I get it. But there's no *way* I will ever get Max MacKilligan into a dress. Not now. Not ever."

Max spun from one side of the room to the other, letting the skirt of her dark gray dress swirl around her. Standing in front of the mirror, as two tailors tried to get the bridesmaid dress clearly designed for much smaller honey badgers to fit her, Charlie watched her sister. "I can't believe you're okay with this."

"Why not? I love going to weddings."

"You do?"

"Absolutely." She stopped behind Charlie, looking at her in the glass. "First, I break out the dance moves." Max began to dance the way she had during Charlie's prom. She'd snuck in with Dutch and together they'd taken over the dance floor until the vice principal caught sight of the two students he continually referred to as "my personal projects because I will not be broken!" and forced them to leave. "Then I watch everybody get liquored up. Then I start taking wallets."

"*No*."

"Oh, come on. I need the practice."

"Absolutely not. We're there to help our aunt because she's giving us a lot of money to do so. We are not ruining everything by going into Dad-behavior. We are there to *prevent* that sort of thing."

"Well, where is the fun in that?"

"You can dance, though. And since I know you'll do it anyway, you can bring Dutch—"

"Already called him. I think he's getting fitted for a tux right now."

One of the tailors, a tough Serbian fox with no patience for what she called, "the idiocy of the badger," suddenly stood straight and yelled at Charlie, "I cannot work with this girl! She is crazy!"

"I don't like to be touched!" Stevie yelled from under a table. "Can't I just give you my size? I don't want your hands on my breasts!"

The fox flung her arms out in frustration, her cold blue gaze on Charlie.

"How about," Max suggested, "we get that giant panda to touch your breasts?"

"I wouldn't mind that."

Eyes wide, Charlie and Max looked at each other, then began laughing.

"He's very nonthreatening," Stevie insisted.

"I cannot make these changes in time if I do not get help from you," the fox said, putting her arms across her chest.

Still getting measured, Charlie motioned to Max and watched in the mirror as her sister walked across the room and kicked the table away from Stevie.

"Out!" Max barked, grabbing Stevie by the arm and yanking her up. "Now let the nice coyote—"

"I am fox!"

"Who cares? Fit you for these not-as-horrifying-as-I-thought-they-would-be dresses."

"These aren't bad for bridesmaid dresses, are they?" Charlie asked, studying the lines of the designer gown on her body.

"Remember the bridesmaids' gowns at Sheila's wedding?" Max asked, dragging Stevie over to the wood riser and forcing her to stand on it. "The giant bow?"

"Oh, God. The bow."

Stevie slapped Max's arms away and growled, "Just do it!" She stood ramrod straight. "Just do it and get it over with!"

"Like you're waiting for the firing squad," Max muttered, stepping away.

The fox stepped close and, with another fox, quickly and silently began to measure a very unhappy Stevie.

A knock at the door had Max twirling across the room, laughing when her skirt swirled around her legs. She opened the door and stepped out.

A few seconds later, there were raised voices and the door was flung back open. A woman who looked a little familiar stormed in, followed by Livy and Max.

"What are you doing with my brother?" the woman demanded.

There was silence and Charlie realized that her baby sister didn't understand who this woman was yelling at.

"Stevie, she's talking to *you*."

Stevie's eyes opened and she looked over her shoulder. "Oh. Hi, Livy."

"Hi, Stevie."

Stevie frowned down at the other woman. "Are you mad at . . . me? Or Max."

The woman pointed at herself. "*I'm* mad at you. *I* am mad at you!"

"Oh. Okay." Charlie waited for her sister to say it . . . she wasn't disappointed. "I don't know who you are, so I don't know why you'd be mad at me."

"What do you mean you don't know me? We've stayed in the same house together. Traveled together."

"I'm . . . sorry. Are you a fan? Do you want an autograph?"

Livy and Max looked at each other, but just as quickly turned away. And Charlie knew she couldn't catch Max's eye. It would be the undoing of her.

"You know me, *Stevie*. I'm Toni. Jean-Louis Parker."

"Are you related to Kyle?"

"I'm his big sister."

"The assistant?"

"Assistant?"

"Yeah. Kyle says his big sister is his assistant. You help with the mundane duties of his career."

Livy looked like she was about to say something, but instead she just walked out of the room. Not that Charlie blamed her. She would have done the same thing in her place.

"I am not Kyle's assistant," Toni responded. "I am his sister. And I want to know what you're doing with my brother."

"I want to know what you're accusing my sister of," Charlie cut in, nodding at the fox now that they were done.

She stepped off the riser and let them unzip and slip the dress off her. Charlie grabbed her T-shirt and pulled it on, then went for her jeans.

"My brother says he's living with you guys. He's only seventeen."

"Kyle's renting a room," Stevie said.

Tugging on her sneakers, Charlie hopped around so she could focus on her sister. "Since when?"

"Since this morning. He says it's impossible to work in the intolerable situation his parents have going at their rental house in Manhattan, and I totally understand that. Not everyone is like my sisters. Respectful of what extraordinary people need to do to create. It sounds like Kyle's family is not like you guys at all."

Shaking, Toni's hands curled into fists and she barked, "*I* am not respectful of extraordinary people? *I?*" she bellowed.

Livy returned, sort of zooming into the room, grabbing the jackal's arm, and pulling her toward the door.

"This isn't acceptable!" she screamed as Livy dragged her away. "He's only a kid! He's only seventeen! If I find out anything weird is going on between you and my baby brother—"

"Done," the Serbian fox said, stepping back.

"Oh." Stevie smiled at her image in the mirror. "That wasn't so bad."

"Nothing is going on with you and that kid, right?" Charlie felt the need to ask.

"Nope. But now we're getting rent that will cover him *and* his security guard, which also means we actually *have* extra security. It's a win-win for us."

"Okay."

"Besides," she added, slipping out of her dress, "I

love Kyle, but if I had to date that boy, I'd put a pillow over his head until he stopped moving. And that would be a great loss for art, don't you think?" Charlie nodded and told her sister, "I love your sound logic."

"It's just one of my many gifts."

Chapter Twenty-seven

Dee-Ann sat in Ric's office. Malone in the chair next to her. They didn't speak. Not because they were mad at each other; they just didn't have anything to say. That's one of the reasons Dee-Ann tolerated Malone as well as she did; she didn't *need* to run her mouth.

Ric walked in. "Sorry I'm late." He dropped into the chair behind his desk, taking a few seconds to bring something up on his computer. He turned the monitor around to face Dee-Ann and Malone.

"These are the Guerra twins. It turns out they're also part of the MacKilligan family. They were, however, never in touch with their father and they were raised by their full-human mother only. They seem to have no idea they're honey badgers, but they have joined forces with one of the younger MacKilligans. A Mairi MacKilligan who is known among her own in Scotland as the Beast of Braewillow, the honey badger village most of the MacKilligans come from. And if honey badgers are giving you a nickname like that . . ."

"Who do you want us to go after first?" Dee-Ann asked.

"We think the twins and Mairi are in the States right now together, but the twins are unbelievably wealthy.

If they run, it'll be harder to track them down. But the Beast . . . considering the body count she had on her when she went into prison in Scotland, I'm sure it will be easier to find her once we've got the twins under control. Although I'm hoping she doesn't do as much damage here as she did in her homeland." Ric looked at Malone. "What's Katzenhaus's direction on this?"

"They're leaving it up to the Group since they don't really have an opinion on badgers. But if you want me to work with Dee-Ann to eliminate this issue, my bosses won't care."

"Should we bring those MacKilligan sisters into this?" Dee-Ann asked.

"I'm surprised you asked, Dee-Ann."

"Me, too!" Malone piped in. "And you were so nice about it."

"I'm just asking whether we should warn them."

"Excellent idea," Ric replied. "I'll take care of it. Now, anything you ladies need, please let me know. I want these twins dealt with. I know they don't know what they are, but it doesn't really matter when they've tried at least three times to kill or capture the MacKilligan sisters. Sadly, they've already crossed a line they can't come back over."

After the fittings, all Charlie and her sisters wanted to do was go home. But in order to keep track of Carrie—who was off that evening with her bridesmaids and some friends for her bachelorette party—it was up to Charlie and Stevie to distract her. Not hard, though, when all Charlie had to say to the bride was, "The gowns are long so we can wear sneakers instead of heels, right?" which led to a whole lot of hysterical yelling—while Max took Carrie's phone and set it up with a GPS app. Then she put GPS trackers into Carrie's multiple bags, which she carried with her everywhere.

Once they'd done that and checked in with a weary Kenzie, they all headed back to the house in Queens.

It was hot, so Charlie changed into jean shorts and a tank top before going outside. Entertaining the idea of treating Berg and his siblings with a little barbecue, Charlie went out the back kitchen door to see if a barbecue was one of the things that Tiny had in his hoarder house garage.

But as she went toward the garage, she sensed something coming at her. Flying at her. She only had time to turn her head as a fist slammed into her jaw, sending Charlie flipping into the middle of the yard.

Her head stuck in the freezer, trying to find at least one more of those frozen honeycomb ice cream treats that Britta had turned her on to, Max didn't hear the yelling. But she heard and felt Stevie run by her.

Stevie didn't run *toward* anything. She always ran away. But there was nothing behind her. And no bears in the house.

Max closed the freezer door, and that's when she did hear the yelling. Charging outside, she came around the corner just as Stevie threw herself at the back of a female that Max recognized but couldn't believe was attacking her sister.

Charlie was on the ground, with five females over her, punching. Her sister hadn't gotten up yet, too busy trying to protect her face and side and, knowing Charlie, trying to figure out what was happening.

But Max didn't need to know what was going on. She didn't care.

Snarling, claws and fangs unleashing, Max crouched a bit, and feeling her anger soar through her, she moved . . .

* * *

Berg and his siblings stepped out of the SUV. They'd been out on the Island all day helping a company shore up their security. But despite all the work he'd done, his mind had been on Charlie. He couldn't stop thinking about her. Not just having sex with her—although he really wanted that . . . soon—he just wanted to see her. Talk to her. See her smile. Hear her laugh. Watch her roll her eyes at something weird or funny her sisters said.

Deciding not to wait, he started down the driveway to go over to Charlie's house. But before he even reached the sidewalk, he watched a souped-up '73 Camaro tear down the street and slam to a stop, double-parking in front of the badgers' house.

Dutch jumped out, tore around his car, and jumped over the fence.

Not liking any of this, Berg continued walking toward Charlie's place. But he'd only gone a few steps when Dutch came running back out and waved at him.

Berg took off running, yelling over his shoulder, "Dag! Britta!"

He didn't wait to see if his siblings were coming. He knew they would.

He heard the screaming and yelling before he even reached the front gate. He charged through and ran around the side of the house. That's when he saw it. A fight. A really nasty, violent fight.

Not between military-trained killers and the MacKilligan sisters either. But a bunch of angry females . . . and the MacKilligan sisters. Even little Stevie was on the back of some redhead, screaming, small fingers trying to dig into the female's eyes.

The weasel was trying his best to separate the women, but he didn't want to hurt anyone so they were ignoring him. And the only rational person who could calm this out-of-control situation was down on the ground getting pummeled.

Berg ran over and waded into the melee, trying to grab hold of one of the viciously fighting females. He didn't care which one.

Dag was already next to him. He'd managed to get hold of Stevie. She was screaming and thrashing. Dag could barely hold onto her.

Wondering how they would get a handle on all of this, Berg tried again to dig in and grab his badger. But just as he caught hold of Charlie's arm, a massive roar startled him, and Dag jerked away.

Britta stepped in, her shoulder hump raised high, and began swinging her arms. Much smaller females flew, tossed across the yard; Berg and Dag ducked.

Once she got the women off Charlie, Britta bellowed, *"That is enough!"*

That same bellow used to send Marines running for cover. Made even generals find the closest exit. But these small women didn't seem to care.

They started to come for Charlie again, but the weasel jumped between them and said, "No, Mia! No!"

Stevie fought her way out of Dag's arms and launched herself at the one called Mia. And instead of stopping her, Max screamed, "Get her, Stevie! *Get the bitch!*"

That's when all the yelling began. Each set of females screaming at the other. Except for Charlie. She was getting to her feet. Berg only noticed her because she was using his leg to help herself get up.

He grabbed her hands and pulled. "Are you o—" was all Berg managed before Charlie, bloody and snarling, pushed her way past Dag and Max. She yanked Stevie away from Mia, tossing her over her shoulder and into Berg's arms.

"What the fuck was that?" Charlie demanded of Mia.

"What the fuck do you think that was?" Mia abruptly grabbed Dutch, pulling him in close. Still clinging to his arm, she grabbed the weasel's face with her hand, squeezing his cheeks hard. "Look what you did to his face! Look what you did!"

"He deserved it! He betrayed my family!"

"Then you should have come to me!"

"I don't have to ask your permission to kick the shit out of your idiot brother!"

Mia shoved Charlie. "Only *I* can call him an idiot!"

"Idiot." Shove. "Idiot." Shove. *"Idiot!"* And that led to a punch.

Berg started to step in again but Britta held him and Dag back with a raised hand. Then she caught both women by their hair. They tried to swing on her, but it was a waste of effort. She was half a foot taller than Charlie and a whole foot taller than Mia.

Britta simply held them off the ground by their hair and waited.

Eventually, they stopped swinging and when they relaxed, Britta dropped them both.

"Are we going to be rational now?" Britta asked calmly, her grizzly hump gone.

"That psychotic bitch," Mia yelled, but still sitting on the ground, rubbing her head, "attacked our baby brother!"

Dutch turned red, his gaze unwilling to meet Berg's or Dag's because he was smart enough to know . . . they were grinning now.

"How would you feel, Charlie?" Mia asked. "If I attacked Max the way you attacked Dutch?"

Charlie leaned forward and growled between clenched teeth, "I'd tell your parents, 'I'm sorry for your loss.'"

"Okay!" Britta barked, before the battle could begin again. "That's enough. We're done."

The She-weasels began to argue that point with Britta but she barely let them get started before she roared once more, sending birds from trees, Stevie back into the house now that her anger had subsided, and the weasels into silence.

"I know you're pissed," Britta said calmly. "I'd be pissed. These are my brothers." She motioned to Berg and Dag. "And I'm very protective. So I get it. But it's over. Charlie kicked Dutch's ass. You kicked hers. We're done now."

Like a group of dancers performing, the five She-weasels crossed their arms over their chests, hitched out their right legs, and let out annoyed sighs. It was weird.

But their actions overall were not that surprising. Wolverine males didn't get along with each other at all, but they didn't mind having wolverine females around. So, males with sisters, Berg had heard, often had their own little pack. They protected each other's territories and, when necessary, fought each other's battles.

Although Berg didn't think Dutch had sent his sisters into this particular battle. He'd probably been hoping to avoid it. Too bad he hadn't been able to manage that.

"So," Britta pushed, "are we all calm? Rational?"

The She-weasels refused to answer and Charlie wiped the blood from her lip before announcing, "I need to bake," and storming back into the house.

They stood for several long seconds in silence until Tiny suddenly loped into the yard. Looking around he finally asked, "Did I hear something about Charlie baking?" He pulled out a piece of paper from his back pocket. "Because I've got a list here . . ."

"You didn't make anything better," Dutch told his big sister while they stood by their cars. "You just made it worse."

"I don't care. The only one who gets to slap my brother around is me, which reminds me . . ." Mia slapped Dutch in the back of the head. "You're working for the Group? Have you lost your mind? You could get killed!"

"It's a good job. They respect my talents."

"What talents?"

"I have talents." When his sisters just stared at him . . . "I do!"

Charlie slipped the cinnamon cake into the oven and informed Tiny, "I do not bake on demand. I bake when I want to."

She heard Berg and his siblings laugh. She faced them and Berg quickly explained, "Sorry. Drug humor. Our mother would get it."

Not in the mood to analyze that, Charlie went back to the kitchen table and finished kneading bread dough so she could let it proof.

. Tiny held the list of neighbors' requests in front of her. "But—"

Charlie pointed her flour-covered hands at the door. "Out."

"Fine." Tiny slammed the list on the table and stomped his way across the kitchen, and Charlie again focused on her work.

"You know," she complained to the three bears passing around a jar of fancy honey that Stevie had apparently ordered, "I had such plans for tonight. I was going to throw a little barbecue for you guys and my sisters, relax, maybe read a book. Just enjoy the evening, ya know? But, of course, I couldn't just have a nice time to myself. Instead—"

"You're not going to blame your father for this, too, are you?" Berg asked.

Charlie's head snapped up but he looked so damn adorable licking the back of the spoon and watching her, she didn't have the heart to rip off his big bear head.

Taking a breath, she admitted, "If I could, I would. And I'm sure if I tried, I'd find a way. But I'll let it go for now."

"That's very big of you," he teased.

Dag was refusing to give up the honey, so Britta went to the cabinet over the refrigerator. She opened it and Stevie, who'd gone inside there when the roaring started, handed her another jar. "This one is infused with lemon."

"Oooh. Yum. Thanks, Stevie."

Britta closed the cabinet door and opened the honey. Dag tried to get a taste, but she moved across the room so she could eat in peace.

"There's no reason we still can't have a little barbecue," Britta said. "Just the six of us."

"I'm not sure I'm in the mood to cook right now."

They silently watched her kneading the bread dough and Charlie pointed out, "This is baking. Not cooking."

"We'll barbecue," Dag said.

"I'll get the supplies," Britta offered.

Charlie used her foot to point out her backpack. "Take the Visa card that's in there," she told Britta.

"It's okay, I'll pay."

"No. I'm going to expense this as a . . ." She thought a moment. ". . . *team* meeting."

"Is that fair to your aunt?" Berg asked.

"My aunt reminded me today that the MacKilligans don't really think of me, Stevie, and Max as family so—"

"Yeah," Berg told his sister. "Use the aunt's card. Let's expense this bitch."

"Get some chicken!" Stevie yelled from inside the cabinet.

Having retrieved the card, Britta asked, "Do you want to come with me, Stevie? Get out of the cabinet for a little while?"

"Uh . . . okay." Stevie eased the door open and skittered out. It was weird because she crawled out of the cabinet and down the refrigerator to reach the floor without grabbing onto anything. Kind of like a spider. But the bears didn't say anything about it and neither did Charlie. It was best not to talk about these things. It just freaked people out more.

"Get stuff you'll eat, Stevie," Charlie reminded her sister.

"That's why I said, 'get some chicken.' Max will want cow. I want chicken."

"Just saying."

"Well don't!"

Charlie waited until Stevie was gone before she laughed. "She's so sensitive sometimes."

"Can you bring over the grill?" Berg asked his brother.

"Yeah. And some charcoal. I'll be right back."

Charlie put the bread dough in a pan and put the whole thing in the proofer drawer. That's when it hit her . . .

"This oven's new." She stepped back to get a good look. "Like . . . super new. And expensive."

"Yeah. I saw the delivery guys earlier today after you all left. Tiny let them in."

"Why would he buy us a new oven when we're just renting the place?"

Smirking, Berg held up the list of treats that Tiny had brought her.

Charlie rolled her eyes. "Come on. Seriously?"

"Well, now you kinda gotta."

"Bears," she complained before snatching the list from Berg.

Stevie was following behind Britta. As they neared Dutch's car, where his sisters were sitting on the trunk and leaning against the doors, the bear stopped and asked, "Still here?"

Dutch stepped forward. "My sisters want to apologize to—"

The rest of what Dutch was about to say was drowned out by his sisters emphatically denying that they were going to apologize to anyone.

Britta roared again but before Stevie could run back into the house, she caught Stevie by the back of the neck and lifted her up so that her feet kept going but she didn't actually move anywhere. It was a little embarrassing.

"Now listen up, ladies," Britta announced. "I'm about to go out and get meat. Lots of meat. For a barbecue. And I could go ahead and pick up some elk, which I hear your kind enjoys. Or I can get just enough food for three bears and three honey badgers. Your decision. Choose wisely."

Stevie felt like flailing her way out of Britta's grip but she was also enjoying the way the bear treated the wolverines. Not taking their shit, but still trying to make it better.

Still holding Stevie, Britta started across the street, but Mia jumped from the trunk and asked, "Are you getting corn?"

"I can. And potatoes." Britta smiled and said again, "Choose wisely."

They reached the other side of the street and Britta finally released her, so Stevie could get into the SUV.

Once they were inside, Britta started the vehicle and immediately turned on the AC.

"I still make you nervous, Stevie?" she asked as she slid on her sunglasses.

"Everything makes me nervous." Stevie thought a moment. "Well . . . not everything. But man-eaters definitely make me nervous."

"But tigers are man-eaters . . . and you're half tiger."

Stevie stared out the front window for several seconds ruminating on that bit of information before admitting, "Dear God. I'm terrified of myself."

Chapter Twenty-eight

Max didn't know when this had turned into a party. She'd been sitting on the metal picnic table—seething, because she loved Dutch's sisters but she wasn't about to let anyone go after Charlie or Stevie on her watch—when Dag walked in carrying a giant barbecue grill. He was carrying it alone. Like one might carry a small carton of apples. The only trouble he seemed to be having was that its dimensions made it a tad unwieldly.

Without saying a word, he'd placed the grill down, walked away, returned with a bag of coal, lighter fluid, and a lighter. He didn't use them, though. Just set them up and walked away.

That was around the time random bears began wandering through their backyard. Peeking into the open window, heads moving as they *sniffed, sniffed* the air. A few sized up the window as if they were wondering whether they would be able to rip it out of the wall so they could just get in there and devour the treats Charlie had started baking.

She wondered if this was how full-blooded bears dealt with cars that had empty fast-food containers in them. Did they look in? Circle around? Debate tearing the vehicle apart? Before simply trying the door?

One of the bears—a sow, of course—did that. She just walked in. And, three seconds later, came running out when a hissing Charlie charged her.

Charlie slammed the screen door shut and that was the last bear that actually attempted to enter their house without an invitation.

Berg came into the backyard, giving Max a sweet smile before getting the grill going. He sure did seem happy. He'd spent only one night with Max's sister, but maybe that was all he needed to know how he felt about Charlie MacKilligan. Wading into a weasel fight to protect a woman was a definite statement for any shifter male.

Now he was getting ready to grill . . . like any middle-class American husband. It was adorable. Who knew that Charlie MacKilligan would have an "adorable" relationship? With anyone?

Max's sister didn't really *do* adorable. Then again, she was a stand-up girl. She could have taken out any and all of those wolverines. She'd had a gun holstered to the back of her shorts. But she hadn't done it because she would never do something like that to Dutch's sisters. Max wasn't sure that she could be as honorable as her sister. Not when a group of crazy broads were screaming at her and hitting.

Eventually, those screaming broads came into the backyard. They barely looked at Max, which was good because Max was eyeing them with great intensity. Honey badgers loved a good "eyeing" as Max's mother called it. Wolverines, although just as ballsy as badgers, didn't go out of their way to challenge anyone. They just moved along, hoping not to be noticed, so they could get what they wanted and then disappear.

Not badgers. They'd go through your garbage with you standing right there, trying to shoo them away.

Dutch sat down beside Max on the picnic table and together they watched as Mia threw back her shoulders and entered the house.

Depending on her attitude, the discussion could go any number of ways. But, after about five minutes, she came back out alone, holding a six-pack of beers. She took one and handed over the rest for her sisters to divvy up.

If Charlie was giving out liquor, they'd made up. Big sisters understanding each other.

Max pressed her shoulder against Dutch's arm and he let out a relieved sigh.

"If there's a barbecue," Mia said after sipping her beer, "how about a little music?"

"Okay," Max replied. By choosing to speak to any of the She-wolverines, Max was saying she was letting all of this go because Charlie had. Stevie might be a little more difficult to make up with, but Max doubted it. Their baby sister didn't really hold grudges the way Max and Charlie did.

Although Max had been super impressed with how Stevie had thrown her skinny little ass into that fight. She'd always been a runner, their little sister. Which had been fine because Charlie and Max had taught her to run since that day. That day they'd all had to run when Charlie's mother had screamed at them to do just that. That day when everything had changed. And the life they'd known had ended.

That was what they'd taught Stevie to do and she'd become really good at it. Sometimes running with so much screaming and roaring that their attackers were thrown off, allowing Max and Charlie to do maximum damage.

But when Stevie had seen that Charlie was in trouble, she had done what both Max and Charlie would have done in the same instance. She went in swinging.

Max couldn't be prouder.

Eventually, Britta and Stevie returned with so much meat and corn and potatoes that another bear brought his own grill over. A much bigger one that the grizzly carried by himself.

In short order, both grills were going strong, music was playing, and Max began to wonder if the neighbor bears would complain. They didn't seem to like too much noise. Stevie's panicked screams really upset them.

But most were still lurking around the kitchen window, hoping for food. At one point, Charlie put a cherry pie on the window ledge. Two males got into a fight over it, allowing a sow to take it for her and her children.

It was pretty funny.

But as soon as a couple of black bears dived into the pool Max and her sisters had yet to use . . . it was officially a summer party.

Berg turned the deer legs over, added some more seasoning, and covered the grill. He then moved to the second grill and dealt with the elk. Then the third grill and dealt with the steaks, hamburgers, and hot dogs.

Britta had already gone back to the shifter-owned grocery store for more meat and sides. Mrs. Fitzbaer was helping out by roasting the corn and potatoes, but she was doing it from her house. She didn't feel like having "some hulking man-bear take my grill away."

Charlie was still in the kitchen baking, getting everything on that list done. Tiny had already gotten his honey-pineapple cake and had happily carried it home to hide away before coming back and invading the pool with a beer and a few of his friends.

Then things got weird.

Dag bumped Berg's arm to let him know that a lion male was walking into what Berg was considering a bear party that just happened to have badgers and wolverines.

That was only a minor weirdness, though. Lion males were always attracted by food and had no problem just wandering into your yard . . . and taking some. Because they were lion males and they thought they could get away with it.

But the big weirdness was that when the lion male walked in—with several wolf females . . . also weird— he threw his arms open and Dutch ran into them.

Dutch, a few inches shorter than the lion, jumped *up* into the feline's arms, wrapping himself around him like they were reuniting after the lion had gone off to war or something.

"I have nothing to say about that," Dag muttered.

"Probably for the best."

"Don't like having cats here, though."

Berg shrugged. "Who does?"

The weasel walked around the party with his lion and the lion's friends, showing them around, introducing them to some people, until they reached Berg and Dag.

"Berg and Dag Dunn, this is Mitch Shaw and his mate Sissy Mae Smith of the Smith Pack."

Berg's neck muscles tightened. "You brought a Smith Pack wolf into bear territory, weasel?"

"Sissy Mae is Alpha female of the New York Smiths with her brother Bobby Ray. Thought it was a good idea for the MacKilligans to get to know her in case they run into any trouble when they're in the city." He winked at Berg—which Berg just found annoying—and took the She-wolf's hand. "Will you and your Packmates be swimming today, Sissy Mae? The MacKilligans have a lovely pool."

The She-wolves looked over at the pool filled with bears. No wolf with sense would get into a watering hole with bears. But despite that belief, Sissy Mae yelled out, "Woooo-hoooo! Let's get wet, ladies!" Extra small T-shirts and tiny denim shorts were dropped, revealing even tinier bikinis, and the She-wolves took off running, jumping into the pool without caring about the bears already in there.

A few seconds later, stripped-down She-weasels in equally tiny bikinis followed the wolves, screaming and diving into the water.

"Isn't my girl amazing?" the lion male asked. "She can start a party at a grave site. Oh wait . . . she did that once," he recalled. "It wasn't planned, of course, but no one really liked the deceased anyway and we all had *such* a great time."

The lion smiled before asking, "So . . . is that zebra I smell?"

Charlie was loving this oven. Loving it like sunshine. She was able to make several of her best baked goods at the same time.

She knew she was missing the party outside, but she was enjoying her time inside baking. With such a big crowd of shifters in the yard, she felt confident she didn't have to worry about any outsiders coming for her sisters or her. So she could bake without worry, without stress.

She got through Tiny's list pretty quickly since there were a lot of cakes and quick breads. Nothing with yeast. While those baked, she worked on the more complicated breads, perfect to go with all the meats and sides grilling outside.

It wasn't until she was taking the last batch of rolls out of the oven that she realized the music outside had increased, as had the sound of voices.

Drying her freshly washed hands, Charlie went out the back door. It was as if she'd stepped into one of those desert raves. Only it was in her backyard. She'd be worried about complaints if most of the neighborhood didn't seem to be in attendance.

Charlie went looking for Stevie first and found her sitting on a low-hanging tree limb with Kyle. His giant panda protection not too far away; amiably chatting with local giant pandas from down the block. Stevie and Kyle were eating grilled meats and corn and people-watching.

Stevie people-watching was a good thing. She seemed to get her best ideas doing that—either for science or music—and hanging around geniuses such as Kyle somehow grounded her. A kid like that, so full of himself, reminded Stevie that she needed to be more human sometimes. That her work affected actual human beings. It kept her from just creating to create without thinking about long-term consequences.

Most scientists and artists were firm believers that to worry about those kinds of consequences stifled creativity. Stifled their work and the greatness that could come out of it.

And, Charlie would agree. Except where her sister was concerned. Because Stevie's creations could not just destroy thousands or even millions. Without meaning to, she could destroy the *planet*. She had that kind of brain. That kind of genius. One of her early physics teachers affectionately called her "the god-killer." He hadn't really been joking either.

So Charlie and Max kept an eye on their baby sister.

One of them always on her. At least from a distance. Just to make sure that she didn't do anything that they'd all end up regretting . . . seconds before the world imploded. Although as Max pointed out, "At least we won't have to feel bad about failing for long . . . you know, with the world ending and all."

But right now, Charlie didn't have those worries. Not with Stevie right in front of her. On a tree limb, laughing and chatting with Kyle. Being part of the human experience and, it seemed, enjoying it.

Charlie could relax. At least for a little while.

Except she didn't really know what to do with it. Relaxing, that is. Not worrying. Not plotting twenty different ways out of any possible situation that might come up. Although she *did* have twenty different ways off this street if it was necessary, but she'd come up with those contingencies the first *hour* after Berg had brought her here.

"Well, hi," a female voice said from beside her.

Charlie looked over at the tall, dark-haired woman smiling at her. She wore a *miniscule* bikini top and unzipped denim jean shorts over her bikini bottoms. She held a beer and had her wet hair gathered in a loose topknot.

"You must be Charlie MacKilligan," she said with a thick-as-molasses Southern accent when Charlie silently stared at her.

"Must I?" Charlie finally asked.

"I'm Sissy Mae Smith."

And she said it like . . . Charlie was supposed to know her or something. But Charlie didn't know her. She'd never seen her before. So she said, "I don't know you."

"Of course. We've never met." She suddenly leaned in and said, "But I *am* Sissy Mae *Smith*."

Charlie leaned in, too, and said, "And I *am* Charlie *MacKilligan*."

The woman straightened up. "I heard you're part wolf. Raised by some Pack in Wisconsin, I think."

"Yeah. So?"

"And you've never heard of the Smiths?"

"I beat the shit out of a Smith recently. That was fun. And my grandfather told me not to date any Smiths. Of course, he also didn't want me to date any Green Bay Packers fans, which was weird because he was born and raised in Wisconsin. He didn't want me to date any boxers, which seemed so random. And really didn't want me dating a cat person. So, you'll have to forgive me if the 'don't date a Smith' speech was lost among all that."

"Wait." The She-wolf sized Charlie up. "Which Smith did you beat up?"

"Uh . . . I think Dutch called her . . . Dee-Ann. That was it. Dee-Ann."

"*You?*" she asked, gawking at Charlie. "*You* beat up Dee-Ann Smith? *You?*"

"Broke her arm." Charlie smirked. "Broke her friend Malone's face. Anyway"—she shrugged—"hope you enjoy the party."

Charlie left the She-wolf standing there, her mouth open, eyes wide and confused.

Berg didn't know what to say when the lion male began the conga line. Mostly because he never thought he'd see bears actually *join* a conga line. But there they were, bears conga-ing around Charlie's yard.

"Where's Charlie?" Britta asked.

He was proud that she wasn't on that conga line. Of course, she hadn't drunk that much. Sadly, Berg couldn't say that about his brother, who'd had a little too much tequila and was now dancing by as Berg and Britta watched.

Pinching the bridge of his nose between thumb and forefinger, Berg asked Britta, "Could you . . ."

She laughed. "Look, I'll take care of stuff here with Max and Stevie. Why don't you find Charlie?"

"I just saw her . . ." Berg realized that Charlie was no longer where she'd been.

"Go," Britta pushed. She kissed her brother's cheek. "I'll make these bitchy weasels handle the cleanup. It's the least they can do."

"If you can do that, I'll get us out of Mom's Labor Day Grateful Dead Celebration Barbecue this year."

Britta held her hand out. "Deal."

They shook on it and Berg went off to find Charlie. He didn't have to look far, though. She was sitting on the trunk of one of the weasel cars—they really had a thing for seventies American muscle cars—drinking a beer and using her bare feet to pet his dog's back.

"Hey," he said when he was close enough not to yell.

She smiled at him and he loved how happy she seemed to see him. She didn't look at people that way very often. "I've got a name for your dog. Benny."

"Benny?"

"He loves it. Licked my foot when I asked him."

"He's weird. He likes to lick feet."

"I thought about other names like Atlas or Titan. But that seems so typical for a big dog. So I went with Benny, which is much better than your nonexistent name."

He rested his ass on the car trunk beside Charlie, but even that little bit—he barely put any weight on it—had the car dropping down as if an anvil had been placed on it. Berg cringed, embarrassed, but Charlie only laughed and handed him her beer.

He took a sip and she rested her head on his arm.

"Thank you for this," she said.

"For what?"

"Bringing me someplace where I can leave my sisters alone for five minutes. It's a nice feeling."

"Are you going to leave?" he abruptly asked.

Charlie gazed at him. "What?"

"Are you going to leave? Like soon . . . or . . . you know . . . ever?"

"Ever? I can't tell you. Sometimes the MacKilligans leave and sometimes we are run off. But I wasn't planning on going anywhere soon."

"This thing with the Guerra twins and your dad all gets resolved, say, tomorrow . . . you're out of here?"

"I don't know. I hadn't really thought about it. I kind of like it here. Except for the weird demands for baked goods. But then again . . . the bears do give me ovens. So that seems fair."

"I don't want you to go," he admitted.

"I'm not going anywhere. Yet. And this seems like a really intense conversation for two people who've known each other for a very short amount of time."

"Did your wolf grandfather have a mate?"

"Yeah. I never had a chance to meet her."

"Is he a good-looking guy? Tall? Handsome?"

Charlie took out her phone, pulled up a picture of her and her grandfather at a Pack Christmas get-together a few years back.

Berg looked and said, "Then the answer is, 'Yes. He is.' Your grandfather is the kind of guy who would have gotten a new woman eventually. Except that he couldn't."

"He dated. I know he dated."

"He had sex. But I bet he never brought anybody home and said, 'This is your new grandma.'"

"No." She gave a small shake of her head. "He never did that."

"Because he'd found the one, and for shifters . . . that's all there is."

"Unless you're a MacKilligan male apparently."

"I can't speak for that . . . bloodline. I can only tell you what I know about the rest of us."

"And you think *I'm* the one for you?"

"I don't know." He was lying. He already knew. "But I won't be sure if you leave suddenly."

"If I leave it's because I need to protect my sisters."

"But they seem happy here."

"Except Stevie's career is in Switzerland right now."

"She doesn't seem to be in a hurry. Actually, she seems really comfortable right now. I mean . . . as comfortable as she can be when she's not screaming and running from bears."

Charlie chuckled. "She does seem comfortable. For her. But my sisters come first. I have to protect them. That's my job."

"I feel the same way about Britta and Dag, but . . . what? Nothing for you?"

"I honestly don't know." She rubbed her forehead. "But I'm not trying to . . . you know . . . get away from you either. Which, for me, is a lot."

"All I ask is that you tell me if you need to go. For whatever reason. Even if it's to get away from me."

She rolled her eyes. "You are the most amiable person I've ever met. Why would I need to get away from you?"

"That makes me sound boring."

Charlie jumped off the trunk and faced Berg head-on. "Dude," she practically snarled, "you can shift into a fifteen-hundred-pound *bear*! How fucking boring can you be?"

Berg gave a little shrug. "Polars shift into fifteen hundred pounds. I only shift to a thousand."

Charlie threw up her hands. "Oh! Well, then."

* * *

He was so frustrating! Cute. Sweet. Goddamn lovable. He could have any woman who didn't have a fear of heights. But he was worried about being too boring for her?

God, she needed boring. If boring meant stable and loving and caring. If it meant taking care of those you loved. Then, yeah, the dude was boring.

The kind of "boring" she'd always wanted in her life. From the moment Charlie had been conceived, everything about her life was a surprise. Even her. Never had anyone been with her just because they wanted to be. Things had worked out, even when she'd been dumped on some unsuspecting person's doorstep—like her grandfather—but it would have been great to know she'd always been wanted. Always been needed. And not just because she could kill twenty people in a room without working up a sweat.

And to her shock . . . she'd finally found that. In a bear who was a triplet.

Could she stay around forever? She still didn't know. But while she was here . . .

Charlie moved in and kissed Berg. Without warning. Just grabbed him and kissed him. Because she wanted to and she knew he wouldn't mind.

And, boy, did he not mind.

His big arms wrapped around her and lifted her up so that she could wrap her legs around his waist and dig her fingers into his hair. That great, thick sexy bear hair.

"Come home with me," he whispered when he pulled away.

The party was still going on and her sisters couldn't be more secure. So she kissed him again and that seemed to be the only answer he needed.

* * *

He carried her back to his house, the pair kissing the entire way. Her body was warm and pliable in his arms, but she was also demanding.

They reached his front door and he carried her inside, closing the door in "Benny's" face, much to his annoyance. Damn dog.

Berg wanted to get her upstairs but he only got her as far as the wall beside the stairs. That's where he pinned her, still kissing her, but now with his hands moving all over her.

She pulled his T-shirt off, forcing him to stop long enough so she could get it over his head. Charlie tossed it aside and then removed her own, her bra quickly following.

Then she wrapped her arms around his shoulders and he knew she'd wanted to feel him skin to skin. Her hands moved over his shoulders, down his arms, back up to his shoulders again.

She dragged her short nails against the tight muscles in his neck.

Berg growled, unable to help himself, praying she didn't get scared off. Then again, this was the woman who'd told Sissy Mae Smith, "I don't know you." The entire party had been talking about it . . . the bears laughing. Mostly because the She-wolf had been so insulted.

But that was not a woman who was going to be frightened off by some growling. Or a little snarling. Or fangs brushing against her shoulder.

He was right, too. It didn't scare her off. It turned her on. Charlie's grip on him tightened, her breath growing harsher, her nipples hard against his chest.

Berg unleashed his claws and shredded the shorts and panties from her body. She shuddered hard and kissed him deeper. He grabbed the condom he'd put in his back pocket in case an opportunity with Char-

lie presented itself that night. Thankfully, it had. Right
now.

Berg didn't believe in missing opportunities.

He slipped the condom on and buried himself so
deep inside Charlie MacKilligan he felt part of her. Until he knew he'd never find anyone who could replace
her. Who could fill the Charlie-sized hole she'd built for
herself inside his heart?

Berg stopped moving, letting himself just feel her
pulsating around him. Warm and needy, loving and demanding, ballsy and ridiculous.

No wonder she'd warned him away from her at the
beginning. Not because of some curse, but because she
was like a drug where one hit was too much and a thousand hits were not enough. She was in his blood now. In
his soul. Her concerns were his. Her troubles his. Her
family his.

Her sisters had problems that he'd feel responsible to
help fix, the same as he did with his own siblings. Because that's what happened when you found your mate.
His father had warned him. "Your mother may drive
me nuts," he'd often complain, "but I can't imagine my
life without her."

Now he understood his father as he never had before.

He pulled out of their kiss and looked down into her
face. Studied it, pushing her curly hair off her cheeks so
he could see her clearly.

"Are you okay?" she asked, stroking her hands down
his chest.

His Charlie. No matter what was going on, she was
always thinking about others. It was her way. He didn't
think she knew any other.

He wanted to tell her he loved her, but it was too
soon. The big shifter world was still kind of foreign to
her. Still an oddity.

So he began to slowly fuck her. Taking his time.

Stroking his cock inside her as he watched her face. Enjoying the way she smiled when he thrust in.

Berg wouldn't tell her he loved her. Not yet. But he would tell her the truth. So she understood.

"You mean everything to me, Charlie," he said, leaning in so his breath hit her ear. "If you have to leave, tell me first. Just tell me."

She gasped, her entire body throbbing around him. Her pussy beginning to squeeze him so hard he was sure he was seeing stars.

"Okay," she said around her gasps. "Okay."

"Promise me."

"I . . . God . . . yes. I . . . I promise," she finally got out before burying her face against his shoulder, her fangs biting down on his flesh, the pain sending him over the edge.

He came so hard he could barely remember his name.

Charlie opened her eyes when she tasted blood in her mouth.

"Oh, my God!" She wiped her hand against her lips. "Berg, I'm so sorry."

He gazed at her, eyes slowly blinking. "For what?"

"I bit you." She examined the wound, wincing at the clear fang marks on his shoulder. "I broke the skin."

"So?"

She lifted her head. "We're not vampires, dude."

"No, but we're predators. Biting's expected." He kissed her and, still inside her, kicked off his jeans and sneakers, and carried her up the stairs.

"We can't leave our clothes and condom wrappers just lying around your house," she warned him. "I'm guessing Britta wouldn't be okay with that. I know I wouldn't be okay with that."

"You grew up with sisters. Britta, sadly for her, grew up with two brothers." He carried her into his bedroom and together they fell onto the mattress. "Trust me. Over the years, my sister has dealt with much worse. But," he added, "don't believe her if she calls you a whore when you leave tomorrow."

Charlie frowned. "Wait . . . what?"

Chapter Twenty-nine

Max tied up the last of the trash bags and tossed it on the massive pile before heading into the house. Stevie and the seventeen-year-old who had been too young to drink but weirdly didn't complain about that had made themselves scarce as soon as the party wound down and Britta began forcing wolverines and She-wolves to start cleaning.

Not surprising. Stevie hated cleaning in general. She always expected someone else to do it for her.

The luxury life of the prodigy, Max supposed.

Once in the kitchen—every last morsel of Charlie's baking had disappeared along with the bears—Max found Britta pouring herself a glass of water.

"Hey, Max, my brother took Charlie back to our house. I'm almost positive they're having sex, which is not a problem for me, but if I find any evidence of that outside his bedroom, I'm going to lose my shit. So can I stay the night here so he has a chance to clean up the place before I get home?"

Max loved Britta. She was a six-foot-seven nut, but she was a hilarious nut. Max enjoyed that in any woman.

"Absolutely. There are extra bedrooms down the

hall. And tons of fresh bedding that suddenly appeared in the closet yesterday."

"Thanks. Dag already nabbed the couch. It's for black bears, though," she said, "so he's all scrunched up on it."

They both laughed at that until they heard it. Not Dag. He was snoring loudly in a cute drunken stupor. This sound was soft. And they'd both noticed it.

Britta lifted her nose, scented the air. She pointed up.

Max reached under the table and grabbed two .45s, tossing one to Britta.

Moving quickly but silently, they went up the stairs and down the hall, stopping outside Stevie's bedroom.

Britta was about to kick the door in, but Max stopped her with a raised hand. She put her forefinger to her lips.

Max eased the door open. While her baby sister slept soundly in the bed—blissfully unaware, probably zonked out on her nighttime meds—their father was busy going through a pile of notebooks that had arrived earlier that day from Switzerland.

He was so intent on whatever he was doing, he didn't even know that his other daughter and a goddamn *bear* were watching him.

Biting back a snarl, Max marched into Stevie's room, wrapped her hand around her father's mouth from behind and pressed her gun against the side of his neck.

"Not a sound. Not a word." She started to drag him to the door, but Britta was suddenly there, grabbing Freddy's legs and lifting them off the floor. Together, they carried him out into the hallway.

That's where they met a shirtless Shen. He had his own .45 out and he was ready for whatever.

Max motioned at Stevie's door. "Close it," she said low. "Then go back to bed. We've got this."

* * *

Britta never expected the MacKilligan sisters' idiot father would dare come back to New York, much less his daughters' house in the middle of bear territory. But here they were.

They carried the honey badger out into the yard and threw him into the garage wall.

When he tried to get up, Britta rammed her foot against his shoulder, pinning him there.

Max crouched next to Freddy MacKilligan.

"What the fuck are you doing here?"

"Nothing. I just needed a place to—"

Max grabbed her father by the throat with one hand and squeezed. He began choking, slapping at her hand, trying to get her to release him. She did. Just when he started to turn blue.

While he coughed and took in big gulps of air, she asked again, "What the fuck are you doing here?"

He gazed at his daughter with bloodshot eyes. "Go to hell."

Calmly, Max let out a breath. "I will have this She-bear break your windpipe for me and then I'll hold your nose closed until you suffocate. And we all know that I am the crazy MacKilligan to do it and not lose a moment of sleep. So are you really going to make me ask you again . . . or are you just going to tell me? Because we both know you're not brave."

Freddy looked up at Britta and she balled up one fist, knowing her knuckles would crack. An irritating sound that drove her brothers crazy but was so effective on others.

Swallowing, Freddy looked at his daughter and said, "Please . . . please don't hurt—"

The damn badger suddenly slipped out from under Britta's foot and with a surprising amount of that hidden strength badgers were known for, he tossed his daughter at Britta.

Britta caught Max, but when she put her down on the ground, one of the worst fathers Britta had ever known was long gone.

When they were back in the kitchen, coffee brewing and open jars of honey out on the table, Britta asked, "Are you going to tell Charlie?"

"I don't hide anything from Charlie. I just delay. So let her have her night with Berg, and we'll tell her in the morning."

"She's gonna be mad, huh?"

"When it comes to my father, Charlie always ends up mad. Not because she's irrational but because he's an asshole."

"What do you think he really wanted?"

"I have no idea. But the good news is, although it has to do with Stevie, it's not Stevie herself. Honestly, that's the first bit of good news we've gotten in a long time."

Britta ran her finger over the rim of her still-empty mug. "Are you guys going to run?"

"No," Stevie said from the kitchen doorway.

"Go back to bed, Stevie," Max said gently.

"I'm up now." Stevie walked over to the double coffeemaker, pulling off one of the carafes and coming back to the kitchen table. She filled up Britta's and Max's cups before getting her own from the cabinet and pouring coffee for herself. Once she put the carafe back, she asked, "When did we get a coffeemaker?"

"I think that's from Mrs. Fitzbaer," Britta offered. "A thank-you for the cinnamon buns."

Stevie sat down at the table, across from her sister. "We're not running," Stevie told Max. "I'm tired of running. Besides," she added, "Charlie's happy here." She thought a moment. "*I'm* happy here." Another pause. "*Kyle's* happy here. And he's not happy anywhere."

"You do know we can't adopt that kid, right?" Max asked.

"Of course we can't. He already has a family that loves him. He just makes them insane, so they need a break from him. I'm happy to help." She peeked up at Max. "Do you want to run?"

"Me?" Max grinned. "I'm a honey badger, bitch. I wanna stand my ground and beat the fuck out of any-body who crosses my path. But if something happened to you . . ."

"Nothing is going to happen to me. I've got you and Charlie." She leaned in a bit and, after glancing at Britta, she whispered, "And I'm surrounded by man-eating bears."

"Says the man-eating tiger."

Eyes narrowing on Britta, Stevie barked, "Stop freaking me out with that!"

Chapter Thirty

Berg was quickly learning that the pleasure of waking up with the woman of his dreams asleep on his chest did not come without a price.

He knew that the second his bedroom door slammed open and a honey badger came into the room to turn on the TV and announce, "We have a problem."

Charlie didn't even lift her head from Berg's chest. "Dad?"

"Surprisingly, no."

Max grabbed the remote from the top of the chest of drawers and began changing channels.

Stevie ran in and jumped onto the end of the bed. "Wow. This is the biggest bed I've ever seen. How fun!" She looked back at them, grinning. "You two are so cute!"

"Here it is." Max stepped back from the TV and Charlie sat up, not really bothering to cover her breasts. Berg wasn't sure if this was a sister thing—he and his siblings might be triplets but with one girl and two males, they had definite boundaries—but when his own sister walked into the room, followed by Dag, Berg yanked the sheet up to cover her.

When the MacKilligan sisters laughed, he had no idea how to respond.

"Awwww, he's shy," Max said.

"Yeah," Stevie chimed in. "I'm easily panicked and terrified, but I'm not shy. And Charlie's definitely *not* shy."

"My mother said that when I was a baby, I used to snatch off my diaper and wiggle my ass."

"Maybe it's because you can't shift," Max guessed. "Instead of being covered in fur and hunting, you run around naked wiggling your ass."

Berg pressed the palm of his hand against his eyes and asked, "Didn't you want us to see something?"

"Oh. Yeah." Max glanced at the remote. "Oh, good. I can rewind." She rewound the local news story and stepped back so Berg and Charlie could easily see.

"Police say, The Ring of Life Jewelry Emporium was hit this morning between midnight and 4 a.m. Thieves opened a hole beneath the store and went into the vault, stealing millions of dollars' worth of diamonds, gold, and other gems."

Charlie gestured to the TV and yawned. "Did Dad do this?"

"No. And we know this because Dad was in Stevie's bedroom last night when it was happening."

Dag suddenly raised his hand but before he could say anything, Stevie clarified with, "He was just snooping for something among my books." She shrugged. "Of all the horrible things there is to say about our father . . . what you're concerned about is, thankfully, not one of them."

Nodding, Dag pulled his arm back and said, "I just needed to know before we kept going."

Charlie, whom Berg was starting to realize liked to talk with her hands, raised her forefinger and said,

"Putting aside the issue of our father"—she moved her forefinger to the right to illustrate—"what does this heist have to do with us?"

Max smirked. "Carrie's polar bear? It's his store. On Forty-seventh. The one he took her to yesterday."

"But her bachelorette party was last night, right?"

"Which, again, we were not invited to," Stevie muttered.

"But all the cousins were," Max said. "All MacKilligans. All honey badgers. All—"

"Thieves," Charlie finished. "She wasn't having an affair with that bear. She was setting his ass up."

"That doesn't mean she wasn't having an affair," Max reasoned. "But I doubt she was really planning to end her upcoming marriage for him."

"What if he knows?" Stevie asked. "What if he knows that she set him up?"

"Then he'll come to ruin Carrie's wedding and demand his shit back," Max guessed.

There was silence on that and, after nearly a minute, Charlie forced her eyes wide open, shook her head, and announced, "All right. We need to move. Quickly. Suddenly this wedding day—"

"That we were originally not invited to."

"You need to let it go," Max admonished Stevie.

"—has gotten a new sense of urgency. Everybody know what they're doing?" she asked the room. When everyone nodded, "Good."

Charlie threw off the sheet and Britta and Dag quickly left the room. Max and Stevie followed but with no real sense of urgency.

"What about your father?" Berg asked Charlie.

"What about him?"

"What does *he* want?"

"I have no idea. We have our money secured, under different names, and scattered over the globe in different accounts or safety deposit boxes in cash just because of our father. The only thing Stevie has that could possibly be important to him or anyone—that Freddy could actually get to—is what she has in her head."

"Do you think they were trying to take her because of something they think she has?"

"It's possible. Who knows what my father told the Guerras. What he's *convinced* himself Stevie has in her notebooks that he must get his hands on because it'll give him everything he's ever wanted." She pointed at her own head. "He's stupid."

"Do you think he'll really show up today?"

"An event with a lot of rich people drinking and showing off their expensive jewelry? And he's desperate and out of control? What do you think?"

They arrived about an hour before the nuptials. The Dunns were sent off to meet up with the security forces Bernice and her wedding planner had already arranged for, while Charlie and her sisters went to find their cousins.

Before walking away, Berg grabbed Charlie's hand, smiled at her. "You look great in that dress."

"Enjoy it while it lasts. I'm not big on wearing dresses. Too limiting. I may know fashion, but I do not *abide* by fashion."

"I don't know what that means."

She tugged on his hand until he leaned down a bit so she could kiss him. When she pulled away, brushing her hand against his jaw, she said, "I know you don't . . . and I'm learning to find that charming."

Grinning wide and shaking his head, Berg followed after his siblings.

Charlie caught up with her sisters by the elevators. They got in, pushed the button for the correct floor, and as soon as the doors closed Stevie suddenly announced, "I sent my resignation to CERN."

Shocked, Charlie gawked at her baby sister. "You did what?"

Stevie let out a sigh. "Do I really have to say it again? Because nothing annoys me more than someone who says 'what' but they actually heard fine and all they really need is a moment to gather their thoughts."

Charlie shook her head and barked, *"What?"*

"I gave my notice."

"Why?"

"I thought we should stay."

"Where?"

"Here?"

Charlie looked around. "In the Kingston Arms? Dude, we can't afford this."

"Oh, my God!" Stevie snapped.

Chuckling, Max offered, "I think, Charlie, she's talking about staying in New York. Most likely the Queens abode we are currently living in."

"Why would we do that?"

Max sighed. "Gee, I don't know . . . maybe because you're in love with that mountain of a man you just soul kissed in the middle of a hotel hallway. We've *never* seen you do that before."

"Look, I appreciate that you guys are happy that I am . . ." she searched for the right words, "finding romance."

Max couldn't even hold back a snort and Charlie glared at her until she looked away. Something she didn't do with anyone else.

"But your career," Charlie said to Stevie, "is more important than whether I get laid."

"My career?" Stevie asked, stepping out of the elevator now that the doors were open. "What does CERN have to do with my career?"

"I don't know," Charlie replied, glancing at an equally confused—but less caring—Max. *"Everything?"*

Stevie's back suddenly straightened and her chin jerked up a notch. "You think that my *brilliance*—"

"Uh-oh," Max warned.

"—is due to where I lay my hat?"

"You don't wear hats," Max unhelpfully pointed out.

"Shut up," Stevie snapped before refocusing on Charlie. "Do you?"

"Of course not," Charlie said quickly. "But I've always thought that . . . uh . . ."

Max blinked when she noticed that Charlie had turned toward her. "What are you looking at me for? I don't know how to help you out of this."

"I just assumed it was . . . um . . . helpful for your career."

"You know what helps my career?" Stevie asked. "Me. Not to sound smug but it's all about me. My brilliance. My skills. My ability to think beyond the plebes of this universe."

"Wow," Max burst out. "Hanging with Kyle has brought out an interesting side of you."

"Kyle is a child. He has years to realize how amazing he is. I, however, already know."

"Dude, you're twenty-three."

"I'm twenty-*four* but that's not the point, you . . ."

"Peons?" Charlie suggested.

"Yes! Peons! I love you both, and I appreciate your protection and absolutely everything you've done for me."

"But," Max pushed.

"But my career is my own. And if you think that CERN—"

"We don't think that CERN defines you," Charlie quickly told her. "I know it has not made you who you are. But I thought it was a good fit for you because you mostly got along with the staff, you got to do whatever you wanted, when you wanted, and they paid for your weird mental health facility obsession."

Stevie shrugged. "Bluntly . . . I can get that anywhere. I can get any job, anywhere I want in the universe. I've got Silicon Valley coming at me. I've got universities from all over the globe coming at me. I'm a girl and I'm smart and I've got two sisters who are women of color . . . I'm their diversity wet dream. So I don't need to lock myself into anything. You two, however . . ."

"What about us?" Max asked, sounding indignant for the first time.

"Not to be rude but if either of you find a man . . . you need to *hold* that man."

"What the fuck does that mean?" Max demanded.

"Yeah," Charlie chimed in, "what the fuck *does* that mean?"

"It's that you need me to explain that hurts."

"Stevie!"

"What? Do you think just *any* guy would be okay with your sisters busting into his bedroom to discuss the thievery of other family members? No. But Berg puts up with it because he loves you and he's already a triplet. He *gets* siblings. He'll understand if you need to take off for Norway because Dad has done"—she sighed—"something stupid and you have to fix it before one of us goes to jail for his fuck-up. He'll be okay with you having weaponry around the entire house. He won't like it, but he'll be okay with it. He won't freak out when he finds me and Max hanging out in his cabinets, eating his honey."

"You don't like honey," Charlie pointed out.

"No, but I really like living in cabinets. And I have to say that my coworkers at CERN . . . they all thought that was a little weird. But not here. For once, do you guys realize, we're not the weirdest people in the group?

I mean, did you see there was a guy with a lion's mane doing the cha-cha at our party with his wolf girlfriend? And we were playing tech music at the time. Or have you noticed that Kyle has a bodyguard that eats bamboo . . . *all*. *The*. *Time*. Or perhaps you've spotted Dag in our backyard doing his full body back scratch on that big oak tree. He was human at the time . . . he could have just used a back scratcher. But no." She circled her forefinger in the air to signify each of them. "Not the weirdest. I say we revel in that and see what we can make of it."

Max smirked. "And you're okay staying on a street with nothing but, as you call them . . . man-eating bears?"

"As long as Charlie keeps giving them baked goods, we should be fine."

Charlie tossed her arms in the air. "So now I'm beholden to bake all the time for demanding bears?"

"You can't give wild animals food and then take it away." Stevie pointed a finger at Charlie and snarled through gritted teeth, "So if that means you need to bake, bitch. *Bake!*"

Max started to laugh but the sound suddenly cut off and her eyes narrowed as she focused down the hall.

Charlie looked over her shoulder, but didn't see anything. "What?"

"I saw Dad."

Charlie didn't question whether her sister had really seen their father. She knew she had. "Go," she ordered Max, then pointed at Stevie. "Tell security Dad's here. I'll talk to the bride."

Stevie cringed. "Good luck with that."

Max ran down one hall, then another searching for her father. She caught his scent when she started past the stairs. Her father wasn't using bear spray this time to disguise his scent. Just a cheap knockoff Paco Rabanne cologne that he'd probably picked up from a street vendor in Chinatown. Idiot.

She ran into the stairwell and started up the stairs.

She'd just gotten two floors up when she caught the scent of another honey badger behind her. Not her father, but a female.

Max turned but just in time to watch a steel pipe collide with her head . . .

Dee-Ann buried her knife into the man's side, a brutal thrust between ribs. She dropped his body and stepped over him to move around the office, examining everything. But they were gone. She knew it.

Malone came out of the hangar office. "They're gone," she said, proving Dee-Ann right.

"I know. We're too late."

"The jet is still here, though."

"They're like bazillionaires. They could have ten jets like that one."

"Did you look at that thing? We are so absconding with it."

"Right now? You just want to drive it off the tarmac?"

Malone laughed and motioned to the two teams they'd brought with them. One from Katzenhaus, one from the Group.

She motioned to the bodies. "Get this cleaned up," she ordered before coming over to Dee's side.

"Now what?" she asked.

"We put out the word to our contacts, try to track the two bitches down."

"Three bitches," Malone corrected. "The Guerra twins and that honey badger."

"She's our problem too?"

"It sounds like it. Word is she's rabid."

"Literally?"

Malone sighed. *"No."*

"Well, don't get that tone. You weren't being clear."

"What I mean is that she's like one of those tigers that sneak into a village in India and start killing everybody but not eating them. She's what we don't need out in the world representing our kind."

Charlie walked into the hotel room where Carrie was about to be helped into her gown. The room was filled with flowers and bridesmaids. There was girlish giggling and open bottles of champagne. There were also three photographers moving around the bride while Max's cousin Livy stood off to the side. She had her own camera hanging from her shoulder, but she didn't seem too interested in taking any pictures.

"Why are you here?" Charlie asked her, still holding the hotel door open.

"They're paying me a shit-ton of money to choose and oversee the photographers and videographer handling the wedding. This is how low I've sunk as an artist."

"Don't worry, Liv. You're about to see something really interesting."

The badger raised a brow just as Charlie slammed the hotel door with as much strength as she could. So hard, she might have damaged the doorframe itself from the force.

Everyone in the room faced her and she asked, "So which of you crazy cunts were involved in the jewelry heist last night?"

Livy rubbed her nose—hiding her smile behind her hand—before she got control and motioned to the photographers and videographer to get out of the room with a wave of her finger.

It took a little effort for them to pull the door back open after Charlie had closed it though.

Once they were gone, Charlie focused on the bride and her cousins again. "Well?"

"What are you talking about?" Bernice asked. "Carrie had her bachelorette party last night."

"Nope. She went a-stealin' last night."

Kenzi dropped the wedding dress to the floor and demanded, "Is that why you kept giving me that black mamba–infused vodka last night? So that I'd pass out?"

"It's not like you would have come with us," Carrie explained to her sister. "You're such a drag about everything."

"Wait . . ." Bernice peered at her youngest daughter. "You mean this is true?"

"Did you really think all we would do was go see a bunch of strippers and drink? What are we? Full-human?"

"You insolent little—"

"The heist isn't the big problem," Charlie cut in. "It's who she stole from."

"Why? Who did she steal from?"

"You going to tell her?" Charlie pushed her cousin. "You're doing such a nice job and all."

"The polar bear . . . he wasn't her boyfriend. He was her mark."

"You thought he was my boyfriend?" Carrie sneered. "I'm about to marry Ronald P. Farmington the Fourth. Do you think I'd really risk that for a *bear*?"

Charlie looked at Livy and at that point her sister's cousin just laughed out loud.

"The bear you're talking about," Charlie explained, "is a dangerous scumbag. A loan shark. A mobster. If you think he won't figure out—"

"I already sent him an 'I love you' text this morning. And by tomorrow I'll be on my honeymoon, so—"

Bernice had her hands wrapped around her daughter's neck, attempting to wring the life from her. Charlie watched impassively as the cousins and Carrie's sisters tried to pry Carrie's mother off her throat.

When they finally pinned Bernice to a chair, she screamed, *"You are the worst daughter ever!"*

"It was a flawless heist! The cops will have nothing!"

"The cops are the least of your worries," Charlie told Carrie. "I mean, does your husband even know you're a criminal?"

"How can I be a criminal," Carrie asked, "when I've never been caught?"

Bernice was almost out of the chair again, but one of the huskier cousins literally sat on her to keep her down.

"Anyway," Charlie continued, "the additional security I employed is already on it, but there are a lot of exits and entrances in this hotel and he is a shifter, so regular hotel security won't notice a polar bear the way they would if we were talking about a full-human. And there's one other thing . . . Max saw Freddy. About two minutes ago."

Bernice shoved her niece off her lap, tossing her across the room, and stood. *"What?"* she exploded.

"Max is already on it and so is the additional security."

"If you need to," Bernice said, pointing at Charlie, "you have my permission to kill him."

"Good to know. Anyway, I strongly suggest we get these nuptials going as quickly as possible. And I also strongly suggest that after the I dos are said, cousin"— she looked directly at Carrie—"you drag that new husband of yours off to a closet somewhere and fuck his brains out. It'll be harder for him to annul this sham

of a marriage if you've already fucked after the ceremony." She spread her arms out. "Are we all clear?
Great!"

She winked at Livy and walked out, leaving a room
full of screaming honey badgers throwing expensive
glass things around in her wake.

As Charlie moved down the hall, she heard the room
door open and looked over her shoulder to see Livy
sticking her head out, her team of photographers standing by.

"Charlie?" she called out.

"Yeah?"

Livy smiled, tears in her eyes. "I love you."

Grinning, Charlie replied, "I know you do."

Laughing, Livy motioned her team in. "Let's go,
people! We have lifelong memories to photograph!"

Chapter Thirty-one

Max woke up as her body was dragged down some hallway. She opened her eyes to see pipes over her head. She was in the hotel basement. Or at least that's what she was assuming. Hotels like this didn't have unattractive things such as plumbing on floors with guest rooms. That would be tacky.

A full-human male dragged her into a room. "Here," he said. Max didn't know, though, to whom he was speaking. She'd closed her eyes to maintain the illusion she was still out cold.

"Where is our little friend?"

"She went to find the notebook."

Ahhh. That's what they wanted from Stevie. One of the notebooks she obsessively wrote in.

Max had no idea what her sister put into those books, but she'd always assumed if it wasn't music, it was probably some amazing Leonardo da Vinci–style prototype that would change the world.

The Guerra twins were the kind who could easily afford to make any of Stevie's ideas into reality with all the money and connections they had. Of course for Max there was another question: Was Freddy also trying to get Stevie's notebook for himself? Or was he still working for the twins?

"Hello, niece," a female voice said above Max. "We know you are awake."

Max opened her eyes and gazed up at one of the women she'd seen in the *Vanity Fair* article.

"It is so nice to meet family, is it not?" she asked with an Italian accent. An accent Max normally found sexy . . . from a man trying to pick her up in a Rome bar. Not on some broad holding a .45 aimed at Max's head.

The mirror image of the woman standing over her stepped to Max's side. "So nice to meet family. Although we must admit . . . you do not *look* like a MacKilligan. But your father assured us that you are."

"Your father," said the other, "has been *so* helpful. He just can't do enough for us."

"He specifically told us to take you. He said . . . what was it, Rina?"

"He said to take the Chinese one, Tina. That would keep the others from doing something stupid."

"Wasn't that helpful?"

Actually, it wasn't helpful. Not to Max's enemies. Unlike her sisters, anxiety and reason did not rule Max MacKilligan. Insanity did. And her father knew that. For once . . . he'd done something right.

"My sisters would never put me at risk," Max admitted. "That's kind of my job."

The one crouching over her—the one who was probably Rina—narrowed her eyes on Max.

Max smiled. Grinned, really. A big, wide one.

Then she unleashed her claws, reached up, and slashed Rina across the face from her jaw to her forehead.

Screaming, Rina fell to the floor, and Max rolled backward until she was able to get to her feet. Tina fired her weapon and Max turned. The bullets rammed her in the back, two hitting close to her spine. But because they didn't actually touch it, she was able to grab the male who rushed into the room, his gun drawn.

Max caught his wrist and twisted until she broke it. She yanked him close, using his body to protect her from more bullets, letting her aunt shoot her gun dry. When she went to reload, Max threw the now-dead male across the room, knocking her aunt to the ground.

The other twin sat on the floor, screaming and crying, blood pouring, flesh hanging off her skull. But Tina struggled up from under the body.

"Kill her!" Rina ordered her sister in Italian—an Italian phrase Max had learned long ago. *"Kill the bitch!"*

Max raised her blood-drenched claws and unleashed her fangs. She jerked her entire body forward and hissed.

Tina, without thought, hissed back and her claws suddenly burst from her fingers. Fangs dropped from her gums.

Shocked, she and her twin gazed at the abrupt change in . . . well . . . everything.

Max grinned. "Welcome to the family, Auntie," she told the females before she charged Tina.

She was almost on her when the door was kicked open and more armed men came in.

Max ripped a line down the skirt of her gown and yanked a blade out of one of the holsters tied to her thigh. She threw it and it slammed into the throat of the first man entering the room. He fell back into the men behind him and Max punched Tina in the face before jumping up onto a nearby desk, ripping out the grate over an air duct and crawling inside. Bullets riddled the tiny shaft as Max crawled her way down to the first exit she could find.

* * *

Charlie was standing near the room where the ceremony would take place. The wedding planner was asking everyone to take their seats because the ceremony was about to begin. The guests showing surprise that a wedding ceremony was about to take place on time.

The music started and the full-human groomsmen began to line up, waiting to make their way down the aisle.

"You guys ready?" Charlie asked with a false smile. "Then let's go, let's go, let's go!"

"Is there a problem?" the groom asked her.

"No. Of course not. The bride is just excited to start her new life with you."

With an annoyed snarl, the wedding planner pushed Charlie away from the groomsmen.

"All right, gentlemen," the She-tiger said, a headset firmly in place, an iPad desperately clutched in her hand. "You remember what to do. And smile everyone. Smile!"

As the men started to go, the She-tiger turned on Charlie. "What are you doing?"

"Trying to get this thing moving."

"It's a wedding. Not a business meeting."

"You can't be in that much denial." Charlie jerked to the side so she could see over the taller woman's shoulder. Her father had crept out of a room where the bridesmaids and groomsmen were allowed to store their stuff during the ceremony and he now held Stevie's backpack. Even worse, when he saw his eldest daughter, he ran.

He ran!

"Get this thing moving!" Charlie ordered the She-tiger before she lifted up the skirt of her gown and took off after her old man.

* * *

Stevie came around the corner in time to hear "Here Comes the Bride" played—rather poorly, in her opinion—by the string quartet.

She waited until her cousin started off down the aisle to let out a relieved sigh.

"Hey!" Dutch said, coming up behind her in a perfectly tailored suit. Thankfully *not* a tux. "Everything going okay?"

"Doubtful." Stevie faced him. "But Carrie's heading off down the aisle, so I think she's ahead of the . . . oh, shit!"

"What?" Dutch looked over his shoulder and he immediately begged, "Please tell me they're not our problem."

"They're our problem."

There were ten of them. Ten *polar bears*. A few seven, others maybe eight, feet tall.

And all Stevie wanted to do was run. She wanted to run and never look back. But she couldn't. She'd made a commitment and she didn't have time to dash off a letter of resignation to her sisters.

"Look," Dutch said, "I'll distract them. You go and get the grizzlies."

"They'll just squeeze you until you pop like a zit." Stevie motioned to the wedding planner to close the doors leading into the wedding venue.

And once she heard those doors close, Stevie grabbed the gun she knew Dutch had holstered under his jacket. Even better, it already had a silencer on it.

She aimed and shot Damian Miller five times in the chest . . . which did nothing really except redirect his focus from finding the honey badger who'd ripped him off to destroying the honey badger who'd fucked up his nice white English suit.

The bear roared and Stevie tossed the gun back to a stunned Dutch.

"Run!" she told Max's best friend. "Run away!"

Then that's exactly what she did.

Charlie caught up to her father near the lobby and threw herself at him, landing on his back and taking them both down to the ground.

They rolled right into the middle of people trying to walk to the nearby stores or to the elevators, but Charlie didn't care.

Grabbing her father by the hair, she yanked him onto his back and straddled his chest.

She had just leaned in to start asking him questions when she felt she was being watched. She looked up to see Bo Novikov standing over her with one child on his shoulders, another in his arms. Beside him was a tall black woman holding onto a baby.

"Seriously, though," Novikov said, "I can teach you and your sister to skate. That's, like, the easiest part."

"What?"

"Hockey. I can teach you to play hockey."

Charlie started to say something, but her father was trying to get out from under her.

She punched the idiot in the face three times before looking back up at Novikov. "Can this wait?"

"Well . . . you're not getting any younger."

"Bo," the woman said. "Later. You can talk to her later."

"Whatever." He sighed, walked off.

The woman smiled warmly, pressing her hand to her chest, and said, "I'm Bl—"

"I don't care—could you go?" Charlie barked.

Looking hurt, the woman walked off but Charlie wasn't too concerned. She had other issues at the moment.

"Help!" her father suddenly yelled. "She's trying to kill me!"

They both waited but everyone kept moving except for a couple of teenagers who started filming on their phones.

"Seriously, Dad," Charlie told him, "if you're going to try that move, you really need to pick another city."

Max was crawling through the air ducts, moving fast, but sadly not really knowing where she was going . . . exactly.

Still, she didn't expect the bottom to go out from under her. Literally.

The hatch opened and Max fell to the floor. She turned over, swinging her fists, her eyes closed. But when she didn't actually hit anything she looked up and saw . . . Dutch and Stevie?

"Told you I smelled her," Dutch told Stevie proudly.

"That's just weird," Stevie replied. "I'd appreciate you not saying something like that to me ever again."

Dutch held his hand out and Max reached to grab it, but then Dutch was gone, picked up and flung across the room by Carrie's polar bear dupe.

He reached down for Max but she grabbed another knife from her holster and slashed. The bear roared, his severed thumb hitting Stevie in the head before bouncing across the room.

Another polar grabbed Max from behind, but Stevie unleashed her ridiculously sized claws and slashed, tearing a massive amount of flesh and muscle from a shoulder. That bear roared in pain and dropped Max.

Now on her feet, Max used her elbow to push her sister toward another door—since her claws were still out—and together they ran, the bears right behind them.

*   *   *

Charlie's father was turning blue by the time Berg was able to pry her hands from around his throat and Dag was able to yank her off.

Freddy rolled to his knees, coughing and taking in big gulps of air. It was quite dramatic until he suddenly grabbed Stevie's pink and burgundy backpack and tried to make a run for it. But Britta caught him around the neck Charlie had tried to wring and dragged him away from the lobby.

Berg took a cursing and hissing Charlie from a terrified Dag and they followed Britta down the hallway. They moved into a room that wasn't near the wedding festivities and carried the two MacKilligans inside.

Dag kicked the door closed and Britta pressed her .45 under Freddy's chin. And before he could speak a word, she said, "Keep in mind, old man, I am not your child, I do not like you, and no one in your family will miss you."

Charlie fought her way out of Berg's arms and adjusted her dress.

"You should have let me kill him," she said to Berg without looking at him.

"You were being filmed. I'm pretty sure that's one of those situations you can't MacKilligan your way out of."

Charlie took in a breath, let it out. "You're right. Thank you." She pointed at her father. "Why did you take Stevie's backpack?"

Her father gave a shrug and false smile. "No reason."

Charlie's fingers curled into fists and, after a few seconds, she said, "Dag . . . rip off his arm."

Dag started across the room like he was going to do it, and Britta even forced Freddy to extend a limb.

When his brother grabbed hold of it and looked like he was going to start pulling while his sister held the other half of Freddy, the badger screamed out, "Okay! Okay!"

Charlie cocked her head. "Well?"

"I needed one of the notebooks . . ."

"Tell me you're not trying to sell secrets to the North Koreans again."

Britta's eyes widened. *"Again?"*

"He never actually did," Charlie explained. "It's just that . . . um . . ." She shook her head. "I'm sorry. It's too stupid a story."

"It's nothing like that. I just, uh . . ."

When Freddy hesitated too long, Charlie informed her father, "If you think that I won't tear strips of your flesh off just to see you cry, let alone get information that will protect my baby sister, you are sadly mistaken. So if I were you, *Dad*, I'd start talking."

But, even after that, he still hesitated. Berg pushed Charlie to the side, got at the head of the long, heavy wood conference table, raised his fist in the air, and brought it down. Once.

The entire table caved inward, folding like a thin sheet of cardboard.

Berg lowered his head a little so that he was sure Freddy MacKilligan could see his grizzly hump. Then he said, "Talk."

"It's account numbers," the badger quickly replied.

"Account numbers for . . . ?" Charlie pushed.

"Every member of the MacKilligan family in Scotland and in the States."

Aghast, Charlie demanded, "How the *fuck* did you get that?"

"I just . . ." Freddy's gaze bounced around the room, examining them all before he told his daughter, "You don't have to worry. I don't have yours and your sisters since you won't give me that information. Spoiled brats that you are!"

"Seriously?" Britta snapped, pissed *for* the MacKilligan sisters.

"They're my daughters. They wouldn't *exist* if it wasn't for me."

Charlie started to go for her father but Berg caught her arm and pulled her back. "Just finish," he ordered Freddy.

"Anyway, I sold Will's info to the Guerras to prove what I had."

"Uh-huh. And?" Charlie pushed.

"But then Will got so mad about it."

"Shocking," Charlie drily replied.

"He owes me!" her father yelled. "Fucking cheap ass."

"Can we just keep going, please?"

"So, I wasn't going to sell the book to the Guerras since Will was all bitchy about it. But then they . . ."

"Then they . . . ?"

He cleared his throat. "Then they got me drunk one night and I must have told them where it was. Or how they could get it."

"How they could get it?"

"Well, I know your sister likes to write in those composition notebooks. So, I just bought one, put the info in there, and then slipped it into the middle of the stack she already had in her backpack. I figured she'd never notice."

Without moving, without blinking, Charlie asked her father, "And when was this?"

He shrugged. "I don't know. A month ago. Maybe."

"You . . . you let your daughter walk around for a month with a target on her back?"

"I wouldn't put it that way."

Her voice tight, Charlie asked, "And how would you put it?"

"Ummm . . . well . . . I guess . . . kind of that way. But," he quickly added, "I knew my little Stevie wouldn't mind."

The problem wasn't Freddy's "little Stevie." It was Freddy's "extremely upset Charlie."

Body so tense that every vein bulged, Charlie reached down and grabbed one side of the table that Berg had broken in half.

Britta and Dag, eyes wide, immediately dove out of the way as that table half flew across the room and rammed into Freddy MacKilligan, battering him into the wall. When the table hit the floor, a brutalized and unconscious Freddy fell on top of it.

Calm again, Charlie went over to her father's side and grabbed her sister's backpack. She dumped everything on the floor and quickly pulled out the notebooks. She handed a couple to Britta, Berg, and Dag. She took the rest. In silence, they all quickly flipped through the pages until Britta said, "All I see are notes for things that I'm not sure are physically possible to make in today's world."

"These are all music and drawings," Dag said.

When Charlie looked at him, Berg just shook his head.

"Someone else must have taken it."

"Who?"

Charlie thought a moment, but when she suddenly closed her eyes and whispered, "Fuck," he knew they were in trouble.

"Come on then, Aunties," Mairi said as she pulled the Guerra twins up, tucking the notebook the two women wanted into the pack before strapping it to her shoulders. "Let's get you out of here."

"My face," one of them sobbed. "Look what that bitch did to my face!"

Mairi understood why her cousin had done it, though. She'd wanted to do something similar. Just so she could tell the two bitches apart.

"It's all right. No need to worry. You'll be better in no time. Plastic surgeons can do wonders these days," she lied. Those weren't just scratches. Her cousin had dug down deep with her claws. To bone. Those were scars that would last, even for shifters.

She led them to the door, stepping over the bodies of the men she'd been forced to kill. Her cousin had only taken out one. Mairi had killed the others because they'd seen too much. She'd walked in when they were talking about claws and fangs. Not a good scenario in her estimation. Best to quiet them all.

So she had. She'd killed every man and hadn't even worked up a sweat. Full-humans were almost too easy.

"Let's get you someplace safe, Aunties. And then," she said as she helped them out, "we'll have a nice, long talk about family . . . and how we're different from the other boys and girls."

They led the bears as far away from the wedding as they could, but when they turned to make sure they were all back there, Stevie realized that only Miller's polar friends had been chasing them. Miller was gone.

"Max!"

Max stopped and turned, quickly realizing the issue.

They were at a dead end, with the bears only a few feet away from them.

One of them threw his arms wide and asked, "So what are you gonna do now?"

Max reached under the slit in her dress and pulled out two blades. She started toward the men but Stevie yanked her back.

"No!"

"Why not?" Max snapped.

"It's wrong."

"And what? You think *they* were going to be nice to us?"

"We don't know if they were going to kill us, though, right?" she asked the men, but they just seemed sadly confused by the situation. "Look at them. You can't just kill them."

"And I still say, 'why not'?"

"What about the bodies?"

Now Max was getting frustrated. "What about them?"

"We can't just leave them here. The cops will come. It'll ruin the wedding."

"The wedding?"

"Look, we want to stay in New York, right? So Charlie can have a chance at what some consider normalcy. Then we can't leave bodies just lying around everywhere."

"So what do you suggest?"

Stevie studied the hallway they were in, her mind calculating every bit of space, noting anything within arm's length, taking into account every defect in the design and architecture before evaluating those things within three dimensions inside her mind.

When she was done, she took one of Max's blades, walked over to the wall on the right, found the patch she wanted, and stabbed it with the knife.

There was a moment of silence before the wall began to crack. The crack spread fast, crawling up the wall, to the ceiling.

The bears were staring up as the crack moved by, a

second before nearly five feet of ceiling gave way and fell on them.

Stevie pulled Max's knife out of the wall and handed it back to her. Then she smiled.

"Show off," Max muttered before she ran around the bears, who were groaning and trying to dig their way out of the rubble.

Barb Malone stood behind the tapestry that separated the prep area from the actual ceremony. Everything was going perfectly. She could see her staff on her tablet as they rushed to get those last-minute details finished in the Grand Ballroom for the reception. She'd been reluctant to move away from her paper and pen days, but high tech was her friend, an extra set of hands that she'd never really had before.

Glorious. Just glorious.

"We are winding down here," she said very softly into her mic. "You have T minus five minutes before the ceremony is over. Be ready. Be smiling."

To her delight she heard that the cake had arrived and it was perfect. The cake always worried her. If that thing was damaged during transport, a bride would forever say her wedding was ruined by "the cake disaster." So Barb only worked with certain bakers and bakeries; she wouldn't tolerate mistakes. Not now, not ever.

She was about to move back to the front of the room when she saw a polar bear come in through one of the doors and start moving toward the ceremony.

Barb quickly and quietly moved across the floor until she stood in front of the man. Why was blood on him? She shook her head. No time for those kind of questions.

"I'm sorry, sir," she whispered, "but you can't be back here."

He tried to push her out of the way but Barb Malone was a Siberian tiger. You didn't *push* her anywhere. She unleashed her fangs and he started to roar. A roar that would travel.

But then two of the bride's cousins were suddenly there, throwing themselves onto the back of the bear, trying to stop him and, thankfully, distracting the polar from roaring.

Unfortunately for the two cousins . . . they were honey badgers. Honey badgers on a polar bear? Seriously?

"This wouldn't be so bad if I could use my knife!" one cousin complained. Too loudly.

"I said, no!" the other barked back.

"Keep quiet!" Barb ordered.

A muffled scream startled Barb, but a wolverine landing on the bear's back startled her more.

What the unholy fuck was happening?

"Dutch! Get him!" one cousin squealed.

"I'm trying!"

Charlie couldn't find any sign of the Guerra twins or Mairi, and she really didn't have time to look. She had to check on the damn wedding.

She eased the door open and slid into the back with the Dunn triplets behind her. She'd just let out a relieved breath—seeing the bride and groom about to take their vows—when she noticed the tapestry in the background was moving.

Then she heard a squeak. She knew only one shifter who ever squeaked like that. Stevie.

She motioned to Berg to keep a lookout for trouble

before lifting her skirt and moving around the perimeter of the room until she reached the tapestry and disappeared behind it.

Charlie was trying to be quiet but she gasped when she saw Stevie and Max hanging onto a polar bear wearing a blood-soaked white suit and desperate to shake them off. Coming around to the front was Dutch. He grabbed the bear around the waist and was using all of his brawny weasel strength to try to take the bear down to the ground. But Miller wasn't having any of it.

Charlie ran toward the bear just as he opened his mouth to roar. She slapped her hand over his face and started pushing him back with Dutch.

"Get him out of here!" the She-tiger wedding planner whispered-yelled at them.

The bear tried to go forward again, ready to ruin everything for a couple Charlie really could not give two shits about, but still . . . She'd been paid to prevent something like this from happening. Sadly, she still felt a sense of commitment.

But just when the bear managed to get within inches of the tapestry, his hand reaching down to pull it off and reveal all of this to the rich full-humans about to marry into this insanity, a big hand caught hold of the polar's wrist and yanked him back.

Max and Stevie were quickly removed from the polar's back, and Dag wrapped his arms around the polar, slapping his hand over Miller's mouth.

Then there was Britta. Standing in front of the polar, smirking, she reached down and grabbed Miller's balls. Then she twisted.

His high-pitched squeal—despite Dag's hand over his mouth—still made every shifter in the place wince, but the full-humans probably hadn't heard a thing.

"Let's go," Britta ordered, and as one, the Dunns lifted the polar up and carried him out.

Just as the door closed behind them, Charlie heard applause and cheers and knew that the bride and groom were now wife and husband.

Grinning, she looked at her sisters and, together, they all did their own little awkward celebratory dances.

Charlie knew it wasn't pretty . . . but she also didn't care.

Chapter Thirty-two

Their table at the reception ended up being all the way in the back, by the kitchen doors, but Charlie still didn't care. How could she when she was just relieved the worst of it was over?

Carrie, for once, had taken someone's advice other than her own and had nailed her husband almost immediately after the ceremony. A good thing because four hours later, after the toasts had been made, the dinner served, and the cake cut, Damian Miller had shown up again with his thumb reattached—shifter surgeons could do amazing work—and his rage unhampered by all the pain meds he was on. He slurred his way through accusations of whoring and thievery, but he was such a mess that Ronald Farmington and the Farmington family didn't believe a word of it.

Eventually, the intruder passed out and he was dragged from the room by the wedding planner's security detail.

Charlie doubted it was over—multimillions had been stolen from that bear—but her involvement in all of it sure was.

She looked out over the dance floor and watched Max and Dutch tango from one corner to the other.

Charlie winced at the bandages easily visible on her sister due to the cut of her dress. Shot in the back and Max refused to go home, to get some rest. Even worse, she'd let Dutch, of all people, yank out the bullets before the area was cleaned and bandages taped over the wounds.

Charlie sighed and focused on the slice of honey cake a waiter had placed in front of her.

Berg came back to the table and, lifting Charlie up, sat in her chair and then put her on his lap.

"Is this a thing we do?" she asked.

"It is now." He gave her a short but warm hug. She liked it.

"You all right?" he asked.

"I'm fine. Did you see them?"

"Nope. If the twins and your cousin were here, they're gone. I did touch base with Ric Van Holtz. He said that Malone and Smith are on their way to Italy, trying to find them."

"According to Max, they know what they are now. This kind of changes everything."

"How? It's not like it's going to make them meaner."

She shrugged. "You have a point."

"Oh, and your father disappeared."

"Of course he did." She rolled her eyes. "Whatever." Although she still wondered how the old bastard had gotten everyone's bank account information. Even worse, he hadn't bragged about how he'd done it. He bragged about everything, which meant he was hiding something big . . . or disastrous. And that worried her more than anything.

Dutch and Max tangoed over to them and Max dipped Dutch so that his head was almost in Charlie's lap.

"Still hate me?" Dutch asked.

"Forever and ever."

"What's wrong?" Max asked before bringing Dutch

up and twirling him away. She dropped into a seat and motioned to one of the waitstaff. She pointed at each of them and asked, "Beer? Beer? Beer? Beer? Four beers," she told the waiter.

Once the waiter was gone, Max asked, "So what's up?"

"Dad's gone."

"Of course he is. Although I have to admit, I was impressed you threw half a table at him."

"It was awesome," Berg said, burying his nose against the back of Charlie's neck.

"He just made me so mad."

"I understand that," Berg said, squeezing Charlie a little tighter. "There is something about your father that just makes you want to punch him."

Bernice stopped by on her way to more drunken schmoozing, repeatedly pointing her finger at Charlie before telling her, "Nice job, pretty girl."

"Thank you."

"Can I pay you tom—"

"Tonight," Charlie insisted. "You promised. The rest of the money *tonight*, including the bonus."

Bernice quickly held up her hands but stumbled a little in the process. "Not a problem. My husband has the cash. I'll send him up to get it for you."

When she'd walked away, Berg asked, "You going to tell her about the account numbers situation?"

"After we get paid, I'll tell her and Will. Not before."

"Especially since we don't know how much longer she'll have access to ready cash," Max muttered, smirking at Dutch.

Stevie came back to the table and dropped into a chair. Dutch motioned to his lap and she kicked off her shoes and placed her feet there. Dutch was smart enough, though, not to actually rub her feet. That she hated.

Stevie looked around the room and admitted, "I'm

so bored here." She leaned in a bit and whispered, "Our party last night was so much better."

"It really was," Max agreed. "Of course, we had zebra legs."

Charlie laughed and Stevie held up her phone. "So I got a call from the CERN director. I think he cried a little."

"You're making the world of science very sad," Charlie told her sister.

"I'm not giving up science. I *am* science."

"I *really* don't think you should be hanging around that Kyle kid," Max warned.

"You need a job, though," Charlie said, pointing at Stevie. "Somewhere, somehow. I don't give a shit. But you cannot just sit around the house doing nothing. We all know that leads to obsessing and possible hoarding."

"I'm well aware of my mental health issues. I've got it all under control."

"You're not going back to Switzerland?" Berg asked Stevie.

"Nope. I already talked to Tiny and he says he'd be more than happy for us to stay."

"Considering what he's charging us—"

"He's willing to work on a deal for the rent if we sign a lease and you continue to make him your honey-pineapple cake."

"You promised him—"

"I said we'd talk about it. Didn't I, Max?"

Max looked at her sister and admitted, "I'm sorry. I wasn't listening because you're boring the fuck out of me."

Stevie's eyes narrowed but before she could say anything, Max took off running and Stevie charged after her.

"Fun is fun," Charlie yelled after her sisters, "until someone gets hurt!"

Charlie cringed when Max slipped in her heels and flipped herself over one of the open bars and into the liquor bottles, sending glass crashing to the floor and knocking the bartender out cold.

Dutch pushed his chair back. "I'll deal with it," he said before Charlie could start yelling at everyone.

Embarrassed, she couldn't even look at Berg. He was probably checking for one of the seven exits she'd noticed and marked in her head in case of emergency. Not that she'd blame the man . . .

Berg tried to calm his mind. Because he knew, if Stevie wasn't leaving New York . . . then Charlie wouldn't leave, which meant she would stay. In New York. With him.

Don't get too excited, he warned himself. He didn't want to scare Charlie off. *Don't say anything that will spook her. Just keep calm and—*

"Are you going to say anything?" she suddenly barked at him, making Berg jump.

"Say anything about what?"

She gestured across the room, and that's when he noticed Max was covered in cuts and, apparently, liquor. She was also laughing hysterically along with Dutch while a tsk-tsking Stevie was trying to help the bartender, and the wedding planner was ordering the waitstaff into action and yelling at the badgers who'd caused a scene.

"What am I looking at?" he asked, confused.

"You didn't notice all that?"

"Notice all what?"

She turned to the side, her butt still on his lap, so she could look him in the face. "You're not embarrassed?"

"By what?"

"By what I affectionately call my family? I mean, look at them over there."

Max had gotten poor Stevie into a headlock, which was doing nothing but pissing Stevie off.

But all Berg could do was shrug. "My sister grabbed the nuts of a polar bear and twisted until he squealed like an otter caught in a hunting trap. You haven't even met my parents yet." Berg suddenly looked off and said, "Oh, God. You'll have to meet my parents."

"So?"

"They're going to embarrass me. And Dag. And Britta. Oh, Britta . . . she's not going to be happy."

"Berg?"

"Yes?"

"Have your parents ever sold you into indentured servitude?"

"No."

"Then I don't think you have to worry about me judging them."

"And you're staying?" the question was out of his mouth before he could stop it. He hadn't meant to ask her so directly.

"Stevie wants to stay. I don't know what Max is doing but that's nothing new."

"But *you're* staying?"

"I have to. I have to bake food for Tiny."

Realizing she wasn't getting what he was asking her, Berg just closed his eyes and came out with it, "I love you and I want you to stay."

Charlie let out an annoyed sigh. "Well . . . that's all on you."

Eyes snapping open, Berg demanded, "What the hell does that mean? You don't love me?"

"Of course I love you." She glared at him and added, "Idiot. But I'm just saying, if you've chosen to fall in love with a MacKilligan, after everything you've seen . . . then that is on you. I will *not* take responsibility for your continued poor decision making."

Instead of responding to that logic, Berg decided to simply keep quiet and hold Charlie on his lap. While they sat there, silent, Stevie ran by yelling, "It was an accident! It was an accident!"

Max chased after her baby sister. Max's nose now bloody from where—Berg was guessing—Stevie had punched her.

Dutch quickly followed, promising Charlie as he ran past, "I'll get 'em. I've got it all under control. Don't worry. Trust me!"

Lips pursed, Charlie looked at Berg. He shrugged and admitted, "Sorry, but I'm *still* glad you're staying."

Crossing her arms, Charlie shook her head and muttered, "*Such* poor decision making."

Epilogue

Dee-Ann walked into the apartment, dropping her duffel bag by the door.

"Is that you?" Ric called from one of the back rooms.

"Yeah."

"I'll be out in a minute."

"Take your time," she called back, heading toward the kitchen.

Dee-Ann really hoped there was some of that angel food cake sitting in the refrigerator. She needed it after that useless waste of a trip to Italy. The Guerra twins and that Mairi MacKilligan were long gone. Not only that but she'd spent several days trapped with Cella Malone in a foreign country.

The fact that she hadn't killed that feline should get Dee-Ann a reward, but it wouldn't. At the very least it should get her a slice of angel food cake from her mate's restaurant.

It did seem perfect, didn't it? A slice of cake, a kiss from her mate, and a big hug from Dee-Ann's baby girl.

But when Dee-Ann entered her kitchen, she froze in the open doorway and stared across the room. She felt the hackles on the back of her neck rise and, for the first time she could remember, she had to fight her urge to shift to wolf. To howl for her mate. To howl for her Pack.

Lizzy grinned at her and waved. "Hey, Mama."

"Baby girl."

The female holding her daughter in her brawny arms looked up and smiled. "Dee-Ann."

"Max."

The She-badger sat cross-legged on the floor, with Lizzy-Ann sitting in front of her, playing with the plastic knife set Dee-Ann had gotten her to train with.

"Your daughter is awesome," the honey badger said. "She's gonna kick butt one day, huh?"

"Yes!" Lizzy cheered, giggling when Max hugged her tight, those brown eyes coldly locked on Dee-Ann's face as she snuggled Dee-Ann's only child close.

Dee-Ann's fingers twitched, ready to grab hold of the blade her daddy had given her all those years ago. Just so she could rip out the badger's guts and show them to her before she died.

"Now, now," the badger cautioned. "None of that's necessary. I'm just here to talk."

"About?"

"Family."

"You mean the Guerra twins."

"I do. And, of course, Mairi MacKilligan. My cousin is dangerous for all of us, I'm afraid. Still, I'm used to working alone. But I was thinking I'll have a better chance of hunting those lovely ladies down with the help of you and your people. Don't you think that's true?"

"So you wanna work for us?"

"No. Work *with*. Because if you think the Guerras are going to back off now . . . you don't know the MacKilligans. And that's what they are, you know. No matter what country they were raised in. How rich they are. In their souls, in their blood, they are MacKilligans. And I'm pretty sure . . . there's going to be a war."

"And you think you can stop this war?"

"No. But I am hoping to mitigate damages. Something you and your fancy teams won't be able to do without me and my sisters, I'm afraid. Because the problem is, the Guerra twins now know what they are. And Mairi will show them what they can do. How far they can really go when they no longer have the boundaries of being full-human to think about. They are just learning what their claws can do." She stretched her arms out, unleashed her claws.

Her grin wide, Lizzy slid her fingers along those claws. Fascinated and eager to get her own.

"My concern," Dee-Ann admitted, "is that this might be more personal for you and your sisters than is good for any of us."

"Don't you worry about my sisters. They're the only reason I'm as loving and caring as I am." Max glanced down at Lizzy, who was still exploring the badger's claws. "They're the only reason I'm willing to work with people I don't necessarily like. Because family is everything, Dee-Ann. And that was the Guerras' mistake. They've messed with the wrong family."

Dee-Ann understood. The badgers didn't have a Pack or Pride. All they had was family or those they considered family. The MacKilligan girls weren't close to their blood relations, but half-sisters or not, they were as close as three sisters could be. And Max was going to make the Guerras and Mairi MacKilligan pay for what they'd done. For trying to use that bond against them.

Still, having her pup in the arms of a honey badger . . .

Dee-Ann fought her urge to just "start the killin'" as her daddy liked to say and instead replied, "I think we can work something out."

"Good." Max hugged Lizzy again. "I am so in love with this kid." She looked at her. "Do you know how awesome you are?"

"Yes," Lizzy replied. "I do."

"Excellent. Never forget it."

She placed Lizzy on the floor and stood. With one more smile at Dee-Ann's daughter, she silently moved through the kitchen until the badger stood beside her. She stopped there, a tiny little thing. And if she were anyone else, Dee-Ann would assume she could crush the bitch under her big She-wolf feet.

But Dee-Ann knew better now.

"Don't feel bad," Max said. "There are very few people who can keep me out of their house." She leaned in close, going up on her toes, and whispered, "I've fondled the Queen of England's crown jewels." She winked at Dee-Ann.

"I'll be in touch. And let's keep this between us, shall we? Like I said, I'll handle my sisters in my own due time."

With that Max walked down the hallway. A minute later, Ric came from the other direction. He kissed Dee-Ann on the cheek and smiled. He'd had no idea that female had been in their house. And he wouldn't until he realized that his only daughter reeked of honey badger.

"I'm glad you're home," he whispered in Dee-Ann's ear. "Want some angel food cake?"

Charlie stood on the back patio of her rental house and yelled up at one of the trees, "Get your ass out of that tree!"

"Why? I'm comfortable."

"Did you go off your meds?"

"No!"

"You should just let her stay up there. She's comfortable."

Charlie looked at the *child* eating her food. "Why are you still here?"

"I live here now."

"You do?"

"I pay rent."

She faced Kyle. "You're not even eighteen."

"I will be."

"Does your mother even know you're here?"

"She will eventually," he said, already walking away. Still eating her food.

"I don't think his mother knows," the panda said from beside her, munching away at bamboo. A noise that was really beginning to grate on Charlie's nerves. "But his sister knows and she's the only one you have to worry about. That's why I'm here. To protect him."

"Does he need protection?"

"No, but his sister thinks he does. Besides, I'd rather stay here with you guys. He's got these twin sisters that freak me out." He finished one bamboo stalk and pulled out another from a small pack. Like a cigarette pack. "One favor, though . . . could you tell your baby sister to stop . . . *hugging* me?"

"Absolutely. But do you really mind?"

"No, and that's a problem. Because she's not actually interested, she just thinks I'm cute. Like a stuffed toy. That can only end badly for me."

"I'll take care of it," Max announced to the panda as she came around the side of the house. "Hey! Crazy!" she yelled up to the trees. "Leave the giant panda alone!"

"But he's so cute!"

"You're making his dick hard! Stop it!"

Charlie laughed as poor Shen, face red, went back into the house.

"Dude."

Max grinned. "What?"

"You're such a fucker." When Max turned to go inside, Charlie caught hold of her arm. "Where were you?"

"Do you really want to know?"

"Not really."

Charlie released her sister and smiled down at the giant dog that was now standing next to her. "Hi, baby boy," she greeted the beast, leaning down to rub his neck and shoulders while he licked her face.

"Who's a good boy?" she asked. "Who is my good boy?"

"It's not him."

She looked up at Berg. "Hey, you."

"Hey." He slipped his arm around her waist and pulled her close, kissing her. But before Charlie could get her arms around his waist, Benny forced his big-headed way between them.

"That's it," Berg growled, pulling away from Charlie.

"Don't get mad at him!" she yelled after him as he went back into the house. "He just loves me. He can't help himself."

Berg came back through the door holding a leash. "I understand. And that's why I brought him a friend of his own."

"Friend?" Charlie cringed a bit. "What is that?"

"It's a dog."

"What kind of dog?"

"No idea." Berg glanced down at the female animal. "Got her at the pound."

All Charlie could see was a hundred pounds of . . . hair. She couldn't even see eyes. She didn't even know if the dog could see with all that hair!

"I'm pretty sure this is not how you're supposed to introduce new dogs to each other."

"I don't care. I need to sleep in bed with you *alone,*

and he's not letting that happen with the whining at the door every night."

"He's lonely."

"Well, this should help with that." Berg unhooked the leash from the new dog's collar.

"I wouldn't do that—" Charlie began, but it was too late. The new dog took off running, cleared the back fence, and was gone. "Well, that was ineffective."

"She'll be back," Berg said, slipping his arms around Charlie's waist and again pulling her close.

"She is not coming back."

"She will when she realizes she's surrounded by nothing but bears."

As soon as he said it, the dog cleared the fence yet again and charged across the yard and crashed through the screen door leading to the kitchen.

Tongue hanging out, Benny went after her. Hopefully he could calm her down.

"Now I need to get a new door or Tiny's gonna bitch."

"You have to start seeing the positive."

"Really? I've got one sister in a tree."

"I'm comfortable!" Stevie yelled.

"Another sister disappearing to who knows where."

"You said you didn't want to know!" Max yelled from the kitchen window.

"And apparently an artistic genius and his panda bodyguard are living in my house."

"I'm paying rent!" came Kyle's response.

"And you want me to be positive?" she asked, smiling up at Berg.

"Yes. Because you've got me . . . and I have a house right across the street that we can live in so you don't have to be here."

"Dag and Britta *are* mostly quiet."

"Quiet and well-mannered. And tonight . . . not home."

Charlie went up on her toes, wrapped her arms around Berg's neck. "That sounds perfect."

"What about us?" Stevie demanded.

"You're in a tree!"

"I'm in a tree, but I'm hungry!"

"I'm hungry too!" Max chimed in. "Let's get Dutch to foot the bill for that overpriced steakhouse. I want to try the giraffe."

"It's overrated," Charlie heard Kyle explain. "And gamey."

"I thought that was the rhino."

Charlie stared up at the bear she loved. "I really hope you know what you've gotten yourself into."

"I'm a grizzly," Berg replied. "If they really get on my nerves, I can just start roaring and gnawing on their extremities. Trust me . . . they'll run."

"I knew it!" Stevie suddenly screamed from the tree. *"You want to eat us—aaaah!"* She fell off the limb and hit the ground hard. "Owwww. That really hurt."

"Or we could move," Berg suggested, lifting Charlie up so she could put her legs around his waist and he could carry her back toward his house . . . and their bed. "I hear Siberia's nice."

"Unfortunately," she admitted, "MacKilligans aren't allowed in Siberia. There was an incident."

"With the bears?"

"Oh, no." She placed her head on his shoulder, snuggling close, before admitting, "Not with the bears. With *everybody.*"

**If you love Shelly Laurenston, don't miss the first
in her new series writing as G.A. Aiken,
THE BLACKSMITH QUEEN.**

When a prophesy brings war to the Land of the Black
Hills, Keeley Smythe must join forces with a clan
of mountain warriors who are really centaurs in a
thrilling new fantasy romance series from *New York
Times* bestselling author G.A. Aiken.

The Old King Is Dead

With the demise of the Old King, there's a prophesy
that a queen will ascend to the throne of the Black
Hills. Bad news for the king's sons, who are prepared
to defend their birthright against all comers. But for
blacksmith Keeley Smythe, war is great for business.
Until it looks like the chosen queen will be Beatrix,
her younger sister. Now it's all Keeley can do to
protect her family from the enraged royals.

Luckily, Keeley doesn't have to fight alone. Because
thundering to her aid comes a clan of kilt-wearing
mountain warriors called the Amichai. Not the most
socially adept group, but soldiers have never bothered
Keeley, and rough, gruff Caid, actually seems to
respect her. A good thing because the fierce warrior
will be by her side for a much longer ride than any
prophesy ever envisioned . . .

The great king had barely taken his last breath before one brother took the head of another.

It happened so fast that I, the Follower of His Word, had no chance to escape. I attempted to run, but the castle halls were quickly filled with battling men and dying women and children. I ended up hiding where I could, but I had to keep moving in order to stay alive.

I could hear the screams of the dying but I was not brave enough to step in. To help. Not with what I already knew.

His Majesty had warned me of this many years before.

"When I die," he'd said, looking at me from his throne, "my sons will tear everything apart. They will destroy everything I've built in their attempt to take my place. But none will be worthy. None."

I don't know the truth of that, but who was I? Just the Follower of His Word. I had no idea if any were worthy or if all were. It was not my job to make those decisions.

But I had no idea it would be like this. This . . . fast.

All the youngest boys were immediately killed by their older siblings. Cut down with their protective mothers in their beds. There was no mercy for them.

The older sons quickly faced off against each other but not all of them were true warriors. The weakest met their ends quickly. Those who could fight did their best but, in the end, it seemed that only five princes remained: Marius the Wielder of Hate, the Old King's eldest and most feared; Straton the Devourer; Cyrus the Honored; and the twins—Theodorus and Theotimus— who were too young to have earned epithets but who were already loathed for their viciousness.

At one point, I saw Straton and Cyrus escape the castle grounds; Cyrus taking as many innocents with him as he could in order to save their lives. I tried to get downstairs to join him, but my path was blocked by fighting men.

It was said that Cyrus had taken half of his father's army, those who were loyal to him, and was even now planning his next attack against his brothers while Straton already had an army of mercenaries waiting for their orders. As the day wore on, no one seemed to know where the twins had gone and no one was looking for them, except maybe the remaining brothers. But, despite their battle skills, they were relatively stupid and I was sure that no one had much to worry about. Even if they appeared again at some point, they would easily be wiped out.

That meant the castle and its grounds were currently held by Prince Marius, who had already taken over the rest of his father's army. At this moment I could hear him moving through the castle, killing all those he didn't believe loyal to him and only him or, even worse, those who might have the slightest chance of obtaining the throne through bloodlines.

Not knowing how I would be seen by Marius—I had always been openly loyal to his father and was a distant cousin to Marius—I scrambled into the Old King's room and dove behind one of the giant pillars.

My timing was quick enough, thank the gods! Because another cousin of mine ran into the chamber shortly after me. He was already covered in blood, but Marius followed behind him and took him to the ground by slicing his sword down the man's spine. Our cousin fell to the marble floor and sobbed. Desperately.

"Prince Marius, please! I am your kin! Please!"

Marius said nothing to his begging cousin, simply slammed his blade through his back and directly into his heart, ignoring the fact that the Old King's body was still in his bed.

I covered my mouth, terrified I'd cry out. I was not meant for battle. I was not meant for war. I was simply a chronicler. I took notes of the Old King's life. But each king picked his own chronicler and Marius would not want to have anything that once belonged to his father except his throne and his crown.

Marius finished his work and straightened. I moved farther back around the pillar, praying he wouldn't search the room. But he didn't leave and I knew he was coming. Coming for me.

Then the gods must have heard my prayers because that sweet voice rang out.

"Marius? Where are you?"

"Mother?"

"Oh, there you are!" I peeked around the pillar again and watched Marius's mother enter the Old King's chamber. Maila had been the Old King's lead consort because she'd given birth to his first son. The Old King never married, so Maila was as close as the subjects had to a Dowager Queen. And, unlike the other consorts, she'd lived almost like a queen because when the Old King needed to entertain, it was Maila that he always had by his side. That also meant she had ample gold and jewels, and could purchase anything she liked whenever she liked. Her gowns were always the most beautiful and glamorous, her hair artfully done. It also helped that Maila had managed to keep her beauty.

"Mother, what are you doing here? You are supposed to be in the safety of—"

Another cousin ran into the chamber, mace swinging. Maila quickly ducked and Marius blocked the weapon with his sword before slamming his dagger into the man's belly. Again and again, then slitting his throat for good measure.

"Mother, you need to go back to my soldiers. They will protect you."

"I needed to speak to you and it cannot wait. Besides, most of your brothers are either dead or gone. The castle is ours."

"Still, I'd feel better if—"

Another screaming soldier ran into the chamber, sword above his head, ready to strike Prince Marius. The soldier wore the colors of Prince Cyrus and was ready to die for the man he hoped would be king.

Marius raised his weapons again but Maila held up her hand to stop him and, a few seconds later, the soldier stopped in his tracks, his sword still raised above his head. He coughed, blood shooting out of his mouth. Maila give a small laugh, covering her mouth as the soldier fell forward, dead.

"Mother, what did you do?"

"I poisoned the soldiers' well. Oh, don't look at me that way," she complained. "We both know I could never stay out of this. I've been waiting since your birth for you to ascend to the throne."

"This is my fight."

"Wrong. This is *our* fight. Do you really think all my other sons actually died accidentally? No. I took their lives because it was my right, as their mother, to do so. I couldn't get near your other half-brothers because of *their* mothers but I knew when the time came, you'd be

...ed. "You are so very much my son."

...the chamber, Marius taking his mother
...ty. I took my chance then and crawled
...hidden door under the enormous bed that
...g had kept secret from all but me.

...was on the other side, I slowly closed the door
...e so no one heard my escape. Once I could
..., I rushed down the narrow, hidden hallway,
...the steel door at the end was not blocked by
...rly soldier who'd wonder what I was "up to."
...escape took me several long minutes but once I
...d the steel door, I opened it just enough to see if
...was anyone in my way. This door led into the for-
...on the west side of the castle. I searched the trees
... my gaze but saw nothing. I eased out and took my
...e closing the door behind me, afraid to make even
... slightest sound. Once I heard the final click, I let out
...breath and—

"Leaving us so soon, Keeper?"

I shut my eyes in despair, barely holding back tears
as I faced Lady Maila.

"Now, now, don't cry. I'm not here to kill you. I'm
here to offer protection from my son." She came from
around the tree where she'd been waiting and took my
arm. "Things here are about to drastically change and
I need my own historian. You can be the Keeper of *My
Word*. Won't that be nice?"

What could I say? No? Not to Lady Maila. Not only
because of her son but because to challenge Maila was
to sign one's own death warrant. And I was not ready
to die.

So, instead, I replied, "That would be lovely, my
lady."

"Excellent." Together, we headed back to the castle.
"And you can now call me Dowager Queen. It's quite
fitting, don't you think?"

able to handle the rest. And here you are doing a brilliant job. So allow me some fun."

The sound of more battling soldiers in the hallway
had the prince pulling Maila closer, moving in front
of her.

"Just tell me what's going on and make it quick,
please."

"A messenger arrived not too long ago. From the
Witches of Amhuinn."

I was surprised by that. The Witches of Amhuinn
usually stayed in their mountainside fortress, reading
their books and keeping their tallies. They didn't dance
naked in the moonlight, they didn't sacrifice bulls in
the early hours of dawn, they didn't make potions for
love or revenge. But despite all that, their declarations
had power. Even the Old King respected what they had
to say.

And what they had to say must be important for Maila
to leave the safety of wherever her son had placed her.

"What do they want?" the prince asked.

"They have called to the gods and—"

One of the prince's uncles charged into the room, but
he was older and didn't move as he once had. Marius
took his head and kicked his body to the floor.

"Mother, just get to it!"

"Their seer has seen a queen. A queen to replace the
Old King."

I frowned in confusion. In all my years, I couldn't remember the Amhuinn having a "seer." It would have to
be someone who'd truly proven themselves since it had
always been said the Witches of Amhuinn relied on statistics rather than those who could see into the future.

"What queen?"

"A girl. A farmer's daughter."

"A *peasant*?"

"*I* was a peasant before being sold to your father."

"Then put the bitch in chains and bring her to me. One way or another, I will be the next ruler of these lands."

Maila glanced at the Old King's body in his bed, and I saw no pain, nor pity at his death. "Your half-brother, Straton, has already gone after this farmer's daughter."

"Good. Let him kill her. I've got other things to—"

"Don't be like your brothers," Maila snapped at her son. "Short-sighted. Whether peasant or royal, if a girl has been chosen by the Witches of Amhuinn, she will be more readily accepted by the dukes and barons of these lands."

"Why would I need—"

"You need their armies. Cyrus has already taken half your father's men. The rest are loyal to you, but if you hope to win against Cyrus and, more difficult still, Straton, who has been building his mercenary army for years, then you need more men. Men willing to die for you."

"Soooo . . . you want *me* to kill her?"

"No! Dammit, son! Think! To have a queen at your side, with the blessing of the Witches of Amhuinn. The same sect that put your ancestors on the throne four hundred years ago."

Marius let out a long sigh. "You want me to rescue her from my brother."

"It's too late for that. Protectors have already been sent to her."

"Protectors sent by you?"

"No. These are not friends of ours. But they'll need to take her to the Witches of Amhuinn for the girl to be confirmed in person. We can find her there. Take her and then you marry her. Make her queen."

"I don't want to get married."

"Your father was the only son of his father. You, my dearest, were not that lucky. But having a wife—

---

a queen—does not ... whores on the side. ... did and your great ... knew her place."

"I don't know—"

"Meet her. She'll be retri... arrange it all. Once we have ... want to keep her or slit her thro...

Marius blew out a breath an... "All right. I'll meet her. But she h... first. I'm not ready to face him yet."

"If she can't manage to out-ma... brother," Maila said, stepping over de... bers, "it's not like she'll be a great loss.'

"You need to promise me something, t... ius said to his mother's back.

She faced him. "And what's that, my love...

"That whoever this peasant is . . . you won... until *I* decide I have no use for her."

"Why would I ever—"

"*Mother.*"

Maila smirked. "I promise. I'll be good." The p... stared at each other until Maila added, "At the ver... least I'll try."

"Thank you. I've always appreciated your guidance, but now that Father is gone, it's time I make my own decisions."

"Of course."

"So please don't force me to put you away in a nunnery until your sudden and tragic death not too far in the future."

"You'd do that to your own mother?" Maila asked her only-remaining son.

Marius stepped close to his mother and gently placed his blood-covered palm against her cheek. "Before you could pray to your chosen gods to save you."

Maila smil...
They left ...
back to saf...
through the ...
the Old Ki...
Once I ...
behind m...
stand up...
praying ...
some b...
My ...
reache...
there ...
ests ...
with ...
tim...
th...
a...

"Yes, my lady."

"And just wait until you meet my son's future queen. She's like no one you've met before."

I hoped the Dowager Queen was correct. Because that poor girl, whoever she may be, will have to be quite special if she's to have any chance of surviving this mother and son.

Connect with U s

Visit us online at
KensingtonBooks.com
to read more from your favorite authors, see books
by series, view reading group guides, and more.

 Join us on social media

for sneak peeks, chances to win books and prize packs,
and to share your thoughts with other readers.

facebook.com/kensingtonpublishing
twitter.com/kensingtonbooks

Tell us what you think!

To share your thoughts, submit a review,
or sign up for our eNewsletters, please visit:
KensingtonBooks.com/TellUs.